A SHARE OF
HONOUR

Alexander Fullerton

A SHARE OF
HONOUR

LITTLE, BROWN AND COMPANY

A *Little, Brown* Book

First published in Great Britain in 1982
by Michael Joseph
This edition published in 2000
by Little, Brown and Company

A CIP catalogue record for this book
is available from the British Library.

ISBN 0 316 84850 6

Typeset in New Baskerville by M Rules
Printed and bound in Great Britain by
Creative Print and Design (Wales)

Little, Brown and Company (UK)
Brettenham House
Lancaster Place
London WC2E 7EN

If we are mark'd to die, we are enow
To do our country loss; and if to live,
The fewer men the greater share of honour.

Shakespeare: *Henry V,* before Agincourt

From a German staff report, late 1941:

'The most dangerous British weapon in the
Mediterranean is the submarine, especially those
operating from Malta . . . a very severe supply crisis must
occur relatively soon . . .'

From Admiral Raeder's reply:

'The Naval Staff agrees entirely . . . [and] considers
immediate measures to remedy the situation imperative,
otherwise not only our offensive but the entire Italo-
German position in North Africa will be lost.'

1

Mist clinging to the sea's dark surface thickened the night: lights on the coast six miles away seemed to quiver through it. The submarine, with her main ballast tanks partially flooded, was trimmed down to lie low in the water, to present a low silhouette and also so that she could dive quickly if she had to, slip under literally in seconds. Her diesel engines growled through muffled exhausts, driving her shorewards at only a few knots but also pumping fresh power into her batteries. That steady grumble and the swish of the sea along her sides were the only sounds, and they'd have been inaudible a few hundred yards away, but here in enemy waters they seemed frighteningly loud. Sub-Lieutenant Paul Everard RNVR, hunched in the front of *Ultra*'s bridge with binoculars at his eyes, wouldn't have addressed the two look-outs in anything above a murmur: you were in the enemy's backyard and you knew it, *felt* it.

Enjoyed it, too . . . Despite the fact that in the forefront of his mind was the knowledge that an enemy could show up at any second, and that when it happened he'd have about one more second in which to react – and react the right way, at that. Straining his eyes, living through them, aware that behind him the look-outs' concentration would be as total as his own, Paul could feel the tension in himself and them, the sense of solitariness in an enclosing perimeter of threat and danger; he could feel the tautness of his own nerves and awareness of personal responsibility for other men's lives racking up the tension. At the same time his mind didn't need to separate itself from the work of probing the darkness to know that this was what he'd wanted, aimed for, that he wouldn't for any price have been anywhere but here.

That land on the bow, with the lights flickering along it, was the toe of Italy.

'Bridge!'

Without taking the glasses from his eyes, he lowered his face to the voicepipe and answered in a quieter tone than the helmsman's, 'Bridge.'

'Captain coming up, sir.'

And he could hear him, clambering out of the upper hatch, the top of the conning-tower. James Ruck, Lieutenant, DSC, RN. Paul edged over to make room for him. Nobody had any reason to speak, for a while: Ruck became another pair of eyes, a fourth probe of the pre-dawn dark and a hostile coast. He asked, after a few minutes, 'How are the Measures?'

'No movement, sir.'

By 'Measures' he meant the pair of shore lights that represented some kind of anti-submarine device, almost certainly direction-finding equipment. Malta submariners had christened them 'Mussolini's Mysterious Measures', short title MMM. The pair of lights burned horizontally to each other: if they swung to the vertical, chances were an E-boat would soon come racing seaward along the beam. So when they changed position you dived, and within ten or twenty minutes heard the A/S patrol pound overhead.

Ruck had his glasses on the local pair now. It was anyone's guess why they worked on some occasions and not on others – like now, when this submarine was well within any directionfinder's range. Perhaps it was because she was almost bow-on to them: trimmed down like this, she'd be showing about as much reflective surface as a floating oil drum. The general opinion was that the lights were an adjunct to the direction-finding apparatus, their only purpose being to guide patrol-craft towards intruders.

Ruck muttered, 'You'd think they'd be on their toes, in a spot like this.'

Paul murmured, 'Probably all pissed.'

Ruck grunted; he was stooped over the gyro repeater, sighting across it for land bearings. He'd get a left-hand edge of land, and a cross-bearing on Cape Spartivento. He said, still at it, 'Dive in about half an hour, Sub. I'll give you a shout.' A searchlight beam sprang out, swinging skyward and then down to sweep along the coastline to the left; as it lifted again another joined it, criss-crossing. Those lights were near Cape dell'Armi and they'd been on and off several times during the night; now they were illuminating the headland on which Ruck was taking his left-edge bearing. He murmured, 'Thanks, chums.' Then he'd gone, to transfer the fix from his memory to the chart; Paul heard the clatter of his boots in the hatch, and he was alone again, taking another quick glance at the MMM lights. They were still horizontal. He pivoted slowly, examining every foot of the surrounding darkness.

Diving in half an hour: that would make it about 0500. Paul's watch now was from 0415 to 0615, so he'd have about an hour's dived watchkeeping while they motored underwater into the approaches to the straits. The Messina Straits, the gap between Italy and Sicily; this was the southern end of them. It was a prime area for targets, but it was also well patrolled, an obvious place for submarines to haunt and therefore to be hunted.

Land, dotted here and there with lights, lay from broad on the starboard bow to fine on the other. Another half-hour, and making-good about five knots, meant *Ultra* would be roughly three miles from the coast when she dived. By the time it was fully light – around the time he, Paul, would be handing over the watch – she'd be getting into the funnel of the straits and probably be less than a mile offshore.

The MMM lights were still horizontal. The closer you got to them, he supposed, the more you'd need to be alert to them . . . This time yesterday, when they'd arrived for their first day of patrol on this billet, they'd approached along the western coast, the Sicilian side, and there'd been no Mysterious Measures there. He shifted to the left, to begin a new sweep on the bow again.

And stopped. Moving the glasses slowly back the other way . . .

A dark patch: something darker than its surroundings. Low to the water, and right ahead. He was holding his breath, taking another moment in which to make certain he wasn't only *imagining* —

'Look-outs down!'

They were in the hatch, tumbling in, one on top of the other. Paul said into the voicepipe, 'Dive, dive, dive!', then dragged down on the lever of the cock that shut it, sealed it against the sea: he'd jumped into the hatch on the head of the second look-out and he was reaching up to drag the heavy lid down over him. The diesels had cut out abruptly and main vents had opened to let air out and water in: the sea was rising, surrounding and engulfing, sweeping over, noisy through the conning-tower's steel. He'd got the hatch shut and he was forcing the clips on, then pushing in the brass cotter-pins to hold them shut; at the same time he called down for the captain's information, 'E-boat lying stopped right ahead, sir!'

In the control room the signalman, Janaway, was standing ready to shut and clip the lower hatch.

'How far off was he, Sub?'

Paul told his CO, 'Mile – half a mile – hard to say, sir. Only just visible, not distinct at all, but low and small, so —'

'Might they have seen us?'

Several other pairs of ears waited for the answer, sharing the captain's interest. The depthgauge needles were swinging past the forty-foot marks. Hugo Wykeham, *Ultra*'s tall and urbane first lieutenant, controlling the dive with an eye on the planesmen and a hand on the instrument through which he passed orders to the trim-tank operators, told Engineroom Artificer Quinn, 'Shut main vents.'

Quinn, bearded – as opposed to merely unshaven, like most of the men around him – slammed the levers back. 'Main vents shut, sir.'

Paul was telling Ruck he didn't think the E-boat had spotted them. At least, he'd no reason to believe it had.

Ruck told Wykeham, 'One hundred feet.'

'Blow Q, sir?'

He'd hesitated, then nodded. 'Yes.' He turned to the helmsman. 'Port ten. Steer three-one-oh.'

Blowing the quick-diving tank, Q, was a calculated risk, because it would make a noise, which in the circumstances was undesirable. But it had to be blown sooner or later: you couldn't easily get the boat into trim when it was full, not without making at least as much noise by pumping for quite a long time on a bow tank. It was better to get it done with. Wykeham nodded to Quinn, and the ERA opened a valve to send high-pressure air thumping down the pipe into that tank to blow the water out of it, back into the sea. When its indicator light went out he reported, screwing the valve shut, 'Q blown, sir.'

'Ten of port wheel on, sir.'

'Vent Q inboard?'

'No,' Ruck told his first lieutenant. 'But I want slow grouped down on one screw as soon as you can manage it.'

Wykeham took stock of his trim, the balance of the submarine. Until you had her in trim you needed a certain speed through the water in order to hold her to the ordered depth; perfection was a 'stop-trim', when she'd hang motionless, with no way on her and neither rising nor sinking. He seemed to have things reasonably in control, anyway – the hydroplanes weren't having to work hard, and the bubble in the fore-and-aft spirit level was just half a degree aft of the centreline. He glanced round at the telegraphman – Able Seaman West, who was also the gun trainer – and told him to go aft and pass the word to group down and stop the port motor. Wykeham was passing the order by word of mouth because the telegraphs made a clanging sound and the E-boat lying up there would have hydrophones, a pair of earphones clamped to some close-cropped skull . . . Ruck asked his own asdic operator, Newton, 'Anything?'

Newton's expression was always vacant when he was listening. He shook his long, narrow head. He was a goofy-looking man at the best of times.

'Are you sure? No HE?'

Another shake of the head, and this time he managed to force some words out too. 'Clear all round, sir.'

HE stood for hydrophone effect, the underwater sound of a ship's propellers. But of course the E-boat might know there was a submarine around and still not have moved: it could be lying doggo, listening . . .

Could be. It probably wasn't, but you couldn't take anything for granted. The telegraphman came back, and reported that *Ultra* was now running on one propeller only, one motor driving it at slow speed, and that the batteries were grouped down. It meant the submarine's two sections of battery had been switched to operate in series, which gave slower speed, longer endurance. Grouped up, they'd be connected in parallel, maximizing the available power. But the slower you moved, the less noise you made and the longer you'd last out.

'Course three-one-oh, sir.'

Paul looked over the navigator's shoulder at the chart over which he was sprawled as if he was trying to convince himself he was still asleep. Bob McClure was an RNVR sub-lieutenant, like himself. He'd pencilled on the diving position and the new course of 310 degrees: Paul saw that if they held to it it would take them out across the wider part of the entrance to the straits. On that course you could run for fifteen miles or more before you'd hit Sicily. McClure yawned; he asked blearily, 'Sure you saw something?'

Paul nodded. 'I'm sure.'

You could imagine things, easily enough. Seagulls had been mistaken for aircraft before now. McClure stood five foot four inches in his socks; he had a swarthy complexion and brown eyes, and came from Oban in Argyll. He complained, 'Well, you interrupted one of the best dreams I ever had.'

'Chasing Highland sheep, I suppose?'

Ruck asked the asdic man, 'Still nothing?'

'Nothing, sir.'

'Right.' He told Wykeham, 'We'll go to watch diving, and stay deep until' – a glance at the clock beside the helmsman – 'five-thirty. Everard's watch still, is it?'

Now it was dead quiet. Softly lit, and warm, with the metallic odour of electrics and behind that the pervading reek of shale-oil. Shale was the fuel on which torpedoes ran, and it was also used for cleaning, for putting a shine on the corticene deck-covering. Every submariner smelt of shale.

But so silent, and peaceful. In your mind you could visualize the scene outside: dawn reaching over the Messina Straits and the Italian mainland, first light fingering the Sicilian coast beyond. Flat shine on the surface, and the E-boat still lying motionless a couple of miles or so to the northeast now. Down here, under a hundred feet of water still retaining darkness, the submarine paddling gently northwestward, slanting across the approaches to the straits . . . Paul moved over to glance at the chart again. There was the fix on it which Ruck had taken not long before they'd dived, then dead-reckoning positions for the dive itself and for where they'd altered course. The pencilled track took them well clear of land: *Ultra* was in five hundred fathoms of water here, and right up to the Italian coast the chart showed nothing less than a hundred.

He went back to inspect the trim. No problems. The for'ard pair of hydroplanes were level, the after ones tilted in a few degrees of rise. Bubble central. Out of habit his eye checked the diving panel, where the ERA of the watch lounged, and saw that all main vent levers were in the 'shut' position. It was ERA Summers on the panel, Telegraphist Flyte on asdics, and the planesmen were Lovesay and Stapleton. The gunlayer, Creagh, was helmsman; he was yawning, displaying broken front teeth – damage incurred in opening beer bottles, it was said. Most faces were well stubbled: *Ultra* had sailed from Malta on Wednesday, and today was Saturday.

Snores from the wardroom. Could be anyone's; Paul couldn't detect McClure's Scottish accent in them, though. He wondered whether the navigator had found his way back into that dream . . .

You had your own dreams, anyway. Waking ones, patterns of awareness behind the conscious mind which you could bring out and inspect when there was time and your thoughts delved back to them. Call them thoughts, perhaps, or worries; but images of the outside world and people, some of them so very distant and all of it so utterly removed from *this* environment, had more dream quality than thought about them. His father, for instance – Nick Everard, somewhere out East and commanding the cruiser *Defiant*, and that whole area crumbling to Jap invasion. The whole of the East Indies and nearly all the Pacific islands had already fallen; Australia was under threat. You could only hope, and pray – and wish to God you'd written a letter, the one you owed him but hadn't had first the courage and then the time to write.

'Hydrophone effect, sir!'

Telegraphist Flyte wide-eyed, bolt upright on the asdic stool: the fore planesman, Stapleton, turning his prematurely balding head to stare at Flyte censoriously as if he'd disturbed *his* dreams . . . Flyte amplified, 'Green one-two-zero, sir. Started up sudden like.'

'Captain in the control room!'

'All right.' Ruck's acknowledgement . . . There were no doors, and the wardroom was so close that if anyone farted in his sleep the watchkeepers in here would hear it. A general stirring in there as others woke: and the captain was beside Paul – a medium-sized, dark-haired and dark-jowled, square-built man in flannel trousers and a torn shirt. Twenty-six years old. He asked Flyte, 'True bearing?'

'Oh-five-six, sir, steady.'

If it had only just started up – and from its bearing it could only be that E-boat – you wouldn't get much of a clue yet as to which way it was heading. It could be coming to drop depthcharges, or just to follow and continue listening while it waited for other ships to join it, or it could be setting out to patrol the coastline, or even going home for breakfast.

'Revs increasing, sir, bearing steady.' Flyte added, 'Closing, sir.'

Two minutes passed like ten. Paul watching the trim. Ears strained, eyes watchful in the subdued lighting, waiting for their own first sound of the enemy's propellers. When they were close enough, you'd hear them without headphones.

'Still steady, sir. Fast turbine, sounds like an E-boat.'

'Half ahead together, starboard fifteen.'

With its own engines and screws kicking up a row, the E-boat wouldn't hear them now. Ruck was moving *Ultra* out of its path, in case this *might* be some kind of attack.

'Fifteen of starboard wheel on, sir.' Creagh was a Londoner, and sounded like it. The messenger reported, 'Both motors half ahead grouped down, sir.'

'Steer three-six-oh.'

The motors hummed. With wheel on, there was a tendency for the bow to rise, and the fore planesman was putting on some dive to counteract it.

'Bearing drawing left, sir. Fast HE, right to left.'

It wasn't going to pass over the top of them, then. For courses to bring ships into collision, the bearing between them had to remain constant.

'Slow ahead together.'

'Course north, sir.'

Wykeham appeared in the gangway by the chart table, the few feet of space between wardroom and control room. Tall, fair-haired, with an aloof expression rather like a camel's. In fact the appearance was deceptive: he was an Old Etonian and a jazz fiend, and in Gibraltar he'd taken on two civilians and a police-man, knocked all three cold and got away undetected. McClure bore witness to it, although their versions of the affair differed slightly.

Ruck raised a finger . . .

You could hear it – the E-boat's screws. Passing ahead, from right to left. A rhythmic, scrunching sound: but it was already beginning to fade, drawing away on the port quarter. Ruck said, 'Stop starboard.'

The question was, would it hold its course and speed, or would it stop and resume listening? Putting the same question another way, had its captain ever been aware that there was a submarine here at all?

'Starboard motor stopped, sir, port motor slow ahead.'

You couldn't hear any E-boat now. Ruck asked Flyte, 'Well?'

'Still going away, sir. Revs constant.'

Five minutes later, even asdics couldn't hear anything. Ruck moved over to the chart. He told Wykeham, 'He'd have been on roughly this course – here . . .'

'Heading for Taormina.'

'Perhaps. We know they have Mas-boats at Catania and E-boats at Augusta, down here. It'd make sense to base some nearer the straits as well.'

Taormina was only about twenty-five miles down-coast from Messina. Very likely that E-boat – or Mas-boat, if it was Italian instead of German – *was* going home for breakfast . . . Ruck craned round to tell Flyte, 'Listen carefully all round. Tell me if you hear anything.'

The asdic oscillator/receiver was housed in a dome at the for'ard end of the boat's keel. The operator here in the control room trained it around inside its dome by twisting a knob with two fingers: Flyte did it delicately, with his little finger raised. The knob was the centrepiece of a compass ring, so he could see which way he was pointing it and from which direction any sound was coming.

'All clear all round, sir.'

Ruck nodded. 'Sixty feet, Sub.'

'Sixty feet, sir . . .'

The hydroplane operators swung their brass controlling wheels. The after planes – manned in this watch by Leading Seaman Lovesay, the second coxswain – dipped first, pulling the

stern down so as to provide up-angle on the boat as a whole.
Then they swung the other way, to join the fore planes in guid-
ing her up towards the surface. Paul meanwhile used the order
instrument, which was up above the planesmen's heads, to
adjust the trim by letting small quantities of sea into the midships trim-tank as she rose. Rising into shallower and therefore
less dense water, a submarine's hull expanded, displacing more
water and thus becoming lighter, and you had to compensate for
it or she'd become too light to be held at that newly ordered
depth.

There she was, now, settled. He reported, 'Sixty feet, sir.'

'Hear anything, Flyte?'

'No, sir, nothing.'

'Slow ahead together.' Ruck told Paul, 'Let's take a look up
top. Twenty-eight feet.'

Bringing her up again, this time right up to periscope depth.
Working at it, watching the planesmen and using the trimline to
compensate again, it occurred to Paul that if the E-boat's skipper
was really crafty he could be sitting up there, waiting for them to
show. He wondered if he'd simulated, slowed and stopped,
fooled old Flyte?

Thirty feet. He switched the order instrument to 'stop flooding' and to 'shut O suction and inboard vent'. Ruck moved to
the after periscope, the small-diameter one, and told ERA
Summers, 'Up.' Summers lifted one of a pair of steel levers, like
a motor car's handbrake, and the shiny, yellowish tube hissed
upwards.

'Twenty-eight feet, sir.'

Ruck grunted acknowledgement; he grabbed the handles of
the periscope as its lower end emerged from the well in which
it lived when it was stowed. He jerked the handles down,
pressed his eyes against the rubber-capped lenses: in that position his body was still straightening as the periscope came right
up and stopped. Now he was pivoting, swinging around for a
quick, preliminary search. This smaller 'attack' periscope had
no magnification in it: its top end was not much thicker than

a Churchillian cigar, and was thus less easy for an enemy to spot.

He'd done one complete circle, and sent it down, moved to the for'ard periscope and gestured for it. Summers had that bigger one shooting up; it had variable magnification and also a tilting sky search so you could look out for aircraft.

'Stop one screw, sir?'

'Yes. Stop port.'

A similar performance now, using the big periscope first in low power, then high. And obviously there were no dangers visible. Ruck was relaxing, circling quite slowly, examining the coastline. He asked the helmsman without taking his eyes from the lenses, 'Ship's head north, is it?'

'Aye, sir —'

'Port ten.' He leaned back to glance at the periscope's bearing-ring, a graduated circle around it on the deckhead. 'Steer three-two-five.' The handles snapped up: Summers sent the brass tube sliding down, glistening with grease and with droplets of water gleaming like jewels as they trickled down. He told Paul, 'Get a fix on the chart, Sub. It's light enough. Then adjust the course to pass one mile clear of Cape dell'Armi.'

He'd gone, to stretch out on his bunk, no doubt, leaving the watch to Paul. You began to notice the quiet again, the peaceful warmth of a dived patrol. A peace that could be shattered very suddenly, of course . . .

But there wasn't much left of this watch, now. In twenty minutes Wykeham would be along to take over, and in less than five the watch itself, these control room hands, would change. Officers changed watches at a different time because during the main change-round the boat's trim needed watching and adjusting.

'Up periscope. Stand by for some bearings, Jupp.'

Jupp, a torpedoman, was messenger of the watch. The ship's company called him 'Dracula', on account of his sunken eyes and rather long, prominent teeth. Paul gave him three shore bearings to write down, together with his own observation of the ship's head by gyro as each was taken. At the chart table, Paul translated relative bearings into true ones, put the fix on and labelled it with the time, 0555. The course to steer to pass one mile off the cape was – he laid it off on the chart, then ran the parallel ruler to the compass rose – 309 degrees.

'Port ten. Steer three-oh-nine.'

Creagh spun his wheel. *Ultra* would have to cover five miles before dell'Armi was abeam, and at this speed it would take two hours. Paul put the periscope up again, made a quick, precautionary all-round sweep of sea and sky, and then took a closer look at the coast as the light increased. Just about on the beam was a river's entrance to the sea, a deep gorge with a stone railway bridge across it. The railway track hugged the coastline from Spartivento right around and into the straits, and if no better targets turned up in the next few days Ruck planned to try some gunnery. A train crossing a bridge would make the best target. There were plenty of bridges and lots of trains, and *Ultra* had a 3-inch gun: she was the first of the U-class boats to have one, the earlier boats having only 12-pounders, which were useless. Until now the flotilla's train-wrecking activities had been carried out by commandos landing in canoes, folboats, and armed with plastic explosive; a platoon of commandos was attached to the flotilla largely for this purpose.

No trains in sight at this moment. They'd seen a few yesterday, and begun to compile a timetable. Paul pushed the handles up: 'Down periscope.'

He was looking forward to turning in, getting an hour's sleep before breakfast. For the duration of the patrol your watches were two hours on, four hours off, but mealtimes, other jobs and interludes of action interrupted those four-hour periods, and it was never much effort to roll into a bunk and fall asleep. He'd have no problem at all doing that now.

'Happy, Second?'

Leading Seaman Lovesay glanced round from his seat at the after planes. Being second coxswain meant he was responsible for gear and operations on and inside the casing – the steel upper deck, the perforated platform built on top of the pressure-hull and on which you walked when the submarine was in harbour or entering or leaving it. The gear included the anchor and its chain cable, wires and ropes and the timber gangplank and so on – everything up there except the gun, which belonged to Creagh. Both men came directly under Paul, since he was both weapons officer and casing officer. Lovesay was in his early twenties, heavily built, with a round, genial face and a legendary capacity for beer. He nodded. 'Bearing up, sir.'

'Time we all got our heads down, anyway. Is it Blue watch, now?' Lovesay confirmed it, and Paul reached for the microphone of the Tannoy broadcast. 'Blue watch, watch diving. Blue watch . . .'

He was busy with the trim then, as the hands changed over. There was a difference of a couple of stone, for instance, in the weights of Leading Seaman Lovesay, who was going for'ard, and the coxswain, Chief Petty Officer Logan, who'd come to relieve him on the after planes. That change on its own would call for several gallons of salt water to be pumped aft as compensation. Other changes would tend to balance it, and you might end up much as you'd started, but if you hadn't taken care during the change-over the submarine could have gone out of control, either diving steeply or breaking surface – which, this close to an enemy coast, was very much to be avoided.

He'd put the other screw to slow ahead, to maintain control more easily. Now he told the Blue watch messenger, a skinny youngster named Furness who'd been in trouble with some woman up on the Clyde, 'Stop starboard.'

'Stop starboard, sir . . .' The telegraph bell rang in the motor room, as Furness passed them the order.

'We're still a touch heavy aft, cox'n. I want to let it settle a bit, that's all.'

'Aye aye, sir.'

Hector Logan's voice sounded as if he had gravel in his throat. He was short, lean, broad-shouldered, with a seamed, weathered face. He'd have been oversized for a jockey, but he had that horseman's look about him. He asked, without turning his head from the gauges in front of him, 'In the straits again, are we, sir?'

'Just easing ourselves in now.'

'Let's 'ope some bloody Wop comes easin' 'imself out, then.'

You could reckon that *something* would. Targets were plentiful, these days, with the enemy struggling to feed Rommel's army in the desert – at this precise juncture, to supply his advance towards Egypt. In fact it had slowed, pretty well stopped, while he tried to build up his forces for a renewal of the push and to take Tobruk – then Egypt, the Canal, the whole Middle East . . . This Malta submarine flotilla existed primarily to stop the supplies – fuel, ammunition, food, equipment and men – from getting across to Africa: and the enemy, well aware of it, were going all out to smash the flotilla. Two boats had been lost last month – February – on patrol: a detached observer might have seen that as natural attrition, because operational submarines did risk being sunk, obviously, and the 10th Flotilla's losses were running at about 60 per cent. But there was more than that to it. The Germans had moved U-boats from the Atlantic into the Mediterranean, and shifted more bombers from their Russian front to Sicily, not only to strike at Malta – particularly its dockyard and airfields – as they'd been doing for a long time now, but specifically to stop the operation of submarines. They were going for the base itself, the Lazaretto building on Manoel Island, as well as for submarines in harbour. Parachute mines last month had destroyed the seamen's messdecks and the hospital; the frequency and weight of the attacks were increasing steadily.

It was quieter at sea, sometimes, even within spitting distance of an enemy beach, than it was 'resting' in Malta nowadays . . . Paul turned towards the periscope, and glanced at ERA Quinn, who'd taken over the panel from Summers; Quinn dropped his hand to the telemotor lever and brought the tube slithering up. For a quick search round, then a new fix on the chart for Wykeham to see when he came to relieve him as OOW. Paul tugged the handles down, twisted the hand-grip to shift the lenses into low power.

It was full daylight up there now. Grey-green sea unbroken – unfortunately, since broken water camouflaged a periscope – but slightly lumpy under high, wispy cloud. The low swell was lining the Italian beaches with surf, a white edging to the land a mile and a half to starboard. Cape dell'Armi broad on the bow: smoke rising from cottage chimneys. Used as barracks probably – there'd hardly be civilians in those houses now.

Activity at one end of the nearer beach – soldiers assembling, or drilling. He circled on, leaving that for the moment, more concerned with completing the all-round check to ensure there was no threat nearby. Swinging left, pausing on dell'Armi with its lighthouse; on again, and now he was looking across the straits towards Sicily. Empty sea, blank sky. Moving on across the bow and down the port side: acres of sea agleam with the hardening daylight. A gull dipping to inspect the periscope . . .

All clear all round. He switched to high power, and began again. Those soldiers on the beach were spread out in lines and doing PT, prancing about and swinging their arms. Local garrison working off yesterday's pasta . . . A goods train was chuffing westward: *Ultra* could have surfaced, manned the gun and blown it to pieces. He swung on, anti-clockwise, and saw a truck moving along the road that ran beside the railway line. A heavy military vehicle painted greenish khaki and going the opposite way to the train. The thing to do, he thought, might be to catch two trains at once as they crossed a bridge: by surfacing in a fixed position you'd have your range established accurately before you opened fire. But Ruck would have thought of that already . . . The truck was hidden by the train as they passed each other: so at this point the road was on the far side of the tracks. He swept on slowly across the cape and the left edge of the Italian toe to the straits again, or rather the approach to them. Fifteen miles of shiny, empty, humpy sea . . .

Aircraft. A Cant seaplane . . .

Search the sea, then, the whole area under it.

Smoke. Gone now. But there *had* been. And was again now: a little greyer than the sky behind it, behind the rim of the low horizon this periscope-view afforded.

He checked the bearing, and snapped the handles up.

'Down . . . Captain in the control room. Slow ahead together. Diving stations.'

A rush of movement: men's faces hopeful, excited. Paul at the trim now, Wykeham pushing up beside him muttering, 'All right, Sub, I've got her', the ship's company already settling at diving stations – which in surface-ship terms meant action stations. Only CPO Logan didn't have to move at all, since the after hydroplanes were his action responsibility anyway. Paul had reported, a few seconds ago in the first moment of the rush and when the periscope had had time only to dip and then rise again into Ruck's impatient grasp, 'Seaplane on red one-oh, then smoke a little to the right of it.'

'Yes. Right.' Ruck had found the smoke too; he was studying it, twisting the periscope a small amount this way and that across it, during the ensuing moments when Paul was being relieved at the trim by Wykeham. Now, as he edged away to his own job at the 'fruit machine', Ruck was making a swift low-power search all round.

'Down.' Blank-eyed, with the picture in his head and his brain applying logical deductions, guesses, to it . . . 'Group up, half ahead together, port ten.'

His orders were repeated by the telegraphman and the helmsman. The extra speed and the change of course would take the submarine out towards the centre of the straits.

'Steer two-seven-oh.'

The chief ERA, Charlie Pool, was waiting near the captain, ready to read off bearings and ranges and set the firing-angle for him when the time came. *If* it did. The smoke might be coming from some tug hauling a lighter full of rubbish – or from one of a group of anti-submarine trawlers on a sweep: in which case the fly was rushing into the spider's web. Paul didn't *think* that such an amount of smoke would be coming from anything but

a biggish ship; half the reason for that opinion was the fact there
was also a patrolling or escorting seaplane.

'Course two-seven-oh, sir!'

'Very good. Slow together. Up periscope.'

Slowing the boat to reduce the feather, the splash around the
top of the periscope, which in such a smooth surface an aircraft's pilot might easily spot. The periscope jolted to a stop.
Wykeham reported, 'Depth twenty-seven and a half feet, sir.'

Having altered course about forty degrees to port the target –
smoke – ought now to be about thirty on the starboard bow:
Ruck had the periscope trained on that bearing before he put
his eyes to it. Adjusting fractionally, then settling; light reflected
down from the sea's surface, glittered in his eyes as Paul
watched him, hoping there *was* a target . . . Ruck muttered
angrily, 'Bloody thing. Why don't you bugger off?' He snapped
the handles up, and ERA Quinn sent the glistening tube shooting down.

'Half ahead together.' Ruck told Wykeham, 'Shagbat was
coming straight at me. Bloody thing.'

The seaplane, he meant. McClure whispered, close to Paul's
ear, 'What d'you reckon this is?'

'Something that smokes, Shortarse.'

'Bonfire on Sicily?'

McClure's job during an attack was to keep a track chart showing the submarine's movements and also the enemy's, plotting
the target by ranges and bearings and thus estimating his speeds
and courses. Paul's was to operate the 'fruit machine', a magic
box of dials and knobs which gave you certain vital information
if you fed it with the right data. It was about the size of a small
one-armed bandit, mounted on the bulkhead near the chart
table.

'Slow ahead together.' Ruck let the reduction in speed take
effect before he gestured again for the periscope. Vibration less-
ened as the revs were cut: when she was grouped up, you could
feel as well as hear the power forcing her through the sea. It
didn't mean she was exactly scorching a path through it: full

ahead grouped up, the maximum dived speed, gave her only
nine knots. The periscope rose into the captain's hands: he swiv-
elled around sky-searching, then settled on what had been the
bearing of the smoke.

Newton reported from the asdic position, 'Confused HE from
green two-eight to green three-four, sir!'

'What's confused about it?'

'More than one ship, sir. It's' – he swallowed – 'one lot's slow,
reciprocating, and —'

'*There*, now!'

Heads turned: expressions brightening . . .

Start the attack.' McClure's stopwatch, and Ruck's, clicked . . .
'Target is a tanker, about ten thousand tons. One destroyer frig-
ging around in front . . . Target bearing – *that*. Range – *that*.'
Chief ERA Pool read the figures off, over his captain's shoulder.
Ruck added, 'I'm – twenty degrees on his port bow. Down
periscope, half ahead together!'

Tankers were worth sinking, and so was the stuff they carried.
Tanks ran on it – Rommel's tanks – and Stukas flew on it.
McClure was putting that range and bearing on his track chart.
Ruck asked Newton, 'What revs d'you give the tanker?'

'One-fifty, sir.'

'Set enemy speed fifteen.'

Paul fed that to his machine. Range, bearing, angle-on-the-
bow, were all in its works already. There was a dial with a shape
representing 'own ship' and another with an outline for the
target. What mattered was their relative positions and the
dynamics of their courses and the enemy's speed, and what the
machine would provide in the end was called the DA, director
angle, which meant aim-off, the angle you'd send your torpedoes out on. If you'd got the figures right the torpedoes and the
target would run to meet each other like old friends.

Ruck told Wykeham, 'The shagbat was way over on the other
side, that time. So it hasn't seen us *yet*. And the escort is a
Partenope-class destroyer. Slow together. Up . . .' The periscope
rose swiftly, its wires hissing round the sheaves in the deckhead.

Ruck had his eyes against the rubbers before it had stopped moving: he'd swung to find the target – or the seaplane —

'*Damn!*'

Flinging the handles up had been an order to Quinn to send it down, fast . . . Anxiety and questions in a dozen faces; Paul thinking, *We've lost out* . . . Ruck muttered angrily, 'Seaplane was right on top of me, and the bloody target's zigged away. I'm about sixty on his port bow now, damn it.' Seconds ticked by while he thought about it . . . Then 'Stand by for a range and bearing. Up . . .'

If the Cant had been over them a minute ago, it wouldn't be there now – with any luck, it wouldn't, slow-flying as those things were . . . And if he could build a picture of the tanker's zigzag, anticipate its turns . . .

'Bearing – *that!* Range – *that!*'

The periscope was on its way down, and Ruck had gone to the chart table to see how it looked on paper. He told McClure, 'I was still sixty on his bow. Extend those tracks, see where he may have zigged.' He glanced round. 'Port ten, fifty feet, full ahead together. Steer two-three-oh.' He checked his stopwatch. 'Five minutes, now.'

McClure showed him the track chart.

'If he turned here, sir, it's giving him a mean course of two-oh-five, zigzagging twenty degrees each side of it. Courses one-eight-five and two-three-five.'

'I'll buy that.'

The submarine was at fifty feet, making her best dived speed and shaking from the effort. Wykeham looking uneasy as he glanced round at his captain. Full speed with the battery grouped up could exhaust it very quickly, and with a whole day ahead and the distinct possibility of having to manoeuvre to evade depthcharging, it wasn't a happy prospect. Battery care was the first lieutenant's – Wykeham's – responsibility. He'd turned back to check the trim, then looked round again. Ruck was preoccupied, watching the circling stopwatch hand in his palm.

Five minutes, Wykeham would be thinking, was a long time to be caning his precious battery that hard.

Ruck glanced up, and found Wykeham staring at him. He nodded. 'I'm going to nail this bastard.'

Wykeham sighed, turned back to the trim.

It was a gamble, basically, on where and when the tanker would make its next change of course. One of Ruck's problems was that with an aircraft over the top you could only take very quick and infrequent observations. The Sicilian coastline did limit the tanker's options, of course . . . Ruck would be hoping that when the target came back on to the port leg of its zigzag he'd have *Ultra* in a position to take a shot at it.

Part guesswork, part mental arithmetic, part logic and a lot of luck. 'Slow together. Thirty feet. Take it easy, Number One.' He meant, *Don't rush it, and risk breaking surface*. He asked the asdic operator, 'Bearing of the HE now?'

Motor noise and vibration fell away as the power was reduced. Newton should be able to hear the enemy's screws again now; in that racket, he couldn't have.

'Target is green five, sir.' His Adam's apple wobbled when he swallowed. 'Bearing drawing left —'

'The destroyer?'

'Right ahead, sir. Drawing left.'

'Depth thirty feet, sir.'

'Twenty-eight feet.' Ruck moved his hands, and the periscope began to move too. Newton reported, 'Still one-fifty revolutions, sir.' Ruck said, 'Port ten.' The periscope stopped, with his eyes already at its lenses. 'Bearing – *that*!'

'Green three degrees!'

'I'm – thirty-five on his port bow. Range – *that*!'

'Oh-three-five!'

Three thousand five hundred yards, that meant. The figures whipped through Paul's consciousness like runners leapfrogging and tumbling, but in the machine as he fed them into it they made sense, built a picture, slotted together to provide answers to other questions, while on Paul's left McClure translated it all into pencilled tracks, positions, courses, each position labelled in terms of seconds since the start of the attack. Ruck had steadied her on the adjusted course.

'Distance off track?'

'Two thousand one hundred, sir!'

The periscope slid down. Ruck confirmed the speed setting of fifteen for the tanker. He was studying his watch again: feet straddled, a frown of concentration on his lightly bearded face. He ordered port wheel again, and steadied her on a new course without taking his eyes off the watch's dial. Then his left hand's fingers curled, summoning the periscope . . . Bearing was green two-six – range two thousand one hundred yards – distance off track fifteen hundred. Periscope flashing down. Ruck was taking his time – and still ignoring, or not mentioning, the opposition, the aircraft and the destroyer . . .

'Open one, two, three and four bow-caps. Blow up all tubes.'

But the target could zig away again, turn its quarter to him suddenly: and the seaplane —

'Up . . .'

'Bow-caps open, all tubes blown up, sir!'

Ruck's eyes were against the lenses. Paul saw him flinch, and catch his breath. Then he'd steadied; he was showing his teeth, lips drawn apart like a dog's snarl as he reset the periscope on the target.

'Bearing *that*!'

'Green twelve degrees!'

'I'm eighty on his bow. What's my DA?'

'DA is eight, sir!'

Sweat gleamed on Ruck's face and neck; knuckles white, gripping the spread handles. 'Set DA eight. What's the firing interval?'

'Fourteen seconds, sir!'

Paul – and the others – heard it then. Fast propellers, a rising note like a train approaching – the destroyer racing directly at them. He put a hand behind him on the corner of the chart table, another on the fruit machine, instinctively bracing himself for the ramming. You visualized, without wanting to or trying to, the split hull, roaring inrush of sea. Seconds passing, CERA Pool reaching over the captain's shoulders to set the periscope on that DA and hold it there. When the target's bow approached the hairline in the sight —

'Fire one!'

You heard and felt the torpedo leave. A thump, and then a sharp rise in pressure as air vented back into the submarine.

'Fire two!'

Yellow light gleaming on carefully expressionless faces. You couldn't see what was happening up there, so you put your faith in the man who could.

'Fire three!' He pushed the handles up. 'Flood Q, sixty feet, full ahead together!' The periscope was already halfway down; the noise of the Italian destroyer's screws was loud, like a train hurtling past overhead. Ruck snapped, going by the fourteen-second stopwatch interval, 'Fire four!'

'Torpedoes running, sir.' Newton's eyes were on the deck-head, as if he was expecting to see the destroyer's stem crash into her. Half a minute ago there might have been such a danger; now, the needles were swinging past forty feet. Ruck said, wiping sweat from his forehead, 'Hundred and fifty feet. Group down. Port fifteen. Shut off for depthcharging.' He asked Paul, 'Running time?'

'One minute seven seconds, sir.'

The length of time it would take the torpedoes to get there, to hit or miss. The quick-diving tank was blown, and the boat sank more slowly, spiralling to port. Ruck told the helmsman, Creagh, 'Steer one-one-oh.'

'One-one-oh, sir . . .' To escape eastward now, across the straits. Ruck muttered, with his eyes on the circling stopwatch hand, 'That Partenope didn't give me much room.'

And the target could have altered course again, zigzagged away after the fish had started on their way.

'Hundred and fifty feet, sir.'

'Slow —'

Explosion: deep, some way off, and on cue, bringing hope. Faces still controlled, though, waiting . . . Fourteen seconds should be the intervals. And there would probably be a counter-attack which with reinforcements to the surface forces might last all day. Fourteen seconds had passed.

Twenty. Twenty-five. Twenty-seven. Twenty —

A second solid, jarring crash. Two hits: quite likely a kill. That first one alone probably wouldn't have sunk the target, and it could have been a fish going astray, exploding on the bottom. Relief all round, satisfaction. CPO Logan chuckled, nodding. Ruck had let out a long, hard breath. Wykeham reported in his mild, totally unstressed tone, 'Both motors slow ahead, grouped down. Boat's shut off for depthcharging, sir.'

'Not a bloody whisper, now. Pass the word.' He asked Newton, 'Where's the destroyer?'

'Green one-four-oh, sir, opening . . . There's A/S transmissions on that bearing. And – right astern, sir, breaking-up noises.'

Quite often a ship broke up as it sank. Bulkheads collapsed or split as the sea took hold of her, and the process was sometimes audible on asdics. Ruck went over to the A/S position, and Newton passed him the spare headset. With the earphones on, he nodded; then passed it back. He told Wykeham, 'No doubt about *that*.' Paul was wondering whether the torpedo tracks would have faded yet, or whether they might still be there for the seaplane to spot so it could then guide the destroyer to the point they'd fired from. But it would still have to guess which way they'd gone. The Italian was searching in the wrong area now and it might be beyond his imagination to guess that they'd fired from pretty well under his own ship's forefoot. And if he thought they'd attacked from ahead, the odds were that he'd expect them to be escaping seaward, southward, rather than on this eastward course.

Another explosion: so far astern it didn't raise an eyebrow. Then three more in quick succession, and a fifth all on its own. All distant, harmless, as the submarine crept away.

2

CPO Gaffney, the senior torpedo rating in the submarine, was cleaning oil off his hands on a wad of cotton waste. He was a tall, bony character, with a deeply cleft chin. He muttered, 'Bit over the hour. Not bad, considerin' the shower of cloth-'eads I got workin' for me.'

The torpedomen, he meant. They were restowing the gear now, dragging it back in from the gangway. This was the TSC, the torpedo stowage compartment, and for the last hour Paul had been supervising the reloading of the tubes, here and in the tube space, the small compartment immediately for'ard of this one, right in the sharply narrowing bow. It was an intricate and quite arduous task. First the TSC, which was also the main living space for the seamen, had to be cleared of its mountain of ham-mocks, kitbags, oilskins, seaboots, crates of stores and other clutter. Then the four reload torpedoes had to be eased carefully out of their racks at the sides of the compartment. Heavy bars had to be rigged for them to rest on and slide on, two down near deck level and the other two roughly at shoulder height, and then blocks and tackle rigged to haul them for'ard through the latched-back watertight doors into the tube space and into the tubes themselves. There were a number of complications to it, and it was heavy work in a very confined space. If you made a mistake at the beginning – like having a steel-wire rope the wrong side of a stanchion, and no one noticing it in time – you'd

find after half an hour's hard labour that the whole process had
to be reversed and then started again from scratch.

Ultra was paddling eastward at slow speed and a hundred feet
below the surface, keeping quiet and level while the reloading
was in progress. They'd begun it at about 0830, after breakfast,
and now it was getting towards 0940. Paul was due to take over
the watch again at 1015, so he'd missed the sleep he'd been
looking forward to earlier.

A small price to pay for a 10,000-ton tanker.

'Your fish ran good and straight, TI.'

'They bloody better, sir.'

Torpedoes didn't always run straight, though. Sometimes they
circled, or dived and hit the bottom, or their depthkeeping
mechanism went wrong and they porpoised, jumping like gamefish. Paul said, 'Touch wood', and looked around for some to
touch . . . The space was rapidly filling up again with gear: the
gangway would be unblocked soon and he'd be able to get aft.
There'd be a little more space in here now, with the spare torpedoes shifted into the tubes and the racks empty.

Gaffney asked him quietly, 'Bit of a close call, was it, sir?'

'Huh?'

'Destroyer close to running us down, was it?'

'Hell, no.' Paul told him, 'Skipper reckoned he had room –
just – so he stayed up and made sure of it.'

But it *had* been a close thing, he thought – half-listening to
torpedomen Booth and Furness arguing as to whether Booth
owed Furness 'sippers' of his rum tot today, as the settlement of
some bet. He knew it had been close by the way Ruck had
looked, by the time he'd squeezed that third fish away and then
realized he couldn't stay up for the fourth. McClure, who'd been
watching him at that moment too, had murmured when they'd
been falling out from diving stations, 'We looking for a VC,
d'you reckon?'

McClure was a stroppy little bastard at times . . . Paul went aft.
The passageway ran down the submarine's starboard side. On
his right he passed first the petty officers' and leading seamen's

mess, then the ERAs', then the galley. Able Seaman Shaw, the wardroom flunkey, asked him if he'd like some coffee.

'Thanks, I would.' Even Shaw's coffee, which tasted exactly like Shaw's tea. You knew which was which by the shape of the pot he made it in.

Wykeham was at the wardroom table, with a mug of the same liquid as well as some paperwork, a battery log, in front of him. Paul said, 'Tubes reloaded. They're stowing the gear now.'

'Shake the skipper and tell him, will you?'

Ruck was asleep on his bunk, under a blanket and with his back to the rest of the wardroom. It was more an alcove than a room, a space about seven feet square with two settee berths and two bunks that hinged up above them. A narrow bench with lockers in it and a chair on the gangway side of the table completed the furnishings.

Paul touched Ruck's shoulder. 'Captain, sir.'

'Yeah?'

The answer came immediately, as if he hadn't been asleep. But it was habit: even in sleep he'd be half-awake.

'Tubes reloaded, sir. They're putting the gear back now.'

Ruck rolled on to his back, and checked the time.

'Good. I've known it done faster, mind you.'

'We'll improve with practice, sir.'

'Who's on watch?'

'Navigator is, sir.'

'Tell him to come round to two-nine-zero and bring her up to sixty feet.'

Wykeham swallowed the last of his coffee. 'I'll see to it.' He capped his fountain pen and slid out.

Reversing course now, Paul thought. Heading back into the straits. It seemed rather soon to do that, when you'd just stirred things up in there. Ruck murmured – as if he'd read that thought, but staring at the deckhead's mass of piping and probably just thinking aloud – 'They won't be expecting anything there now. They'd expect us to be miles away and legging it like hell.'

He was probably right, at that. Shaw brought the coffee . . . Sipping it, savouring its distinctive aroma of metal polish, Paul thought again of McClure's critical *Looking for a VC*? There was one VC in the flotilla already: Wanklyn, captain of *Upholder*.

Ruck said, 'Seems you've brought our luck back to us, Sub.'

Paul had gone sick in Scotland, just when *Ultra* had finished her work-up period on the Clyde and had been about to sail for the Mediterranean. He'd come out eventually as a passenger in a freighter which had been part of a Malta-bound convoy. Ruck had promised him, when his appendix problem had come up, that if he could get himself to the island quickly enough he could have his job back: he'd taken out a spare-crew officer as a temporary replacement. But Paul had been lucky to make it to Malta at all: the ship he'd taken passage in had been sunk, and he'd ended up in one of the escorting destroyers, finally arriving with nothing but the salt-stained clothes he'd swum in.

He'd missed *Ultra*'s first two patrols, on each of which she'd sunk one small ship. This morning's tanker was therefore the first major success Ruck had scored out here. Perhaps he *had* been over-anxious not to miss? As a newcomer to the flotilla of seasoned veterans, he'd have wanted to prove himself worthy of that company, and it was an exceptionally high standard to live up to.

You could feel the movement and angle on the boat as she planed up to sixty feet and the rudder pulled her round through 180 degrees.

When he'd arrived at the Malta base, Paul had learnt that *Ultra* was at sea, due back in two or three days. He'd been sent for, and welcomed over a glass of gin and water, by 'Shrimp' Simpson, the flotilla's commanding officer – Captain S10. It was a considerable honour for a young RNVR sub-lieutenant, but Shrimp happened to be an old friend of Paul's father, Nick. He was a short, sturdy, fiercely energetic man with a fine sense of humour and a friendly, easy-going manner. About forty, Paul guessed. He'd seen Paul's father in Malta a couple of times, he said, when Nick had been there for short periods with his destroyer flotilla; more recently, of course, Captain Sir Nicholas Everard had been appointed in command of the cruiser *Defiant*, and taken her to join the Eastern Fleet.

Captain Simpson asked Paul, 'Am I right in thinking you were at school in America when the war started? Came over and joined on the lower deck?'

'I was at college, sir.'

'I beg your pardon.' Shrimp smiled. 'But your mother lives over there, is that it?'

'Yes. She married an American, after she and my father divorced.'

'She was a White Russian, wasn't she? And your father married her in the Black Sea in 1919, when we were fighting the Bolsheviks . . . Yes, and I met her here in Malta – oh, years ago . . . Where were you born?'

'In England, sir. Yorkshire.'

'But here in Malta, in the late twenties – your father was a three-striper, in a battleship, they had a house here and there was a child – son – was that *you*?'

'Must have been, sir.'

'I'll be damned.' They both laughed. Shrimp asked him, 'I don't suppose you'd remember much about the place?'

'Not much, sir. I remember the house, and a children's party on board that battleship, and my father teaching me to swim . . .'

'Just as well he did.' Shrimp frowned. 'You chose a peculiar way to get out here, Everard. From Gib you could have cadged a lift in one of our supply submarines. You'd have saved yourself that wetting.'

'Couldn't get to Gib, sir. Nothing that was calling there had room for me.'

'In a hurry, were you?'

'Lieutenant Ruck might not have been able to keep the job open for me, sir. If my replacement had had too long to settle in.'

Shrimp had nodded. 'In those circumstances, if you're anything like your father you'd probably have cut his throat.'

He'd had two days with nothing much to do except familiar-
ize himself with the base and get to know some of the other
junior submarine officers. Some were his friends already, from
meetings in home waters. There were ten submarines in the
flotilla at this juncture, including one Polish boat, and at any one
time about six out of the ten would be on patrol.

The base itself, Lazaretto, was on Manoel Island in
Marsamxett Harbour, which was to the northwest of Valletta;
Valletta in fact stood on a promontory dividing Marsamxett
from Grand Harbour. Lazaretto was an old sandstone complex
which in years gone by had been the island's quarantine estab-
lishment, and among names of detainees carved into the stone
on one high, sheltered balcony was that of the poet Byron,
who'd languished here and complained about it later in his
verse. But the Luftwaffe were out to demolish the place now,
and in February they'd made a start by hitting the seamen's
messdecks, leaving them roofless and gutted. Raids were so frequent that they were almost continuous on some days – the
Sicilian airfields were only fifty miles away, and the RAF were
always short of fighters.

There was alternative accommodation for officers and crews
in flats in the nearby suburb of Sliema, and there were also rest
camps in which ships' companies could spend some harbour
periods, right away from the base. And Shrimp Simpson had
had burrowers at work ever since he'd been here, tunnelling
into the sandstone cliff which was right up against the back of
the Lazaretto building. He'd told Paul, in that interview, that in
1934 there'd been a proposal to excavate submarine shelters
that would have made a Malta flotilla safe from bombing and
would have been easy to accomplish in that soft stone, but the
Treasury had vetoed it. The total outlay would have been the
same as the cost of building one U-class submarine now, in
1942.

The flotilla had its own farm, right in the Lazaretto base. The
important part of it was a piggery, but there were also chickens,
rabbits, goats, and a turkey that had a foul temper as a result of

sailors feeding it dried peas soaked in rum. Pork from the piggery provided most of the submariners' meat, and the pigs ate
all the flotilla's garbage. It had been Shrimp's idea, and the project had been set up with private money of his own. He was a hell
of a guy, Paul thought – the sort of man who *would* be a good
friend of his father's.

'Your watch now, is it?'

He looked up at Ruck, and nodded. 'Will be shortly, sir.' The
tannoy hummed, at that moment, as McClure switched it on in
the control room: the Scots voice rasped, 'White watch, watch
diving!'

Shrimp had said, finally, 'When you next write, give him my
regards and tell him I'm delighted to have an Everard here.'

He hadn't written yet. Because he knew that when he did he
ought to tell his father about recent happenings in London:
about the girl – Fiona Gascoyne – whom it was rumoured Nick
intended to marry, and Jack Everard, Nick's half-brother. Paul
had been with Jack in London when he'd first set eyes on her –
knowing damn well she was Nick's girl . . .

There was no doubt that if his father did marry Mrs Gascoyne,
Paul thought, he'd be landing himself in a hellish situation. Jack
wouldn't let her go: he'd said as much. He'd also proved how
little she was worth: he'd set out to do it. He was a hard case, he
didn't give a damn, and he had his own strange, family-back-
ground reasons for hating Nick. Also, although he was Nick's
half-brother, he was of a different generation: only two years
older than Paul, in fact. Fiona was young too – much younger
than Nick – and sensationally attractive; and a thoroughgoing
bitch.

How did you put *that* down on paper – to your own father,
about a woman he was in love with and planned to marry?

The relieving watchkeepers had all passed through to the
control room, and the men they'd taken over from were filtering
back for'ard. Wykeham returned, and confirmed to Ruck that
the boat was at sixty feet, course 290.

'Good.' Ruck sat up, and tied the laces on his canvas shoes.

He murmured, 'We'll come up and take a squint around. Perhaps Everard can find us another tanker.' He edged out, and into the control room. They heard him order 'Thirty feet.'

Wykeham told Paul, 'I want some shuteye now, Sub. If you see anything, keep your trap shut, eh?'

'Oh, sure . . .'

He'd keep the thing about Fiona Gascoyne and Jack to himself too. Because he didn't have the guts to write that letter. It shamed him that he didn't, but he'd been thinking about it for quite a while and he knew he wasn't going to be able to do it. If he could have seen his father and talked to him – if he could have led up to it gradually, and had a chance to find out first whether he did really intend to marry her . . . Paul sighed, wishing to God his father was still in the Mediterranean.

'Something worrying you, Sub?'

Wykeham was looking at him curiously. With his eyebrows hooped up like that he really did have the look of a camel: haughty, rather supercilious . . . Paul shrugged. 'Personal. A bloody awful letter I'm going to have to write and wish I didn't.'

'What's her name?'

He got up from the table. It was twelve minutes past the hour, time to go next door and take over from McClure. He told Wykeham, 'Fiona.'

In London it was twelve minutes past nine, and still half dark behind the drawn curtains in Fiona Gascoyne's flat in Eaton Square. She lay with her eyes open, studying the outline of Jack Everard – on his back beside her, his chest expanding and contracting with deep, even breaths. She thought, looking at him across a few inches of crumpled pillow, *He looks like a thug. A real bastard.*

Even in his sleep, relaxed . . .

There was a very slight resemblance to Nick, when you looked at him not in profile like this but full-face. Only a hint – and you wouldn't have seen it if you hadn't actually searched for it, and if you hadn't known them both about as well as it was possible to know anyone . . . But why bother, why look for a resemblance anyway?

Because you need to find a common element so you can link them, merge two men into one so you could love just one?

She was as deeply involved as he was, now. It was a bloody mess, and she hadn't asked for any of it. It had been just – *fun*, to start with: flirtation with an attractive man who also happened to be Nick's young half-brother. And from his side of it – well, she'd attracted him, and he'd been intrigued very much as she'd been because of the relationship with Nick: she'd only come to understand later that half the attraction sprang from the fact that she *did* belong to Nick – or Jack *thought* she did . . .

He said, 'You're twitching.'

'I thought you were asleep. I haven't moved.'

'You're like an electric charge, sometimes. You – have a magnetic field around you . . . What are you worrying about?'

She sighed. 'Take your pick.'

He hadn't opened his eyes yet. He said, 'No point in worrying. On a weekend morning, when I'm with you. It's the one time there *isn't* anything to sweat your brains about.'

He thought he was going to get killed. He'd told her so, when he was drunk. Twice . . . In the sober light of day neither of them had referred to it, but she knew he did believe it, and it had become part of the jumble of thought she groped around in and became lost in so often. In that clutter it was like a joker in a pack of cards. If you let yourself accept it, it swept the board: and then, because it eliminated the confusion that enveloped her relationship with Nick now, it created a new and sickening problem of its own. The idea of losing Jack, of Jack being dead – dead, but still part of her as she couldn't imagine him *not* being now, and trying to live as if he wasn't there – especially in a relationship, marriage even, with Nick?

Even loving Nick, the thought of it loomed like nightmare.

'I have to go back tomorrow night.' Jack turned his head to see what time it was. Nine-thirty . . . 'So we have thirty-six hours. Think we could spend it all in bed?'

'Of course not!'

'You want me to take you out?'

'Bet your ugly mug I do. I'll make us a snack for lunch, but —'

'No, we'll lunch at the Gay Nineties. I'll ring and book a table. Don't want to use up all your points.' He stroked her cheek with the backs of his fingers. 'You're still the most beautiful thing I ever saw in my life. Let's paint the town tonight!'

'I thought you wanted to stay in bed.'

He swung over, and his arms slid round her.

'We'll come back here for the afternoon. And we don't have to hurry now, do we?' His head moved forward and down; he muttered with his jaw abrasive against her neck and shoulder, 'There aren't many weekends left. If any. I want to make the most of the time we have.'

Now he'd said it sober.

Or perhaps she was jumping to a wrong conclusion . . . She asked him, 'D'you mean you're being sent away somewhere?'

He didn't answer. He was beginning to make love to her. Touching, stroking: hands, mouth, body. From outside, the sounds of London made erotic background music. It was the contrast, the prosaic noise of the streets while here, *now* —

'You'll have to get used to not having me around. There's nothing else could have done it. Broken us up, I mean. If any human being tried, I'd kill him. But – look, this is the stupid bloody truth of it, it's what's likely to *happen* . . . Will you still marry Nick?'

Motionless, waiting for her answer – which she didn't have . . . She whispered with her eyes shut, hiding from it, 'You haven't made it easy.'

'D'you expect me to regret that?'

'You're so wrong about him, Jack —'

'It's not *him* I think about. Not now, anyway . . . D'you wish it hadn't happened?'

'You *know* I don't . . .' She did, though. She wished with all her heart it hadn't. That she'd had the sense to realize how it might turn out, or just never to have met each other; and not, certainly, to be in love with him now – as she was, painfully – or have him in love with her, as he was beyond a shadow of a doubt.

He said roughly, 'You'll have him to yourself soon, anyway. Back to square one. You and him, and no complications.'

'You're trying to *hurt* —'

'For Christ's sake, I'm solving all the problems for you! Look, my darling, it's going to happen whether you like it or not, so —'

'So it could happen to Nick too . . . Jack, I think you're scared – and jealous – of the fact it *could* happen. I suppose because you're doing something dangerous. So I'd be left, with Nick. You want to hurt me because the thought of it hurts you and you want to see me suffer too – isn't that it? For what's purely in your imagination, and jealousy, and bitterness towards Nick – isn't it?'

He moved, for the first time in several minutes. Stroking her back. He said, 'You don't want to face facts, that's all.'

'No, *let's* face them. Tell me all about it. *Explain* the facts!'

'You know damn well I can't . . .'

Even if he'd wanted to, he couldn't have told her much. He still didn't know what it was that he was part of. He knew what he had to do, or try to do, once he got to whatever the target area was; he knew all that down to the smallest detail, and also that it would be soon now, that this was likely to be his last weekend in London. But that was as far as his knowledge of it went.

He'd been messing about in boats, in an outfit that came under Mountbatten's new Combined Operations set-up. Jack was in it because he'd volunteered and because of experience he'd gained in Crete, where he'd spent most of the previous year. He'd been sunk during the Crete evacuation, and left behind when the Germans took over. He'd worked with the Cretan partisans, mostly in getting British and Australian soldiers away by caique and submarine, but also taking occasional swipes at the German garrison – cutting a throat, blowing a bridge, sabotaging transport. There were people and materials to be brought in – often by caique, island-hopping from the Levant. Eventually he was brought out himself, and sent back to

England, but he'd acquired a taste for clandestine operations
and he volunteered for special service. By chance he'd timed it
well, since Lord Louis had recently been appointed to run
Combined Ops and suitable personnel were being recruited.

For a long time it was all training and exercising, in secluded
Scottish sea lochs. They'd used Fairmile motor launches. All the
ML skippers and officers were young reserve – RNVR – people,
and as Jack was now a senior Lieutenant with a lot of seatime to
his credit he found he was caught up in planning and instructing. And getting fed up with it, fast. Then there'd been a raid
planned, and he was to command the naval force; like everyone
else he'd been mad keen to go, but at the last minute the operation was called off. This happened just after he'd met Fiona: on
both counts, confinement in Scotland became intolerable. It
was at precisely this low point that he was sent for one morning
by the base commander: he had a visitor with him, an RN captain from Mountbatten's staff, who'd had him sent for.

There was a certain amount of preamble, including questions
about Jack's career to date, and a hint of a new appointment,
possibly a move south. Jack would have grabbed at anything at
all that might put him within reach of Fiona.

Finally the man came out with it . . .

'I believe you'd fit the bill, Everard. It's a very special job –
that's to say, you'd have to volunteer for it. And to start with – as
I said – we'd need to have you down south. A few weeks' special
training. Interested?'

He'd nodded. It didn't matter what kind of a job it was. 'Very
much so, sir.'

'I must warn you that, if it goes ahead, it will be an unusually,
a *quite exceptionally*, hazardous undertaking. You'd have ten or
twelve chaps in your own team, and you'd be landing to – well,
with a certain precise objective, although in fact you'd be part of
a somewhat larger force. I can't go into detail, obviously. But it's
a task requiring naval expertise, and quite beyond the scope of
our brownjob friends.' The military, he meant. He finished, 'I
think it might be rather up your street. But the risks, I repeat,

are about as steep as they could be. Are you sure you want the
job?'

'Certain, sir.'

'H'm . . . You're not married, I believe?'

'No, sir.'

'Very well, Everard, I'll put your name in for it . . . By the way –
what relation are you to Sir Nicholas Everard?'

'Half-brother, sir.'

'*Really* . . .'

The usual series of questions followed. And the usual praise of
Nick. It was a familiar, boring litany.

At his next interview, which took place in London, the project
was described to him in somewhat starker terms by a
Commander Smith, also from the planning section of
Combined Operations. He asked Jack, again after some preliminary chitchat, 'Do you understand the nature of the job?'

Smith had grey hair and a limp: he'd obviously been called
back from retirement. Jack told him, 'Don't know the first thing
about it, sir.'

'The aspect I have to impress upon you at this stage – and I'd
want to off my own bat even if I hadn't been instructed to – is
that it's going to be bloody dangerous.' Jack nodded. It was a
description applicable, he thought, to just about any commando-type operation. The commander added, 'To put it very
simply, the chances of your returning from it at all, let alone in
one piece, are so small as to be negligible.'

Jack laughed.

The commander raised his eyebrows. 'That's funny?'

'Sorry, sir. It sounded a bit – well, dramatic. Errol Flynn stuff.'

'Yes.' The grey head nodded. 'My apologies for the cliché,
Everard. It just so happens that it's the truth, and not a bit exag-
gerated. *If* the operation goes ahead, it'll be as I say – your
chances of survival will be as near as dammit nil. Barring mira-
cles, of course.'

Jack nodded. 'May I smoke, sir?'

'Yes . . . You still want to do it?'

'Yes.'

'Why?'

'Oh . . . Well, sir' – his lighter flared, and he borrowed that four-striper's phrase – 'it's sort of up my street. And one can get bumped off here in London – in bed or in a shelter. Then – well, in and around Crete I saw quite a lot of people get killed, and' – he shrugged – 'it's the same risk, isn't it?'

'Yes. I suppose it is. Except the odds are much worse.'

'Then it must be something really useful, *important* —'

'Yes, it's that, all right.' This seemed to clinch it. Smith looked satisfied as he took a pipe out of his pocket and began to fill it. He said, 'I can't tell you much at this stage. You'll train on a mock-up of the actual terrain, and you won't be told where or what it is. Your team will comprise ten volunteer other-ranks – six naval, and four Royal Marines. There'll also be an ML with its own officers and crew, for your transportation. They'll be provided from where you've been in Scotland.'

'May I pick that boat myself, sir, since I know them all?'

'No reason why not. Subject to their being available, and the CO's approval. But they'll come down in a fortnight or so; there's no need for them yet. You'll be going down to Cardiff, Everard. We've got a house near the docks as our accommodation and headquarters. I'll be with you most of the time, by the way.' He glanced at his notes. 'Monday. Report on Monday evening, by 1800. Here's the address. They'll give you a railway warrant in the outer office here. I think that's about all . . . D'you have any questions?'

'Will there be any weekend leave from Cardiff, sir?'

'Yes. Subject to' – he quoted the jargon – 'the exigencies of the Service . . . That is, until you know where you're going. After that, there won't. You'd better give me a contact address or telephone number, by the way.'

Jack gave him the telephone number in Fiona's flat. Smith noted it down, and asked him whose it was.

'It's – my sister's, sir.'

The commander glanced up, quizzically. 'Indeed.' He pointed

at his file. 'The record doesn't show you have one.' Jack said
nothing; Smith frowned. 'All right. Cardiff, Monday 1800.'

When he arrived down there, after spending the weekend
with Fiona, he found that the naval members of the team had
already reported. There were four torpedomen – a petty officer
and three leading seamen – and two engineroom artificers. They
were all volunteers and they'd all completed assault-course training. Commander Smith introduced them to him individually.
Later, when he and Jack were alone, he dropped his bombshell.

'You've got those fellows on their own for the first five days,
Everard. The leathernecks will be joining after that. By that time
you and this bunch will have learnt to handle a German E-boat.'

'Up periscope.'

The big one: ERA Summers sent it up. This first look round
would be with the sky search, because earlier in the watch
there'd been another Italian seaplane, a Cant, patrolling
between Calabria and the Sicilian coast. It had been a long way
off, mosquito-like in the circle of the periscope, but its presence
was still a warning.

It was eleven-forty now and the course was 270 degrees, due
west, to take the submarine out across the bottom of the funnel-
shaped straits. Ruck was being cautious, staying out of those
narrower waters higher up. There was a pair of trawlers trailing
each other around up there – obviously sweeping for submarines – and two A/S schooners nearer, inshore to starboard.

No aircraft now, anyway. He switched to high power and
began another, slower search. Cape dell'Armi was five miles on
the starboard beam, and beyond it to the left the land fell away
northward into the straits, with Reggio Calabria halfway up
towards the actual narrows. Just off that point was where the
schooners were hanging about, no doubt listening through
hydrophones, but at this range they didn't present much of a
threat.

He could see only one trawler now. The other must have
shifted up higher. The sea was as it had been since dawn: a low

swell and an unbroken surface reflecting the greyness of the sky. Earlier it had looked as if a lot of A/S activity was developing, presumably as a result of the sinking of the tanker, but it had settled down and what was visible now was probably no more than routine patrolling. Ruck might have been absolutely right when he'd said they wouldn't expect him to be in here now.

Paul took some bearings – Spartivento, a left-hand edge and a distant summit called Montalto – and went to update the position on the chart. He was tired, and once again looking forward to the end of his watch.

'All right, Sub?'

He glanced round. Ruck was looking at him from his bunk. Paul nodded. 'All serene, sir.'

'What's up there now?'

'Only one trawler in sight northward, sir. The schooners are still inshore, about where they were before.'

'The heat's off, then.' Ruck slid off his bunk. 'Not that it was ever exactly hot . . . No aircraft recently?'

'None since that Cant.' He showed him the new fix on the chart.

Ruck went into the control room. 'Let's take a shufti.' He lifted his hands, glancing at Summers: a moment later he was circling, the toes of his plimsolls stubbing against the raised lip of the periscope well.

Slow search now . . . A torpedoman – Leading Seaman Winter – came from for'ard, asked Paul, 'All right to go aft, sir?' Paul nodded. For the trim's sake, movements had to be limited. The ship's company's heads were back aft, beside the stokers' mess, and if someone had been visiting there already he'd have told Winters to wait. Ruck said, clicking the handles up, 'Down . . . Come round to three-one-oh, Sub.'

Turning up – towards the narrows where the trawlers were messing around. Paul told Creagh, 'Starboard ten. Steer three-one-oh.'

Creagh spun his wheel. 'Ten of starboard wheel on, sir.'

Stapleton, the fore planesman, put on a few degrees of dive, to counteract the bow's tendency to rise as she turned. He was levelling them again as Creagh eased the rudder.

Ruck had gone back to his bunk.

'Course three-one-oh, sir.'

'Very good.'

Stapleton was turning his head to look at the clock. Rather a protracted glance; Paul realized he was having his attention drawn to it too. He said, 'There's a minute to go yet. What's the matter – hungry?'

The bald head nodded. 'Peckish, sir. Peckish.'

It was time not only for the watch to change, but also for the midday meal. It would be a cold snack, as usual – pilchards, sardines or corned beef. The main meal was always in the evening, after the boat surfaced and you could use the galley stove. You could smoke, too, when the hatch was open and the diesels were running, sucking air through.

He unhooked the microphone from its deckhead stowage. 'White watch, watch diving . . .'

He was asleep, in mid-afternoon and in the deep, warm, underwater silence. The sleep was deep too – the kind submariners referred to as being at sixty feet. Sixty was a safe depth: down there you were under any bad weather that might be making surface life uncomfortable, and well hidden from your enemies. You always felt safer underwater than you did on the surface.

Surfacing now, though . . . Becoming aware, through the vague edges of some unpleasant dream, of voices, movement. Then he'd slipped back into the dream state: he was in the Gay Nineties club in London and Jack was crushing a naked Fiona Gascoyne in his arms and shouting at Paul over her head, 'Nick left me to *drown*!' But then it was Nick drowning: alone and half a world away, trying to call to him – to Paul – to tell him something terribly important . . .

'Diving stations, sir . . . Torpedo officer, sir?' Shaw, the wardroom flunkey, raised his voice higher: 'Sub-Lieutenant, sir!'

'Right!'

It wasn't, though: not until another second had passed and he knew where he was, that he had *not* been watching his father drown. He was half off the bunk by then, Wykeham vanishing into the control room, crewmen hurrying past in both directions.

Ruck was at the small, after periscope. Paul asked McClure, 'What's the excitement?'

Ruck ordered, 'Shut off for depthcharging. Silent routine. Hundred and fifty feet.'

The periscope hissed down. McClure murmured, 'Several little widgers up there hunting us. Too close for comfort. Been dodging 'em all this watch, but they seem to know we're here. And some weird tapping noise.'

'Tapping?'

'Like knocking on the hull. God knows. Some new —'

'Boat's shut off for depthcharging, sir.' Chief ERA Pool made the report. 'Auxiliary machinery's stopped.'

In silent routine, to give the enemy as little as possible to listen to, you switched off everything except main motors and the gyro compass.

Ruck asked Newton, the A/S man, 'Tapping, still?'

Newton nodded. His eyes were fixed rather dreamily on the deckhead: his ears, tuned to the underwater sounds that were reaching him through his set, were the only link *Ultra* had now with the hostile world outside.

'Port beam, sir. Moving aft a little.'

Asdic pings, when a destroyer had you in contact, were like squeaks, little *peep* noises as the impulses bounced off the hull. Nothing in the least like tapping.

'Hundred and fifty feet, sir.'

'Very good.'

'HE on green one-five-eight, sir!'

'What sort?'

'Reciprocating, sir.' Piston-engined, that meant, as distinct from turbine. Newton was counting, nodding very slightly to the rhythm in his ears. Like a doctor counting heartbeats: blank-eyed, wrapped up in it . . . 'One-eighty revs, sir.' He added, 'Drawing left now.'

'Are the trawlers still astern?'

He nodded. 'Astern, sir. And – red one-four-oh.'

Paul shifted to the chart table, and McClure obligingly pointed to the last fix he'd put on. They'd come well up into the straits, but not into the real narrows. It was eight miles from coast to coast here, and the submarine was just about in the middle. Paul heard Ruck order, 'Steer one-five-oh.'

Watertight doors had been shut all through the boat: it was part of the 'shut off for depthcharging' routine. The compartments were isolated from each other, except for telephone communication and also a small tube that pierced each watertight bulkhead just beside its door and through which you could yell if the screw-down valves at each end were first opened. The same tube was for use after heavy damage to check whether or not the adjacent compartment might be flooded.

'Course one-five-oh, sir.'

It was a line of retreat: if it proved possible to keep to it, *Ultra* would leave Cape dell'Armi four or five miles abeam to port and plug on out into open water.

'That HE's on the starboard beam, sir. Slowing.'

'What about the tapping?'

'Can't hear it, sir . . . HE green eight-five, one hundred revs. This one's transmitting, sir!'

Asdic transmissions, that meant – from the trawler, or whatever it was. It had come up to starboard on a course parallel to their own and now it had slowed down to probe for her with its asdics.

Directed this far by the mysterious tapping?

'HE closing from astern, sir, fast diesel!'

E-boat, presumably. Or something like it.

'Exactly astern?'

'Yes, sir.' Newton swallowed. 'Bearing steady, closing fast, sir.' Across the control room Paul met Quinn's eyes: both men

looked away. At times like this you tried *not* to show your
thoughts, or study others'. Quinn had looked puzzled, Paul had
noticed in that very brief exchange of glances. And *he* was, too.
It wasn't that there was necessarily anything particularly dangerous about this present situation; but it was unusual. The
tapping, and the different types of craft up there seemingly
acting as a team . . . The tapping, he guessed, might have come
from some shore installation, some new adjunct to the
Mysterious Measures.

Ruck had one foot on the bottom rung of the ladder that
slanted up to the lower conning-tower hatch, and one arm up,
ape-like, gripping the ladder above his head. The other hand
was in a pocket. Listening, and thinking . . . Paul was trying to
make his own brain work too, make sense of it, see some pattern
to the surface forces' tactics. A trawler on the beam; tapping
which had now faded and might have been from some coastal
installation from which they'd now removed themselves; and an
E-boat chasing up from dead astern . . .

'Trawler to starboard is in contact, sir!'

'*Sure?*'

Newton nodded. 'Turning towards, sir.'

Ruck pushed himself clear of the ladder. 'Group up, full
ahead together. Starboard twenty.'

From silent running, Paul thought, to making about as much
racket as you *could* make . . . But with the trawler already fingering them with its asdics, it wouldn't make all that much
difference.

'Both motors grouped up, full ahead, sir!'

'Twenty of starboard wheel on, sir!'

Ruck nodded. Waiting . . . Then: 'Stop together. Group
down.' The submarine was spinning round to starboard, driven
by rudder and that thrust of power. Ruck told the helmsman,
'Steer two-three-oh.'

'Both motors grouped down, sir.'

'Slow ahead together.'

The one in contact had been on green eighty. And Ruck was

turning her eighty degrees to starboard, therefore directly *at* it. In turning, with that burst of speed he'd have stirred up a whirlpool, churned up a disturbance which might – just *might* – hold the trawler's attention for a while.

'Where's the E-boat?'

Newton began to train his receiver round to find it. Ruck asked Wykeham, 'Can you hold her on one motor, Number One?' Wykeham said yes, he could. Ruck ordered, 'Stop starboard.'

'Course two-three-oh, sir.'

Southwest. Not the way they really wanted to go. But if the trick worked, *Ultra* would shortly be passing right under the trawler, and with any luck the Italian asdic operator would be concentrating on that centre of disturbance.

'The diesel HE has passed astern, sir.'

'Where's the other?'

'Green one-oh. Transmitting.'

'In contact?'

Newton's long head shook. 'No, sir.'

'Starboard motor —'

A depthcharge exploded on the port quarter. The boat shuddered a little, but not badly. Two more explosions – three – four . . .

'Starboard motor stopped, sir.'

'Very good.' Ruck added, 'Bloody mile out!'

Wykeham raised his right hand, crossed his first and middle fingers, then lowered it again. ERA Quinn grinned, scratching at his beard. McClure muttered, behind Paul, 'What did we do to deserve this?'

'You tell me.' Paul's whisper couldn't have been heard a yard away. 'You had the bloody watch.'

'HE astern, sir – that's the trawler – astern, drawing right. Diesel HE slowing, on red one-four-oh. Slowing and opening, sir!'

'Opening' meant opening the range, going away. Ruck murmured, with a glance upwards towards the surface, 'Keep at it, boys.' He told Wykeham, 'They're looking for us inshore. Bloody fools think we turned to port.'

Minutes ticking by . . .

Ruck had been silent, listening and watching Newton. *Everybody* listening. The enemy might discover their mistake, return, regain contact . . .

Might. Might *not.*

Newton confirmed, after ten minutes, that both lots of HE were a long way astern and fading. Ruck waited, making sure of it for a while longer; then he nodded.

'Open watertight doors. Pass the word – quietly – that we'll continue silent routine and I don't want to hear a bloody hiccup. What's our course now?'

'Two-three-oh, sir.'

'Port ten. Steer one-one-oh.'

'Stand by to surface.'

Wykeham said, 'Check main vents.'

Ultra was at twenty-eight feet, at diving stations, and Ruck was at the big periscope. It was dark now, up top, and the control room was dimly lit for the sake of night vision. If you went straight into the dark bridge after bright lights you'd be blind for some possibly crucial minutes.

The clock's hands pointed at seven-thirty.

'Main vents checked shut, sir.'

'Ready to surface, sir.'

Ruck was dressed for the bridge, in an Ursula suit and seaboots. An Ursula was a waterproof jacket and trousers; first used in a submarine of the same name, it was now standard submarine issue.

'Listen carefully all round, Newton.'

To make as sure of the situation as was possible . . . In the moments of surfacing in enemy waters a submarine was at its most vulnerable – wallowing with only half buoyancy, and blind, until men were functioning in her bridge . . .

Paul had come off watch at six-fifteen; he'd had only the last

hour of the watch, in fact, after they'd fallen out from diving stations. Ruck had held to the easterly course, so as to get out to
where he could surface as soon as it was dark. The night would
be spent – as usual – charging batteries, and his plan for tomorrow was to close in to the approaches to the straits again and
spend the forenoon in hopes of a target coming through. If
none did, he'd carry out a bombardment of some suitable railway bridge during the afternoon, selecting one on either the
Italian or the Sicilian coast according to the disposition of A/S
craft. Then tomorrow night he was thinking of retiring down-
coast to Catania, giving the hue-and-cry up here a day or two to
tire itself out. Shrimp Simpson's orders for the patrol, scrawled
on a sheet of signal-pad in Shrimp's own hand, did allow him
that line of withdrawal.

Newton reported, 'Clear all round, sir.'

Ruck completed his own visual check. You could imagine the
darkening night, the empty sea with the white feather of the
periscope's top cutting through it . . . 'Down periscope. Surface!'

Wykeham ordered, 'Half ahead together. Blow one and six
main ballast.'

ERA Quinn wrenched open those two valvewheels on his
panel. High-pressure air was noisy as it pounded into the bow
and stern main ballast tanks, forcing seawater out of them. The
signalman, Janaway, had unclipped and pushed up the lower
conning-tower hatch; he got off the ladder now so that Ruck
could climb up into the tower. He'd get up close under the top
hatch, ease the pins out of the clips and take one clip off; he'd
be up there in wet-metal-smelling dark, listening to reports from
the control room below him as the boat rose towards the surface. When he took the second clip off, the hatch would fairly fly
open, its heavy weight flung back by the air pressure that had
built up in the boat during the day, mostly from the torpedo-
firing. Janaway had disappeared into the tower now. Wykeham
called, 'Twenty-two feet . . . Twenty . . .'

Air still roaring, as the tanks fore and aft were emptied.

'Fifteen . . . Twelve . . . Ten . . . Eight feet!'

The top hatch clanged open. Air whooshed up and out: pressure dropped sharply, and a sprinkling of sea splashed on the control room deck. Shaw, the wardroom flunkey, held a bucket under the helmsman's voicepipe: as the cocks on the pipe – one in the bridge and one down here – were opened, about a gallon of water sloshed out.

'Stop blowing. Open one and six LP master blows.' Wykeham had had to yell to make himself heard. 'Start the blower.' The captain's voice boomed in the voicepipe: 'In both engine clutches, half ahead together, running charge starboard!'

It was already cooler and fresher: stale air had rushed out with the release of pressure. Now as the diesel engines exploded into sudden, noisy life, sucking air down through the conning-tower, there was a powerful, cold wind blowing through.

Wykeham said into the Tannoy microphone, 'Carry on smoking.' All through the compartments, matches and lighters flared. Cigarettes had been ready in men's lips and lights in their hands for the first smoke of the day. Wykeham added, 'Patrol routine. Red watch. Red watch to patrol routine.'

'Only a running charge, sir, one side?'

Roffey, leading LTO, the senior electrical rating, looked indignant. Wykeham assured him, 'Don't worry. Only for an hour or —'

He was dealing with some other questioner at the same time.

'Box is bloody low, sir.' Roffey was a short, rotund man, pale-faced from the motor room's constant warmth, and with bulging, heavily muscled forearms from years of slamming the big copper switches in and out. Wykeham turned back to him. 'I know it is. About one hour, then we'll have a standing charge. All right?'

The diesels could drive the boat along and at the same time put some of their effort into battery-charging. But a standing charge, using one engine for propulsion and the other for charging only, did the job a lot more quickly. You needed all the dark-hours time there was, because the night patrol was very often interrupted, by patrol-craft or other interference . . .

Roffey had gone, and Wykeham was heading for the wardroom to get dressed for the bridge; this was still his watch and Ruck would be getting impatient up there. ERA Quinn stopped him: 'Start the compressor, sir?'

'Yes, please.'

To replenish the air in the high-pressure bottles, the stuff you needed for blowing tanks with. It was as vital as battery power. He reached the wardroom, and got his bridge watchkeeping gear out from behind the watertight door. Paul was sitting at the table, smoking, fiddling with a set of poker dice. Wykeham suggested, 'Game of liars later, Sub?'

'If the skipper'll join us, why not?'

'Double cameroon perhaps, for a change?'

'Hardly be time.' You played double cameroon with two sets of dice and a scorecard to fill, and his next watch started at ten-fifteen. He said, 'Feels like it's getting a bit bumpy . . . *Cochon Lazaretto* for chow, I'm told.'

The pork would be in the oven by this time. Wykeham headed for the bridge. Bob McClure came from the heads, lighting a fresh cigarette from the stub of his first one. Paul said, 'You'll never grow to a normal size if you smoke that fast.'

The navigator sat down beside him. He nodded. 'And fuck you, you half-Yankee prick.'

It was a happy time of day. The fresh air, the smokes, for the ship's company a tot of rum and for everyone the prospect of a good meal. 'Forces' Favourites' from the BBC over the loud-speakers: Vera Lynn belting out 'We'll Meet Again' and the Inkspots keening 'Don't Get Around Much Any More' . . . Paul said, 'Number One tells me you may have given those Gibraltarians water on the knee.'

'What's this cock?'

'He told me you were, quote, valiantly belabouring their kneecaps, unquote. Eye to eye with the policeman's shins, he said.'

'He's an amusing shit, isn't he?' McClure rolled two more kings, making five. He added bitterly, 'To think I went tae the bastard's help!'

'Other way round, according to him.'

'Och, well. Only because the dagoes picked on me to start with.'

There'd been a party in the submarine flat on Scudd Hill, and apparently there'd been a very pretty little Gibraltarian girl at it, as well as a bunch of Wrens. The local girl had suddenly realized how late it was – there was an 11 pm curfew in force in Gib – and was almost in tears with worry about going home alone. Nobody seemed to know who'd brought her or invited her, so Wykeham with Old Etonian gallantry had offered to escort her, and McClure, who'd been trying to chat her up all evening, insisted on going along too. Somewhere near where the girl lived they were intercepted by two of her male relations, both of whom had immediately attacked McClure, either because he looked easier meat than Wykeham or because he'd happened to have his arm round the girl when the meeting occurred.

'You were reaching up to embrace her hips, Number One says.'

'I'd ignore anything that long streak of piss dreams up.'

'How did the cop get into it?'

'The family were yelling for help, that's how. Soon as they found they weren't getting a walkover. By the time the rozzer arrived one of 'em had scarpered and the other was on the deck. This clown comes running with a bloody great truncheon up over his head, shitface belts him and I join in, and that's that.'

'Wouldn't the girl have told them where you'd come from?'

'Might've.' McClure threw a full house in one. 'But we were sailing in the morning. That's what the party was for.'

Ruck said, pulling off his waterproof jacket as he arrived down from the bridge, 'Bunch of bloody hooligans . . .'

They'd told him about it – Wykeham had – in case of repercussions, so he'd be prepared with a defence. Ruck had thought about it and agreed that they'd acted wisely; they'd committed an offence, but if they hadn't taken decisive action they'd have ended up in the slammer and *Ultra*'s sailing would have been delayed.

Ruck kicked off his seaboots. 'What's for supper, anyone know?' Shaw stuck his head round the corner from the galley, and made his 'oink-oink' noise. The captain nodded, reaching for one of Paul's cigarettes. 'Good-oh.' He pulled the only chair back, and sat down. 'All right, boys. Ace up, king towards.'

'Captain, sir . . .'

It was the petty officer telegraphist, Parker. He handed Ruck a sheet of pink signal-pad. 'To us from S10, sir.'

Ruck took it from him, and scanned it rapidly.

'Well, *well* . . .' He read it aloud. 'To *Ultra* from S10. *Two large troopships now loading in Taranto, destination probably Benghazi. Establish patrol forthwith vicinity 39 degrees 05 north, 17 degrees 45 east.*'

He passed the signal to McClure. 'Time to earn your keep, pilot. Course to steer, and what speed do we need to get there by first light?'

3

'My sister and I remember still . . .' The dance band moaned softly in a pinkish glow, and the girl singer was tiny, bare-shouldered, blonde. The lyrics were slop, Jack thought, but the melody was all right, adequate as a background against which to smooch around the little patch of floor. Not now, this minute, because Fiona had gone to the girls' room; he'd made her cry, and she'd gone to repair her face.

What the singer and her sister remembered still was a tulip garden and an old Dutch mill. Then certain glossed-over events connected – one gathered – with the Nazi invasion of Holland, and the last line of each verse was, 'But we don't talk about that.'

Jesus. He thought, mesmerized by the yellow glow of his whisky glass, that you couldn't safely talk about any bloody thing at all. You wanted to shout it, howl it at the moon, and you couldn't even whisper it without – he reached for a cigarette, opening the case and fingering it out one-handed – tears . . .

To start with they'd been sparring, about the same old things. Because these were the last minutes – twenty-four hours yet, roughly, but that short space of time was easily broken down into minutes and seconds – you wanted things clear, understood, explained. Some people might have been noble about it and tried to shield her from the truth, but he didn't see what kindness there'd be in that, in the long term. Facts emerged and became events: you *had* to face them then, so why not be prepared for them . . . He needed – not wanted, *needed* – to be inside her skin, have her inside his, so he could leave knowing that what he felt, she'd be feeling too. And to know what she'd do, what he'd be leaving. If he could be certain she'd be throwing herself back at Nick it would almost make the whole thing easier – in the sense of a door slamming and nothing else mattering all that much . . .

Confusing. Maudlin, perhaps. Drink didn't help. He tipped some Scotch into his glass, replaced the stopper in the bottle, and gave himself a squirt from the soda syphon. Like most other members of this club he had his own locker and kept gin and whisky in it – duty-free, at that. If you bought bottles here, from the head waiter, you had to pay a small fortune for them and you were inviting a hangover that could last for days; the only genuine thing about those bottles was the labels. Fiona was drinking Scotch tonight: she liked it with ginger ale, though, which you had to buy from the waiter and cost about as much as the liquor had.

Thinking back – with the drummer's wire brush rhythmic in his ears, and a girl who was with an RAF man at the next table smiling faintly when she caught his eye – to how that last conversation had started . . . Fiona had said – he remembered – 'Oh *Christ*, how I hate this war – and this year specially, this *bloody* year —'

'Thanks.'

'Oh, don't be *silly* —'

'Well, Nick's away, *I'm* here – barging in and upsetting your life, splitting you from him —'

'But I'm *not* split from him!'

He'd told her, 'You see – I love you . . .'

It was muddled now in his mind, and he'd forgotten some bits of the conversation just before that. But he'd said it, just as he'd decided earlier in the day that he *had* to tell her – except he'd intended saving it for later, for when they'd be back in her flat some time around dawn. It had been a pressure in his mind, and he'd just let it out; then he'd explained, 'I didn't expect to. You know that, of course, it wasn't – serious, to start with. But I've got to tell you this – I never felt it or said it to anyone in my life before. It's all yours – sort of a parting gift.'

'*Please*, Jack . . .'

'I'm sorry. It's true, you see. Why can't I —'

'Nick. *He's* why. There, now I've —'

'*Damn* Nick, and —'

'Listen to me, Jack.' She'd been twisting her glass round and round, and not looking at him. The floor was crowded with dancers who hardly moved, only swayed and shuffled, girls with their eyes shut or half-shut, dreamy, lost, their arms tight round their partners' necks. Not a man in the club, apart from waiters, who wasn't in uniform. Fiona turned her face towards him: light radiating from the bandstand shone in her wide, slanting, incredibly beautiful eyes. She told him, 'I've been thinking – this afternoon, while you were asleep, I was getting it all a bit straighter in my mind. It isn't really complicated: it's just been getting over our heads so we haven't been able to see it properly . . . Listen. First – you *will* come back, from whatever you're about to do. And Nick will come back from where he is, and I'll marry him if he still wants me to, and we'll forget – you and I, Jack – all of this, what we're – what we are to each other now. I'll be a faithful wife to Nick, and you and I will be *friends*, and —'

He'd laughed. She went on doggedly, 'And you'll marry someone else —'

'Fairy tales.' He shrugged. The band was playing 'Honeysuckle Rose'. 'Believe it if it makes you happier.'

'All you want to do is make me miserable!'

She'd said that loudly, angrily, and the girl at the next table had turned to look at them, interested in seeing a quarrel developing. Interested in Jack, too. Fiona caught on at once, and turned her back on her. She put her hand on Jack's, on the table between their glasses. 'I'm sorry . . . But listen. I did a *lot* of thinking, this afternoon. And another conclusion I came to was that we don't have to be ashamed of this, Jack, not the way I've felt a few times lately. Because I'm not Nick's wife – not yet – and I'm not even his fiancée, in any formal or definite sense. What's more, he knows I've had boyfriends. I've been careful to *let* him know, because – well, never mind, but that's how it's been . . .' She shook her head. 'I didn't want to be tied down. Not for a while, anyway. He knew it and accepted it – that's what matters. But – this thing between us is different, isn't it? And – Jack, don't tell him, please. Don't even let him *suspect* it? And when I am his wife —'

'I'll be your lover.'

She frowned. 'There has to be a solution, Jack. And this is it, what I'm telling you now. You've simply *got* —'

'Wait.' He took both her hands in his. With her back to that other table, she was facing him on the velvet-covered seat. 'A better idea still . . . If we make your fairy story come true – if I *did* come back – would you marry *me?*'

That was the point at which she'd begun to cry.

They were supposed to have intuition. Perhaps she'd sensed the truth which up to now she'd been shutting her mind to?

In a sense, his own mind was shut to it too, though. The odds were – as Smith and the other man had warned him – against one's surviving this expedition. That was plain fact, unarguable; you could only accept it and, at one level of awareness, believe in it. In your heart, you didn't. It wasn't a matter of odds or logic, just a natural trust in your own fate. He *thought* that was it. All he *knew* was that he and his team were to be landed on a jetty in some enemy port, in the face of heavy opposition, then sprint some five hundred yards – by night, under fire, with enemies in defended points and gun emplacements determined to stop them; then reach another quayside – presumably an inner harbour – where they'd take over a berthed E-boat and fire its torpedoes at a static target 150 yards away.

That was *all* he knew. Nothing about where, when or what for.

Commander Smith had told him on that first evening in the house at Cardiff, 'I've got an E-boat here. Only one in captivity, so far as I'm aware. Someone caught it off the Dutch coast and brought it back alive, and I've been allowed to borrow it for you to practise on.'

With his team of engineers and torpedomen he'd spent that week getting the hang of it. They'd christened the boat *Sauerkraut*: it had an S identification letter on it, not E as one might have expected. They'd taught themselves to start it up and get it away from a quayside in a hurry while at the same time checking that its two torpedoes, German 50cm, were 'armed', set to detonate on impact.

At the end of the week the Royal Marine section had arrived; one sergeant, one corporal and two marines, all commando-trained. And the instructors, themselves commandos – a captain named Trolley, and two sergeants, Woburn and Hislop. They started at once on a rigorous training programme: endless physical training, close combat and weapons drill and route marches by day, and by night practising the assault over a specially set-up course on land that was being reclaimed as an extension to the docks. The ML and its crew joined them. Then in later stages a force of commandos under training was brought in to act as defenders opposing them. The mock assaults were conducted in all kinds of weather, with real explosives being thrown around, searchlights blazing in their faces . . . They could do the whole thing now in about one-twentieth of the time it had taken them to start with, and after that considerable expenditure of energy they were still able to do their stuff with the E-boat quickly and smoothly and without using lights. When it came to the real thing there'd be plenty of light anyway, from gunfire and explosions; *if* they got that far alive, Trolley pointed out, when the ammunition wasn't blank and the grenades weren't thunder-flashes.

Jack detested Trolley. He shaved his head, didn't drink or smoke, and disapproved of Jack's weekends in London. The four Royal Marines comprised the 'protection party'. It was their job to ensure that the naval group did get through to the E-boat and that the opposition was held off while they took control of it and loosed off its torpedoes.

Local inhabitants and dock workers had been allowed to believe that the exercises were being held to train personnel in guarding shore installations against enemy raiders. There'd been a larger group training here over the same ground, apparently, shortly before Jack's team had arrived; they'd all been commandos, army men.

Jack had begun to think they wouldn't get much better now, and that there was a danger of going stale. Smith had agreed with him: but it hadn't bothered him at all. This, plus certain other clues, indicated that the deadline was approaching. Jack had recalled that the man who'd recruited him, up in Scotland, had said they'd be part of a larger force, and it seemed to fit in with there having been others here before them; Smith hadn't mentioned such a thing, but when Jack asked him a question about withdrawal from the target area – responsibility for ordering it was surely his own, but there seemed to be some confusion about it – the commander had begun, 'Well, the military force commander —'

Then he'd seemed to bite his tongue. He'd demanded, 'What makes you think other people might be involved?'

Jack told him. The commander swore. Obviously the main force, which must have a naval and a military component, had to be assembling and training somewhere else, in great secrecy. And a raid on the coast of Europe would hardly be sent off from Wales; this group must surely move to a jumping-off point somewhere on the south or east coast, joining up with the main body after they'd reached that stage in their own training.

It was at about this point that Tubby Sharp, the RNVR lieutenant commanding the Fairmile launch, had come up with a good idea. He'd suggested to Smith that the E-boat, if they might be allowed to use it – keep it – would be a lot more suitable for the job than his ML would be. The German boat had a lower profile, much greater speed but still more than adequate range; its twin high-speed MAN diesels could push it up to more than thirty knots when necessary; and its torpedoes might come in handy if the raiding force met seaborne opposition. And – most cogent point of all – the motor launch had been giving a lot of trouble with machinery breakdowns, and its unreliability had been worrying them.

Smith went up to London rather doubtfully, but returned to announce that the proposal had been approved. Sharp and his crew were to transfer to *Sauerkraut.* But modifications were to be made. The one-pounder AA gun aft was to be replaced by a 20-millimetre Oerlikon – she already had a 20-millimetre for'ard, between her torpedo tubes – and extra armour plating was to be fitted to the front and sides of the bridge. From the orders that Smith gave to the two ERAs it seemed likely they'd be sailing from Cardiff not later than the middle of next week. There was also a suggestion – it fitted in with what he'd already guessed – that they'd have a week or more in some other harbour for any finishing touches that might still be needed.

One way and another it was pretty obvious, Jack thought, that there'd be no more weekends in London. He'd asked Smith a personal favour.

'If this operation does go ahead, sir, and I get bumped off, would you mind letting someone know what's happened?'

The commander hadn't looked too happy. He'd pointed out that next-of-kin would automatically be notified.

'This isn't kin, sir. It's someone who wouldn't hear, and who'd really need to know.'

Smith sighed. 'Better give me the name and address.'

'Just a telephone number, sir. The one you have already.'

'Your sister?'

'Well. Not exactly.'

'So?'

'If you'd ask for Mrs Gascoyne. Just say – well; that I'd asked you to call her, in certain circumstances, and just not to expect me back.'

Smith hated it. It showed, clearly. And very likely it was the 'Mrs' that irked him particularly. He said disapprovingly, 'Not a very pleasant task you're asking me to perform, Everard.'

'I'm sorry, sir. But I'd be extremely grateful. Frankly, there's no one else I could ask. Especially in view of – well, security —'

'Speaking of which – does this Mrs Gascoyne know what you're involved in?'

'She knows nothing about it, sir.'

'Well.' He was still frowning. 'I sincerely trust the occasion will not arise.'

He didn't look at Jack as he said it. From his position on the sidelines, of course, all Smith could see would be facts, probabilities, the odds against. He'd see Jack, as the team's leader, as the least likely of them all to get out of it alive. You could understand this, because in his place you'd take the same detached view of it; but you could guess, too, that if Smith were in *your* shoes he'd have the same instinctive trust in personal survival that you had yourself.

They'd begun to play 'Don't Get Around Much Any More'.

'Oh, I've been an age. I'm sorry, darling!'

Fiona, back from her excursion. It was extraordinary; you could let her out of your sight for just ten minutes, and then suddenly seeing her again be astonished, knocked for six all over again. Nobody, he thought, could ever get *used to* Fiona . . . He eased the table back to give himself room to stand up and to let her in, but she'd noticed the girl at the next table giving Jack the eye again, and she'd turned to her. 'Hello.'

The girl smiled, glancing again at Jack. 'Hello.' She was about nineteen.

Her Air Force escort beamed up at Fiona: 'Why, *hello*, there!'

Fiona ignored him. She told the girl, 'If you haven't managed it yet, my dear, you never will. I'd give up, if I were you.'

'I – beg your pardon?' Blushing . . .

Fiona pointed at the airman. 'Make the most of *that.*' She slipped in behind the table, sitting so close against Jack that she was almost on his lap. She murmured, 'Poor little thing. But beggars can't be choosers, can they? . . . Darling, I feel absolutely *marvellous.* The old duck in the lav sold me a pill for

half a crown. It's called benzedrine. Isn't it what they give commandos?'

'I wouldn't know.' He warned her, 'Better watch the booze,
though, if you've had that.'

'Oh, phooey! Anyway, let's dance!'

'All right.'

'No. Wait.' Her hand cool on his. 'Let's just listen to this one.'

'Anything you say.'

'I'm crazy about it . . .' She did a double-take: 'Well, I say! Give
me a drink, you mean bum!'

He poured her one. Then she wanted a cigarette. She held
his hand with the lighter in it, stared into his eyes while the
pianist repeated huskily that he kept pretty much to himself.
She murmured, blowing smoke out with the words, 'You're
awfully sweet, Jack.'

'No, I'm not. Not *sweet.*'

'The rest's an act. All the tough-guy stuff.' She asked him,
'Would you *really* want to marry me?'

Wykeham grunted, 'All right, Sub. Go get your head down.'

Quarter past midnight. Paul lowered the binoculars which
he'd had at his eyes for the last two hours. The night air was
cold, with spray in it now and then as the submarine lanced her
way eastward through a slightly choppy sea. The fore casing –
looking down on it from this bridge – was a jet-black finger with,
up near the pointed bow, two great bat-ears that were the
turned-out hydroplanes a few feet above the jumpy surface. The
steel was wet, glimmering from a faint radiance of stars. The
clouds were shredding, which was bad luck on Bob McClure
because they'd be out of sight of land at diving-time tomorrow –
no, *today* – and Ruck would be sure to insist on starsights for a fix
of their position. Bob was still rather slow at working out his
sextant observations, and morning stars invariably left him in a
bad temper.

There was a certain fascination, Paul found, in his messmates'
idiosyncrasies. He dropped into the hatch and climbed down

into the control room. The coxswain, CPO Logan, was PO of the watch. 'Kye, sir?' he offered.

'Thanks, cox'n. Just the thing.'

The chart table light was burning, and Ruck was there, checking courses and distances. He too had a mug of the coxswain's cocoa at his elbow. Paul took his and put it on the wardroom table while he pulled off his wet Ursula suit and extra sweater.

Beside Ruck: 'Excuse me, sir. Just the log . . .'

Ruck pushed it over to him. At the end of each watch you had to enter a weather report: wind, sea, visibility, sky conditions. Ruck asked him, 'What's the sea like?'

'Should have some broken water tomorrow, sir.'

Earlier, Ruck had been in something of a quandary: the problem being that if he'd set a course directly for the position ordered in that signal, *Ultra* would have had to dive at first light still fifteen or twenty miles short of it, and in the time it would take to cover that distance at dived speed the enemy could pass unseen and unheard. He'd discussed it in the wardroom with Wykeham. They could have made it on time, or nearly on time, but only by going flat out on both engines with no battery charge: then they'd have been in the right place, more or less, but in rotten shape to start the day.

His decision had been a compromise. If the troopship convoy was routed directly from Taranto to Benghazi they'd be steering a course of 165 degrees, following a track that did pass through the position given in Shrimp's signal. To be on that track was more important, Ruck had decided, than to be in that particular position on it; and he could get to it sooner by joining it forty-eight miles farther south, approaching it at right-angles and then, when he was on it, turning up towards Taranto. He'd be on the enemy's route, and dived before the light came, and he'd have at any rate *some* power in the batteries.

It was a good solution, but one danger in it was worrying him: Shrimp might have ordered some other boat to a waiting position fifty miles downtrack of *Ultra*'s. He would, undoubtedly, have deployed other submarines to intercept; the doubt was at

what intervals he'd have disposed them. And you couldn't signal
to ask: breaking wireless silence would alert the enemy to submarine activity on his convoy's route.

'Read my night orders before you turn in, Sub.'

'Aye aye, sir.'

Ruck moved away – into the control room. Prowling, thinking, sipping at his mug of kye. Paul reached for the night-order
book, and studied his captain's neat, sloping handwriting. After
0200, any submarine sighted was not to be attacked without
prior challenge and identification. That was the only point that
would affect him, during his next watch: and one always made
sure of knowing the challenge and reply letters for that two-
hour period, anyway. Ruck's other instruction was to McClure:
morning stars, before diving . . . Paul chuckled as he put his ini-
tials to the orders as confirmation that he'd read them. Then he
drank the kye, returned the mug to the control room messenger, and turned in.

Engine noise was a loud and constant rumbling. He could
also hear, as he pulled the blankets up, the sea crashing and
banging along the hull inside the casing, booming against the
tower. Four hours' sleep now – three and a half anyway – *if* there
were no interruptions. Then he'd be taking over from McClure
at 0415, allowing the diminutive Scot to get busy with his sextant
and logarithm tables.

Paul wondered where his father was, right at this moment.
Judging by the BBC news of Jap successes in the southwest
Pacific there'd be no bases for Allied ships to operate from, by
this time. If any Allied ships still floated . . .

Jack Everard hated his half-brother Nick, Paul's father. Paul
suspected the influence of Jack's mother, Sarah, Nick's step-
mother: she was a dried-up, bitter creature, and *she* hated Nick,
for sure. Impossible to know why. The Everard family past was a
murky area, impenetrable to the outsider – the term 'outsider'
including himself, because though he was very much his father's
son he was also something of a mixture: part-Russian parent-
age, and upbringing in the USA . . . It seemed quite natural to

him that others – Jack, for instance – should see him as an outsider. And yet if Nick Everard should be killed out there he,
Paul, would become *Sir* Paul Everard, with the family house and
estate in Yorkshire on his hands and those back-biting relations
to deal with. He thought, with his eyes shut and the regular
thumping and slamming of the sea in his ears as *Ultra* drove on
eastward, that it would be a hell of a lot better all round if his
father survived.

Fiona hugged herself against him. She muttered through
clenched teeth, 'Thank God for a bit of warmth!'

They'd had no luck finding a taxi when they'd left the night
club. London was gripped in a freezing fog, air like ice and the
colour of dirty bathwater. They'd walked all the way to Eaton
Square, and the flat felt like an igloo too. She'd piled extra blankets on the bed, they'd torn their clothes off at frantic speed and
leaped into it. Trembling, she pressed her mouth against his
chest: his hand slid down over the hollow of her back, and
cupped her bottom. He said through gritted teeth, 'Hell, but
that's cold!'

'Didn't I *tell* you?'

His hand was warm there, though. And getting warmer.
Warmth creeping right through her from that hand. Except she
still couldn't feel her feet.

England had been cold for weeks now. Right through
February and now into March. People said it was the longest
cold spell the south had had for centuries.

Jack kissed her neck. 'Just lie still, while we thaw out.'

'I'm thawing a bit already.'

'We don't have to get up before midday or so, do we?'

'I think *I'm* here for the duration.'

The manic state she'd been in after she'd swallowed the benzedrine tablet hadn't lasted. It might have been frozen out of
her, he guessed. And he felt strangely sober, considering how
they'd spent the night. Sober, and soberly aware of how little
time he had left to spend with her.

Except he *would* come back . . .

'Listen. While the ice melts, I want to explain something.' His chest hair tickled her nostrils and made her sneeze. He added, 'Thanks. Cold shower's just what I needed.'

'Sorry.'

'Listen. This thing I'm doing – *about* to do. It'll be soon, now. I don't know for certain, but I doubt if I'll be seeing you for a while . . . Did I tell you that earlier on?'

'Only nineteen times.'

'You can believe it, anyway.'

'You didn't say "for a while", though. It was going to be per-manent.' She rubbed her face against him, like a cat rubs itself on furniture. 'Or so I was given to understand.'

'That's what I want to explain.'

'All right, go ahead.'

'It's another fact – which is why I'm bound to tell you that the odds against me *ever* seeing you again are fairly daunting. When I say it's fact, I mean my boss, for instance, would tell you so if he was talking openly and honestly. He warned me about it when I took the job on, and now I know more about it I know he wasn't talking through his brass hat either. Follow me, this far?'

'I suppose so.'

'Well, the other side of it is that although I know it, I don't *feel* it. I feel like anyone else does – with a life ahead. I don't know if that's only because it's a natural way to be – you know, nobody ever believing the bullet's got *his* name on it – or whether the idea of being separated from you is – well, it's inconceivable, it couldn't *happen* . . . Are you getting any of this?'

'I'm not stupid. And you *will* come back.'

'Is that an order?'

'Yes.' The thawing process was more or less complete. 'Yes, it is.'

'So what about Nick?'

'*What* about him?'

'If I come back, for Christ's sake . . . If I don't – all right, you'll marry him, I can see that. But suppose I —'

'Jack, wait.'

He waited.

'Listen. If I say I'll marry you – *you*, not Nick – would you do two things for me in return?'

He'd stopped breathing.

'Jack?'

He whispered, 'I'd do a hundred things. *Anything.*'

'Two'll be enough. First, come back from whatever this beastly thing is. Second, stop hating Nick, so we can be his friends if he'll let us.'

Near-dawn: and surely it was time to get under, out of sight, Paul thought. The sea was lively, white-streaked, seething around the gun and pounding against the front of the bridge, foaming away along the after casing and sluicing out along *Ultra*'s sides. Spray flew over streaming as she pitched and rolled. It didn't take much of a sea to put quite a lot of motion on any surfaced submarine, and these little U-class boats only displaced 600 tons.

The port screw was driving her. The starboard tail clutch was out, the engine on that side providing a standing charge to the batteries. At about three o'clock Ruck had decided he could afford to slow down a bit, since the night had been uneventful and they'd made uninterrupted progress eastward.

Nearly five-twenty now. He took one of his last bits of periscope paper out of the Ursula pocket, to clear the front lens of his binoculars. Salt spray on them did nothing to improve one's vision . . . Darkness definitely thinning now, though. Ruck was chancing his arm somewhat, in order to have the battery as well up as possible, presumably; also, to dive as near as he could get to what was alleged to be the troop convoy's track.

It would be a convoy of soldiers bound for the desert, reinforcements for Rommel. The sort of target you longed for: big ships, the kind it was vitally important to stop, destroy . . . He was sweeping slowly across the bow and down the starboard side. Acutely aware of the possibility of encountering another boat from their own flotilla – and of the need, if he did see one suddenly, to flash the challenge and identify oneself. Also of the likelihood that a flotilla-mate, having no reason to suspect that a friendly submarine might be here, would be readier to fire first and regret it afterwards. Instant response to threat was part of the submariner's equipment, essential to survival . . .

Still, if either got a good sight of the other, the difference between these U-class submarines and the bigger German and Italian U-boats ought to be fairly obvious.

Ought . . .

Training back towards the bow: and thinking that one submarine bow-on and about to fire would look very much like another.

'Captain coming up, sir!'

And thank God. They'd be diving now – getting down to where it was safe and peaceful, and some shut-eye before breakfast.

'Morning, sir.'

'We're about there, Sub. They're breaking the charge.' As he spoke, the starboard engine's noise died away. Ruck hadn't bothered to get dressed up for this quick visit to the bridge. He had his glasses up and he was examining the horizon on the port bow, the sector from which the troop convoy *might* appear. He muttered, lowering them and blinking at the sky, 'It's damn near light, for God's sake!'

He'd cut it finer than he'd intended.

'Starboard tail clutch in, sir, engine clutch out!'

'Half ahead on starboard main motor. Stop port, out port engine clutch.' Straightening from the voicepipe as the other diesel cut out, Ruck glanced behind him. 'All right, look-outs. Down below.' The silence without engine noise was sudden and dramatic. It wasn't silent, of course, but the sea made *all* the noise, now. Ruck said, 'Down you go, Sub.' Moving quickly to the hatch Paul saw Ruck shut the voicepipe cock. 'Call down to open main vents will you?'

Diving quietly 'on the watch' – without waking the men who were off-watch. But Wykeham was in the control room yawning behind the planesmen as the submarine slipped under.

Bob McClure boasted, as Paul pushed by to get his Ursula outfit off, 'That was a spot-on fix I took, boy.'

'Might even find you're earning your keep one of these days, Shortarse.'

'Here. *Look* at it!'

According to his starsights, they were within half a mile of the spot Ruck had been aiming for. At normal dived speed it would take all day now to reach the position they'd been ordered to by S10. He heard Wykeham's report of 'Twenty-eight feet, sir' and the helmsman's 'Course three-four-five.' So *Ultra* had already swung her sharp snout towards Taranto. Wykeham murmured, 'Slow ahead together', as the trim settled. The asdic operator was reporting that there was nothing to be heard, all clear all round.

'All right, Number One. I'm going to get my head down.' Ruck hadn't slept much during the night, and he was delaying any attempt at it now, stopping beside McClure at the chart. 'Let's have a look at some alternatives, pilot. Suppose those boys left Taranto at dusk yesterday. Giving them – oh, let's say twenty knots.'

'That much, sir?'

'Troop convoys are always fast-moving. Always well protected, too. Two big liners should have about four destroyers, I'd guess. Plus maybe a seaplane or two . . . If they sailed at eight last evening, at twenty knots, what time do we run into them?'

Paul took over for the last half-hour of his watch. All that stuff was just guesswork, he thought. They'd meet the convoy, or they wouldn't. Today, or just as likely tomorrow . . . Except that the signal had said 'now loading', and maybe you didn't put troops into ships unless you were going to sail them quite soon?

Down here at periscope depth there wasn't a hint of any movement. It was still, and warm, and quiet, shale-scented. He glanced at Summers: 'Up periscope . . .'

Lunch was corned beef, pickles and baked beans. They were drinking so-called coffee in the wardroom at 1415 when

McClure went next door, wiping his mouth on the back of his hand, to take over from Wykeham. Then the first lieutenant's contrastingly tall figure drifted in and folded itself down at the table, and Shaw brought him his ration of corned beef.

'Special today, sir.'

'What's special?'

'Had me thumb in the beans, sir.'

Wykeham sighed. He said to Ruck, 'Troopers usually get a solid destroyer screen, don't they?'

'Usually.' Ruck smiled. 'What's the matter? Nervous?'

'I was only thinking – these lads of ours' – he gestured towards Paul, and nodded in the direction of the control room – 'haven't heard any really close depthcharging yet. Might be their day of baptism.'

Paul thought he'd seen enough of other kinds of action to be able to put up with most things. Of course, depthcharging would be frightening, and one didn't expect to enjoy it, exactly . . . Ruck observed, 'There's one benefit can apply sometimes, with troopships. If you put enough men in the water, their own side aren't usually so keen on dropping charges.'

Paul nodded. 'That's a happy thought.'

'Don't count on it,' Wykeham said, chewing. 'If the troops are Germans, the Wops mightn't be so squeamish.'

Tea was produced at 1600. There were biscuits too. Ruck and Wykeham stayed in their bunks, merely stretched out to the table, but Paul was due on watch at a quarter-past so he'd turned out. In any case from his own bunk, which was one of the hinged top ones, he'd have needed arms five feet long.

He heard McClure's quiet order, 'Up periscope.' And it was time to go in there and take over, except the tea was too hot to drink quickly. He decided he'd take it along with him, and he was on the point of moving when the Scots voice turned sharp and loud: 'Captain in the control room!'

Ruck's departure was like an act of levitation. He'd been here, horizontal, and now he was in there, vertical.

McClure's voice: 'Seaplane, sir. Last on green two-oh flying left to right.'

Thump of the periscope stopping. Wykeham slid off his bunk. 'Here we go.'

Ruck said, 'Messenger. I want Able Seaman Newton closed up on asdics, *now*.'

The messenger shot for'ard past the wardroom. Ruck murmured – he'd be at the periscope – 'No reflection on you, Flyte. I want the expert, that's all.' Then: 'Depth?'

'Twenty-nine —'

'Keep her up for Pete's sake!'x

'Sorry, sir . . . Twenty-*eight* feet now.'

The broken surface would be a help, today. In a sea that was patched white a periscope was like a needle in a haystack. Newton, following the messenger, came shambling past. They heard Ruck telling him, 'We're expecting a convoy from somewhere ahead. Probably two big ships, with destroyer escort.'

'Aye, sir . . .'

Periscope going down. Now it was coming up again. You never let it show for too long at a time. Just quickly dipping it made it much less likely to be spotted.

'Depth now?'

'Twenty-eight feet, sir.'

'Come up to twenty-six.' Wykeham slid out into the control room. Ruck was muttering to himself: 'The Cant seaplane's there . . . Only one, I think . . . And – ah!' He paused for about long enough to blink, then: 'Diving stations.'

Paul stayed clear of the sudden rush. He only had about one yard to move, and that spot, his diving station at the fruit machine, made for a bottleneck. He heard Ruck announcing, 'Destroyer foretops – two of 'em so far . . . Newton, hear anything?'

'Trying to sort it out, sir. There's HE – faint – red five to green one-four. Seems like several different —'

'Starboard ten, steer oh-one-oh. Sixty feet. Group up, half ahead together.'

'Ten of starboard wheel on, sir . . .'

Turning to cut across the line of advance of the oncoming convoy? But he couldn't know yet whether or not it was zigzagging, or what pattern of zigzag it might be following . . .

'Tell me when we've run five minutes, pilot.'

McClure started his stopwatch. Paul trying to guess at what was in Ruck's mind, what the surface picture might be.

'Five minutes, sir.'

'Group down. Slow together. Twenty-eight feet.'

There'd been some report from Newton, and then questions and answers between him and Ruck. Lost in thought, Paul hadn't caught it. He'd been remembering a remark of Shrimp Simpson's, at that interview he'd had with him: Shrimp had said that at the present rate of submarine losses and replacements, a sub-lieutenant brand-new to the job today could, if he was right up to scratch, hope to get his own command in two years. It was a mind-boggling thought . . .

'HE extends from red oh-five to red two-nine, sir.' Newton listened with his eyelids drooping, training his receiver slowly to and fro across that sector. Then he amplified, 'Three destroyers, sir, two big ships.' He gave the destroyers' bearings.

'What about the troopships?'

'Red eleven, sir. Two hundred revolutions. And – red one-five, sir. Same.'

Wykeham reported, 'Thirty feet, sir . . . Twenty-nine . . .'

'Up.'

The day's brightness reflected down the tube through its prisms and lenses, flashed and flickered in Ruck's eyes. Greenish-glowing, like a cat's in the gloom. He'd taken a quick check on his target: then he spun right around before settling on it for a longer look.

'Target is a troopship, three-funnelled, about twenty thousand tons. Start the attack. Bearing is – *that.* Range – *that.* I am – thirty-five on his starboard bow.'

He'd slammed the handles up: the tube was already speeding downwards. Paul read off from his machine, 'Enemy course one-three-five, sir.'

'Probably dead right.' Ruck nodded. 'Starboard ten. Blow up all tubes, open one, two, three and four bow-caps.' He muttered, watching the circling hand of his stopwatch, 'There are two of them, as expected. About the same size. One with three funnels, one with two. And only three destroyers. I'm going for the leading troopship. Set enemy speed twenty.'

'Twenty knots set, sir.'

Ruck told McClure, 'He's on the port leg of his zigzag, pilot. So the starboard leg will be one-*nine*-five. But he might steer the mean course between those stretches.' A glance at ERA Quinn: 'Up periscope.'

They knew the convoy had come from Taranto on a mean course of 165. And if he was steering thirty degrees to one side of that course now, he'd have to spend just as long steering thirty degrees the other side of it too.

'Midships. Steer oh-three-oh.' The periscope was in Ruck's hands; he put his eyes to the lenses. 'Bearing – *that*. I am – forty-five on his starboard bow. Down.'

Chief ERA Pool had read off the figures again. He was a tall man, which fitted him for the job, because he had to see over Ruck's head.

'Enemy course still one-three-five, sir.'

McClure offered, from his track chart, 'Enemy speed nineteen, sir.'

'Set nineteen.'

Paul adjusted the setting on the machine. Newton said, answering Ruck's questioning stare, 'Two hundred revolutions, sir.'

He nodded, thinking about it. You reckoned about ten revs to the knot, for merchant ships, but obviously there were variations to the rule. Everything depended now on the zigzag pattern: whether at the next alteration the enemy changed course by thirty degrees to the mean course – or sixty, to the zigzag's starboard leg . . . 'Up periscope.'

'Target is on red one-two, sir.' Newton, from the asdic set. 'Destroyers are – right ahead, and – red five, and – third one's —'

'All right.' Grabbing both the handles, jerking them down. 'Stand by. Bearing *that.* Range is – *that.* I am – eighty on his starboard bow. *Down . . .*'

He'd stepped back – breathing fast . . . 'Seaplane was right over the top of us, blast it.' Glancing at Quinn, hands curling upwards; Quinn stopped the periscope, brought it shooting up again. Ruck said, with his eyes against the lenses, 'Zigging *now.*' He pulled his head back, and shot a glance over the planesmen's heads at the depthgauges. 'Twenty-seven feet, Number One.'

'Twenty-seven —'

'Bearing *that.* Range *that.* Target's steadying. I am – fifteen, on his starboard bow.' He shoved the handles up and Quinn depressed the lever.

'Makes enemy course one-nine-five, sir.'

As predicted. Thirty to starboard of the mean course.

McClure reported, 'Averaging the enemy speed over all those stages and over the whole distance suggests nineteen point five, sir.'

'Set that.'

Paul did it. 'Nineteen and a half knots set, sir.'

'Sir –' McClure, looking down at his track chart – 'problem over here . . .'

Ruck went over. Impatient, frowning. McClure pointed out, 'He must stay on this leg at least *this* distance – same as the other leg. So here's where he *might* alter to the mean course. Or he might hold on as he's going. But isn't that where you'd expect to fire, sir? And if he zigged *there —*'

'How long before he gets there?'

McClure was working it out. Ruck told the helmsman, 'Starboard fifteen.'

McClure said, 'Eleven minutes, sir.'

'Time it for me . . . Steer one-eight-zero.'

Ruck was carrying the whole picture in his head. Speeds, angles, and the minutes ticking by, the picture changing in his mind as they passed. He was tense with concentration, sweating as if he was playing squash. Quite a lot like squash really: a new figure came flying like a ball and he had to stop it with his brain . . .

'Stop starboard. All right on one motor, Number One?'

'Quite all right, sir.' Wykeham's eyes stayed on the gauges, the plane indicators and the bubble. The submarine was swinging round faster now, with that screw stopped. Paul, having McClure's track chart to look at now and then, could see roughly how Ruck was manoeuvring to put *Ultra* where she'd be able to turn and attack whichever way the zigzag pattern developed.

'Course one-eight-zero, sir.'

Motoring southwards, with the convoy coming up – converging slightly – on the submarine's port quarter.

'How long to go, pilot?'

'Three and a half minutes, sir.'

'Slow ahead together. Twenty-eight feet. Up periscope. Stand by for range and bearing.' The periscope wires, glistening with grease, gleamed as they hissed around the deckhead sheaves and the shiny tube slid up between them. 'Bearing – *that*. Range – Christ – *that* . . . Down, forty feet!' He then added, 'I was thirty on his bow. Destroyer'll be passing over in a moment . . .' *Ultra* planing down, to give the Italian room. Eyes upward, watching the deckhead – as if its steel might be transparent and they'd see the enemy keel pass over . . . In your mind you *did* see it: now – noise like a train rushing through a tunnel. If depthcharges were coming they'd be floating down now, all round . . .

'Twenty-eight feet.'

'Twenty-eight, sir.' She'd only reached thirty-four. The hydroplanes swung, reversing their angles in the water to level her and bring her up again. Propeller noise fading – and no depthcharges, that time. Ruck muttered, wiping his eyes, 'That's one of 'em out of the light.' He meant one less between *Ultra* and her target. 'Time, pilot?'

'Minute to go, sir. Fifty-five seconds.'

'Twenty-eight feet, sir.'

'Up periscope . . . Bearing is now – *that*. Range is – *that*. And I'm forty on his bow.'

He pushed the handles up. McClure was keeping an eye on the stopwatch as he simultaneously put that range and bearing on the track chart.

'Twenty seconds to go . . . Fifteen . . . Ten . . .'

Ruck raised his hands, nodded to Quinn.

'Five —'

'All right.' He'd spun round swiftly, checking the positions of the escorts and the seaplane. Muttered, 'Bastard . . .' Something on the beam, that had been: he was on the target again now. Another range and bearing: and *Ultra* now sixty degrees on the troopship's bow. Ship crammed with soldiery, relaxing, never dreaming . . . The periscope slid downward; Ruck stock still, then telling Quinn, 'Just dip it.' Quinn obliged: and Ruck's eyes were at the lenses again. 'Holding its course. Port fifteen. What's my course for a ninety-degree track?'

'One-one-five, sir.'

'Steer one-one-five. What's the DA?'

You jerked a handle round to align pointers between the enemy and the own-ship dials. Paul gave Ruck his aim-off angle, reading it straight from the machine.

'Course one-one-five, sir.'

'Stand by all tubes.'

He'd set the periscope on that director angle: Chief ERA Pool was reaching over to anchor it on the bearing. Pool shaved every day: it made him look out of place here, like a politician down a coalmine.

'Stand by!'

You held your mental breath. Literally months of preparation and years of training had gone into these few seconds, but one tiny error could abort the whole thing. While out there the target was a transport packed with troops who'd either get to join Rommel's desert army, or would not – depending on the accuracy of figures you'd been reading off these dials, or a detail in the little Scotsman's track chart, or Ruck's eye and judgement . . .

'Fire one!'

Jolt, and the jump in pressure.

'Torpedo running, sir.'

'Fire two!'

Paul swallowed, for his ears' sake. Newman said, 'Both running.'

'Fire three!'

Ruck with that characteristic snarl, lips drawn back to show his teeth. Now he'd opened his mouth to order the fourth and last fish on its way. Paul saw his expression change . . .

'*Damn!*' Slamming the handles up: 'Down periscope . . . The sods are zigging, damn them! Zigging *now*, blast 'em!'

All a waste. Three torpedoes already on their way, and the target altering course. Just exactly at the crucial moment.

'Destroyer green two-five in contact, sir!'

'Hundred feet. Group up, half ahead together.'

'Hundred feet, sir.' The telegraph clanged. They'd missed, wasted three valuable torpedoes, and now a destroyer had them on its asdics. It would whistle up its two friends, and *Ultra* would shortly be on the receiving end. For *nothing*.

'Closing, sir, in contact, bearing steady!'

'Starboard fifteen. Full ahead together. Shut off for depthcharging.' Ruck's tone was calm, no tension in it now. He added, shrugging, 'Can't win 'em all.' This was the same tactic he'd used yesterday: stir up the sea and charge right under the attacker. Even if it didn't work as it had then, it would have the advantage of confusing the Italian in his judgement of the moment of passing over. This was one of the two things he'd have to get right, if he was going to do any real damage with his depthcharges; that, and having the charges set to whatever depth *Ultra* was keeping.

Watertight doors were shut and clipped.

'Boat's shut off for depthcharging, sir.'

'Fifteen of starboard wheel on, sir.'

'Steer one-four-oh.'

'Hundred feet, sir.'

The deep *boom* of an explosion shook the boat, and came as a surprise. From somewhere to port, and fairly distant. Reverberations dying like echoes . . . And it had, undoubtedly, been a torpedo hit. Wykeham glanced round at his CO. 'Never say die, sir.'

Grins, all round. Paul heard the first murmur of the approaching destroyer's screws. Ruck looked utterly astonished; he muttered, '*Bloody* lucky!'

Wykeham suggested, 'Might have got the second one, sir – before it turned? Something like that?'

'Destroyer coming over, sir . . .'

Everyone could hear it now. Rising note as distance shortened, the rhythmic thrashing of fast propellers. If the man up there knew his business, the canisters of explosive would be smacking into the water about – *now* . . .

'Hundred and fifty feet.'

A pattern of charges began to explode astern. One – then three, four – and another. Astern and above: set shallow, evidently. The boat rattled a bit, but the pattern hadn't been close enough to be very worrying. However – Paul reminded himself – there were three destroyers up there, and they knew where the submarine was now, so —

'Red nine-zero, HE slowing – stopping, sir.'

'Group down, slow together.' He met Wykeham's eye. 'Probably the one we hit.'

'Destroyer closing on red eight-oh!'

'In contact?'

Newton shook his head. 'Transmissions on red one-six-oh and green five-oh, but —'

'Port fifteen. Steer oh-five-oh. Silent routine.'

'In contact, sir. Red seven-oh, closing . . .'

No point in being quiet now.

'Group up, full ahead together, port twenty.' Ruck shook his head, like a dog coming out of water. He said, as much to himself as anyone else, 'We *got* the bugger. God knows how, but we *got* him.' He laughed. *Ultra* speeding up, turning to port and still nosing deeper.

'Twenty of port wheel on, sir.'

The helmsman's tone was so calm it was positively soothing. The sound of the enemy's screws came like a whisper, grew to a murmur, scrunched overhead in a sudden grinding rush.

Exactly overhead, Paul reckoned.

Fading . . .

'Hundred and fifty feet, sir.'

'Very good.'

The sea astern broke up in thunder. The submarine lurched, from solid blows against her plating. Four – five . . .

Ruck said casually, 'That Wop's a learner. Starboard fifteen, slow both.'

'Motors are grouped up, sir.'

'So they are. Group down.'

'Fifteen of starboard wheel on, sir.'

'Steer oh-five-oh.'

'Destroyer closing, green four-oh, in contact!'

'Two hundred feet. *Damn* his eyes.'

'Two hundred, sir. Motors are grouped down, slow ahead.'

'*Half* ahead together.'

Angling downward again, into denser, darker water. Wykeham adjusting trim as she sank, pumping water out of O, the midships trimming-tank. Ruck waiting, listening . . . Ruck snapped, out of a long silence, 'Group up, full ahead together, starboard fifteen!'

Paul could hear it too now. McClure touched his arm. He turned round; the navigator was offering him a pencil and a game of noughts and crosses on a signal-pad. He shook his head, turned back, listening to the enemy coming at them.

'Two hundred feet, sir.'

Ultra trembling from the grouped-up battery power and her own racing screws. Perhaps the Italians would have set their charges deep this time. But then again, maybe they wouldn't have . . .

'Steer one-four-oh.'

Churning over – now.

You could only wait for it, and noughts and crosses wouldn't have helped. He told himself, *Might as well get used to it, there'll be lots more before we're through.* Explosions to port rolled the boat to starboard and lifted her stern a little; the planesmen were having to work to level her. Deckhead paint had been loosened by the shock, and cork chips rained like snowflakes.

'Group down, slow together. Port ten. Steer oh-five-oh.'

'Deeper setting on that lot, sir.'

Ruck agreed. 'Might have been . . . Where is he now, Newton?'

'Red one-two-oh, sir . . . One-one-five. Transmitting.'

'Not in contact?'

Newton blinked, swallowed, shook his head.

'Course oh-five-oh, sir.'

Ruck murmured, 'Very good.' Waiting, listening: feet spread, hands in pockets.

'Red eight-oh, sir, moving right to left, transmitting, not in contact.'

Searching, though, to regain contact. Where the hell was the *third* destroyer? One had continued south with the other troopship, one was hunting them, and the third was lying doggo. Getting a towline over to the ship they'd hit?

'Still drawing left?'

A nod. 'Abaft the beam . . . Revs increasing, sir.'

Wykeham said, 'Looks like you've lost him, sir.'

Faces all round the compartment showed the same hope. Nobody counting on it yet. Ten minutes ticked by very, very slowly. Glances tending to be upward – to where your thoughts were, in deep water.

'Passing astern, sir, fast HE.'

'Revs?'

'Three-four-oh, sir.'

High speed, and southward. Summoned to join the others, the survivor that was continuing towards Benghazi?

They surely wouldn't send that trooper across the Mediterranean with only one destroyer to look after it, Paul thought. This one had been allowed to hang around as long as he had a contact on the submarine, but now he'd lost it maybe he'd been told to leave it and rejoin?

'Ninety feet.'

'Ninety, sir.'

'What was the distance off track when we fired, Sub?'

'Twelve hundred yards, sir.'

Mental arithmetic going on, in Ruck's head. But if he could work out even vaguely how far they might be now from the stopped troopship, after all the twists and turns, he'd have to be some kind of Einstein.

Maybe practice did it. Experience. There was a hell of a lot to learn, skills to acquire, experience to gain. And maybe not everyone *could* make the grade. Which would account for Flag Officer (Submarines) having told his flotilla commanders – so rumour had it – that submarine captains were to be treated like Derby winners.

'HE on red five, sir!'

Ruck looked surprised. 'What sort?'

'Destroyer, sir. Moving left to right. Transmitting . . .'

Behind Paul, McClure whispered, '*Shit* . . .' Ruck was watching the needle swinging slowly round the depthgauge. It was the only one in use, since the shallow-water gauges had been shut off as a precaution against depthcharge damage.

He'd come to a decision. 'Twenty-eight feet.'

'Twenty-eight feet, sir.' There'd been a note of surprise in Wykeham's acknowledgement. He'd been just about levelling her at ninety; now the planesmen put up-angle on her again.

'Be ready to flood Q and take her down fast.' Ruck turned to Newton. 'Where is it now?'

'Green one-five, sir, opening. Transmitting.'

'Just *keep* opening . . .' Ruck was waiting with his toes against the well of the after periscope, the little one, as *Ultra* nosed upward towards the surface. Forty-five feet: forty . . . This third destroyer had obviously been lying stopped, perhaps alongside the damaged trooper. It was looking for them now, but fortunately – for the moment – out on the wrong side. Thirty-five feet. Ruck glanced at ERA Quinn, and wiggled his fingers: the attack periscope slid upwards, shimmering. He met it, unfolded its handles, circled . . . 'Down.' He moved to the other one. 'Steer ten degrees to starboard.' Gesturing again, then waiting impatiently with his hands up, ready to snatch the handles and snap them down, flicking into low power for an all-round sky search. Pausing . . . He muttered, 'The Cant's still with us, sod it.' Circling on. Now he'd settled on what could only be the target.

'Destroyer bearing now?'

'Red five, sir. Moving right to left.'

Shifting fractionally. 'I see him. He was hidden by the trooper.' He was on the target again now, in high power.

'Course oh-six-oh, sir.'

'Stand by number four tube. You were right, Number One, it was the one we weren't aiming at. She's stopped and down by the stern. Destroyer out beyond her, circling round northward.'

'Number four tube ready, sir!'

'Ship's head?'

'Oh-six-one, sir.'

'Steer oh-six-three.' Sky search again, rapidly, right around. Back to his target. He leaned back from the lenses and set the periscope on the fore-and-aft line. Back on target again now . . .

'Ship's head oh-six-three, sir.'

A pause that lasted a few seconds: it felt like minutes . . .

'Stand by . . . Fire four!'

You swallowed, to clear your ears. Newton reported, 'Torpedo running, sir.' Ruck was circling again, checking on the seaplane probably. Back on the for'ard bearing, motionless, intent. 'Running time for 900 yards?'

'Forty seconds, sir.'

'Dip.' The periscope shot down, stopped, rushed up again. Any second now: so long as that fish ran straight . . .

The explosion was deep, close-sounding.

Ruck, at the periscope, let out a grunt of satisfaction. Now he'd stepped back and pushed the handles up. 'Sixty feet. Port ten. Steer' – he thought about it for a moment – 'two-three-oh.'

'Ten of port wheel on, sir.'

And *Ultra* was nosing down. Ruck told Wykeham, 'The seaplane was heading our way. But I hit under her second funnel. Engine room. Ought to do the trick, on top of the first one . . . Where's the destroyer, Newton?'

Training his receiver this way and that, Newton was looking puzzled. 'Can't hear him, sir. Might've stopped again, or —'

'All right.'

He'd have to look after survivors, anyway.

'Sixty feet, sir.'

Newton reported, 'Breaking-up noises, sir!'

'Course two-three-oh, sir.'

Ruck took the Tannoy microphone off its hook.

'D'you hear there. Captain speaking. We had a lucky hit earlier on, on a troopship of about twenty thousand tons. It stopped her, and now we've hit her again with our last remaining fish, and she's going down. Probably won't be any counter-attack – the sea must be full of Germans or Italians, and the escort'll have its hands full. But we'll stay shut-off and keep quiet until we're right out of it. Nice work, lads.' He switched off. 'Anything, Newton?'

'There was slow HE for half a minute but it's stopped again, sir.'

Picking up swimmers? Behind Paul, McClure murmured, 'Home, James . . .'

4

At Cardiff on Monday, Commander Smith announced that there'd be no more leave. Jack was glad to have it confirmed. He'd hung around for long enough: it was time to get on with it, get it over. And get back. There was more to get back *for*, now, than there'd ever been.

'Are you – er – fit, Everard?'

He knew what lay behind *that* question. His weekends in London were disapproved of by Trolley, the chief instructor, who had complained to Smith about it. As a captain in the Army, Trolley was the equivalent rank of Jack as a naval lieutenant; he could throw his weight around so far as the training programme was concerned, but he had no administrative authority. Smith had warned Jack before that physical fitness was of paramount importance: late nights, smoking and drinking and what the commander in his old-fashioned naval terminology called 'poodle-faking' could impair Jack's stamina and thus threaten the success of the operation and the lives of his team. Jack had assured him this wouldn't be allowed to happen: within twenty-four hours of any weekend leave he'd be in as good shape as anyone – including Trolley.

He told him roughly the same thing again now, and Smith accepted it. He was the sort of man who'd avoid a row, just for the sake of peace and quiet. Extraordinary, really, when you considered the characters he was handling here and the kind of

operation they were facing. But he'd promised there'd be weekend leave, at that first interview; and he may have thought that
Jack, in the circumstances, was entitled to some home comforts.
Like a condemned man's last meal . . . He told him, waving him
to a chair, 'You'll be leaving here before the end of the week. For
your private information, not to be discussed with anyone else,
you'll be going round to Falmouth.'

That was where the raid was to be launched from, then.

'There'll be a minesweeper laid on to escort *Sauerkraut* round,
and you and your team will embark in her – the sweeper. When
you get there, you'll be accommodated ashore. You'll have long
enough cramped up in the E-boat later on.'

'D'you mean it's a long haul from Falmouth to the target
port, sir?'

Smith frowned. He said, 'I can't tell you how long you'll be in
Falmouth. But you'll be joining up with the larger force which
you asked me about a few days ago. You'll train with some of
them while you're there.'

More bloody training . . .

'Your part of the show's got to be fitted in with the rest of it,
you see. And we don't want you and your lads going to pot in the
last week or two. Trolley is absolutely right, you know – physical
fitness is half the battle; it's vital – in your own interests, apart
from everyone else's . . . Now, the programme for *this* week.
First, there'll be the usual PT, runs and route-marches, as laid on
by Trolley. Also, we'll have stores arriving, for embarking in
Sauerkraut. Sharp will take charge of that, of course, but it'll
include your own equipment, ammo and so on, so you'd better
take an interest in where and how it's stowed. And there's one
new angle for you – concerning your torpedoes. An emergency
drill we want you to practise.'

'What would the emergency be?'

'Well . . . Obviously you've realized that we're attacking an
enemy-held port, and that your part in the raid is to get right
through to a certain inner basin and make use of an E-boat – as
you've been practising . . . Right?'

Jack nodded.

'The background to the plan is that there is always – or has always been – an off-duty or stand-by E-boat, and sometimes two of them, berthed on that quay at night. Aerial photographs taken just before dusk have invariably shown one lying there, and with its torpedoes in the tubes. But it's been suggested now – this cropped up during the weekend – that when the boat's brought inside the docks the pistols may quite likely be removed from the torpedoes. And not only removed, but *landed*.'

'If that's the case, we're scuppered.'

There were various safety devices on German torpedoes, just as there were on British ones, but nobody had suggested the Germans would go so far as to take the pistols out. Pistols were cylindrical primers inserted in the front ends of the warheads.

Smith told him, 'This has cropped up because someone in Naval Intelligence has discovered it's laid down in their torpedo manual, under the heading "Safety Precautions in Harbour". Whether or not they've found they can observe it, in practice and wartime conditions, we don't of course know.'

'But we can't chance it.'

'Quite. So we're proposing to issue you with a quantity of plastic explosive with detonators and time-fuses. This is the emergency drill. If the pistols are not in the fish, you pack the apertures with plastic, fit detonators and fire the fuses.'

'But —'

'Wait, wait . . . You use the E-boat itself to get the torpedoes there. You set the boat on course for the target with its wheel lashed, and abandon ship.'

'Christ . . .'

Smith's eyebrows twitched. 'A bit startling at first glance, I admit. But on reflection, I don't believe it really increases the – er – hazards. You'll get wet, that's all. The big snag, I suppose, is that the boat becomes an obvious target for enemy guns on the other side of the basin, and they might well blow it up before it gets across. On the other hand, it *is* a German boat, and they may think its own crew's still manning it.'

Its own crew would be dead by then. But it was news to Jack that there'd be guns on the far side of the basin. Nobody had mentioned this before. It seemed strange to him that there'd be defences along an inland waterway – dock, whatever it was . . . Then he thought, *A ship – or ships, berthed on the other side* . . . He asked Smith, 'Could I make a guess that the target is some large ship berthed on the quay facing us? A pocket battleship or something?'

'You could guess it, but you'd be wrong.' Smith sighed. They were all trying to squeeze information out of him, all the time. He said, 'They'll tell you the whole story in Falmouth, Everard. There's really no need for you to know it any sooner.'

Jack nodded. It seemed the interview was over, and he began to move. Smith stopped him. 'Hang on. Haven't finished, quite.'

Subsiding, he saw that the commander was going through the process of 'choosing his words carefully'. It was a look he tended to get, at such times: a frowning pause, lips shaping themselves for speech.

'One aspect of all this – which I *can* tell you, without giving away anything that matters . . . You may find, when you get to Falmouth, that not everyone there is overjoyed by your arrival. I don't mean in a personal way, of course – I mean the fact of you and your crowd being tagged on to the operation. You'll be known as the Naval Task Unit, by the way – NTU . . . The point is, you've been put in as an extra, and not everyone concerned approves of it entirely. The operation itself has one essential and *very* important target; but in the same immediate area there happens to be another. Both, I may say, of considerable strategic importance. Now, when the Prime Minister was having the plan explained to him – chiefs of staff having already approved it – he put his finger on the secondary target – yours – and demanded 'What about *this?*' Well, the planners already have enormous problems, and see very high risks in achieving the *first* objective. On your end of it, there are some people who consider the risks too high in relation to the chances of success. Others appreciate that the value of doing substantial damage to it would be significant enough to justify those risks. *And*, the Prime Minister was very strongly opposed to our passing up the chance of killing two birds with one stone.'

Jack Everard being one of the two birds, no doubt. He wondered who the other one might be . . . He said, 'So we're just a sideshow, while a raiding force happens to be there.'

'I'd rather say you were an *addition*.'

'And mine's a tougher proposition than the primary object of the operation.'

'Well – yes . . . If you remember, Everard, I did try to impress on you —'

'Oh, you did, certainly. I've no grouse about that, sir.'

Surprisingly, the commander smiled: it was a warm, friendly smile. He murmured, 'I'll be glad to see you back, I must say.'

Half an hour later Jack was outside on the roadway, in thin, cold drizzle that felt it might easily turn to sleet. He mustered his party, called them to attention, and reported them to Trolley as present and correct – except for the two artificers, Pettifer and Wood, who were working on the modifications to *Sauerkraut.*

The army man's pale eyes held his. Trolley had a smooth, pink-and-white complexion. Jack thought that perhaps he shaved the sides and back of his head to make up for not needing to shave his face. That was how he looked, anyway.

'In good shape, are you. Everard?'

'Good enough.'

'We'll see.' He gave his orders. A rapid march – a lot of it would be at the double – to a group of disused slagheaps about eight miles away. When they got there they'd be running up and down them for a couple of hours, carrying weighted packs; then there'd be an equally fast return to base. Slagheaps were bastards for running on. But it would sweat the whisky out, all right. He was tough, and confident of his own strength and staying power: he could wallow in the fleshpots and then come back and cope with this without making heavy weather of it. He was twice the man Trolley was, he thought, and he enjoyed the sort of weekends Trolley probably yearned for: also, he'd soon be leading this team into action, and the fresh-faced commando would be staying behind, instructing . . . Jack saluted him, thinking, *I could take you, boy, whatever shape I might be in. And what a pleasure!*

Violence was a relief, sometimes. A thing you needed – like a stiff drink, or a woman. He'd have *liked* to have flattened Trolley: here, now. It wasn't anything he could analyze, understand in himself; it was simply how he felt. And a thing Fiona hated – had called, when he'd described it to her, 'sick-making'. But Trolley's cold eyes, slightly contemptuous disapproval . . .

It occurred to him, as he marched back to his platoon to move them off, that before he left Cardiff he might even do it.

Late that afternoon, aching in a lot of muscles but being careful not to let anyone know it, he went along to visit *Sauerkraut*. Lying near her in the same dock was Sharp's ML, once again immobilized by engine trouble. A crew was coming down from Scotland to remove her next week, but they were going to have to mend her first.

Tubby Sharp joined him on the jetty. Sharp was round-faced, curly-haired and slightly mad; he'd been at Oxford when the war had started. Now that he'd become an E-boat commander he was working up a Nazi act to go with the job – strutting, shouting, Heil-Hitlering. He said, 'Just as well we don't have to go on this jaunt in my old wreck. Highly unlikely the old bitch would have got us there. Wherever *there* is . . . Smithy tell you this morning, did he?'

'No such luck.'

'Just a natter, was it?'

'More or less.' Jack pointed at the auxiliary petrol tanks fitted on the ML's upper deck. There were two tanks, each holding 500 gallons, to give the Fairmile the extra range she'd have needed for the expedition on which she would not now be going. He said, 'That little lot's worried me all along. I told Smith, but he brushed me off. For God's sake – timber boat, and all that gas on deck, and half the German Army blazing away at it as we go in?'

Sharp nodded. 'True . . . Mind you, our *Sauerkraut*'s also timber-built.'

'Doesn't have exposed fuel tanks, though. Whoever thought *that* up, for an opposed landing?'

'For want of anything more suitable?'

'Obviously. But it's high time we *had* something more suitable. Your MLs are useful craft for lots of jobs, but not for this kind.' He added, 'By the way, we won't be crowding you out when we leave here. There'll be a sweeper escorting you, and we'll go in that. *That's* what Smithy told me, this morning.'

Sharp asked him, 'Going where?'

Jack shrugged. 'Smithy'll tell us when he's ready. The thing is, you'll have plenty of room in *Sauerkraut*. Let's decide where the spare ammo boxes are going, when it arrives.'

They boarded *Sauerkraut*. He told the ERAs, 'You two missed a jolly little run this forenoon.'

Pettifer looked at Wood. 'Dash it all, Humphrey, some fellows get *all* the fun!'

That night they went over the assault course several times, starting 'dry' because they had no boat to start from, and doing it repeatedly because Trolley said the first attempts weren't fast enough. He might have been right, but it was very easy to resent Trolley's decisions. Next day, Tuesday, the stores arrived, and had to be checked and stowed, and that afternoon Jack and his torpedomen conducted some preliminary experiments with plastic explosive, detonators and time-fuses.

'Stand by to surface . . .'

Tuesday, 10.50 am.

Ruck, at the periscope, wasn't dressed for the bridge. Wykeham, at the trim as usual, would be going up in his place and conning *Ultra* into harbour. He told Quinn, 'Check main vents.'

Faces around the control room were clean-shaven – except Quinn's – and the ship's company smartly uniformed. Except for Ruck himself, who was still collarless and tieless.

This surfacing routine had been ordered by Shrimp Simpson recently, after the Luftwaffe's blitz on the flotilla had extended to machine-gun attacks on submarines returning from patrol. Fighters and fighter-bombers had taken to ambushing the boats as they surfaced at the end of the swept channel; it was a smart idea from their point of view because the submarine was helpless in those few moments and because the first man into the bridge was always the captain, who was the most valuable human target for them. Two COs had been wounded in this way since the beginning of the year. Shrimp had decreed that submarines were in future to surface only one mile from the St Elmo lighthouse, and they weren't to come up at all if the red air-raid alert flag was flying from the battlements of the Castille. Also, commanding officers were not to show themselves in the bridge until their boats were right inside the harbour entrance.

'Main vents checked shut, sir!'

'Ready to surface, sir.'

Ruck muttering to himself, daylight from the surface flickering in his eyes . . . 'No red flag. Getting a quiet forenoon, ashore.' He swept round again, using the air search. Then another inspection of the Castille flagstaff. He pushed the handles up.

'Surface.'

'Blow one and six main ballast!'

Wykeham had given that order, while the signalman, Janaway, was opening the lower hatch. Now Janaway was off the ladder and Wykeham was climbing up into the tower, while Ruck took over the surfacing process and air roared into the tanks. Janaway scooping up two rolled flags, tucking them under his arm before he started up behind Wykeham . . . One was a White Ensign, the other this submarine's own Jolly Roger, a black flag with a white skull and crossbones in its centre, and symbols marking successes sewn around it. During the dived passage southward yesterday Janaway had spent some time squatting in a corner of the control room with the black flag across his knees and needle and thread in hand, adding this patrol's score to what was

already there. Two more white bars for the tanker and the troopship; there were two there from the first two patrols out here,
and a red bar above that for the U-boat they'd sunk during their
work-up patrol in the North Sea.

If Ruck had had his way, there'd have been crossed gun-
barrels now in the top right corner, and a star below them for
Ultra's first gun action. There wasn't, because Shrimp Simpson
had ordered them back to Malta instead of allowing another
visit to Cape Spartivento for a bombardment of the railway
sidings. *Ultra* had surfaced on Sunday evening as soon as it was
dark enough, and immediately wirelessed an enemy report
giving the position of the day's sinking and the course and speed
of the surviving troopship and its two escorts. He'd also reported
the destruction of the tanker and stated his intention of returning to the Messina Straits for some trainwrecking. Within an
hour S10's reply had come in: their recall to Malta. Shrimp had
added 'Well done.'

Paul called up to Wykeham in the tower, 'Fifteen feet. Twelve.
Ten. Eight. Six —'

Clang of the hatch opening: looking up as drops of water
spattered down, he saw daylight and the two men clambering
out into the bridge. Behind him Ruck ordered, 'Stop blowing.'
The voicepipe was opened, and a moment later the diesels were
in action. In the bridge, Janaway would be flashing *Ultra*'s pendant numbers by Aldis lamp to the Castille signal station.

Paul went into the wardroom to put on a battledress jacket
over his white submarine sweater. Before long the order
'Harbour stations' would be passed, and his job was on the fore
casing with the berthing party. McClure said, as Paul passed the
chart table, 'Neat landfall, eh?'

Meaning he'd done well to find the way back to Malta: a joke
against himself, an admission that he still saw himself as a
learner-navigator, delighted with every good result he got.

With this patrol's results, everyone was delighted. There
could be no question that *Ultra* had now qualified as a full
member of the fraternity.

Ruck came in, fished a stiff collar and back tie from the drawer under his bunk, and began fastening it to his shirt. Paul asked him, 'What'll the form be now, sir? Alongside Lazaretto?'

'Expect so.' Fixing the tie, Ruck leaned back against the table for support. *Ultra* was jolting around a bit, as the diesels drove her through a choppy sea towards the harbour entrance. 'Or they'll put us between buoys.'

Shouting, from the control room . . .

Ruck shot out, sending McClure staggering. The diving klaxon roared twice, diesels cut out, main vents opening: Q tank was flooded, the submarine lurching downwards. There was a fast, loud hammering from somewhere up top, and as she dipped under a jarring explosive *thump* in the sea to port. McClure had sprung to the chart table and leaped back again with the chart, getting out of the rush of men hurrying to their diving stations. He shouted towards the control room, 'Less than fifty feet of water, sir!'

Ruck's voice: 'Forty feet. Blow Q.'

'Blowing Q, sir.' Quinn, at the panel.

Then Wykeham, out of breath: 'Forty feet, sir . . . You all right, signalman?'

The lower hatch thumped. Paul had been keeping out of the way, out of the gangway. He heard Janaway mumble, 'Reckon so, sir. Except – well, seems —'

'Q blown, sir.'

'He's all blood, sir!'

Lovesay's voice, from the fore planes . . .

'Forty feet, sir.'

'Group down, slow ahead together.' Ruck ordered, 'CPO Gaffney in the control room . . . Cox'n, he can take over after planes. You see to Janaway.' Paul was in there, crouching beside the signalman, who was sitting on the deck at the base of the ladder with his legs stuck straight out in front of him and his submarine sweater turning pink, reddening, beginning to glisten at the shoulder as blood thickened and seeped through. McClure was there too.

'Here —'

'Let the cox'n see to him, Sub.' Gaffney, torpedo gunner's mate, arrived. Ruck told him, 'After planes, TI.'

Logan was already off the stool: Paul made way for him. Submarine coxswains were put through a short medical course to equip them for emergency doctoring. Logan muttered, 'We'll get 'im aft, sir. POs' mess, if you'd give an 'and.' He growled at the signalman as they helped him up, 'What you fussin' about, Bunts?'

'I'm not fuckin' fussin', I'm —'

'Don't bloody argue, then. Come on . . .'

'Twenty-eight feet.'

'Twenty-eight, sir . . .'

'What happened, Number One?'

'Messerschmitt 110, sir. One bomb in the sea to port, and it strafed us with its guns. Came out of nowhere. Sorry, I should've —'

'Spilt milk.' He looked angry, all the same. 'Port fifteen.' He steadied her a minute later on the reciprocal of her former course, heading seawards. He was at the periscope, looking astern at the island, when Paul came back. He'd muttered, 'We're well out of *that*.' Then the periscope was hissing down. He told the men around him, 'They're bombing the be-Jesus out of the place.' He glanced at the clock: it was eleven-thirty. 'Trouble is, if we bottom here, we won't know when it stops.'

To settle her on the bottom in water shallow enough to use the periscope would mean leaving the swept channel, and then you'd be risking mines. The enemy were sowing them in the harbour approaches most nights now, and it wasn't practicable to clear more than the channel.

He reached for the Tannoy. 'D'you hear there. There's an air-raid in progress ashore, so we'll stay out here until it finishes. No peace for the wicked . . .'

Janaway was going to be all right. He'd passed out while CPO Logan was probing for the bullet, but it had turned out there wasn't one in there anyway. It had passed through, doing no serious damage. Logan had cleaned both ends of the wound and dressed it with sulphur powder, and dosed his patient with some pain-killer. Janaway was fed up – he called it 'chocker' – at the prospect of missing the next patrol. The coxswain explained, 'Reckons it ain't safe ashore, sir.'

He was probably right, at that. The raid was still in progress four hours after it had started. With Sicily so close, of course, the bombers could run a shuttle-service. When Paul came off watch at 1415 the sky had been foggy with shellbursts and with smoke and dust rising from the battered island. He'd seen a lot of Junkers 88s and some 87s, Stukas, and the assault was still in full swing when Shaw dumped a tray of tea and biscuits on the ward-room table. It was in Wykeham's next watch, an hour later, that the red flag crawled down the mast on the Castille fort.

Ruck looked up from an Edgar Wallace thriller. 'About bloody time. Bring her round, Number One, and let's crack on a bit of speed. Pilot, put a fix on and give me an ETA one mile from St Elmo.' He looked down at his book, then up again at Paul as a new thought struck him. 'Sub, you can be first up, this time. Just in case.' Paul stared at him, wondering in case of what. Ruck explained, 'I'm not risking a valuable first lieutenant again.'

Paul nodded: he was stuck for a suitable comment. Ruck added, returning to his novel, 'One of the telegraphists can take Janaway's place.'

Half an hour later he was at the top of the ladder inside the tower, with Leading Telegraphist Dawson close below him. He'd taken both pins out, and released one clip; he waited with a hand on the other, hearing Wykeham chant, 'Twelve feet – ten – eight – open up, Sub!' He pulled the lever of the clip down and felt the lug swing free, forced up with his other hand on the handle underneath the hatch: it swung up, thudded back. Then he was in the bridge with sea still sluicing away out of the drain-down holes, fore casing awash and the turned-out hydroplanes just clear of the surface, running with white foam. He'd checked all round and overhead with the naked eye by the time Dawson joined him with the Aldis lamp. It was plugged in inside the tower, its rubber-coated cable snaking through the hatch. The signal station was already calling on the submarine to identify herself.

Paul had the voicepipe open and they'd drained it down: he called down, 'Tell the captain, all clear all round.' Engine clutches were in; the diesels started banging away, all of it happening without his having to pass down any orders.

'Pendants and message passed, sir.'

The pendants were P40, *Ultra*'s call-sign, and the message was to S10 requesting medical assistance be made available for Janaway.

The Jolly Roger hung like a dead cormorant from the after periscope. The Ensign was a lifeless-looking object too, drooping forlornly. Both of them had been dragged through the sea for half a day. It was disappointing: you only flew the Jolly Roger when you were returning from a successful patrol, and you liked it to be seen.

There was a signal coming. Paul bent to the pipe, adjusting course by a few degrees, aiming for the gap in the anti-torpedo boom. Dawson had put his lamp up and flashed a go-ahead.

P40 from S10. Berth alongside Lazaretto. Sorry you have been kept waiting at the door. Then confirmation that an ambulance would be waiting to transfer their wounded man to hospital. Paul passed it all down the voicepipe to the control room, adding, 'Tell the captain we're about to enter, there are no aircraft in sight and no red flag.'

Only the *slightest* touch of sarcasm. But there'd have been a smile or two, down below. Ruck came up a minute later – immaculate, fit to appear on a flagship's quarterdeck. He told Paul, 'That's your regular job from now on, Sub. We'll get you a tin hat.' He bent to the voicepipe: 'Harbour stations!'

Paul went on down – over the side of the bridge, down cutaway footholds and round a narrow ledge to the fore casing, then for'ard past the gun. There was a gathering of Maltese on the foreshore to port, and more of them up higher on the stone balconies on that Valletta side. They were cheering and waving as *Ultra* slid into harbour. Ruck seemed not to have noticed them, so Paul waved his cap, and the cheering rose to a howl of welcome. They could see the black flag was up there, anyway: the Maltese loved the 10th Flotilla, for going out and attacking the people who'd been bombing and half-starving them for the last two years, and they knew all about Jolly Rogers.

Lovesay, the second coxswain, arrived, with the other four men of the casing party. They made their preparations for securing alongside, then fell into line, Paul right for'ard where the casing narrowed, the leading seaman next to him, then the others. Facing to starboard, because that was where the Lazaretto base would be when they reached it – passing the entrance to Sliema Creek and then the eastern point of Manoel Island, its massive fort dominating this view of it. There was a strong smell in the air – burning, and dust, and oil-fuel. Shale, too. Lovesay muttered, 'Some sod's caught a packet.'

'Smells like it.'

'Reckon it's *Talbot*, sir?'

The base was officially known as HMS *Talbot*.

Beyond Lovesay, Dracula Jupp observed, 'Fryin' tonight.' He got a chuckle from his mates. But the submarine base *was* the Luftwaffe's prime target now – or at least of equal attraction to them as the airfields. Further cheers, and clapping – from a crowd on the Valletta side again, and also from a group on Manoel Island. Soldiers among that lot – probably gunners, the Royal Malta Artillery, who had AA guns on the island and Bofors around the submarine base. *Ultra* was altering slightly to starboard, and round the bulge ahead was the Lazaretto building. *Should* be, if it was still standing. Paul smelt shale-oil very strongly now. Not just as a mild aroma, the perfume they all lived in and were so used to that they didn't notice until girls complained about it, but a powerful, penetrating stink.

Lovesay's nostrils twitched. 'We been clobbered, all right.'

Coming into sight of the base now . . .

Engine noise ceased suddenly. *Ultra* moved on under her own momentum while the engine clutches were being disengaged. You had to use the motors for manoeuvring in harbour, because the diesels couldn't be put astern. He felt the thrust of her screws again as the main motors took over.

There were no flames, or smoke. At first sight the sprawl of weathered stone seemed to be just as it had been when they'd last seen it. The building stretched along the water's edge with a stone gallery a few steps above water level and an equally long balcony above it. There was a U-class submarine alongside already, and another in the process of securing between buoys just off shore. Both were gleaming wet, obviously just up from hiding underwater. The one alongside – Paul read her pendant numbers on the side of the bridge – was *Unslaked*. Groups of officers and ratings on the balcony and in the gallery below it had stopped to watch their arrival, and on *Unslaked*'s casing a berthing party stood ready to receive them. Then suddenly, looking to his right, he saw the new bomb damage. The wardroom area, the officers' cabins at the eastern end – a lot of that part was roofless, ruined. Two-hundredweight slabs of quarried stone had been scattered around like playing cards.

'See that, sir?'

'Yeah. I see it.'

He also noticed that *Unslaked* was flying her Jolly Roger.

From *Ultra*'s bridge, the shrill note of a bosun's call . . . Paul said quietly, 'Casing party, 'shun.' Ruck was saluting Shrimp Simpson. A pipe from the balcony shrilled in answer: and there was Shrimp – a short, stocky figure in his gold-peaked cap, at the salute. Then the falling note of the 'carry-on', and an echo of it from *Ultra*. Formalities completed. Paul said, 'Right turn, dismiss, get a line over, Second.'

Heaving lines soared and dropped as the motors went astern to stop her; then she was sliding gently in alongside the other boat. Paul saw that *Unslaked*'s third hand, an RN sub-lieutenant called John Hewson, was with the berthing party. Or just loafing there. He called, 'Hi, John. Bad news here?'

Hewson nodded. Tall, red-haired. 'Plenty. But did you hear we sank the other troopship?'

'You did?'

He nodded again. 'Got back here at first light. Been sitting on the putty all day. What's the ambulance for?'

'Tell you later.' He was supposed to be at work, and he didn't want Ruck or Wykeham bawling him out with Simpson watching from the balcony hardly ten yards away.

As soon as the plank was down, linking the two submarines' casings, Ruck went ashore to report to Shrimp. And Hewson prowled across to talk to Paul. Then some of the base specialists, technicians, came across and went below, to consult with Wykeham and Chief ERA Pool about defects and repairs. It had been a hell of a raid, Hewson told Paul. Two-thirds of the officers' quarters had been opened to the sky, electric light, telephones and mains water had been cut, the submarines P36 and P39 had been damaged, and the fuelling lighter had been hit, set on fire and sunk. There'd been some casualties, too – the list of dead included the captain, first lieutenant and two officers of the Greek submarine *Glaukos*. They'd been running – too late – for the rock shelter.

A young naval doctor, an RNVR two-striper, came aboard with two SBAs and a stretcher. The doctor found the plank tricky to negotiate, treating it like a tightrope and seeming to hold his breath as he tottered over it. Panting, he stopped on the casing, waiting for the sickberth attendants to join him.

'How the hell do we get a stretcher with a man in it over *that*?'

Paul moved closer. 'I think he'll be able to walk. It's only a shoulder wound. He'll give *you* a hand over, I expect.'

The SBAs laughed. The doctor grinned. 'All right. All right . . .' He climbed gingerly down into the TSC. Paul asked one of the SBAs, 'Where's our PMO?' The letters stood for principal medical officer. The base had its own surgeon captain, even though he'd lost his hospital in an earlier attack. The SBA said, 'He's dead, sir.'

'*What?*'

'In his house, ashore. Bomb. Two days ago.'

Janaway came up on his own two feet and with one arm in a sling. He was arguing about having to go to hospital at all, but the SBAs hauled him off and the doctor made the return crossing in the same odd, teetering manner. Logan went along too, taking Flyte and another telegraphist, Braidmore, with him, and they came back with two sacks of ship's company mail. Then a messenger arrived, one of Simpson's base staff, with a message to Wykeham from Ruck: one half of the ship's company was to stay aboard, and the others were to be ready in half an hour to board transport that would take them to the rest camp. This started a stream of men, hammocks and kitbags out of the hatch and across the planks. Everything seemed fairly chaotic for a while.

One of Paul's letters was from his father. For some considerable time after the mail had been distributed he made attempts to settle down and read it, but there was a lot to do and Wykeham kept giving him one job after another. Finally, when he'd actually got as far as slitting it open, Ruck came back aboard, took over the chair from McClure and demanded their attention.

'Listen, all of you. Here's the position – and it's not good . . .'

He gave it to them haphazardly, as items occurred to him, as he recalled what Simpson and his staff officers had told him . . . The damage to the base and to submarines, services cut off. Work in progress now to restore lighting, water and communications. Base officers whose cabins had been wrecked were shifting whatever remained of possessions or furniture to a former oil tank, a rock cavern with a floor area of one hundred feet by forty and a ceiling height of twenty. It had an uneven floor with pools of oil in the depressions, and the stink was horrible. But it was underground and safe, and there were dry areas of floor which were being connected by plank bridges laid across the foul areas. Shrimp's secretary, Miss Gomer, was transferring her office work, desk and typewriter, down to this reeking dungeon because his day-cabin had had its roof blown off.

All personnel, officers and men, would henceforth mess together in the open air, using trestle tables. Submarine officers were to be put on lodging allowance and to sleep in the flats in Sliema, but they could use the oil tank as a changing room. Despite, presumably, the presence of Miss Gomer. All other sleeping accommodation would now be in double-tiered bunks in the rock shelters – which Shrimp Simpson, during the past eighteen months, had had burrowed into the sandstone cliff which backed the whole building.

As of tomorrow at sunrise, submarines would spend their days on the bottom of the harbour. Only one boat would stay alongside Lazaretto, risking bombs, while the entire base staff concentrated on readying just that one submarine for sea. All other work on submarines would be done at night. Periods in harbour would be reduced to a minimum, partly because of the problems here in Malta and partly because with Rommel preparing for a resumption of his offensive – an assault on Tobruk was expected, followed by an attempt to drive through into Egypt – the only good place for the 10th Flotilla submarines to be was out on patrol, cutting the Axis supply lines.

Ruck asked Paul, 'Think you could take the boat out and dive her on your own, Sub?'

Paul stared at him, wondering if he was serious. It looked like it. The idea in its first impact was startling . . . He nodded, hoping he hadn't shown the sudden fright that he'd felt.

'Don't see why not, sir.'

'Nor do I. You can do it once under the first lieutenant's supervision. If he tells me you're competent, you and he'll take alternate days.' He looked at Wykeham. 'All right with you?'

'Well . . .' Wykeham looked scared. 'Sounds dicey, but I dare say we'll survive it.'

McClure was looking at Paul enviously. Paul was 'third hand' and the Scot was fourth, because Paul had finished the submarine training course at Blyth a few months before McClure had started his, and he'd done a stretch in a training boat before being appointed to *Ultra*. Both he and McClure were still what sailors called 'as green as grass', but Paul was slightly less so. It seemed a lot of responsibility to be given, this soon; but he guessed that after he'd done it a couple of times he'd think nothing of it.

Ruck gave them the better news now, recent patrol successes. *Ultimatum* (Harrison) had blown a U-boat apart off Sicily somewhere, and *Unslaked* had completed the destruction of their troopship convoy. Both those former liners had been identified now, and Intelligence reported that the troops aboard them had been German.

Unslaked had hit with two torpedoes out of a full salvo of four, and like *Ultra* had escaped without a counter-attack. Several supply ships had been sunk off the Tunisian coast, and a convoy rounding northwest Sicily and steering for Cape Bon had turned back after a freighter had been hit and a destroyer sunk. The freighter, with a deck cargo of German army vehicles, had beached itself, and the RAF had been invited to finish it off before the trucks could be got ashore. And *Torbay*, from the 1st Flotilla at Alexandria, had been right inside Corfu Roads, torpedoed two ships in broad daylight and sneaked out again.

Wykeham handed Ruck his mail.

'Ah. Thanks.'

'One of 'em's scented, sir.'

'From my grandfather, I expect . . . Listen. We're getting three days in now, four at the most. Means the watch ashore gets two full days in the rest camp . . .'

Later, and after he'd read his mail, Paul went ashore, for a stroll and to look around. Only he and Wykeham and the duty watch were sleeping on board, so as to be on the spot to take her out at first light and dive her. *Ultra*'s diesels were pounding away and so were *Unslaked*'s, the combined racket shattering the night's peace while the batteries were charged. Diesel exhaust drifting in near-still air added to the reek of shale. When the fuel lighter had been hit, the entire area had been sprayed with it.

Three other submarines lay at buoys, a floating brow reaching to them like a water snake lying black on the water.

The wardroom, although its eastern end had suffered and its messing facilities had ceased to exist, was still in use. It was a big, cellar-like space, entered from the long waterfront gallery. Dim now, candle-lit . . . A fireplace in the centre of it was open on four sides, so that in cold weather it could be surrounded by yarning, gin-drinking submariners. There were only a few groups of officers in here now: one of them, comprising only COs, included Ruck and the tall, ragged-bearded David Wanklyn VC. And Johnny March, *Unslaked*'s captain, and beyond him – Paul *thought* that was Tomkinson, captain of *Urge*. Another of the aces. Might Ruck, he wondered, become one of the top scorers before long?

McClure's mutter echoed in his memory: *Going for a VC, are we?* After Ruck had sunk that tanker. It had been a silly thing to say. They were all here to sink enemy ships; if someone happened to get this or that medal in the course of doing it, OK, he got it. It could certainly never have been in Wanklyn's mind, and it wouldn't be in Ruck's either.

He joined a group of junior submarine officers. Someone offered him a drink, but he didn't have time to hang around.

'Thanks, but I'll be getting back to the boat. Our flunkey's doing a fry-up.'

Hewson of *Unslaked* said he'd be getting along too. For a similar reason . . . 'But I might offer you a swift tot on your way across. How's that?' A drink in *Unslaked*, he meant. Paul nodded. 'OK. Thanks. Just a quick one.' He felt sad, a sense of loneliness or loss; it had come to him, he thought, when he'd been reading the letter from his father. There was really no sound reason for it: only a feeling, a kind of sadness that had been growing since then in his mind.

Hewson said, pausing at the scoreboard, 'Couple of items to be filled in here now, h'm?'

It was a large sheet of cardboard on the sandstone wall beside the door, and it showed the results of all the submarines' patrols. The names of the boats were in the left-hand column, then vertical ruling provided rectangles in which the results of each

patrol were recorded graphically from left to right. Little
sketches of ships sinking, U-boats blowing up, trains wrecked,
commandos landing in canoes. And some of the boats' records
ended with a rectangle blanked off by diagonals.

Those could haunt you, if you let them. You could only guess
at what had caused each loss: a mine, depthcharge, ramming, U-
boat's torpedo, an E-boat at night . . . Mines, it was thought, were
the biggest killers. There were so many of them around, and if
you'd taken much notice of them you could hardly have operated at all.

Upholder – Wanklyn's boat – had completed twenty-three
patrols in fifteen months. His first four patrols had been blank,
until he'd got his eye in. Since then, his score had been phe-
nomenal.

Thumping drone of diesels: and it would be going on all
night. The wind was down, the surface of the creek barely disturbed. Sentries on the submarines' casings were jet-black
silhouettes against the gleaming ripples. Paul thought about his
father, and the letter he'd had from him. Dated early February:
an air letter-card . . .

HMS Defiant
c/o GPO London

My dear Paul,

By the time this reaches you I expect you'll be under the
wing of an old friend of mine known to us all as 'Shrimp'.
Give him my regards, please. I can't even guess where I'll
be when you're reading it. In case we don't see each other
in anything like the reasonably foreseeable future I want to
tell you, though, that I've been consistently delighted at
news of your progress and achievements, and wish you con-
tinuance of it as well as personal happiness in all other
spheres as well. I look forward immensely to seeing you at
Mullbergh, God willing, when this wretched war is won
and we can all become human beings again. We have a
great deal to catch up on, you and I. I often think about it,

and regret that we've been so far apart in recent years. My consolation is that it obviously hasn't done you any harm; you've turned out splendidly.

I shan't go on with this now. It's said, in case I don't have another chance to say it. Good luck. Write when you have time . . .

In *Unslaked*'s wardroom – which was a duplicate of *Ultra*'s – while Hewson uncorked a bottle Paul took the letter out and checked the date again. His father had written it only days before the fall of Singapore. You could understand that line: *Can't guess where I'll be* . . . 'Water in it?'

'A little, please.'

There'd be absolutely no point, he thought, in writing to him about Jack and Fiona. He was glad, now, that he hadn't.

5

On the Friday when they sailed from Cardiff it was blowing up for a gale, and Tubby Sharp – former ML skipper, now CO of the E-boat – was prophesying that *Sauerkraut* would founder a long way short of Falmouth. Jack told him, caustically, to make sure he had lifebelts for all hands, including the two ERAs. Jack and his team were taking passage in the minesweeper HMS *Gourock*, but he'd lent Pettifer and Wood to Sharp in case of any trouble with the E-boat's engines. The artificers hadn't been too pleased about this, but nobody had any way of knowing how an E-boat might behave in bad weather.

It was a northerly blow, and once they were out of the Bristol Channel they really felt it. They'd pushed off from Cardiff at 1630; even just outside the harbour it wasn't exactly comfortable, but by the time the light was gone it was truly miserable. *Gourock* led the way, showing a blue stern light for the E-boat to follow, and Jack's torpedomen stood watches at the after end of the sweeper's bridge solely to keep track of the boat plunging along astern. Nobody had realized how near to impossible this would be, and after a while *Gourock*'s captain signalled Sharp to burn a masthead light. In the waste of rolling, driving sea it wasn't easy even then; when the E-boat was in a trough, the crests were higher than the light.

Off Ilfracombe at 11 pm course was altered to southwest, for the run of about a hundred miles inside Lundy to pass Hartland

Point, Tintagel Head, Newquay . . . The alteration put wind and
sea astern: there was less rolling but more savage pitching, and
a danger of the screws racing through coming clear of the water
when her snout went down. *Gourock* reduced to revs for eight
knots. Jack had intended to turn in and leave the worrying to
this ship's captain, but he found he couldn't. Most of the time
he stayed with the look-out – one hand for binoculars and the
other for holding on with, and jammed in against the end of the
sweeper's flag-locker – straining to keep that speck of light in
view. Then searching for it again – anxiously, when its disap-
pearances were prolonged – when they lost it. Seas burst
regularly over *Gourock*'s quarter, drowning her afterpart in foam
while spray sheeted like ice on the cutting wind. *Gourock*, ancient
though she was – she'd been launched in 1919 – displaced 700
tons to the E-boat's sixty.

Departure from Cardiff could have been postponed; it would,
Jack knew, have been *sensible* to have waited. *Seamanlike*, some
might say. But the weather wasn't expected to moderate for several days, and there was a worry that if they didn't get to
Falmouth in time to dovetail with whatever else was happening
they might be cut out of the operation altogether, if the commanders of the main force – or the planners, whoever it was –
already disliked having to include them.

Smith, the commander, had agreed that the risk did exist.
And despite his gloom Tubby Sharp had opted to set out. He'd
suggested to Smith, 'If it's all that bad, we could turn back,
couldn't we?'

He was paying for it now, Jack thought. In that tossing, gyrating little craft there could well be broken legs and ribs . . . And
why *not* have waited for the weather, for Christ's sake? When all
he had to do to get Fiona was stay alive!

Incredible. Too marvellous to be real. It justified every damn
thing that was happening or ever had happened. As if sea and
sky had changed colour and the world assumed a different
shape . . .

Trolley and his sergeants hadn't been around to say goodbye

to. Or to say anything else to. They'd pulled out on Friday evening. It hadn't been easy to get the loan of their services in the first place, Smith told Jack, and they'd been in a hurry to get back to wherever they'd come from.

In the enclosed, central part of the minesweeper's bridge her skipper, an RNR lieutenant-commander, seemed rooted, as much a fixture as the binnacle. And he made sure the air in here stayed foul from the shag tobacco he smoked incessantly. He was a strange, rough-looking individual, with one eye wild that didn't look at you: he took a pipe out of his mouth now and shouted, 'Kye?'

Jack shook his head. He wasn't seasick and didn't expect to be, but he wasn't going to invite trouble either by staying in this atmosphere or by filling his stomach with liquid.

'What are you up to with a bloody E-boat, then?'

Bawling, over the noise of wind and sea and the old ship's rattles, Jack yelled back, 'Can't tell you. Don't know myself.'

It might be a raid on Brest, he thought. He didn't know whether any part of the docks there bore any resemblance to the mock-up he'd been training on, or what the purpose of such a raid might be, but with Falmouth as starting-point it seemed reasonable geographically. For the same reason he'd considered the Channel Islands as a possibility, but decided that neither Jersey nor Guernsey could possibly have dock installations of the kind they'd been training to deal with.

'Q-ship operation, is it?'

'I suppose it could be.'

'Some kind of cloak-and-dagger stunt, eh?'

Jack shrugged. The skipper roared with laughter. 'Read about it in the papers, will I?'

Dawn came up silvery under a funeral sky somewhere off the coast between Newquay and St Ives. Growing light revealed that *Sauerkraut* hadn't noticeably changed shape: she was plunging like a gamefish on a taut line, battling through seas that swept up from astern and rolled right over her, hiding her for minutes at a time. They were being set inshore, and *Gourock*'s skipper altered out to counter this. At the same time he discovered that despite having revs on for only eight knots they'd been making ten over the ground, thanks to having this wind astern.

Back at the rail, watching the E-boat's erratic and violent motion, Jack thought about his promise to Fiona to try to make friends with Nick. Get on a brotherly footing with him, was how she'd put it. He'd told her, 'Not so easy, considering he's old enough to be my father.'

'Why are you like you are about him, Jack?'

It would have been very difficult, and taken a long time, to explain in any detail. Old history, the whole atmosphere in which he had been brought up; and other relations involved, including two dead ones . . . He'd tried to give her an idea of it, and to explain that in essence, going back to the start of it from his own point of view, it was Nick's attitude to *him* more than his own towards Nick.

They'd left it at that. And even to himself now the past seemed unreal, irrelevant. Either it was through having tried to talk about it, describe it to her, or because the future was suddenly so full of promise.

They were off Cornwall's southwestern bulge when he went down to breakfast. At 0900 course was altered to due south, to pass Cape Cornwall and leave the Longships lighthouse close to port. An hour later the wheel went over again, after which *Gourock* was leading the E-boat southeastward with Wolf Rock coming up to starboard and Lizard Point ahead, progress much easier as they moved into the shelter of the land. By the next change of course – off the Lizard at 1300, and fish pie for lunch in the sweeper's smelly bridge – they were making twelve knots instead of ten, and the E-boat was having a comparatively easy time of it. Still rollercoastering, but she was in sight all the time and Sharp was having no difficulty keeping her in station.

Crossing Falmouth Bay at two-thirty, *Gourock* signalled to *Sauerkraut* to report any damage and/or injuries. Sharp replied, *One broken wrist, one ERA concussed, minor breakages and leaking shaft gland.*

So he'd be minus one ERA. But a shaft gland wouldn't take much fixing.

Falmouth's Port War Signal Station ordered them to a jetty where a whole fleet of MLs was berthed. They were in trots three and four deep, and some of them were still in the process of tying up, having shifted to make room for the minesweeper. *Gourock* squeezed herself into the vacated space, and after she'd secured the E-boat berthed alongside her. Jack didn't wait for a gangway; he climbed over the rail, and jumped. He called to Sharp, 'Which ERA's concussed?'

Sharp walked slowly towards him down the boat's port side, staring at him strangely. He began, making a performance of it, 'How *are* you, Tubby? What sort of a bloody awful trip did you have, you poor fellow? Lucky to be alive, aren't you? While some of us lie around in the lap of fucking luxury and then don't even bloody well *enquire*—'

'Ah.' Jack was looking past at him as ERA Pettifer rose from a hatch. 'What's the score?'

'Woody got chucked clear across the engine space, sir, cracked his nut on the gear casing. Went out cold. I thought he'd had it.'

'We've asked for an ambulance. Where is he?'

'Below, sir. Still unconscious.' Pettifer glanced at Sharp. 'Officers' quarters.'

'In my bunk, to be exact. Had to lash him in, what's more. It hasn't been any bloody picnic, I assure you. And the smashed wrist, in case your interest should extend that far, is one of a pair attached to young Bellamy.'

Bellamy, an RNR sub-lieutenant, was Sharp's first lieutenant. Jack went below to see ERA Wood, and the ambulance team arrived when he was down there. They strapped Wood in a Neil-Robertson stretcher and carried him ashore, and Bellamy went with him, his arm in a sling. He told Sharp, 'I'll be back when they've fixed this up, sir.' He was tall and very thin, a schoolboy who'd temporarily outgrown his strength. Sharp told him, 'Just do what they tell you. If they want to keep you, you stay. I'll get out there later on.'

'I'll be back.' He looked aggrieved. 'I'll be perfectly all right.'

'No, you won't. You'll need two hands, and you've only got one. I'm sorry, Tim.'

Signals arrived, by hand of messenger. The minesweeper, it now transpired, was to boiler-clean here, and would serve as accommodation for the Naval Task Unit. There'd be plenty of room, since two-thirds of her ship's company were being sent on leave, and it was a lot more convenient than having to move to some shore billet. Jack sent for PO Slattery and Sergeant Bowater to give them this news. There was a sheaf of other stuff addressed to him – Officer Commanding NTU – on domestic matters such as victualling, pay, leave – *no* leave – shore recreation facilities and censorship of mail, and the originator of all the signals was shown as Senior Officer 10th Anti-Submarine Striking Force.

He asked the signalman who'd brought the messages down to him, 'Who's this SO 10th A/S Force?'

'Naval HQ's on the seafront, sir.' He pointed. 'Over that way. Used to be an hotel. Can't miss it – sentry on the door, an' that.'

'And who's this individual?'

'You mean Commander Ryder, sir?'

Sharp was on the jetty, staring at the trots of motor launches . . .

'Seen those?'

The numbers painted on their sides weren't familiar; they weren't from the base in Scotland. Jack frowned. 'Of course I've seen them.'

'Observe the fuel tanks too, did you?'

He was right . . . Each of the Fairmiles had two auxiliary tanks on deck, just as Sharp's ML had. Jack murmured, 'God help us.' Sharp corrected him: 'You mean God help *them*. At least after our little joyride I know old *Sauerkraut*'ll stand up to just about anything that comes.'

'I'm sorry you had a bad time, Tubby. Dare say we should have waited.'

'Except we wouldn't have been here, would we? . . . What'll you do about your ERA?'

'Nothing I *can* do. ERAs with commando training don't exactly grow on trees. We'll manage all right, as long as Pettifer doesn't crack up. You'll replace Bellamy easily enough, won't you?'

'Might even be time to get a bloke down from Scotland.' Sharp nodded. 'I know who I'd ask for, too.'

'You'd better come along with me now, and see if we can fix it. I'm off to call on the SO 10th A/S Striking Force.'

'The SO what?'

'*This* chap.' Jack showed him the signals. Sharp said he'd had a batch too, but he hadn't looked at them yet; there was a direct connection, he explained, between peace of mind and the non-receipt of orders. Jack interrupted this philosophical dissertation: 'It's a seafront hotel that he hangs out in. He's away, but there'll be someone around. Coming?'

There was a gathering of ML personnel on the launches' sterns, with binoculars trained on the unfamiliar shape of the E-boat. They'd need to keep souvenir-hunters from stripping her, probably; Sharp would need a harbour watchkeeper on his boat, as well as the minesweeper's gangway watch. He was suggesting this when they heard a rumble of powerful engines: it was a motor torpedo boat, puttering up towards the ML berths. And something odd about it, even at this distance . . . It would be passing, in a minute. Then he spotted the peculiarity, which at the first glance had told him this MTB wasn't the same as others; instead of having a torpedo tube on each side of her, she had both tubes mounted for'ard, on her foc's'l. They'd fire over her bow, and it was a totally new arrangement.

Sharp said, shielding his eyes, 'Peculiar-looking object.'

'Certainly is.' The number on its side was 74. 'By the way – what about your shaft gland?'

'My blokes'll have it fixed by tomorrow evening. With Pettifer's help . . . What's this fellow call himself – SO A/S Force?'

'A/S Striking Force.'

'Codswallop.'

'Camouflage, anyway.' It had to be. If these MLs belonged to it, at any rate. Not only did they have the fuel tanks on deck, but their dinghies had been removed and the space on their sterns taken up by an extra Oerlikon. You caught submarines with depthcharges, not Oerlikons . . .

They walked on. Seeing a lot that was of interest. Including, on their way out of the docks, a grey-painted passenger ship secured alongside. Men in khaki were visible along her rails, and there were groups of them lounging on her well-deck. Also, there was an armed soldier as well as a naval quartermaster on her gangway.

Sharp commented, 'Looks like we've come to the right place. *And* it's a bigger show than anyone has so far bothered to mention to yours truly.'

Jack pointed ahead. 'Here come some more of them.'

This was where he got the biggest surprise. A platoon of soldiery was doubling towards them along the quayside. They looked as if they'd been worked hard: they were sweating under the weight of their packs and equipment. And the officer doubling alongside them was Trolley. Jack stopped, watching them approach. A strange element was the sound – how little there was of it; you heard the pounding feet but not the usual crash of service boots bashing the ground in unison. It was so quiet, in fact, that you could hear the runners' hard, rasping breaths. Soldiers in soft-soled boots, for God's sake; and of all people, *Trolley*. He'd stopped beside them. Shouting after his platoon, 'Carry on aboard ship!' He grinned at Jack; he didn't seem to be breathing very hard. He said, 'Surprise, eh?'

'Say *that* again.'

'Lucky meeting like this. I'd have been round to see you, later.' Trolley was wearing what looked like two days' growth of yellow beard. Jack realized he'd been wrong in that particular. Wearing, also, a friendly grin, nothing like the Cardiff sneer. He asked them, 'Was it a rough trip round?

Sharp shrugged. 'Bit choppy, don't you know.'

'They're taking us out to the Scillies and back tomorrow.'

The soldier waved a hand towards the ML jetty. 'Idea being to get the boys used to being seasick. Not sure I *want* to get used to it.' He laughed. 'But listen, Jack. Since I'm the devil you know, so to speak, I've been told to liaise with you. First thing is that if you want to, you and your team can exercise with my lot. Runs and so on, and weapons training. It's for you to say, but you'd be welcome.'

'Thanks.' Jack nodded. 'When?'

'Not tomorrow. We'll be on the briny. Day after – Monday? About Tuesday or Wednesday I believe we'll be getting briefed, and you may be included in that, I think.'

'Well, one might *hope* —'

'The thing is – well, no doubt your boss will explain all this, but he's away today, in Plymouth, although he's probably left orders for you with his minions – the point is, I've been told your briefing will be military more than naval, at this stage. We're being briefed earlier than your people, because we've got so much detail to work out. *And* then to fit you into it . . . But anyway, I'll contact you on Monday.'

Sharp said, 'Enjoy your outing tomorrow.'

'Weather's improving, they say.' Trolley glanced seaward. 'Forecast's pretty good.'

Jack asked him, 'Like to come aboard for a drink tonight?'

'Thanks, but I'm still on the wagon.' He laughed. 'See you Monday.'

At Cardiff, he'd seemed poisonous. Jack said to Sharp as they walked on to find the naval headquarters, 'Extraordinary. He's quite a decent bloke.'

'Bit scary, all that fitness lark. Never saw much wrong with him apart from that.'

You're so mulish, Jack. Fiona's voice, echoing round his head. *And so damn moody! You're your own worst enemy, anyone tell you that before?*

At Cardiff he'd been restive, pent-up, ready to go, and sick of the interminable training sessions. He'd felt like a boxed-up stallion; violence of any sort would have brought relief. But here – well, it was all around you, everywhere you looked you saw the imminence of action.

That – and in the background, Fiona . . .

Monday, 0045 . . .

Steering 215 degrees, nine knots, running charge. Moon hidden behind low cloud, wind northwest force two to three, low swell on the quarter. *Ultra* had sneaked out of Malta before dawn on Sunday, dived at the outer end of the swept channel and surfaced last evening at 1900. Shrimp Simpson's orders to Ruck were to establish patrol across the northwest approaches to Tripoli, within certain limits and with a line of withdrawal – if that became necessary – towards the Kerkennah islands. They'd be on the billet by tomorrow afternoon.

Paul had taken over the watch from Wykeham half an hour ago. Ruck was awake, though, down there, and fidgeting around. Judging by what he'd written in his night-order book, he was worried about the danger from E-boats in this area. It made sense, too: this was the direct route from Malta to Tripoli, and Tripoli was an obvious place for the Malta submarines to watch. It was a major port, one of the most important off loading points for Axis convoys which – usually – made the short crossing from the western tip of Sicily to Cape Bon in Tunisia and then slunk down-coast across the gulfs of Hammemet and Quabes to Tripoli or even, now, to Benghazi. But they were under such pressure to get supplies to Rommel at this stage that they were taking the risk of sending convoys straight across, as well; two such convoys had been reported to be at sea yesterday, and surface forces – Admiral Vian with three cruisers and nine destroyers – had left Alexandria to intercept them. Vian was aiming to kill another bird with the same stone – to destroy those convoys if he could catch them, but also to cover the withdrawal from Malta of the cruiser *Cleopatra* and the destroyer *Kingston.*

Paul glanced round, to check that the look-outs were doing their job. As they were, of course. Stolid, silent figures braced for support against the periscope standards as *Ultra* pitched and rolled to the swell that was running up on her starboard quarter. White foam framed her, sluiced across the small amount of her that showed above water: the long bow swung up, axed down, hydroplanes slamming flatly on the white out-curving bow-wave. The diesels rumbled in unison, and the wind was carrying their exhaust away to port.

The harbour diving business had gone off well enough. He'd done it on the first day with Wykeham watching every move and teaching him to flood her down very carefully so she'd settle gently and evenly on the mud. On the second day he'd been allowed to take her out on his own, and there'd been no problems. He'd known he could manage it, of course, but there'd still been some internal twinges of alarm. He'd had a day off on Friday, but most of it had been spent in the underground shelter, and it would have been more comfortable on the bottom of the harbour, where at least you had a bunk to sleep on. On Saturday, *Ultra* had been the boat selected to lie alongside Lazaretto, with the base staff all concentrating on her and the surrounding Bofors guns to keep the bombers from her. The Luftwaffe weren't all kept high, though: the pilot of a Messerschmitt 109 flying up-creek at two hundred feet had waved an ungloved hand to a spare-crew officer on the Lazaretto balcony, who'd sworn that the airman had red lacquer on his fingernails. 'Probably Goering's nephew,' someone had commented that evening in the wardroom. But that same afternoon a Ju88 dropped its stick of bombs down the centre of Lazaretto Creek, and it had certainly looked like a deliberate probing for dived submarines.

On Saturday evening the other half of the ship's company returned, and that night all hands worked hard storing ship and to have her ready to slip out at dawn. Everything else – torpedoes, fuel, fresh water and so on – had been replenished during the previous two nights.

1 am, now . . .

You tended to spend more time examining the starboard

side, the direction of Lampedusa – sixty miles away on that
beam – where you'd naturally expect E-boats to be coming from.
It was a tendency to guard against, though, because they could
be anywhere. Returning from wide, searching sweeps, for
instance. It was also an E-boat tactic to lie stopped, silent and
practically invisible, waiting for unwary victims. A craft that
small, with camouflage painting and showing no wake or bow-
wave, wasn't an easy thing to spot.

'Bridge!'

He answered, 'Bridge.'

'Captain's coming up, sir.'

Ruck heaved himself out of the hatch and stumbled into the
front of the bridge on Paul's right. *He* was concentrating on that
starboard side, now. Then all around . . . But only for a couple of
minutes, before he lowered his binoculars.

'I'm turning in now, Sub. Keep your eyes skinned.'

'Aye aye, sir.'

Searching across the bow and then slowly down the port
side. Following the line of the horizon, vague as it was, looking
for any break or interruption in it. He hadn't heard Ruck
leave, and when he swung back to search the other side he saw
he was using the 'pig's ear', the funnel-shaped bridge urinal. A
pipe led from the base of the funnel down outside the bridge
casing to the sea: it was washed through every time the boat
dived.

Glasses misty again: he fumbled in his pocket for some
periscope paper to wipe the lenses with . . . Ruck had gone down
when Paul resumed his inspection of the dark, murmuring sea
and the dim, hard-to-define horizon.

Unslaked had sailed the day before *Ultra*: she'd gone northwestward, through the Sicilian minefield, to patrol off Palermo.
Upholder, *Unbeaten*, P31 and P34 were also on patrol. Dotted
around this central basin of the Mediterranean in their various
patrol areas, they'd all be on the surface now, all charging batteries, all keeping the same intense and vital look-out . . . He'd
checked suddenly, thinking he'd seen something: something

dark, fine on the bow to port. Sweeping back across it, keeping the glasses moving because you didn't see much at night by looking straight at it . . .

Nothing. Resuming the search now. It was easy to imagine things; and when it happened your heart jumped, the breath stuck in your throat. Sweeping on now, down the port side, *Ultra* corkscrewing to the quartering swell. Pivoting slowly, he swept on past the beam, catching a noxious whiff of diesel fumes . . .

'Object on the starboard quarter, sir!' A yell from the starboard look-out . . . 'E-boat I think, sir!'

'Down below!'

He'd shouted into the voicepipe, 'Port fifteen!' Turning her stern to it. Glasses up on that bearing, searching. And he'd got it: white flare of bow-wave. It was far enough away to get under, anyway . . . 'Midships. Dive, dive, dive!' He'd shut the cock on the pipe and he was jumping into the hatch, vents already open, diesels stopped and sea piling, swelling round the tower as she pushed down into it.

In the control room the look-out – it was Furness, a torpedo-man – was telling Ruck what he'd seen. Paul confirmed: 'It *was* an E-boat, sir. Starboard quarter, but I turned stern-on.'

'Forty feet. Group down, slow together . . . Hear anything, Newton?'

Newton, freshly roused from sleep, looked like a corpse. He shook his head: his expression suggested he didn't *want* to hear anything, either. Then he sat up straighter, and his eyes were suddenly fully open; a forefinger pointed upwards. 'Fast HE, sir . . . E-boat . . . Coming over us, sir . . .'

In less than a minute they heard it, right over the top. Then fading, holding the same straight course.

Ruck said – straightening from the ladder, against which he'd been reclining – 'We'll wait a little while. May have a chum tailing him.' But ten minutes later, with nothing on asdics, he brought her up to twenty-eight feet, then twenty-five, for a periscope search. Not that he'd be seeing much, in

this moonless night . . . 'Down periscope.' Looking over at
Newton again: 'Still nothing?'

'Clear all round, sir.'

He nodded to Wykeham. 'Stand by to surface.'

You had to press on – to get to the billet, and to have the readings well up before you dived for the daylight. Ruck said, a few
minutes later – on the surface again, with 300 revolutions per
minute on the diesels and a running charge port side, everything as it had been half an hour ago except that the bridge was
running wet – 'It doesn't matter a damn being put down. I don't
care if we dive and surface like a bloody porpoise all night long.
So long as we don't stay up when we ought to dive, that's what
matters.'

0150, now. Incidents like that one did tend to make a two-
hour watch pass quickly. Less than half an hour, and Bob
McClure would be up here. The little Scot had been as dour as
hell ever since he'd come back from the rest camp on Saturday
evening. Paul hadn't heard him speak a dozen words since then,
off duty.

'Bridge!'

'Bridge.'

'Relieve look-out, sir?'

'Yes, please.'

He heard it happening, behind him. When a man was taking
over, you waited until his eyes had adapted themselves to the
dark before you left him to it.

'Port look-out relieved, sir.'

'All right, Flyte.'

Then the other one. He told him, 'Glad you saw that,
Furness.'

'So am I, sir.'

Next man up would be McClure. Paul didn't think he'd have
turned in again for so short a time, but it might be just as well to
make sure, perhaps. He called down, 'See if the navigating officer needs a shake, will you?'

'Aye, aye, sir!'

McClure came up seething with ill-temper.

'What the hell would I want a shake for? You knew I was awake, didn't you? Think I can't tell the fuckin' time, or something?'

Paul had his glasses up, searching the sea ahead. He asked him, 'Are you crossed in love, or something?' He got no reaction . . . 'What is it? Shoats wouldn't let you catch 'em, out at the camp?' Shoats were Maltese quadrupeds, half sheep and half goat. Paul swept on, slowly and carefully, round the bow and down the starboard side.

McClure muttered after a minute, 'If the witty stuff's over, I'll take her now.'

'Right.' He told him the revs, course, running charge . . . 'Skipper wants a sharp look-out kept for E-boats. Motto for the night is dive first, ask questions later.'

'I did read the night-order book.'

'You're all right then, are you?'

'Sure. I've got the weight.'

Flat as hell . . . Paul asked him, 'What's wrong, Bob?'

Silence. He'd begun his own looking-out. Then: 'You want to know?'

'Christ's sake, I *asked*.'

'My brother's dead. Shot down in his Lanc. Letter from home, Saturday.'

'Bob – I'm so damn *sorry* —'

'So're my folks. They're bloody desperate . . . Look, I've got her now, all right?'

War . . .

People got killed. Surprise, surprise . . . But – all very well flying Jolly Rogers, winning medals, staying alive and cheerful, having other people *consistently delighted with your progress and achievements* . . .

No. Take that back. *Anyone* could drown. As he'd known, and clearly had in mind, when he wrote that. Embarrassed, finding words for it.

David Wanklyn, everyone said, was a gentle, quiet man who

hated the fruits of his own success. It was said that he despaired, privately, in the knowledge of young men killed, wives made widows, parents broken.

But either you did it, or you lost the war – to people who did *not* mind doing it. It really was that simple. It meant shooting, burning, drowning your fellow humans, and inflicting deep, lasting sadness on those others. But what else, what alternative —

'You all right, Sub?'

Ruck, from his bunk. In the dim light you couldn't see much more than the whites of his eyes watching from where the pillow was. Paul hadn't been aware of arriving in the wardroom; he'd been climbing down the ladder, thinking . . . He nodded towards the eyes.

'Yes, sir. Fine.'

'Standing like a graven image for the last two minutes.'

'I was' – he leaned forward on to the table – 'just thinking . . . Sir, did McClure tell you – his brother, the one who's a bomber pilot – shot down?'

'Oh, *Christ* . . .' Then: 'How did he hear?'

'Had a letter from his parents – yesterday. When he got back from the camp, I suppose.'

He kicked his boots off and climbed on to his bunk. Some minutes later, in the fringes of sleep, he heard Ruck murmur, 'Thanks for telling me', then the helmsman calling 'Captain's coming up, sir . . .' He didn't want to know, or think: he drifted back into sleep and the next thing he knew was a fist banging on the wooden edging of the bunk and a voice insisting, 'Five past six, sir, your watch now. Torpedo officer, sir?'

'All right. Thanks. Good.' Muddled: remembering last night, what McClure had told him. And what day was this, for God's sake? Monday? Could be one of seven: you still had to turn out, get in there . . .

The boat was at periscope depth: they'd dived her quietly on the watch, Wykeham told him. The dead-reckoning position on the chart put them fifty miles north of Tripoli. There'd been no chance of starsights, because of cloud cover. Course was still

215, motors slow ahead and grouped down. Wykeham said, 'Fairly light up there now. Nothing in sight a minute ago, but d'you want to take a shufti?'

He nodded. 'Right.'

Low swell, and low cloud: cloud and sea different shades of grey. And nothing else . . . He sent the periscope down. ERA Summers was on the panel, Flyte on asdics, Lovesay and Stapleton on the hydroplanes and Creagh helmsman. Main vent levers were in the shut position and the trim looked good.

'OK. I've got her.'

'Skipper told me about young Bob.' Wykeham spoke quietly. 'Poor little bugger.'

Paul nodded. 'He used to talk about his brother quite often. Sergeant-Pilot, flying Lancasters, and he'd just got engaged, remember?'

The watch passed uneventfully. Just after 0730 Shaw roused the wardroom with breakfast, the watch changed at 0800, and ten minutes after that McClure shuffled in to take over. He told Paul, jerking his head towards the wardroom and speaking very quietly, 'Skipper offered to take my watch last night.'

'*Did* he . . . ? Look, I'm sorry, Bob, I really did have to tell him.'

McClure shrugged. 'Doesn't matter.'

It was a very quiet day. The sea was whipping up a bit, but it wasn't anything you'd feel at periscope depth. At about eleven, in Wykeham's watch, when they crossed the hundred-fathom line Ruck had the course changed to due south, and by 5 pm they were twenty-three miles northwest of Tripoli with nothing in sight except some fishing boats and an occasional aircraft. They ran on inshore for another hour, then turned about and back-tracked, surfacing in the dark at 2030. Ruck turned her to 215 degrees: he'd decided they'd spend the night patrolling to and fro over a twelve-mile track, reversing course every two hours. Making six knots on one engine, with a standing charge on the other: they'd be roughly twenty miles from Tripoli all night, and in a position to intercept any convoy from the north-west.

That evening, it was wardroom versus stokers in the ship's uckers tournament. Uckers was a game like ludo and a favourite sailors' pastime. The wardroom team consisted of Wykeham and Paul, and their opponents were Leading Stoker 'Sinbad' Seager and Stoker Maskell. The venue was the wardroom; it was a semi-final, each team having won one previous round, and a group of spectators had collected in the gangway.

Just as play started, Ruck came down from the bridge. *Ultra* had reached the inshore end of her beat, and he'd gone up to see McClure bring her round on to the northeasterly course, 035. The wind was about force four now and Ruck looked as if he'd had his head in a shower, from the spray up there as they'd turned into it.

Seager, who came from Derby, muttered, 'Don't like to count me chickens, Ginger, but we're liable to bloody walk this one.' Maskell grinned as he shook the dice-pot.

Paul said to Wykeham, 'You can't blame 'em for trying to put a brave face on it. They know when they're up against real champs.'

Seager had given himself a coughing fit, from laughing . . .

'Captain, sir?'

Ruck, among the spectators, turned to see Parker, petty officer telegraphist, trying to get through to him.

'Signal from S10, sir.' He made a long arm, passing it over two stokers' heads. 'Lot of stuff on the air tonight, sir. Something's going on somewhere, I reckon.'

Vian's sortie, probably. Or the enemy's response to it. Convoys picking up their skirts and running? If the Italian fleet made any move southward they'd have three or four 10th Flotilla submarines to get past, up around Taranto: and there'd be prayers rising from those boats that they *would* come out. Why wouldn't they, when British naval strength in the Eastern Mediterranean consisted now of that handful of light cruisers and destroyers, and the Italians had twice as many *heavy* ones, and battleships?

They enjoyed *having* them. So they kept them tucked up in their harbours.

Uckers was temporarily suspended. On the *Forces' Favourites* programme Pat Kirkwood was singing 'The Only One Who's Difficult Is You'. Maskell wagging his head and listening to her with his eyes half-shut, all other eyes on Ruck as he read the signal, which would have been received in cipher and decoded in the wireless office. He raised his voice, to be heard in the control room: 'Tell the officer of the watch I want him to come round to two-seven-oh.' He told Wykeham, 'Supposed to be an ammunition ship aground, some way west of us.' He turned to the chart table, to put the position on and lay off a course to it.

Seager returned to the business of uckers. 'My go, was it?'

'Might as well be,' Paul suggested, 'unless you want to throw the towel in?' *Ultra* rolled harder as she turned, swinging her bow across the direction of wind and sea.

Pitch-black night: weather on the bow, sea slamming against the casing and geysering around the gun and bridge, *Ultra* demonstrating her favourite corkscrew motion as she drove westward – a little north of west, a course of 290 degrees – with the Libyan coast twelve to fifteen miles to port and about thirty-five miles to cover in the next four hours. With only a running charge now, and making nine knots, Ruck expected to dive her at 0500 not far from the position of the allegedly beached freighter.

About 0100 now. Tuesday morning . . . He *thought* it was Tuesday. In this two hours on, four hours off routine, one twenty-four-hour period was so much like another that putting a name to it was a largely academic exercise. You kept track of dates, because they appeared on signals with the time of origin, but the day of the week only mattered when you were leaving the base or returning to it.

He had a towel around his neck inside the Ursula jacket, but several streams of cold water had already found ways past it. The wind was rising force five, he guessed.

The stokers had wiped the board with them, of course. McClure, when he'd come off watch, had stated that they wouldn't have if he'd been playing. You could see him making

his effort, and the others seeing it and liking him for it. Training
his glasses right now, across the bow – feet straddled for balance, and his back against the for'ard periscope standard – Paul
recognized that it wouldn't be at all easy for him. You could
admire the tetchy little bastard . . . Binoculars getting wet twice
a minute: if anything did turn up it would be *bloody* hard to see
it . . .

He'd stopped, about fifteen degrees on the bow.

Imagination?

Swinging slightly right: intending to sweep back across what
he *thought* he'd seen . . . But – *it had a twin!*

Two destroyers, in line abreast? A screen ahead of something?

Well out on the bow. If he dived her now, Ruck wouldn't see
a thing. Not with the sea this high, and no moon. There was
time, anyway, to let him make his own decision.

'Captain on the bridge!' Then – 'Starboard ten. Steer three-
oh-five!' Straightening, with his glasses on those shapes again:
dark, low, appearing and disappearing, white flashes of bow-
wave catching your eye when they showed . . . Christ, *three* of
them!

'What is it?'

Ruck bawling the question as he arrived like a missile in the
front of the bridge and a flying half-ton of sea drenched over to
welcome him. Paul yelled, 'Three destroyers – ahead and fine on
the starboard bow – I've turned to three-oh-five. Looks like a
screen —'

'Look-outs down!'

Diving?

But he had his glasses up: motionless, so far as that was possible – like being motionless on a bucking horse. Paul swept the
darkness to his left, down the port side. Ruck shouted, 'Stay at
the voicepipe, Sub – diving stations, stand by all tubes! Three-six-
oh revs!'

Paul called the orders down the pipe. Ruck howled, '*Four*
destroyers. And something bigger astern of them, going like a
dingo . . . Steer' – he checked the dimly lit gyro repeater, his wet

face ghostly in its faint radiance right on top of it – 'three-two-oh!'

'One, two, three and four tubes ready, sir!'

Less than half a minute had passed since he'd made the sight-ing. Instinct as much as reason had induced him to stay up instead of doing the safe thing, diving. He'd found reasons, but only because some inclination had made him look for them. But now, the fact they were still up here made it seem that his decision had Ruck's endorsement. Paul was at the voicepipe but he was now using his glasses too, sweeping all round – except for the blanked-off sector astern, behind the swaying periscope stan-dards – while Ruck concentrated on his target, dark shapes racing eastward, four destroyers and 'something bigger' behind them . . .

'Damn, he's *seen* us!' Then correcting himself: 'No . . . Zigzag, that's all. All turning towards . . . Down, Sub! Klaxon on your way!'

Paul leaped for the hatch, straight into it, thumbed the button twice *en passant*: the jarring double roar of the klaxon alarm echoed through the boat's interior. Ruck's boots were coming down on top of him so he let go of the ladder, grabbing at it a couple of times to slow his descent but still cracking one knee painfully on the rim of the lower hatch and landing sprawl-ing backwards on the control room's wet corticene. Ruck, landing on his feet, just managed to avoid adding further injury.

'Forty feet . . . We're ten degrees on the target's bow and it's doing maybe twenty knots. Fruit machine – Sub, for Christ's sake —'

'Sorry, sir.' He'd got to it now. 'Enemy course one-two-oh, sir!'

'Blow Q.'

'Blow Q, sir . . .'

'I'd say its course was about oh-nine-oh before it zigged. So the mean might be one-oh-five. Pilot, how would that look for a course to Benghazi?'

McClure was checking it on the chart. Q quick-diving tank was blown and the boat was at forty feet. Ruck said to Wykeham, 'It's not big, God knows what it might be. Six or seven thousand tons, *something* like —'

'That course would be about right, sir.'

Newton squawked, 'Destroyer HE – ahead – closing —'

'Forget it. I want the target, not the escorts. Motor vessel, bearing – roughly – three-two-oh.' He told the helmsman, 'Starboard ten. Steer north.'

'Ten of starboard wheel on, sir . . .'

'Large vessel, reciprocating engines – one-eight-oh revs, sir!'

'That's him.'

'Destroyers passing over, sir.'

'Target bearing?'

Creagh reported, 'Course three-six-oh, sir.'

'Bearing is red one-six, sir.'

'Thirty feet.' Ruck looked over at Paul. 'Set enemy speed eighteen knots, range – let's say two thousand yards – and give me a ninety track. What's the DA?' Then, abruptly, he changed his mind. 'No. Forget it.' He glanced round at Wykeham. 'Stand by to surface.'

He'd have no idea, of course, when the next zigzag might come. The periscope would have shown him nothing except blackness and a lot of angry sea close up. He'd be surfacing to make sure of it; or rather, to be less *un*sure . . .

'DA seventeen, sir.'

Even if he didn't need it. It was all hypothetical anyway. He'd guessed the range, from the memory of what he'd seen in the dark: and he certainly couldn't be sure of getting into a position where he'd have a ninety-degree approach track for his torpedoes. It depended on that zigzag.

'Target bearing now, Newton?'

He got it, and adjusted the course by ten degrees. Wykeham reported ready to surface.

'Surface!'

It would seem like pandemonium or black magic, to an outsider. But there was method in it. *Ultra* had dived under the

screening destroyers – who were moving too fast to use asdics
effectively, and even if they'd slowed couldn't have made much
of it in this weather – and now she was coming up again, a fox
inside the henrun. Tibbits had reopened the lower hatch. Ruck
told him, 'Won't need you up there.' He shouted to Wykeham
over the racket of air rushing to the bow and stern tanks, 'Stay
on main motors grouped up . . . Sub, I want you behind me.'
He'd gone fast up the ladder; Paul climbed with his chest against
the heels of Ruck's seaboots, leaning back from the ladder to
save his face from getting kicked.

'Fifteen feet! Twelve! Ten! Nine feet —'

The hatch slammed up and Ruck was out, in the bridge,
which was only about as dry as a half-tide rock in those first seconds. A bathful of cold sea slopped into the tower as Paul
climbed out of it and pulled the voicepipe cock open. Ruck was
at the gyro repeater; then he'd shifted over to the torpedo night-
sight, to set it to enemy course and speed. Paul yelled down,
'Stand by all tubes!'

It was a gamble. A degree this way or that would make all the
difference, and *Ultra* was swinging several degrees each way as
Creagh fought to steady her. Ruck was using his binoculars lined
up over the top of the night-sight, shifting his head up and
down, eyes slitted into the darkness and the sheets of spray.

'Fire one!'

It would be about as chancy, Paul thought, as shooting snipe
from the hip. Salt water blinded him: seas were crashing against
the tower and the boat was still only at half-buoyancy, low to the
waves, lurching and hammering through them . . .

'Fire two!'

He screamed it into the voicepipe, beating the noise of wind
and sea.

'Fire three!'

Solid water flying up, dumping itself right over them, sluicing
away aft . . . 'Fire four!' Ruck's eyes were at his soaking wet binoculars. 'Down you go, Sub!' Jumping into the hatch, Paul heard
him order, 'Open main vents' before he shut the voicepipe and

followed. Climbing down at a more reasonable speed than last time, Paul was thinking, *Two thousand yards at forty knots: torpedo running time – ninety seconds . . .*

If the range *had* been 2000 yards. Not 1800 or 2500. And if the target hadn't zigzagged again in the last few seconds.

'All torpedoes running, sir.'

'Forty feet. Group down, half ahead together. Port fifteen.' Ruck asked McClure, 'How long since I fired the first one?'

'Forty-nine – fifty seconds, sir.'

Forty seconds to go, then.

'Fifteen of port wheel on, sir.'

'Steer two-nine-oh.'

Thirty seconds. Expressions tending to be deliberately blank. As if it mightn't be too wise to look hopeful.

Twenty.

Ruck murmured, 'Never know your luck.' He looked relaxed now, as if it didn't much matter either way. Ten seconds to go. Wykeham making his routine gesture: right hand up with two of its fingers crossed. If it annoyed you, you didn't have to notice.

'Forty feet, sir.'

Time, now. Paul leaned against the glass front of the fruit machine, and shut his eyes. At least one torpedo had already missed, was trundling on into empty sea. He'd forgotten about the freezing water inside his shirt.

Explosion: on the starboard quarter . . .

And total surprise – on all faces except Ruck's. He was staring at the deckhead, probably counting the seconds as they passed. Or just thinking . . . One hit would be enough to have stopped that ship, whatever it was. With four destroyers there'd be at least an attempt at a counter-attack, but the state of the sea wouldn't make asdic conditions very easy for them.

Second hit!

Wykeham glanced round, grinning. Paul was staring at McClure – who still looked half asleep . . . Silence now, for several drawn-out seconds . . . Waiting for a third hit? Ruck murmured, 'God knows what it was. Except it was middling

large, two-funnelled and fast, and rated an escort of four destroyers all to itself. *Something*, all right . . .' He was looking over at the
helmsman. 'Creagh! With all that yawing around you were
encouraging her to do – five degrees each way – you had her
swinging. Hell, *you* did it for us!'

In fact – Paul realized he'd fired on each yaw, using the swing
to spread his fish across the target.

'Target stopped, and there's breaking-up noises, sir.'

CPO Logan growled, 'That'll learn 'em.'

It wouldn't be a comfortable sinking. In the dark, and with
the sea high enough to make rescue operations tricky.

'Destroyer HE closing, sir!'

'Slow ahead together. Silent routine . .

Paul took over his morning watch an hour late, at a quarter past
seven. They'd dived at 0500 and gone to forty feet, and he'd
been occupied since then up for'ard, reloading the tubes. It was
done now: he'd reported it to Ruck – who'd grunted and gone
back to sleep – and now he was in the control room to relieve
Wykeham.

After sinking that unidentified ship last night *Ultra* had surfaced again at about two-thirty. There'd been no depthcharges
dropped and no A/S contact made by the destroyers, but the
hunt had still been in progress, at some fair distance. The enemy
would have left a couple of the escorts to search for them, probably, while the others took survivors into Tripoli. They'd have
had no clue as to where the attack came from, though, and in
these conditions not much hope of finding her. While from
Ultra's point of view, with an hour and a half lost and the battery
distinctly in need of charging, it was going to take a bit longer
now to reach the position of the beached ship.

Wykeham said, handing over the watch to Paul, 'There's a
complication – or may be, if that position's anything like accurate. Skipper only caught on to it after we dived just now. Our
wreck's supposed to be near the Zera Spit. Here.' He tapped the
chart with a pencil. 'See the point?'

'Shallow approach, you mean?'

'I mean the Libya–Tunisia border, chum.'

The Zera Spit – shallows and little bits of island, extending about ten miles off the coast – was on the wrong side of that border, in Vichy French territory. If there *was* a German or Italian ship stranded there, its crew ought to be interned and its cargo impounded. In fact, of course, a lot of the Vichy people weren't all that neutral, and the cargo of ammunition might well find its way onward to its destination. You weren't supposed to mess around with the French, all the same.

He got Ras Zera, a very small islet, in the high-power periscope about ten minutes after taking over. At 0830, by which time he was eating breakfast and McClure had the watch, it was a mile and a half abeam to port. Ruck was in the control room, spending a lot of time at the periscope, with the boat up at twenty-six feet for better visibility.

Since dawn, the wind had been moderating a little.

Wykeham said, 'May well not be any ship here now. They could have pulled it off yesterday. Could even have been the one we sank last night.' He rolled sideways off the bench seat and on to his bunk. 'Wake me early, mother dear, for I'm to be Queen of the May.'

Shaw, collecting breakfast plates, nodded. 'Wouldn't want to miss *that*.'

Ruck's voice from the periscope: 'There she is!'

Silence. You could hear the log ticking, and the slight movements as the planesmen held her at the ordered depth. Soft hum of the motors. Warmth . . . And Ruck's voice again: 'Port ten.'

Turning inshore . . .

'Ten of port wheel on, sir.'

'Steer – two-four-five . . . I'll be damned . . .' More heavy silence. Wykeham murmured from his bunk, 'We're twenty miles inside the Frogs' border.'

Also, *Ultra* was moving into some very shallow water. Or at least, *rather* shallow water with *very* shallow patches in it.

'Stand by to take down a fix, pilot. And let's have the echo-sounder going.' They heard it switched on, and the noisy whirring. Ruck was giving McClure shore bearings, using the islets and the right-hand edge of Ras Marmour. Then: 'Down periscope . . . Where does that put us?' He was in sight from the wardroom now, leaning over the chart beside McClure. 'Yup. Just about where we thought . . . The ammo ship's in here – *right* in. Only see her upperworks. But – well, this course is OK. Three miles, say. One hour. Subject to what the echo-sounder may tell us . . .'

He straightened up, dropping the dividers on the chart, and McClure went back into the control room. Ruck pulled back the wardroom chair, and sat down.

'I'd guess she's four or five thousand tons. Flying an Eyetie flag. She's hull-down, from here, behind one of the islands, tucked right in. So we've got to get in there too, somehow.'

Paul nodded. Wykeham got up on one elbow. 'We're well inside Vichy territory, sir.'

Ruck stared at him. 'How do I know where the frontier is?'

'Marked on the chart, sir.'

'On Chart 446?'

'I don't know which —'

'There's no frontier marked on the chart I'm using, Number One. Anyway, if you ignore those islands, which are only pissy little sandbanks, she's more than three miles offshore.' He looked up at the clock. 'One hour on this course, if the water stays deep enough. Then diving stations and stand by gun action.'

6

On the Tuesday, after a run of about ten miles in company with a body of commandos under Trolley, they stopped for a turnip-shoot on a hillside some miles inland from the port. Men higher up bowled the turnips downhill: they came flying and bouncing, and as they passed the waiting marksmen Colt automatics and Thompson and Lanchester sub-machine guns shattered the still, spring-like air.

Not only spring-*like* it *was* spring, and it was beginning to smell, feel and look like it. Soft, mild days and cool sparkling nights, dewy mornings loud with birds; clear skies, blue sea, and the scent of new growth, of a new year budding.

How many here would see it bloom?

Petty Officer Slattery, torpedo gunner's mate, diced a passing turnip with a second burst from his Lanchester, and the rest of the crowd applauded. Slattery was a medium-sized man, dark and stockily built, with heavy shoulders and a receding hairline. After he'd had his turn the three leading torpedomen came forward, and all of them scored. Don Merrit, dark and smooth-faced, known to his mates as Romeo: Pug Rayner, a thickset, bearded Londoner: and Barty Lloyd, a smart, well-educated young Welshman who could have gone in for a commission except he said he wouldn't touch one with a barge-pole. Then the Marines. Sergeant Bowater – a big man with the look of an amiable St Bernard – and Corporal Dewar, contrastingly compact and tough-featured. And Marines Laing and Bone: Laing fair, quiet, a farmer's son from East Sussex; and Bone red-haired and wiry, wild-looking. Bone was Romeo Merrit's main rival for any female talent that happened to pass within striking distance.

Finally, Harry Pettifer, the ERA. His exceptionally large hands, wrapping themselves around the Lanchester – the naval version of a Sten gun – made it look about half-sized. A number of turnips hurtled past before he grooved one and then missed the next. He shook his head as he turned away, working the bolt to clear his gun's chamber. 'Not my day.'

Slattery asked Jack quietly, 'When d'you reckon the day *is*, sir?'

He shrugged. 'Can't be far off now.'

He *hoped* it couldn't be.

The briefing was to be held tomorrow, on board the commandos' troopship, the *Princess Josephine Charlotte*. The audience at this session was to consist of thirty-nine commando officers and Jack Everard. Other ranks, and naval personnel, were to get their briefings later. The Army did of course have a lot more detail to absorb than the Navy had. The ships had only to get the troops to the target and – with luck – bring some of them back.

Slattery sighed, stretching his short, thick arms. 'Shan't be sorry to be on the move.'

A quiet voice, and a mild, thoughtful manner. You might have expected men who volunteered for this sort of work to be thugs, killers, but they weren't at all. They were physically tough – if they weren't so to start with, the training brought them up to scratch – but the real hallmark was intelligence and individuality.

Courage? Jack thought that perhaps it was at this stage the real guts were called for. In the long, often boring waiting period, when you had time to think about it, wonder why the hell you were doing it anyway . . .

The *Princess Josephine Charlotte* had brought the soldiers down from Ayr in Scotland, which apparently had been their main base. They were hand-picked men, drawn from about eight different commando outfits, and during recent weeks they'd trained in several different places. Some, on demolition training, had been at Cardiff before the naval team was sent there. Others had been up at Rosyth, and a lot of them had trained for a while in Southampton. Before they'd been earmarked for this particular operation they'd done stints in the Outer Hebrides, climbed mountains in the Highlands: there didn't seem to be much they *hadn't* done.

The code-name for the operation was 'Chariot'. And at this stage Jack was wondering whether the target might be Brest. Except he couldn't think of what naval target might be in Brest now, considering that *Scharnhorst, Gneisenau* and *Prinz Eugen* had got away upchannel from Brest a month ago . . . And there were no clues to be picked up from the fact that a consignment of tropical clothing had been delivered to the MLs and other ships in the last day or two. The indication was supposed to be that the 10th A/S Striking Force was about to set off for foreign parts, and a rumour had been started that their destination was Freetown in Sierra Leone. At the naval headquarters nobody made any attempt to deny this: it was obviously a red herring, to confuse Nazi spies who might or might not have been thronging the Falmouth pubs.

Jack had picked up only dribbles of information. The officer driving that MTB with the bow torpedo tubes, for instance, was a man called Wynn. There was an MGB too – motor gunboat – involved, and some destroyers. Two of these, Hunt-class, were already in Falmouth, and another – about which there was a lot of secrecy – was in Devonport, Plymouth's naval dockyard, undergoing some kind of refit. This was why the naval force commander, Commander Ryder, had been away in Devonport. What else . . . Well, the military commander was a colonel by the name of Newman. And *all* the commandos had been as sick as cats all the way to the Scillies and back again.

Trolley came down the hill, looking for Jack.

'Ready to move off?'

'Absolutely.' He got off the wall he'd been sitting on. Eyes still resting on the downward sweep of greenery, green turning hazy where it ran to merge with a distant and even hazier blue. Deep shadow where a belt of still mostly leafless woodland dipped through a valley, a cleft between the hills. You could see roofs down there, and a church spire, chimney-smoke hanging like paint on canvas. Timeless, and precious: and – oddly, when you first recognized this – not at all in conflict with the sense of purpose that imbued them all. Because for centuries Englishmen had left for war with such pictures in their hearts, and God knew how many had died still treasuring them. From this very coast-line, for instance, Drake, Frobisher, Grenville . . . A muscle worked in Trolley's jaw as his eyes moved across the landscape. Harbouring similar thoughts, Jack wondered? Thoughts of the summer you mightn't see? You'd need to know a man a lot better than he knew Trolley before you spoke about it. And in any case, this – groping for a half-formed concept, he told himself that the summer still would come, would come and fade and come again a thousand times: and this hillside, England itself —

'Making new friends, last evening?'

'What?'

Trolley had turned his back on the view. '*Very* smart little number. Can't say I blame you in the least!'

'Oh . . .' Back to earth: he realized what Trolley was on about. He told him, 'Happens to be the girlfriend of – well, a relation of mine.'

'Really?' Trolley laughed. 'Nice story, anyway!'

Late yesterday he'd dropped in at the naval HQ on the seafront, to confirm that he'd received his summons to the military briefing. While he was there, he also visited the SDO – signals distribution office – to pick up anything that might have been in the NTU's pigeon-hole or in Sharp's. In fact both were empty. But as he was leaving through the former hotel's foyer he heard quick steps behind him, and then a girl's voice calling his name.

'Lieutenant Everard?'

He stopped. It was a young Wren, and he'd noticed her in the SDO. Not only because she was attractive, but also because she'd stared at him while he'd been in there. She looked *very* young: he'd have guessed she wasn't more than seventeen. Dark hair and blue eyes – a combination that had always attracted him – and a wide, rather sensual mouth. It was her mouth he was looking at as she asked him diffidently, 'Excuse me, but – could you be a relation of *Paul* Everard?'

He nodded. 'I'm his uncle.'

Her expression changed. She thought he was giving a silly answer . . .

'All right. Sorry. I just thought – well, your name isn't all that usual, and in the Navy it does seem to have – well —'

'Connotations? I know. Relations by the score, and most of them ancient mariners. I *am* Paul's uncle, though. Half-uncle, actually. His father and I are half-brothers, you see, although I'm only a couple of years older than Paul.'

'Oh.' She was *very* pretty when she smiled. 'I see!'

'And who are you?'

'Sally Thirsk. I knew Paul up in Scotland. I was stationed at Greenock for a while, when —'

'You *poor* little creature! Greenock, of all —'

'— when he' – she'd faltered – 'was up there in his submarine. I think he must be in Malta now, but I haven't heard, since —'

'Lazy young swine. In his shoes, I'd be writing to you twice a day. Reams and reams . . . I'll tick him off, if you like.'

'Don't bother. But I'll write and tell him I've met you.'

'You'll scare the daylights out of him. In his book I'm a bad hat.'

'*Really?*'

He nodded. 'A really dangerous character. You just ask him.'

If her eyes hadn't been blue, he thought, she'd have had a look of Dorothy Lamour. In fact she *did* have.

She asked, 'And *are* you?'

'Of course not. It's a total misconception.' It was also one of

the most kissable mouths he'd ever seen. He thought, *Paul's
as well as Nick's*? It was an amusing thought, and it certainly
wouldn't have involved any hardship . . . But – he thought, looking down into the intrigued and fascinatingly innocent blue
eyes – it was *no more than* an amusing thought. The fact was, he
felt sure he *could* have: that was the pleasure in it . . . Her smile
had faded. 'May I ask you a question?'

'Why shouldn't you?'

'Shall we go outside for a moment?'

Past the sentry in his gaiters, and a short way down the
seafront, eastwards. Presumably she wanted to be out of earshot
of the sentry before she asked him something about Paul. But
make a time-change and a clothes-change, he thought: himself
in flannels and this girl in a cotton frock, strolling on a seaside
esplanade on a warm evening . . . If you took away those barbed-
wire barricades —

'What I wanted to ask – although I suppose I ought not to –
what *is* all this about?'

'All what?'

'Well, the whole thing. I've only been here a few days, but
nobody seems to know *anything*. Then this rumour about
Freetown – but – well, it all seems so peculiar, and it doesn't
seem to have anything to do with anti-submarine work, or —'

'It doesn't?'

Facing her, on the seaside pavement. Smiling, as if her question puzzled him. And it did, really: what the hell did *she* care?

'Evening, Jack.'

Trolley, with a commando major: in step, and heading for
the hotel entrance, glancing at the girl, grinning at Jack. He
turned back to her, as the sentry came to attention and saluted
the army visitors . . . 'Sally – if you're writing to Paul, give him a
message for me? Tell him I got engaged, before I left London.'

Tubby Sharp's new sub-lieutenant, a Canadian by the name of
Dixon, had arrived down from Scotland, and Bellamy, pro-
nounced fit for shore duties only, had been given a job in the

naval HQ, helping with the administration of the ML flotilla.
ERA Pettifer reported late on Tuesday that *Sauerkraut* was fit
and ready to go: the stern gland had been repacked, various
engine adjustments made, and the modifications which had
been started in Cardiff were complete. The new Oerlikon
needed testing, though, and Sharp decided he'd take the boat
out for machinery trials and gunnery practice on the
Wednesday. Pettifer and the rest of Jack's team opted to go along
for the ride, but Jack couldn't because he had to attend the military briefing.

The door of the troopship's wardroom was shut and locked
before the briefing started. Colonel Newman, the military force
commander, had the floor; he also had a scale model of some
dockyard port, and a large wall-map. Jack had barely had time to
do more than glance at either of them before he had to take his
place, beside Trolley, in a suddenly hushed and expectant crowd
of commandos.

Operation Chariot . . .

No notes were taken, and a lot of ground was covered very
fast. When it was over and he was walking back along the quays
to where the minesweeper was berthed, Jack set himself to
rerunning everything he'd heard, putting it together in his
memory, particularly the parts of it that affected him and his
Task Unit . . .

There'd been a warning, to start with, that what they were
about to be told was not to be divulged to anyone at all. It wasn't
even to be discussed with their naval colleagues – the ML skippers, for instance. And this briefing was to provide only a broad
outline of the nature of the operation: details would be given in
the Operation Order – which they'd find to be a forty-page doc-
ument of close type and diagrams – and in separate briefings of
individual parties.

They were not going to be told, at this stage, the geographical
location of the target area.

Security was vital, the element of surprise paramount. They
would be making a landing and carrying out demolition work

deep inside enemy-held territory, and it was known that, apart from fixed defences, guns, searchlights, etc., a strong garrison force of German troops was barracked no more than a mile from the target area.

Here was a scale model of the port; and here, a large-scale diagram of its layout. The assault would be timed to take place at 0130, and re-embarkation should be completed by 0330. In those two hours, or possibly in less than two hours, a number of specific targets would be destroyed.

There would be an air-raid by RAF bombers starting at 2200, opening with an attack on the dockyard and shifting at midnight to the town. Bombing would continue even after troops had gone ashore. The object of this air attack was to distract and confuse enemy gunners, and particularly to occupy the German dual-purpose, high-angle/low-angle guns during the ships' approach to the landing points.

Ships allocated were as follows: two Hunt-class destroyers, HMS *Tynedale* and HMS *Atherstone*, as escorting ships in both directions; one ramming destroyer, HMS *Campbeltown*; one MGB, motor gunboat, the headquarters ship in which the military and naval force commanders would embark; one MTB, with delayed-action torpedoes for use against lock gates; and sixteen MLs, of which twelve would carry commandos and four would have torpedoes for use against enemy patrol vessels which might be encountered *en route*. It was very much hoped, of course, that no such contingency would arise: the object was to achieve total surprise.

The primary target was the outer gate or caisson of this very large dry dock. The destroyer *Campbeltown* would cut through the anti-torpedo boom protecting it, and then ram it head-on. *Campbeltown*, formerly the USS *Buchanan*, an old four-stacker and one of the famous fifty lease-lend destroyers received from the United States, was at present in dockyard hands, in Devonport. Among the changes being made to her was the installation of an exceptionally powerful explosive charge in her bow. This would be set off by time-fuse some hours after she embedded herself in the caisson. But she would also be carrying commandos who would land over her forepart on to the caisson and thence ashore.

Object of the operation: why it was so important to destroy this particular dock . . . It happened to be the only dry dock on the European Atlantic coast big enough to accommodate the new German battleship *Tirpitz*, sister ship to the *Bismarck*. *Bismarck* had been hunted down and sunk by the Royal Navy about a year ago, and the Navy was hell-bent, naturally, on bringing the sister ship to battle and destroying her in a similar manner. Meanwhile, however, she was at Trondheim in Norway, posing a considerable threat to our convoys supplying the Russian armies through Murmansk. Even more important, there was a danger of her breaking out into the Atlantic, where our convoy routes were already in mortal danger from the U-boats. If *Tirpitz*, a monster of more than 40,000 tons, added her firepower to that effort, the Atlantic might well become impassable to convoys. Not only would Britain starve, but the enormous effort of building up forces and munitions for an eventual Allied landing in Europe would be halted. But for *Tirpitz* to set out on such a foray, she'd need to be assured of having a base on the Atlantic coast where she could be docked for maintenance and repairs. This – the port represented by the model – was it. The only possible one. There was no other dock large enough to hold her. If it could be smashed, the Atlantic would be closed to the *Tirpitz*; consequently its destruction was of the greatest strategic importance.

In addition to the giant caisson at the outer end of the deck, there were other important installations marked down for destruction: for instance, the mechanism for sliding the huge gates to and fro, certain bridges and other lock gates, a power station, pumping equipment, and fuel storage tanks.

There was one other major target not directly connected with the primary object of the operation. For this, a separate team of Royal Navy and Royal Marine personnel had been added to the landing force. Their part of the operation, which was linked with the main one but basically separate, would be described later. First, a look at the general topography . . .

The big dock – the primary target, with the caisson that would be rammed at its south end – was also the entrance to an inner basin. You could see it as a sort of wide canal with gates at each end: it became a dry dock by shutting the gates and then pumping the water out of it. It was nearly 1200 feet long and 165 feet wide. The caissons were vast constructions built of steel and sliding on rollers: each was 54 feet high, 167 feet long and about 36 feet thick. No pushover . . . And the King George V dock at Southampton, on which many of the demolition experts present at this briefing had spent so many weary hours, was virtually a twin of the target dock. In that Southampton dock they'd learnt to place their charges by feel alone, in pitch darkness, and they'd find they could do the same thing on this German – well, French – dock too. Similarly, the teams who'd be blowing up pumping equipment and winding-gear would find that the games they'd played had been very close indeed to the real thing.

The big dock that was the primary target led into the inner, northern basin. It could be seen on the diagram and on the model. It had a name, but at this briefing names weren't being mentioned. The northern basin was divided by a swing bridge from this large rectangular one immediately to the south of it. This one too could remain nameless for a while, but it was roughly 800 yards long and 150 wide. At its bottom end was another entrance and/or exit, again with lock gates at each end, also one lifting bridge and one swing bridge and the machinery to operate them. And a power station. This southern entrance was in fact the main entrance to both those interleading inner basins, and it was approached from seaward through a harbour area, enclosed by a jetty and a breakwater, known as the *avant-port*. But all those lock gates and installations were listed for destruction.

Northeast of the *avant-port* was the Old Town. From its east side protruded the Old Mole. North of the Old Mole lay the

warehouse area, and on the northern edge of that was the Old
Entrance. Close to the primary target and at a sharp angle to it,
this Old Entrance led directly into the large inner basin: and
here again, lock gates and a swing bridge were to be demolished.

In all, there were twenty-four targets, which explained why
the demolition parties would be carrying so much explosive.
Some individuals would be loaded with as much as ninety
pounds of it. And this of course was why those engaged on demolition would be armed only with Colt automatics, and
accompanied by protection parties who'd have Tommy guns,
Brens and grenades.

The bridge between those two inner basins also connected
the whole dock area to the mainland. When it was blown, enemy
troop reinforcements would be prevented from entering the
target area. Similarly, on completion of the operation – all
troops would withdraw to the Old Mole for re-embarkation –
blowing the bridges over the Old Entrance and Main Entrance
would have a further isolating effect. And – while on that subject – destruction of the dock gates at those points would make
the large inner basin become tidal. It was used by U-boats, and
destroying those locks should at least interfere with their use of
it. *But* this brought one full-circle, back to the job that was to be
done by the Naval Task Unit.

Jack Everard had it fairly clear in his mind after he left the
briefing. The inner basin with its two entrances and its link to
the northern basin: and on its western quay, his own team's
target. Very large, new, bomb-proof, reinforced concrete U-boat
pens. Some of it was still under construction, but two-thirds of
the shelter was complete and now in use by U-boats resting
between Atlantic patrols. And more or less opposite it – actually
a bit farther north on the near side of the same basin – was
where the Germans were making a habit of berthing one or
sometimes two E-boats. Escorts for departing or returning U-
boats, perhaps. He had to get his party to that quayside, seize
one boat, move it out into a position where its torpedoes could
be fired directly into the completed part of the U-boat shelter.

While the building was designed to resist attack from the air, it was believed that *internal* explosions might be very effective: you'd hope simultaneously to wreck or damage severely the shelter itself and sink a U-boat or two inside the pens.

Think only of using *one* E-boat, he told himself. You'd be damn lucky to get away with that much, let alone with repeating the trick. And his small party certainly wouldn't be able to handle two E-boats at once.

What he had to work out now was where his team would fit into the scheme as a whole: where they'd go ashore, for instance, and at which stage, and so on. Listening to the briefing, he'd considered various possibilities as the commando operation was sketched out. There were five commando assault parties: Captain Birney's and Captain Hodgson's landing at the Old Mole, Lieutenant Roderick's and Captain Roy's from the *Campbeltown*, and Captain Burns' at the Old Entrance. He'd thought about where he'd fit in with them or behind them while the picture as a whole had been filled in piece by piece. The commandos were organized as assault parties – those five – and demolition parties and protection parties: the first category interested him most, since they'd be faster-moving – if his NTU could, so to speak, travel *with* one of them. Because they wouldn't be stopping to blow things up – except guns, since it was their job to knock out the defences as they moved in . . . Move in behind one of them?

His choice of landing place was obvious: from a glance at that map, he'd seen that the place to take his people ashore would be the Old Entrance. From there, there'd be considerably less distance to cover than the way they'd practised it. And if he had an assault party moving ahead to clear the way for him – or at least part of the way, until they reached that frighteningly exposed quayside . . .

Captain Roy's assault party, he'd heard then, who'd land over the *Campbeltown*'s bow, were to take care of some guns on the roof of the pumping station and then push on through to hold an area on the north side of the bridge over the Old Entrance.

So they'd be on that same quayside and within about a hundred yards of where the E-boat was supposed to be. They'd draw at least some of the fire from across the water: if they made enough of a shindy they might even take all – or most – of those guns' attention. Take it *away from the NTU.* At least until – well, if the E-boat could be taken charge of quickly and unobtrusively? Once its torpedoes had been fired in the right direction, it didn't matter a damn *what* —

Don't be bloody silly. Of course it mattered. But that party – Captain Roy's – would be the crowd to fall back on afterwards. From them, then, the NTU could retire to the Old Mole for re-embarkation.

Wishful thinking?

Yes, of course it was. You didn't have to be a commando to know what action was like, how everything changed, how nothing looked as it had been planned to look or worked quite as it had been expected to work . . .

He'd gone on thinking about his own options while the briefing continued with a filling-in of all sorts of items to complete the general picture. Signals for withdrawal: two stages of withdrawal, one to be ordered with a red-rain rocket and the second with a green-rain one. All commandos to wear whitened webbing equipment as an aid to recognition in the dark. They'd carry blue flashlamps too, fixed to their automatic weapons. Rubber-soled boots would be worn by everyone: so if boots *scrunched* through the dark towards you, you could safely shoot whoever was occupying them. Then passwords: the challenge was to be *War Weapons Week,* and the reply *Weymouth.* If a German tried to pronounce those words, you'd know it.

There'd been laughter, at that point. Jack made a mental note to tell Tubby Sharp about it, as soon as he was allowed to do so. Tubby would love it.

There would be separate briefings for each commando party. That was when detail would come into it: the military commander would conduct these sessions himself, and each party would be rehearsed until no individual would be capable of

putting a foot in the wrong place. But first – tomorrow – there'd
be a briefing for other ranks.

One other, memorable point had been made.

Mountbatten had told the military commander, 'We're writing you off. I'm confident you can get in and do the job, but we
can't hold out much hope that you'll get out again . . . I want you
to tell all those who have family responsibilities, or think they
should stand down for any other reason, that they're free to do
so. Nobody'll think any the worse of them.'

Nobody had moved or spoken. Or would tomorrow either,
Jack guessed. Nor had they – he remembered Nick telling him,
years ago – in 1918, when Roger Keyes had delivered an almost
identical message before the raid on Zeebrugge. Nick had been
in that raid – and, come to think of it, at exactly the same age
that Jack was now. Twenty-three: and he'd come out of that one.
Wounded, but he'd come out of it . . .

He lunched aboard the minesweeper. The E-boat was still at
sea: probably hadn't yet sunk all the oil drums that Sharp had
taken along for floating targets. Only *Gourock*'s engineer and
first lieutenant were on board the sweeper; the other officers
were on leave, and boiler-cleaning was in progress. She'd been a
coal-burner, the engineer told him, and they'd converted her to
oil just before the war. He went into a lot of detail and gloom
about her mechanical condition, while Jack ate lunch and
thought about Operation Chariot.

He wondered if the port they were to attack might be Lorient.
He had no idea whether it had a dry dock of that size, but the
fact they were building U-boat shelters made him think of
Lorient, which was, after all, Admiral Dönitz's submarine command headquarters. And the distance from Falmouth would be
about right, justifying the auxiliary fuel tanks on the MLs.

Correction: explaining, not justifying. Nothing, he thought,
justified that feature. It could be explained, by the fact that
motor launches were the only craft available and that it wouldn't
have been possible to find space for the extra fuel storage below
decks. Even those facts didn't seem to him to warrant carrying

petrol on the decks of timber-hulled boats that were going to be shot at, though. He thought, *Thank God for* Sauerkraut . . .

After lunch he walked round to the naval HQ to keep an appointment with someone called Hawkins, one of the planning team, in order to discuss the details of the NTU's part in the landing. They knew he'd have had the military briefing by now, and his proposals for where and when his team would land had to be fitted into the naval plan as well. Or, if they didn't fit, he'd be told to think again. But this would be his first insight into the Navy's side of it.

Hawkins was an RNVR lieutenant-commander. He walked with a limp: Jack heard afterwards that he'd been shot up in an MTB action in the Channel a year ago. He did notice that he sported the ribbon of the DSC, when they met at the reception desk in the ex-hotel's foyer.

Hawkins asked him, bowing and rubbing his hands together, 'A *double* room, sir, was it?'

Jack thought, *I've got another Tubby Sharp, here* . . . He told him, 'Unfortunately she's in London.'

'What dashed bad luck.' Hawkins straightened. 'Take it you're Everard?'

'Yes, sir.' They shook hands. The lieutenant-commander said, 'Come along to the conservatory. That's where we've got all the gubbins.'

The hotel's conservatory had been turned into an Operations Room. Charts, maps, desks loaded with paperwork, and a clutter of stores and navigational equipment. The chart most noticeably on display, stuck to pegboard on an easel, was of the West African coast at Sierra Leone, with a blue crayon ring around the port of Freetown. Hawkins murmured, 'Nerve centre of the 10th A/S Striking Force. Pretty terrifying, isn't it? But sit down, anyway. The big white chief's away again today, I regret to say. All in a good cause, though – he's over at Devonport, where *Campbeltown* is supposed to be ready for us. He's gone to cast an eye over her. You know all about *Campbeltown* by now, I suppose?'

'All I know —'

'Smoke if you want to.' Hawkins stopped, rummaging in a cupboard. Getting up again, as Jack pulled out his cigarette-case, he had some large flag bundled in his arms. 'How about *this*, now?'

Draping it around himself: a big German naval Ensign . . .

'Do we fly that thing?'

'Not on your E-boat.' Hawkins was rolling it up again. 'Might be a little *too* realistic . . . What were we saying about *Campbeltown?*'

'Well, all I know about her is she was once the USS *Buchanan* and she's having an explosive bow fitted.'

'A bit more than that, actually.' Hawkins sat down. 'She had four funnels, for instance, and two of 'em have been removed, and the other two have had their tops sliced off, raked, you know, to make her look like a Hun. They've taken out all her guns, tubes, depthcharge throwers and suchlike, too, to lighten her so she'll make it up the river without grounding. We *hope* . . . Then, as you say, there's the fireworks for'ard. Colossal. Two dozen full-sized depthcharges – that's getting on for five tons of high explosive – fitted in a special tank they've built for it in the seamen's messdeck just abaft the for'ard gun support. That'll protect it when she rams the dock, you see – they reckon her bow'll crumple to that point and no further, so the explosive will end up just where it's wanted – stuck in or right up against the lock gate . . . They've given her some extra armour too, around the bridge and the steering position, and armoured screens on deck for pongo-protection purposes. What else . . . Oh, some extra weapons – Oerlikons. And it's all been done in ten days. Not bad, eh?'

'Terrific.'

Hawkins was studying him. Serious, behind the jocularity. 'What d'you make of it, Everard?'

'*Campbeltown?*'

'The whole scheme.'

'Well.' What to say . . . It was going to happen, anyway. And he, Jack Everard, was as much a part of it as one of those depthcharges. He nodded. 'It's a job worth doing, obviously, and I don't know how else we'd tackle it . . . I think it'll work, all right. One thing that does worry me is the MLs having all that petrol on their upper decks.'

'Worries us all, old horse.'

'No alternative?'

'The only possible one would have been one additional destroyer instead of all the Fairmiles. But there isn't a destroyer available and expendable. Well, *you* know that – destroyers are like gold to us . . . But also – and this *is* a valid argument – we'd be putting all those separate eggs in one basket.' He shook his head. He was greying at the temples . . . 'We have to live with it, anyway. Effectively, there's *no* alternative. And now, my lad, brass tacks. Did you form any ideas this morning for your own deployment?'

'Yes. I believe it's fairly straightforward, actually.' There'd been a question in his mind, but for the moment he had to leave it. 'May I use that map?'

'Be my guest.'

It was a hand-drawn outline, like the one the military commander had displayed at the briefing. With no names on those locks and basins, no clues therefore to the geographical location.

'*Campbeltown* rams the dock gate here. Commandos on board her then land to the right and to the left. The party to the left – an assault party – is No. 5 Troop, under a Cameron Highlander by the name of Donald Roy. They go ashore here, over the caisson, and their first job is to knock out some guns that are on top of this object here. It's a pumping station, and after Roy's chaps move on the demolition team nips in and blows up everything inside it. But sticking to the assault party – when they've fixed those guns they break through to this quayside here, and hold a defensive perimeter around the bridge over the Old Entrance. Well, the location of my own action, the moored E-boat I've got to make use of, is just along this same quayside, about a hundred yards along this way. So I'd propose landing fairly promptly after *Campbeltown* hits the caisson. I'd envisage getting ashore either just to port of where she hits, or in the approach to the Old Entrance itself, and then moving up behind the commando assault party. So we'd have our way cleared for us as far as that quayside, and all we'd have to do is sprint along it until we come to the E-boat. Then when we've finished, back the same way into No. 5 Troop's perimeter.'

'Sounds reasonable.' Hawkins reached for a buff-coloured folder, and turned its pages. Cruising diagrams, Jack saw. The third one he came to showed a formation of ships in two line-astern columns, with a small ship and a larger one placed centrally between the leading ships of those columns.

'This is the disposition for the attack, the approach to the target. There are two cruising formations as well, a daylight and a night one, but this is the one that counts. That little dodger in front is the motor gunboat, and by the time you're in this for-mation she'll have the force commanders in her. Astern of the MGB, this bigger lozenge is *Campbeltown*. The two columns flank-ing her are of course the MLs, with the torpedo-carriers at the front and back of each line. One at each corner, in fact.'

'And this?'

A tail-end Charlie, right astern and between the tails of the ML columns.

'That's MTB 74. Have you seen her around?' Jack had, of course: the boat with tubes mounted right for'ard. Hawkins told him, 'Those fish have delayed-action pistols in their warheads. She was fixed up like that originally for an attack on *Scharnhorst* in the harbour at Brest. The plan was that Wynn would shove his boat's stem right against the anti-torpedo nets they had sur-rounding her, so the fish would be fired *over* it and then explode later on the seabed under the target, with obvious advantages in terms of destructive blast.'

'Not bad thinking.'

'Right. Not at *all* a bad idea. But unfortunately, as you know, *Scharnhorst* and bloody *Gneisenau* scarpered before we could get a crack at them. So MTB 74's job now is to act as a reserve to *Campbeltown*. If she doesn't manage the ramming, then Wynn will put his two fish into the caisson instead. If *Campbeltown* does her stuff, though – which, touch wood, she will – then the naval force commander will direct him to use them elsewhere. But now look here. Here's the attack formation. Where do we put your E-boat?'

'In the centre, astern of *Campbeltown*?'

Hawkins stared at the plan, frowning. The suggestion seemed to have surprised him.

'I suppose it's – not altogether out of the question . . . You see, the MGB will be leading almost right up to the lock gate, then swerving off to let *Campbeltown* push on in . . . And if at about the same time Sharp turned off as well – *without* getting across the bows of those MLs, mind you . . . Well, they'll have peeled off themselves, of course, by then. The MLs have two landing places for their troops, by the way – some at the Old Mole, and some at the Old Entrance. At both those spots there's bound to be a certain amount of congestion, so —'

'What if we went ashore over *Campbeltown*? Run alongside her after she's rammed the caisson, then board her and go over her bow right behind the commandos . . . Alternatively, directly on to the caisson, after she's crashed into it?'

'The caisson would be too high to get on to, from that craft of yours.' Hawkins tapped the plan with a finger that lacked its top joint. 'But to land over *Campbeltown* – I think that might be rather a good idea. You'd be right out of everyone else's way, and there'd be nobody in *your* way, either.' He thought about it, staring at the plan. 'Of course, if *Campbeltown* bungled it and went adrift, you could plug on into the Old Entrance and take pot luck.'

'Yes.'

'You'd have the guns on that pumping station shooting at you, of course. I mean if *Campbeltown* didn't reach her target, nor would the assault parties that are landing from her.'

'We have to assume, I imagine, that she *will* hit her target?'

'True.' Hawkins nodded. 'One has to make a fair number of assumptions, on a lark like this. But in fact that's a reasonable one to make, I think. Anyway' – he sat back – 'I'll put these ideas to Commander Ryder. Then we'll have you along here again, Everard. And we're having a dress rehearsal, in a few days' time – attacking the dockyard at Devonport. Operation Vivid, it's to be called. If it's all agreed we'll test your scheme then, see how it goes.'

Jack was looking at another copy of the outline plan: it was the same drawing of the target area, but the fixed defences – German guns – were marked on it. All along the sea frontage, and on the Old Mole, and on every roof and other vantage-point. He glanced up at Hawkins. 'Might be a bit of a duck-shoot, from the Germans' point of view?'

'Well – not *quite* that bad.' Hawkins made a face. 'I'm not saying it won't be a rough passage, because obviously it will be. But during your approach, a hell of a lot of Oerlikons on *Campbeltown* and the MLs will be giving as good as they get. Also, there'll have been an RAF bomber force over the target area for a couple of hours before you get there. And then of course the commandos'll make short work of those defences once they get ashore.'

It sounded all right. It looked, he thought, bloody awful. But he'd remembered his question now.

'You said *Campbeltown* was being lightened to reduce her draught so she can get up some river, sir. May I ask what river?'

'You may. What's more, I'm allowed to tell you. Reason being that for the purposes of discussions you'll need to have now with Commander Ryder, you've got to know it anyway. But I'm also to impress on you that the rest of our chaps won't be briefed until after the dress rehearsal; so for God's sake —'

'I know.'

Hawkins pulled out a chart.

'Here. The river is the Loire, and your target is six miles up it. And the deep-water channel – this, the Charpentier – as you'd expect, has shore gun-batteries zeroed-in on it every yard of the way. It also winds around, which would make the approach longer. So you'll be taking a straight course – another reason for using MLs, of course, with their shallow draught – slam-bang across the mud-flats. Look.'

He went on with his explanation – a planner explaining the logic of his planning, pointing out the features of the approach, the river passage through six miles of enemy-held territory. Jack staring down at the chart, seeing only the name – *St Nazaire* . . .

7

Ruck was on his knees at the periscope as *Ultra* crept in towards her target, the beached ammunition ship. He was down on the boards like that in order not to show too much periscope up top: they were in shallow water and holding a depth of only twenty-five feet because of the sandbanks under the boat's keel.

'Stop port.'

'Stop port, sir.'

If he did hit bottom he wouldn't want to hit it hard or twist a propeller blade, for instance. He pushed the handles up and sat back, squatting on his heels as the long brass tube slid down into its well.

'Got that fix on, pilot?'

McClure nodded, glancing around. 'Won't get in much closer, sir.'

'Then we'll have to get out and walk.' He gestured for the periscope.

'What's on the sounder, Sub?'

Paul checked it. 'About five feet under the keel, sir.'

Ruck circling again, crouched like some kind of ape, daylight flashing weirdly in his eyes. Using the air search on this circuit: it did seem likely there'd be aircraft patrols along the coast, particularly with this Italian ship stuck on it. There had to be some kind of life on the surface too, because there was a lighter alongside her and they were using the ship's derrick to unload her, or possibly just to lighten her so they could get her off. But that lighter alongside had come from *somewhere*: and Ruck's guess, propounded half an hour ago over the wardroom table, was that there'd be a tug and another lighter, and the tug would currently be hauling a load inshore before returning with the empty lighter and taking this one in. It was possible, in fact likely, that the ship had been beached deliberately after damage from an RAF bomb or some other submarine's torpedo. About seven miles up-coast – eastward – there was a little harbour called Zarzis, which was the likely off-loading spot.

He'd settled on the target again now. *Ultra* was rolling a bit: she was close up under the surface turbulence, and although the wind had dropped the sea was still lively over the shallows.

'Gunlayer?'

'Here, sir.'

Creagh moved up beside Paul. The other four men of the gun's crew were in the gangway by the wardroom. Other hands, the ammunition-supply chain which would establish itself after the boat surfaced, were clustered beyond them. The magazine hatch was open, with a few rounds of HE, high explosive, out on the corticene-covered deck beside it, and Shaw was down inside there, like an old buck rabbit looking out of its hole, waiting to pass more up.

Ruck told Creagh, 'Target's a merchant ship, about four thousand tons. She'll be on our port bow when we surface. Range 030. Point of aim the after well-deck. There must be a hatch open over one of the holds there: try to drop your bricks right into it. Got it?'

'Aye aye, sir.'

Creagh's mouth, part-open, revealed those broken teeth. Ruck finished, 'No deflection. Shoot.'

That told him to open fire when his sights were on the target. He didn't have to wait for any further order.

'Stand by to surface!'

'Stand by to surface, sir . . .' Wykeham ordered, 'Check main vents.' Ruck had gone over to peer at the echo-sounder, while the periscope went down behind him: now he'd come back to it. 'Up.' The lower hatch was open and Creagh was on the ladder, waiting, with his gunlayer's telescope slung from a lanyard round his neck. The trainer, next behind him, had his slung similarly. Normal gun-action drill was to take the boat down to forty feet, blow her tanks and hold her down by hydroplanes alone, at speed enough for them to grip the water to that extent, until she was so buoyant she couldn't be held much longer: then you'd reverse the planes and she'd come up fast, fairly exploding into the daylight. You could open the hatch a few feet lower than usual because her upward momentum would carry her through that, at the cost of a bit of a wetting down the tower, and the end result would be the gun manned and in action before the enemy had even realized there was a submarine on the surface.

But here, there wasn't enough water for going deep. And anyway the target was a sitting duck.

'Ready to surface, sir.'

Ruck grunted acknowledgement as he started a final air search.

This would be the first gun action of the commission. And Paul's first submarine gun action ever, apart from innumerable drills and practices. Detailing the system for getting the gun's crew out and the gun into action had been his own job: he'd had a drill-book to base it on and Ruck to check it over and approve it, but it was still his own initiative – and an original one, to some extent, since *Ultra* was the first of the little U-class boats to have a 3-inch gun, and she had no gun-tower hatch as the S and T classes had. How well or how badly this went was his own personal test: in particular, how many seconds passed between the order 'Surface!' and the first shell leaving the barrel of the gun.

Then, how many rounds it would take to score a hit, and continue hitting . . . He could feel the imminence of the test like a fist tightening in his gut.

'Switch off the echo-sounder.'

Still circling with the periscope . . . You could visualize the
submarine's keel with only a couple of feet of water under it
now: that one screw turning in thick, stirred-up silt . . .

'Twenty-two feet.'

'Twenty-*two*, sir . . .'

Surprise in Wykeham's tone. At that depth the periscope stan-
dards – the heavy steel structure through which the periscopes
moved, immediately above the bridge – would be just about covered, but only just . . . And she was rolling more as she rose
higher. Ruck right down on the battery-boards with his eyes at
the lenses blazing like a cat's with the surface light in them.
McClure with his back to the chart, biting his fingernails: he'd
grown a lot of black beard very quickly but it grew unevenly,
sprouting in some places and thin in others. The gun's crew
were fidgety, like horses under starter's orders with the start
delayed. Gunlayer, then trainer – West – then Hayward and
Booth, respectively breechworker and loader . . . While Creagh
and West were unclamping the gun and getting it on to the
target, those two would wrench open the watertight ready-use
lockers for an initial supply of shells. Bewley, sightsetter and the
fifth man up, would meanwhile be setting the range and the
zero deflection. Behind him up the ladder would go Paul, and
then Ruck, and after Ruck the two Vickers gunners who for the
moment were waiting at the after end of the control room near
the W/T office. Each of them carried his own machine gun and
had a pan of ammunition slung round his neck; the second man
would also bring up the top end of a rope which, with a bucket
at its lower end, would constitute the ammunition hoist.

Ropes passing through hatches were a submariner's nightmare, but there was no other way to do it.

'Twenty-two feet, sir.'

A lot of movement on her. If she hit the ground like this she
could do herself some damage. To the asdic dome, for instance.
Ruck slammed up the handles.

'Surface!'

'Blow one, three and six main ballast!'

Happening now, the thing you'd worked out on paper and then
played like a game with the only enemy a stopwatch . . . Air roaring into
the tanks: then there was room on the ladder and the tower was
a vertical tunnel, boots and bodies filling it, a voice below shouting the depths and others passing the message on, echoey in the
steel, wet-smelling enclosure as the hatch flew open crashing
back to daylight, an upward rush into the bridge still awash with
foam, sea noise and a cold, stiff breeze, the submarine wallowing
in spray-topped waves. Paul got to the front of the bridge and
leaned over, getting his binoculars on the target just as the gun
fired, about eight feet below him, its noise penetrative, deafening. Breech open, new round slamming in, cordite smell
familiar . . .

The Italian freighter was obviously well and truly aground,
listing this way – to port, towards the lighter. There was a load of
ammunition boxes in a cargo-net suspended halfway down her
rusty-looking side. Italian colours flapping briskly, and no sign of
any French flag . . . No fall of shot yet either. Could have missed
seeing it, in so much broken sea? A natural guess was that it
might have been in line, but over . . . With a static target and
Ultra virtually stopped, thus no deflection, you'd hardly be
wrong for line – particularly at this close range, 030, meaning
three thousand yards, one and a half nautical miles . . . Then the
splash went up, a narrow white column – in line, and short.

'Up four hundred, shoot!'

Another shell went on its way. The time-standing-still effect of
action was what had made him think he'd missed spotting that
first one's fall. Ruck was bawling down the voicepipe and the two
Vickers gunners had mounted their weapons, one each side of
the bridge, and fitted the pans on them: a spare pan for each
would be coming up on the rope.

Hit. Orange-coloured burst smothered immediately in black
smoke, on the Italian's stern. West, the trainer, had muffed that
one. Paul yelled, 'No correction, shoot!' Ruck was turning the
submarine to point her seawards, one screw ahead and one
astern. And searching overhead for aircraft: that would be the

danger, if there was one at all. It was also the purpose of having the Vickers guns up here: in such shallow water it mightn't be possible to dive quickly, and it might become necessary to hold an attacker off while you got the gun's crew down . . . That load of ammo boxes had been let go, gone down with a run into the lighter as some Italian panicked. And a hit flared now on the freighter's well-deck. *Ultra* swinging to starboard so that the target was already on the beam, the gun training slowly round as she swung. And a hit – orange spurt, then drifting smoke – on the listing side just near the lighter . . . 'No correction, shoot!' A fire had started, aft there, by the looks of it. Mostly smoke, at the moment, and men jumping overboard from the lighter as another shell struck above them. The ship *was* on fire, and it was spreading, smoke thickening above a lick of flame. Ruck had his glasses on the target while the Vickers gunners watched the sky; then he'd dipped to the voicepipe to steady her on her present course. Paul yelled again, 'No correction, shoot!' Firing over the quarter, and not waiting to see each fall of shot now: when one shell hit there was another in the air and a third in the breech about to follow it. The Italian's afterpart was well on fire, smoke rising a hundred or more feet in the air above her and pouring landward on the wind. 'No correction, shoot!'

It was surprising that anyone could hear his voice; he couldn't, now. But Ruck was sending the Vickers men down, and he'd stopped the flow of shells . . . Reckoning he'd done enough and that the flames would finish it?

'No correction, *shoot*!'

Hitting every time: but there could only be another half-dozen shells there. Plus a few ready-use, if Ruck gave them time to use them. There'd been an explosion in the lighter: he'd thought it had been just a shell falling short, but it was more than that, a small eruption outwards. He shouted again, 'No correction, shoot!' Then heard, as the gun cracked and recoiled, breech opening and the empty shellcase flying back, Ruck's voice bellowing, 'Down! Cease fire, send 'em *down*!' Paul blew the whistle on his lanyard, and to the gun's crew it was an alarm

signal – meaning, roughly, *get below or drown* . . . Ruck pointing –
at two aircraft, coming this way from over Libya. Below, West had
trained the gun fore and aft and unshipped his telescope;
Creagh, telescope already slung over one shoulder, was engaging
the clamp, down at casing level below the breech. The breech
was open and empty, smoking; West slammed it shut as the last
empty shellcases splashed into the sea alongside. Hayward
appeared over the side of the bridge, his face streaked with
cordite smoke. He'd have shut one of the ready-use lockers, and
Booth – arriving now – would have fixed the other. One – two –
three men inboard, in the hatch, Ruck roaring at everyone to
get a bloody wriggle on: now West, and last Creagh. The aircraft
were Heinkels, coming with their snouts down from way above
and behind the cloud of smoke pouring out of the Italian ship.
Ruck snarled, 'Down, Sub!' and yelled into the voicepipe, 'Open
main vents!' He was shutting the voicepipe cock as Paul dropped
into the hatch – thinking about the shallowness of the water, the
likelihood of bouncing off the bottom. In the same moment
the ammunition ship blew up: Paul saw nothing, only heard it, a
roar of sound that broke out like any other explosion but was
then prolonged, a *continuing* roar as the whole of the Italian's
cargo went up, hold by hold. He fell as far as the lower hatch,
then climbed down into the control room, Ruck above him
shouting, 'Twenty-four feet!'

'Stop together. Fore planes hard a-rise.'

To level her, keep her off the bottom. But you had also to get
her down and hidden: not that she'd be completely hidden, to
an airman's view, in water this shallow. Wykeham had to do the
impossible anyway: get her under fast, and not hit the mud . . .
Ruck was off the ladder and Tibbits was dragging the lower
hatch shut. Twenty-three feet – twenty-six —

'Half astern together!'

She jolted hard as her forefoot hit the bottom, bounced,
struck again.

'Stop together.'

There was a harsh, unpleasant scraping noise from under her

keel. Twenty-seven feet showed on the gauges. Bow coming *up* now. Wykeham and the planesmen had been fighting to get it up, until a couple of seconds ago, but now as the bubble ran forward in the spirit-level there was a danger she'd start porpoising, break surface. Logan had a lot of rise on the after planes, to lift her stern and take the up-angle off . . . Explosion in the sea to starboard. A hard *thump*. And a second one, ahead and to port. Just the sound, and a slight tremor, as if the sea on that side had quivered against the hull. Then silence: and she was level, at twenty-five feet. That had been one pair of bombs: two from one aircraft, and another two to come? Ruck said, 'That was the Eyetie blowing up. Beautiful . . . I'll have a word with your gun's crew later, Sub.'

'Aye aye, sir.'

'Slow ahead together.'

Explosion astern, closer than the other two. Nothing to sweat about, though. Wait for the next . . . You held your breath and didn't really look at anything: it was your mind waiting, other thoughts suspended, needing this bit over before it began to work again. The bomb went in and burst ahead – like a steel door slamming in your face. That had been the nearest of the four.

'Report any damage or leaks for'ard. I want the bilges checked too, please, Chief.' Pool moved aft to the engineroom to tell Fry, the stoker PO, what was wanted. Ruck asked, 'Ship's head?'

'Oh-four-oh, sir.'

'How's that, pilot?'

'Take us out nicely, sir.'

'Why are we at twenty-two feet, Number One?'

'Getting her down again now, sir. I'm sorry.'

'You'd have been sorrier, if those bastards hadn't been such lousy shots.' He moved closer to the periscope and stood watching the depthgauges, waiting until she was deep enough for him to put it up. He muttered, 'Anyway, we aren't out of the woods yet.'

'Twenty-five feet, sir.'

He crouched down beside the well, glanced at Quinn and lifted his hands. He murmured as the glistening tube began to move upward, 'My *God*, what a sight that was . . .'

As soon as they surfaced that evening Creagh went down on to the casing to do a maintenance routine on the gun. It was mostly a matter of greasing it, with the grey grease called 'non-floaters', a special submarine lubricant that left no oily trail in the sea. Creagh did the job fast, at least as keenly aware as Paul was in her bridge that if an enemy showed up suddenly *Ultra* would have to dive and leave her gunlayer to swim around until she could surface again and try to find him. He sponged out the bore, and coated the breech mechanism and other moving parts with the heavy grease; then shells were brought up and passed down to him, and he refilled the ready-use lockers and screwed their lids down tight. He was below now, on watch as helmsman, patched grey with non-floaters and noticeably cheerful. Ruck had summoned him and his team to the control room earlier, to congratulate them on their first gun action and its success. It wasn't every 3-inch gun, he'd pointed out, that opened its career by bagging a 4000-ton ship and a full cargo of ammunition – ammunition that would *not*, now, be used against the Eighth Army in the desert.

Ultra had been clear of the Zera Spit and its sandbanks by noon, and she'd paddled eastward all day at periscope depth without seeing anything except a few passing aircraft. Some of which, probably, would have been scouting for *her* . . . The course now was 100 degrees, to bring her back to the billet northwest of Tripoli. With seventy miles to cover and all night in which to do it she was using only one diesel to push her along, while the other put new life into the battery.

Moon streaked the sea. Before long it would be hidden behind cloud, but at its present low altitude it would be silhouetting the submarine to any observer astern or on the quarter. It gave one an unpleasantly vulnerable feeling to know it – particularly with

Ruck's fresh warnings in mind, his lecture on the subject of the
U-boat threat. According to Intelligence reports, there were
twenty-one German U-boats here in the Mediterranean. One
had also to keep in mind, he'd pointed out this evening in the
wardroom before they'd surfaced, that *Ultra* had sunk one ship
last night not more than fifteen miles south of her present track,
and blasted another into scrap-iron a few hours ago in the Zera
shallows. The enemy would hardly be unaware of the presence
of a submarine on this stretch of coast: and they wouldn't be
well-disposed towards it, either.

'Port look-out relieved, sir.'

That was the second one. Paul asked, without interrupting his
own looking-out, 'Who's taken over?'

'Stapleton, sir.'

Baldy Stapleton . . .

'Need to be on our toes tonight, Stapleton. They're likely to
be looking for us.'

'Aye, sir. I was just thinking it's a bit lit-up, like.'

Searching: swivelling slowly, probing the peculiar areas of
light, half-light and blackness. *Hating* that low-slung moon – at
which, elsewhere, lovers might be gazing. In no danger from
anything but romance, wine, soft music . . . Might one in years to
come remember how it had looked on this night, and on others
like it?

'Bridge!'

He bent to the pipe: 'Bridge.'

'Relieve officer of the watch, sir?'

'Yes, please.'

Food, then sleep: both were attractive propositions. Corned
beef hash tonight, Shaw had said it would be . . . McClure
emerged from the hatch like a black gnome, and lurched into
the space beside him.

'Shit. Bloody illuminations . . .'

'Not for long. It'll be in that cloud pretty soon. How was the
hash?'

'Smashing. There's not much left, I'm sorry to say.'

'*Very* funny.' McClure seemed to have come to terms with the death of his brother rather quickly. Perhaps the two successes *Ultra* had chalked up in the last twenty-four hours had cheered him. There'd certainly been a very cheerful atmosphere in the boat, since the forenoon's gun action. Paul said, 'Been a good day, eh?'

'Bloody marvellous.' The little Scotsman had his glasses up, getting his eyes tuned in. 'He's good, our skipper. I mean, one of the best, don't you think so?' He leaned closer: his voice was covered by the rumble of the diesels. 'I heard some of the lads chatting – outside the galley, when I was in the heads. What it comes down to is they reckon he's tops.'

'Glad to hear it. It should help.'

'*Sure* it'll help. And I *agree* with 'em.'

'So who's arguing?'

It *would* help, certainly. It would put an edge on the ship's company's performance as a team: it was natural to take pride in being winners. And Ruck did look like one, right now . . . But McClure, Paul thought, had changed his views dramatically: less than a fortnight ago, on that patrol up near Messina, he'd been making snide remarks about medal-hunting – *going for a VC* . . .

Ruck had, of course, offered to stand a watch for him. It reminded Paul of a dissertation on leadership he'd once had in a letter from his father: the essential attributes had boiled down to a combination of professional competence and care for the men you led. Maybe Ruck *did* have that combination.

McClure swung slowly, studying the moon-dappled seascape. Dangerously *pretty* seascape. The sea was almost flat, the wind right down . . . Paul lowered his own glasses.

'Right, now, Bob. Three hundred revs starboard, standing charge port, course one-double-oh. Got it?'

'Yeah. Bugger off, will you?'

There was plenty of the hash left. He'd finished his meal, and he was smoking a cigarette over a mug of coffee when the BBC news bulletin started. It opened with a statement to the effect that Rangoon had fallen to the Japanese.

Wykeham muttered, 'They'll be into India now. Little yellow sods.'

Ruck winked at Paul, '*Floreat Etona.* Wish *I'd* had the benefit of a first-class education.' Backchat faded suddenly – none of them had realized, as the announcer went on in much the same tone, what they were hearing: it was an Admiralty communiqué, just released, on recent naval action in the Far East. There'd been a battle, three weeks ago, in the Java Sea: ships taking part had been HM Australian Ship *Perth* (Captain H. M. L. Waller, DSO, RAN), HMS *Exeter* (Captain O. L. Gordon, MVO, RN), HMS *Defiant* (Captain Sir Nicholas Everard, DSO and Bar, DSC and Bar, RN), the United States cruiser *Houston* and the Dutch cruisers *De Ruyter* and *Java* . . . Plus destroyers: and the whole force under Dutch command . . .

Ruck said, 'Wait for it, Sub. He'll be all right.' He and Wykeham met each other's eyes, and looked away again. Wykeham was in his bunk: he'd turned his head to stare upwards, listening . . . The announcer's familiar voice continued:

At 4.14 pm on 27 February this Allied force made contact with a Japanese force halfway between Bawean Island and Surabaya. Action was joined at extreme range. The Japanese force consisted of at least two Nati-class cruisers of 10,000 tons and a number of other cruisers. They had with them thirteen destroyers organized in two flotillas . . .

Paul's brain urged, *I don't give a damn how their bloody destroyers were organized, I want to hear just one simple, vital —*

HMS *Exeter* was hit by an 8-inch shell in a boiler room . . . Dutch destroyer *Kortenaar* hit by a torpedo and sank . . . Three British destroyers ordered to counter-attack: HMS *Electra* not seen again.

Droning on. Dull, matter-of-fact, cold-blooded. Ruck's face between his hands, elbows on the table, eyes fixed on the leather cup of poker-dice. Wykeham flat on his back, staring up. Paul hunched forward, trying to be ready to cope with the news of his father's death.

Underwater explosions occurred in the *De Ruyter* and *Java*. Both Dutch cruisers blew up and sank at once . . . Impossible to assess accurately the damage inflicted on the enemy . . . HMAS *Perth*, who had received some damage, reached Tanjong Priok at seven in the morning of Saturday, 28 February. With the enemy in command of the sea and air in overwhelming force, Allied command was faced with the problem of extricating the remaining Allied ships from a very dangerous situation. The way to Australia was barred by the 600-mile-long island of Java, with the straits at either end of it under enemy control . . .

After dark on 28 February HMAS *Perth* left Tanjong Priok. During the night a report was received which indicated she had come into contact with a force of Japanese ships off St Nicholas Point at 1 pm. Nothing has been heard of HMAS *Perth* or the US cruiser *Houston* since that time.

Paul muttered – talking to himself, not meaning to do it aloud – '*Defiant* – what about —'

'Hang on, Sub.' Ruck, shaking his head . . . 'Hang on.'

The same night HMS *Exeter* left Surabaya accompanied by HMS *Encounter* and the US destroyer *Pope*. Forenoon on Sunday, 1 March, HMS *Exeter* reported she had sighted three enemy cruisers steering towards her. No further signals were received from HMS *Exeter*, HMS *Encounter*, or the American destroyer.

Wykeham murmured, 'What a *bloody* awful —'

Dutch destroyer *Evertsen* encountered two Japanese cruisers in the Sunda Strait. She was damaged and was beached . . .

The destroyer HMS *Stronghold* and the sloop HMAS *Yarra* are also missing and must be considered lost.

The announcer's voice rose a little:

All other Allied warships which were in Java waters are known to be safe, except for some small craft and auxiliaries about which information is not yet available. Next-of-kin of all known casualties have been informed.

Pause: deep breath; change of subject . . .

Paul wondered, *That's all?*

'*Defiant*'s all right, then.' Ruck said it: a flat statement. 'Your father must have brought her out of it, somehow, Sub.'

He couldn't believe it yet. He'd been so keyed-up, defences raised and ready for that name *Defiant* to be the next one mentioned. He shook his head; Wykeham told him sharply, frowning at him from the bunk, 'Of course she's all right. The man just said so. There's no question about it, Sub.'

'None at all.' Ruck's stare was almost angry – at his lack of faith? He pointed out, 'They've admitted all those losses – poor bastards. There's no earthly reason they'd have kept quiet about one light cruiser if she'd gone too.'

'More than that.' Wykeham pointed at him: 'That communiqué said *all other warships are known to be safe.* Not *thought* to be safe, *known* to be. So stop twitching, now. Your old man's having a hell of a good time in Colombo, by now.'

'Or Australia.' Ruck nodded. 'Somewhere in Aussie would be my bet.'

'Yes.' He looked at them both. 'Thanks.' Stubbing out a cigarette, and reaching for another. They were right, and there was no reason to doubt it: his father *must* have brought his ship out of all that mess . . . Ruck told him, 'Turn in, Sub. Get some sleep.'

When he was next on watch, from midnight to 0215, there was no moon and the sea was barely ruffled. A long, low swell from the northwest was enough to give the boat a lazy corkscrew motion as she ploughed her white track eastward, still charging with one engine.

McClure had heard about the Java Sea battle: Wykeham must have told him. He was glad for Paul, he said, that his father's ship hadn't been among those lost; Paul wished he could have been glad for that brother, the airman. You realized, at times like this, that it was the people left behind who felt the hurt and whose lives were damaged, and the dead who suffered least. He turned over the watch and went below, more than ready for another few hours' sleep; getting off the ladder he had to step around Roffey, the leading LTO, who was crouching to take battery readings, prising up the brass inspection plate in the control room deck to take a sample of electrolyte for testing with his hydrometer.

'How's it coming, Roffey?'

Roffey nodded rather pompously, with the manner of a doctor taking a patient's temperature and reading more from it than a layman could be expected to understand . . . 'Coming up nicely, sir. Couple of hours'll do it.' He was a short, tubby man, and captain of *Ultra*'s football team. 'They say your guv'nor come out of that shambles all right, sir.'

'Yes, thank God.'

CPO Logan, PO of the watch, joined in. 'Good news, that, sir. Must be the only ship as *did* come out of it.'

Roffey went on for'ard, to check the pilot cells in number one battery section, which was under the POs' and ERAs' messes and that end of the gangway. Number two section was under the control room and wardroom, with the two periscope wells passing down through it. In fact each section was a tank holding fifty-six cells, each cell standing waist-high and needing either a crane or about four men to lift it. There was a lot to be learnt about battery management, and Paul was aware he'd have to learn it before he could hope to become a first lieutenant.

Not right now, though. Sleep, now. Thinking, as he turned in, that if that catastrophic action in the Java Sea had taken place three weeks ago – end of February – pretty soon now there might be a letter from his father. Maybe not after this patrol – but after the next, there might be one. And a rider to the news of his father having survived what must have been a massacre out there was the thought that with three Everards at sea the odds against all three of them coming out of the war alive had to be fairly heavy. So, if it was true that the real sufferers were the survivors, would you volunteer to be the one who did *not* survive?

The hell you would.

But Jack would have heard that communiqué, too. So would Fiona Gascoyne . . .

Dreaming. Back in something like last night's action: *Ultra* on the surface, himself on the bridge with Ruck; destroyers rushing towards them, their bow-waves high, white, menacing; Ruck's mouth gaping wide like a frog's as he screamed 'Down, Sub, *Klaxon!*' Falling . . . Reaching for the klaxon button and not able to reach it, falling past it and panic rising because he hadn't pressed it and she wasn't diving: but Ruck must have done it anyway because he heard it now, sudden skull-splitting racket . . .

'Blow Q!' Wykeham's voice: 'Shut main vents!'

You heard them thudding shut as Quinn slammed the levers home, his hands travelling fast across the panel's gleaming steel. The quick-diving tank's indicator light went out and he shut that blow-valve too.

'Main vents shut, Q blown, sir.'

'Sixty feet. Group down.'

Orders, acknowledgements, reports, all so familiar that they ran on as background to what might still have been a dream: but he was in the control room, beside the fruit machine, awake – *just* . . . And McClure standing crookedly, clasping one elbow with the other hand as he told Ruck, 'Destroyer was broad on the bow, sir —'

'Turbine HE green four-oh, sir, moving right to left!'

'Hundred and fifty feet.' Ruck spoke quietly, with no trace of urgency in his tone. 'Stop starboard. Starboard ten.'

Paul checked the time, and realized he'd only been in the sack for twenty minutes. The deck slanted as *Ultra* nosed downward. McClure telling Ruck, who had time to listen to him now, 'It was broad on the bow and steering to pass ahead, sir, but if I'd stayed up it'd have seen us for sure.'

'You were right to dive.' Ruck glanced over towards Creagh. 'Midships. Steer one-three-oh.'

'Turbine HE on green three-oh, sir. And there's another lot – green *one*-oh, farther off —'

'Anything astern of them? To the right of them?'

History repeating itself: like last night, the destroyer screen. And there was still that dream-like quality, a kind of unreality about it . . . Newton shaking his head: 'No, sir. No others.'

Destroyer sweep, then. A hunt for *Ultra*, very likely, for an enemy who'd made monkeys out of them last night and created a nuisance along the coast since then. And it sounded as if they'd come from the direction of Tripoli, so they *might* have been part of the escort with that ship last night.

'Depth one-fifty feet, sir.'

'Course one-three-oh, sir.'

McClure muttered as he pushed past Paul, 'That was what the newspaper and film people call a *crash* dive. Crashed my fucking elbow, in the hatch.'

'Clumsy bastard.'

'Oh, *thanks* —'

'The HE's ahead now, sir. Moving right to left. Slowing . . .' Newton's eyes half-shut, his brain out there in the sea, on its own, nurtured by sound-waves. 'Coming towards, sir!'

It wasn't good news. You could see in more than one face a desire for Newton to be wrong about it. But when a transmitting ship was coming towards you, you got a rising note, called a Doppler Effect, that was unmistakable. The hunting ship wouldn't mistake it, either.

'In contact, sir!'

'Damn him.' Ruck scowled. 'Shut off for depthcharging. Silent routine.' He shook his head. 'Bloody nuisance . . .'

'Second one's red two-oh, drawing slowly left, sir.'

Watertight doors were swinging shut, and the heavy clips sliding over to secure them. Shallow gauges, outboard valves on the heads and various other outlets or potential inlets were being shut or screwed down.

'Second one's in contact, sir!'

You could hear the asdic impulses like squeaks on the boat's hull. 'Destroyer ahead has stopped, sir. Maintaining contact. Other one's speeding up, closing.'

Ruck frowned: listening, thinking it out, translating Newton's reports into a mind's-eye picture of the scene up there.

'One holding, one attacking, sir . . .'

An attack was really a charge, using depthcharges instead of a lance. While one Italian held the contact the other would rush in and try to centre a pattern of depthcharges over the right spot. He had also to have them set to the right depth, if they were to be effective. A depthcharge pistol was about the size of a can of beans, and perforated with holes whose size could be adjusted. The pistol fired by water-pressure when it was full, so by reducing the size of the inlet holes you made the setting deeper.

Ruck pointed a finger upwards. 'Here he comes.'

Newton moved the headset off his ears.

It was a murmur at first, distant and rhythmic. Ruck leaned back against the ladder – waiting, listening. Wykeham watched the trim. Newton's head was bowed, his hands locked together in a tighter grip than he'd have wanted anyone to notice. Creagh moving his wheel a little this way and that, minute adjustments of rudder to hold the submarine on her course. The planesmen were barely touching their brass control-wheels: the boat was keeping her depth all right, with both sets of hydroplanes level most of the time. Quinn squatted on the deck in front of his assembly of HP air valves and vent levers. Bearded, narrow-eyed, square-jawed . . . The other ERA, Summers, would be in the engineroom, isolated by the shut watertight doors at each end of it. And their chief, CERA Pool, was leaning against the wireless office bulkhead. Clean-shaven, and with thin, dark hair neatly brushed.

Lovesay, on the fore planes, shifted his bulk slightly, and yawned. CPO Logan turned his head and scowled at him.

The Italian destroyer was passing overhead *now* . . .

'Starboard twenty.'

'Starboard twenty, sir.' Light flashed on the wheel's spokes as Creagh spun it. The rhythmic thrashing of the Italian's screws had begun to fade. The best the destroyer captain could have done would have been to centre his pattern of depthcharges at the point where he'd passed over them; to do better, he should have crossed the submarine's track just a little way ahead of her. Italian depthcharge patterns consisted sometimes of nine charges, but more usually of five, arranged in a diamond formation. A destroyer made the diamond by first dropping a charge from her stern rack – to make the lower point of the pattern – and simultaneously firing a charge out on each side from the throwers. Because of the ship's forward motion these two were flung ahead as well as outward, and fell to make the diamond's outer points; just as they hit the water the ship would drop another from her stem, midway between them and filling in the centre of the pattern. Then, a short way on, the final charge would roll out of the stern rack.

Ruck pushed himself off the ladder, where he'd been reclining.

'Midships. Steer —'

Exploding depthcharges interrupted him. One on its own first, somewhere overhead; then two more. Those two had been a bit closer. Now the fourth and fifth.

'Wheel's amidships, sir.'

'Starboard twenty.'

The ship's head was on about 180 degrees, due south, but he was taking her on round. He added, having thought about it, 'Two-fifty feet.'

'Two hundred and fifty, sir.'

Spiralling downward to the right . . .

Newton reported – he had the headset on his ears again – 'HE fading on green one hundred. No contact, sir.'

'Where's the other?'

'Turbine HE on red eight-oh, sir.'

Paul leaned against the end of the chart table. Shaw, in the wardroom, was reading a copy of *Good Morning*. It was a paper produced by the *Daily Mirror* and issued gratis to submarines; the copies were numbered instead of dated, and the contents included photos and items about submariners on leave, or getting married, and general entertainment more than news. An important ingredient was the 'Jane' strip cartoon: accent on strip.

'Red two-oh – in contact, sir. Red two-four – two-eight —'

'All right.'

The other one, roughly astern now as *Ultra* circled, would take its turn to attack this time, while the previous attacker held the contact. When a destroyer passed over it lost contact, but when a pair worked together like this there was always one to hold it.

'Midships.' Ruck padded across to glance over Creagh's shoulder. 'Steer three-one-oh.'

'Steer three-one-oh, sir. Wheel's amidships, sir.'

'Two-fifty feet, sir.' Wykeham was still working at the trim, though, pumping water ballast out of her midships trim-tank to allow for the increased depth, the extra weight it gave her. He was passing his orders, over the electric telegraph just above the planesmen's heads, to a torpedoman squatting in a cramped, damp space in the bilges of the torpedo-stowage compartment up for'ard. Each time the pump was started it made a noise that would be detectable on asdics: in fact an expert listener might be able to guess from that sound that the target submarine was changing depth.

With luck, the Italian operators up there might not be all that clever or experienced.

'One in contact red two-oh, sir. One astern – attacking, sir . . .'

McClure nudged Paul's arm. Just for a game of noughts and crosses . . . This was the trouble – having nothing at all to do except stand around and listen, wait . . . He took the pencil, and put a cross in the middle.

'Starboard fifteen.'

'Starboard fifteen, sir. Fifteen of starboard wheel on, sir . . .'

Screws approaching; then churning over. One Italian, eighty yards overhead . . . 'Group up, full ahead together!'

Accelerating away from the patch of sea in which, in about half a minute, charges would be bursting. *Ultra* trembled as her motors speeded and her screws thrust her forward.

Maybe you didn't *need* to volunteer, to become the one Everard out of three . . .

'Steer three-six-oh.'

'Three-six-oh, sir . . .'

The sea erupted, thundering – above them and astern. Shock-waves pummelling the hull were like the buffeting of a rough sea. Echoes fading: and the last charge of that pattern was the closest.

'Group down. Slow ahead together.'

It was surprising to remember that it was dark up there on the surface. Here in the submarine things were the same by day or night, once she was below periscope depth. Up top, after each attack the Italians would be straining their eyes through binoculars and imagining every shadow or hump of water to be a submarine rising helplessly to the surface.

Reassembling the picture now . . . Sweat on Newton's goofy face as he slid the earphones on and gave Ruck news of the Italians' current positions and activities. *Ultra* meanwhile motoring slowly northward – like a mouse resuming its crawl for safety after each mauling by the cats. Ruck explained to Wykeham quietly, 'I've let them see us working our way around to north, and I'll hold this course through one more attack. With any luck the Wops'll have it in their heads that north is the way we want to run. The attack after next, all things being equal, we'll try to lose them with a smart about-turn.'

Wykeham nodded. The explanation could only have been for his sake, part of his education.

McClure told Paul, 'Your go.'

'Why don't you get a chess set?'

'Or have a billiard room built on?'

They'd agreed to play five games, and McClure had won the first two. Paul made sure of losing again. He handed the pencil back, and turned away: with Ruck's qualifying phrase *All things being equal* ringing in his head.

'Attacking, sir . . .'

Eyes glancing upwards: which was pointless, but natural. Asdic pings were clearly audible: that hateful fingering on her hull. This attack was coming in from astern again; the other destroyer, holding them in contact, was out on the port bow, northwestward. In that one they'd be preparing for the *next* attack: hoisting another pair of depthcharges into the throwers, and perhaps resetting the depth on the pistols to try their luck at another level.

Screws thrashing up from astern. Newton's head nodding to the rhythm as he counted revs. His eyes half-closed, expression dreamy, face gleaming in its coating of sweat.

Coming, coming . . .

'Stop together. Group up.'

Ruck listened intently, judging his moment as the sound of the enemy propellers rose to about its peak.

'Main motors grouped up, sir!'

'Full ahead together!'

No rudder, this time, no change of course. Just the burst of speed: as if the mouse was pointing at its hole now and wasn't going to let itself be turned aside.

The first charge was a close one – to port, really *quite* close, its blast rolling the boat the other way. Cork chips scattered down from the deckhead paintwork . . . Paul had gone skidding to fetch up hard against the other side of the gangway; CERA Pool had been careless too, forgetting to hold on to something: he'd bounced off the cage which held electrical gear opposite the

W/T office. Ruck *was* holding on, to the ladder. That had been only the first charge of the pattern: it had been closer and obviously set deeper than the previous ones, and there were another four to come – in *this* helping.

Ruck began, 'We'll be away —'

Three explosions to port, farther off.

He finished, '— from these bastards in a minute or two . . . Group down, slow ahead together.'

Fourth charge: it was the least dangerous of the pattern. From the Italians' angle that had been a badly executed attack: only the first depthcharge had been close and the rest had gone wide. The destroyer couldn't have passed directly overhead; it had sounded as if it had been right up there, but when the propeller-noise was loud you tended to imagine it was closer than perhaps it was. In fact he must have been off beam to port, and overshot a little.

But by so small a margin. Just that small calculation or miscalculation made the difference between killing and not killing – between another square on the flotilla scoreboard being neatly illustrated or crossed off with bare diagonals. But the first charge of that pattern had been a frightener. It was comparative, though, Paul realized: any exploding charge would worry you, until you'd heard closer ones and survived them. Maybe they'd have some much closer than *that*, before much longer.

'Both motors slow ahead grouped down, sir.'

'Very good.' Ruck emerged from a period of thought; he nodded to himself, confirming the decision before he gave the order.

'One hundred and fifty feet.'

'Hundred and fifty, sir . . .'

Gambling on charges being set to explode deeper now, as the last lot had been. There was no guarantee of it: he *could* be taking her up to exactly the depth for which the next pattern was being set. *Ultra* could be rising gently now into the centre of her own destruction . . . Decreed by fate how long ago? When she'd been no more than a set of plans delivered to a builders' yard? And taking that fantasy on further, as each man had received his appointment or draft to her, had fate thrown *his* card on to the pile of discards too?

'One destroyer stopped. Right ahead . . . In contact, sir. The other's – on red four-oh, sir, closing.' Listening to the underwater world, the deep black night-time water and the hunters in it: narrow head seemingly squeezed in by the headset clamped on it. A forefinger touching each eyelid in turn, delicately removing sweat. 'Red four-two, attacking, sir!'

The needle in the only depthgauge that hadn't been shut off was swinging up past one-seventy. Wykeham using the order instrument, the electric telegraph, to have ballast flooded into the midships trimming tank. The torpedoman in the TSC bilge didn't have to use the pump for this: he had only to open certain valves to let sea flow in along a pipe known as the trimline.

Hundred and sixty feet. Wykeham reached up again and turned the switch so that the order in the little box became 'stop flooding'. The planesmen eased the angles of their hydroplanes to level her as she came to the ordered depth.

'Hundred and fifty feet, sir.'

Ruck nodded, listening to the Italian destroyer, her pounding propellers just audible now, the sound coming from just for'ard of the port beam. After the demonstrations he'd been giving them, that routine of speeding up just as the attacker came over, they *might* have become well trained enough to aim ahead this time – *expecting* the submarine to crack on speed, rush into the maelstrom of their depthcharges.

Louder than before. But at this depth, Paul realized, it would be . . . Newton took the phones off his ears and told Ruck, 'Drawing right, sir.'

To pass ahead . . .

'Group up, full ahead together!'

Power shook her as the note of the motors rose, matching the overhead crescendo of Italian screws.

All eyes on Ruck . . .

'Stop starboard. Starboard twenty.'

'Stop starboard, sir . . .'

'Starboard twenty.' Creagh flung his wheel round. 'Twenty of starboard wheel on, sir!'

With that screw stopped and a lot of rudder, she was already turning fast. Enemy propellers fading over. Dive-angle on the fore planes as Lovesay worked to counter the bow's tendency to lift as she swung round.

'Steer one-eight-oh.'

Explosions to port – and *deep* . . .

'Stop port. Group down.'

Ultra's bow was swinging through east as more charges burst on the quarter and below her. She was turning her stern to an erupting sea in which the Italians would be expecting her to be suffering agonies at this moment.

'Main motors grouped down, sir.'

'Slow ahead port.'

The last explosion was almost directly astern. Ruck's hunch about the change of depth had been exactly right. Paul thought, *No such thing as fate . . .*

Too soon to count chickens, though.

'Course one-eight-oh, sir.'

'Where are they, Newton?'

'Both astern, sir.' Listening, frowning in concentration, breathing faster than usual; and Ruck watching him, impatient for news. Newton glanced up, blinking. 'Both of 'em's back there astern, sir, both transmitting. Trying to pick us up again, sir.'

They might even imagine they'd sunk her.

Ruck nodded. Running wet with sweat, Paul saw. The cold prick of it over his own skin too: until this moment, he hadn't noticed it. *Ultra* silent, holding her breath as she crept south.

During the next few days' uneventful dived patrol – *Ultra* motoring slowly up and down a northeast–southwest patrol-line between ten and fifteen miles from Tripoli by day and moving farther out for the battery-charge at night – Paul found himself thinking quite a lot about that brush with the Italian destroyers.

Ruck had got them out of it: his dodge had worked, and the Italians had been left hunting northward while *Ultra* escaped south. In fact she'd surfaced again at about 0400, for a final hour's charging before daylight put her down again.

But what if it hadn't worked? What if the Italian senior officer had been smart enough to guess that he was being led to think in a certain way? If he'd followed his own ideas instead of the ones Ruck had fed him? If, instead of the last report *Both of 'em's back there astern, sir*, Newton had had to tell him *Closing, sir, in contact* . . .

How bad would it have felt, the shock of that disappointment?

Well, Ruck would have tried again. Another ploy, a new sequence of three-dimensional manoeuvres, while attacks continued. And – quote – *all things being equal* – unquote – he'd eventually have brought the new plan to a similarly climactic stage, the point where he'd again have been making his decisive move.

And – if that one failed?

In contact, sir, attacking . . .

The only answer was not to think about it: simply to control the imagination and tell yourself that Ruck had got her out of it that time, and would get her out of it next time too.

There wasn't any *other* answer.

8

A quiet smoke now, he decided: one cigarette and a few minutes' solitude before turning in. A few minutes in which to forget Falmouth and St Nazaire and think about Fiona . . . He'd stopped at the guard-rail, to look out over the placid harbour with its glimmering reflections of stars: it was a very spring-like night, the air decidedly cool but holding the promise of warmer days and nights to come. It was in your mind, most of it, the way you felt, always *had* felt, right from childhood, at this time of year. But that wasn't – as he'd assumed, without giving it any thought – someone's wireless playing, it was music and voices, laughter, from the E-boat down there alongside. With an unlit cigarette in his mouth, lighter in hand, Jack looked down at the slim, ninety-three-foot-long shape of the German boat, and realized that Sharp had female company aboard her.

He checked the time. Nine-forty. He'd just returned from spending the earlier part of the evening aboard *Atherstone*, the Hunt-class destroyer in which the naval force commander was living; she'd be one of the escorting warships when the force sailed, in a few days' time . . . He'd come back to get an early night – the rigorous commando physical-fitness programme wasn't geared to late ones. But – nine-forty, and the Wrens were supposed to be tucked up in their Wrenneries by ten. They could only be Wrens, he guessed. Unless Sharp had gone *really* mad . . . He slid the cigarette back into his case and pocketed it as he walked aft, towards the plank connecting the two ships.

Whoever the girls were, Sharp ought not to have been entertaining them on board. Security regulations were strict, with good reason, and there were clues in *Sauerkraut* that might be noticed by people with sharp eyes and inquisitive minds. Which was a description that fitted every woman he'd ever met . . . Things like small arms and ammunition and other equipment more obviously suited to commando-type operations than anti-submarine work. All right, so the Wrens weren't likely to be spies, but they were capable of chattering, and the chatter could be heard by the wrong ears. What was more, Sharp did know now where they were going and what for, because on Sunday, yesterday, the naval force commander had briefed all ships' COs and first lieutenants. Who could be sure that the eccentric Tubby Sharp mightn't be talkative when in his cups and provided with an audience of girls?

The E-boat's sentry rose from her dark bridge to challenge him as he crossed the plank. Then, seeing who it was, he up-ended his rifle and saluted. Jack returned it.

'Party going on?'

'Bit of a one, sir, sounds like.'

'Thought I'd join it.'

'You know your way, sir.'

It was a sort of joke. Knowing that Jack and the rest of the team could have found their way to any square inch of this craft in pitch darkness. Jack climbed into the bridge, and went down inside.

'Hey, look who's here!'

Light was blinding for a moment: he pushed the door shut behind him. The little wardroom space was crowded: with Sharp, and his Canadian first lieutenant, Dixon, and young Bellamy still with one arm in a sling, and the little Wren who knew Paul, and a blonde a couple of years older. They were all laughing and jabbering at him: Sharp offering him a drink, a cigarette, a space at the table . . .

He lit the cigarette, then told Sharp – exaggerating, in order
to make the point – 'I heard this going on from up by the ML
berths. Sorry, but I've come to tell you to pack it in.'

Cries of dismay from the girls. Hostility from Sharp. Jack
showed the blonde the face of his watch. 'Don't you have to be
in by ten? Or do you have late passes?'

'No —'

'What were you going to do, run all the way home?'

The blonde, whose name was Maureen, said she hadn't
dreamt it could be that late . . . Sharp wanted them to have one
more for the plank. Jack told him, 'You'd only land them in
trouble, Tubby.' He asked Bellamy, 'Did you bring them down?'

'Yes.' Bellamy added, 'Sir.' And – 'I didn't see there could be
any harm in just —'

'Take them back, please, Sub. And get them into the
Wrennery by ten if you can. Better get moving.'

Sharp began, 'Jack, this is *my* boat —'

'If you want to keep it, get these girls ashore.'

Sharp changed colour. The others showed mixed surprise
and embarrassment. But they were moving. Jack smiled at Sally
Thirsk. 'I'll be writing to Paul in a day or two. I'll give him your
love, shall I?'

'If you like.'

He hadn't the slightest intention of writing to Paul: it had
been something to say, an olive branch. Dixon muttered, 'I'll see
you all to the jetty.' The blonde was thanking Sharp for his hos-
pitality, and trying to include Jack in her smile as well. Sally,
Paul's girlfriend, seemed nervous and tongue-tied: she was, of
course, extremely young. It was very awkward for Sharp, obviously, but it was his own fault because he shouldn't have had
them on board in the first place.

Paul's girl said abruptly, as if the words were forcing themselves out, 'I heard that news broadcast about the battle in the
Far East and your father's – I mean *Paul's* father's – ship . . . I do
hope he's all right.'

He told her drily, 'He will be. Don't worry.'

'Yes, it did *sound* as if —'

She'd blushed. The blonde one, Maureen, interrupted: 'Coming, Sally?'

They straggled out, silent now with embarrassment. Sharp looked furious. Alone with him, Jack said, 'I'll accept that drink you were offering me, now. Just to show we're still on the best of terms.'

'Think we are, do you?'

'Well. Put it this way. If we aren't, it'd be your loss, not mine. I'm running the NTU party; I'm totally responsible for it, and I'm not risking having anything go wrong, not even for the sake of your sunny smiles.' He shook his head. 'Cut out the nonsense, Tubby. I'll have a drink with you here, or you can come inboard and have one with me in *Gourock*. Take your choice.'

'Here.' Sharp poured a tot of Plymouth gin, the neck of the bottle rattling a little on the glass. Jack took it and added water to it. 'We'll forget it now, Tubby. But you won't have any more Wrens on board this boat. Or any other outsiders either.'

'You'd get me fired, is that the message?'

'Without a moment's hesitation.'

'Sure our masters would oblige you?'

'Certain. Not only is this my show, but I'm irreplaceable and you're not. Frankly, yours is a chauffeur's job, to get us there and possibly bring us back. I could take a spare ML skipper and teach him to drive this craft in half an hour. I could do it on the way to you-know-where, if necessary.'

'You don't mince words, do you?'

'No reason to, is there?'

'In fact you're quite a shit.' He wasn't smiling. And he'd had quite a lot of gin, Jack guessed. 'I mean frankly and privately, just between the two of us.'

'I told you, Tubby. Being liked or disliked doesn't matter to me in the least. What does matter is getting the job done and if possible staying alive. If you and I can work together without friction, fine. If we can't, you don't fit.'

Sharp smiled. 'On which happy and fraternal note —'

'Up yours.'

Drinking . . . Sharp studying him, over the glass. Then he put it down, and sighed. 'OK. I should *not* have had them down here. But Bellamy's working in their outfit, and they've been pestering him to wangle a visit for them, so —' he shrugged. 'I said OK, just this once. There's no damage, is there?'

'They could spot something, and talk about it afterwards. To friends, or family, or even to be overheard in some pub. A spy doesn't go around in a black cloak and clutching a dagger, these days. He might even look like a naval officer. And this thing's dicey enough without risking leaks. Just imagine the reception they'd lay on for us, if they guessed we were coming!'

It was why he hadn't telephoned Fiona during the weekend. He'd wanted to: to hear her voice, tell her he was still alive and crazy about her, that he *would* be back. And to hear from her that it was all solid and watertight between them . . . But there could, remotely, have been a risk in it. Suppose she'd told some close friend that she didn't know whether she'd see him again – even that he was off on some kind of special operation? And someone else picked it up and wanted to know about the operation? There *were* such people, they existed . . . Suppose her telephone was being tapped, and a call came through from him at Falmouth? Then they'd know where to start sniffing. The odds might be thousands to one against, but the possibility was there.

It had taken a lot of self-control, not to pick up a telephone. She might have been working, anyway, though. She was in the MTC and they did have weekend duties, and she'd owe her friends a few after all the time she'd spent with him, swapping duties to match his own weekends in London . . . Which seemed so long ago, now. At least six months, it might have been, since he'd said goodbye to her on that last Sunday evening.

He'd write to her, before they pushed off. To his mother, too. For no reason except it was the sort of thing one did, that was expected, in circumstances like these. Several of his team had been drawing up wills, and asking him to witness them.

A formality, he thought. A precaution. Like looking left and right before you crossed a street.

Sharp asked him, 'What was that young one – Sally – saying about some relation of yours in the Far East?'

'Well.' He sipped his gin. 'There was a news release a few nights ago about action in the Java Sea. Did you hear it?' Sharp shook his head. Jack told him, 'My half-brother is captain of *Defiant*. One of the old Dauntless class. And it seems she was the only ship to come out of it intact. The only one they didn't mention as being sunk, anyway.'

'He *is* all right, then.'

Nick, Jack thought, would *always* be 'all right'. As if it had been ordained, right from the start, that he was to be the survivor. Right from Jutland in 1916, when the elder brother had drowned and Nick had come out of it by the skin of his teeth and with the first of his many decorations – as well as having become the heir to the baronetcy. He'd hogged it all, and the luck seemed still to be sticking to him. Leaving it to Messrs Jack and Paul Everard to pay the family's dues to *bad* luck?

But – lucky in war, unlucky in love. Nick didn't know it yet . . .

Sharp murmured, staring down into his glass and looking sad, 'Four days. It's going to be bloody difficult, keeping my hands off Maureen for four whole days.'

Making an attempt at a joke: accepting *force majeure* and deciding to remain friends in order to keep his job . . . Dixon came back, and his relief at finding the atmosphere so cordial was plain. Sharp told him, 'Pour yourself a drink, Harry.'

'Right.' He asked Jack, 'You – sir?'

'No more, thanks . . . Whereabouts in Canada are you from?'

'Toronto.' He put the bottle down. 'Know it?'

'Halifax is the only bit of Canada I've seen.'

'Oh. Well, there's a hell of a lot of it west of there.' The Canadian raised his glass. 'Here's to Friday.'

Friday, which would be the twenty-seventh, was the day the Chariot force was scheduled to sail for St Nazaire. If it *did* sail. There'd been a problem brewing up in the past few days, and

Hawkins had told Jack about it. There'd been some mention of it this evening, too, on board *Atherstone*. It was the business of the RAF's contribution, the diversionary air attack they were supposed to be laying on in order to distract the attention of the German gunners. To start with, Churchill had vetoed the second stage of it, the bombing of the Old Town area, for fear of killing Frenchmen; and now the RAF had cut the bomber force from seventy to thirty-five – the aircraft were required for some other purpose, apparently. The army brigadier in charge of planning was raising hell about it; C-in-C Plymouth – Admiral Sir Charles Forbes, who carried the overall naval responsibility now – seemed to think it didn't matter; a lot of tempers were rising to boiling-point, and Mountbatten was being asked to intervene. It was being hinted that without the promised RAF co-operation the Chiefs of Staff Committee might, on the Army's recommendation, propose cancellation.

Nobody believed it *would* be cancelled. But the mere possibility of that happening was dispiriting. Trolley had told Jack that the effect on the commandos' morale would be devastating. They were at a peak of readiness, really straining at the leash.

The dress rehearsal, Exercise Vivid, had gone off quite well. The ships had been able to practise their different steaming formations and other manoeuvres, and the commandos had familiarized themselves with the processes of embarking and disembarking, settling down for the sea passage, and so on. They'd simulated an attack on the docks at Devonport. The main lesson had been that powerful searchlights at close range had a blinding effect that could lead to a lot of confusion if you weren't ready for it. The NTU knew it already, but the ML skippers had found the experience salutary. Officially the object of the exercise had been to test the dockyard defences, and the defenders – including Home Guards – had beaten off the assault, to their own considerable satisfaction.

Campbeltown, the former American destroyer which had more recently become British, now looked decidedly German with

her twin raked funnels. Other changes gave her a grimly com-
bative appearance: with armour plating all round her bridge
and wheelhouse, armoured screens welded to her decks as protection for her commandos during the approach to the lock
gate, eight new Oerlikons crouching in circular armoured nests
and a 12-pounder on her foc'sl, she was more missile than ship –
especially if you happened to know that her foc'sl was packed
solid with high explosive.

She'd been lightened, and drew three feet less than she had
originally, but it was still touch-and-go whether she'd manage to
scrape over the Loire estuary mudbanks, and the need for the
highest possible tide was one consideration in the timing.
Another was the fact that the nights were becoming shorter, and
a reasonable period of darkness was essential for the withdrawal.
They would be sailing from Falmouth on Friday 27 March, and
the assault would take place at 0130 on the twenty-ninth.

If *Campbeltown* ran aground in the river, her commandos
would be taken off her in MLs and the force would go in without
her. The caisson, the one target that *had* to be destroyed, would
then be dealt with by the commando demolition experts with
plastic explosive, and by MTB 74's delayed-action torpedoes.

If MTB 74 made it to the target area. She'd been getting a lot
of machinery problems lately.

Hawkins had told him, 'There are always last-minute snags, on
this kind of jaunt. It'll be all right on the day . . .'

The reason *Ultra* had been recalled, less than a week after she'd
sailed for that fourth patrol, was that a new convoy operation was
being organized from the Alexandria end. Four ships were to be
sailed for Malta under the protection of Admiral Sir Philip
Vian's small force of cruisers and destroyers, and Shrimp
Simpson was preparing as many of the 10th Flotilla boats as possible for patrols off the Italian ports as distant cover to the
convoy.

Vian hadn't caught up with the two enemy convoys he'd gone
hunting for, apparently, but he'd collected the cruiser *Cleopatra*

and the destroyer *Kingston* out of Malta, despite heavy Luftwaffe attacks; having gained one cruiser he'd then lost one – his own flagship, *Naiad*, who'd been torpedoed and sunk fifty miles north of Sidi Barrani, during the return to Alexandria. He and most of her ship's company had been picked up by *Naiad's* sister ship *Dido.*

Ultra entered Marsamxett harbour at dawn, Roger flying, and berthed alongside Lazaretto for long enough to de-store and get the sailors' gear ashore, and to land half of them for a two-day sojourn in the rest camp. Paul had volunteered to stay with the boat. For one thing, there were torpedoes to be embarked, but anyway this was to be only a short spell in harbour. Also, he could make himself useful in the harbour diving routine – which, since it was still a novelty, he enjoyed. A final consideration was that a short stand-off might be good for McClure, who was still suffering from the news of his brother's death and the effect of it on his parents. He'd been doing a good job of trying to hide it, but you couldn't hide much for long when you lived at such close quarters.

Wykeham decided he'd stay too. In fact he had little choice, because there was a lot to be done before they sailed again. Wednesday night was scheduled as departure time. Ruck had accepted an invitation to stay with friends of Shrimp's, a retired officer and his wife who had a house on the other side of Valletta: the husband had some job on the Governor's staff, and kept open house for submarine captains.

Janaway, the signalman, had reported on board as soon as *Ultra* came alongside. He'd been passed fit for duty. He was critical of Tibbits' workmanship on the Jolly Roger: the stitches were too big, he complained, and so was the star under the new crossed gun-barrels. He refused to accept that a 4000-ton ship did warrant a bigger star than would have been accorded to a tug or a schooner. Lovesay, the second coxswain, teased him, saying the only thing Janaway didn't like was the fact he'd missed the patrol: if he'd been along with them, he'd have sewn on a star twice that size. They nearly came to blows about it.

But there was also a new bar sewn in the upper left quadrant of the flag, for the fast escorted ship they'd sunk in that night action on the surface, a week ago. Shrimp Simpson knew all about it, even before they'd got back to Malta, from Intelligence sources. The ship had been the German motor vessel *Vulkan*, 7300 tons, and she'd been carrying a load of Tiger tanks to Benghazi, replenishments for Rommel's armoured divisions. Transporting tanks had been the *Vulkan's* specialist role, and there'd been several attempts in the past to get her. Her sinking was a feather in Ruck's cap, and the loss of the brand-new battle tanks could be reckoned as a serious one for the Afrika Korps.

The main successes by other 10th Flotilla boats during the past week had been two U-boats sunk, one by *Unbeaten* (Lieutenant-Commander E. A. Woodward) and the other by *Upholder* (Wanklyn), both in the Adriatic. It was a second enemy submarine kill for both of them: they'd each sunk one in January.

On the debit side, *Sokol* had been near-missed while lying alongside Lazaretto. Thirty-six battery containers had been cracked, and she was now in dockyard hands. And a major set-back had been the destruction of Shrimp's pig-farm and the rest of the menagerie with it. A direct hit during one of the many air attacks had killed all the livestock, including the bad-tempered turkey. All the meat that had been recoverable was being minced up to provide a final boost to the flotilla rations; but those roast pork dinners would be sadly missed . . . Also, there'd been bombs dropped two days ago on Sliema, the north-ern suburb not far from the base in which submariners had flats with the object of getting *away* from the bombing. Those used by the wardrooms of *Sokol*, *Urge*, *Unbeaten*, P34 and *Unslaked* had been virtually demolished. Luckily none of the sailors' flats had been hit; and whether the Luftwaffe could have known they were attacking submariners' accommodation was a matter for speculation. The loss of the farm was the more serious of these mishaps anyway. Malta was down to siege rations: the workmen tunnelling out new underground workshops at the Lazaretto base, for instance, were now reduced to 900 calories a day, as opposed to the official 'norm' of 3000. That convoy was needed, all right.

Paul took *Ultra* out for her daily dip, on that first day back from patrol. As they cast off from Lazaretto, Janaway carefully lowered and folded the Jolly Roger; he was intending to unpick the offending stitches during the day. And Paul had unopened mail in his pocket, for perusal in the underwater peace and quiet. There was nothing from his father, but there were two letters from the USA, one from his mother and one from a girl he'd known in college. He took the boat out to her allotted buoy – just around the bulge of Manoel Island and in the wider part of Marsamxett harbour – and Lovesay secured a bow-wire to it; then he backed her so she was just clear of it, and flooded her down gently to rest in about sixty feet of water. He wondered, reading letters in his bunk, whether any of his correspondents could have believed that their letters would be opened and read on the bottom of a Mediterranean harbour.

He heard a few explosions during the day – they'd be bombs falling in the harbour, probably aimed at the base and landing in the creek – but nothing came near *Ultra*. When he surfaced her that evening the skies were clear of raiders: within minutes, half a dozen gleaming wet submarines were queuing to get in alongside Lazaretto or to the off-lying buoys. Paul secured *Ultra* between buoys, and two other boats berthed on her, with the long floating gangway linking them to the gallery steps.

That evening, best of the week, was *ITMA* night. Tommy Handley, with Colonel Chinstrap and Mona Lott, and others . . . Every loudspeaker in every submarine as well as in the base itself had the familiar catch-phrases rolling out. Then the BBC news from London: it started with an admission that the Japanese had landed in the Andaman Islands – a stepping-stone from Burma to Ceylon? – and continued with an Admiralty announcement of new successes by our Mediterranean submarines. Those selected for mention were the two U-boats and the German tank-transport: the names of Wanklyn, Woodward and Ruck were given as commanding officers of the submarines concerned.

So Ruck was one of the greats, now?

Most of the flotilla was either here already or due back within the next day or so. *Unslaked* wasn't back: but she had a long haul from her billet off Palermo – round the top-left corner of Sicily and then the dived passage through QBB 255, the Sicilian mine-field. The base was crowded, with so many in at the same time, all preparing for the convoy operation, and there were a lot of friends around, some of whom he'd missed seeing for some while through being at sea when they were in harbour, and vice versa; there was a very cheerful atmosphere in and around the heavily bomb-damaged base.

Work went on all night. In *Ultra*, four torpedoes in the tubes had to be hauled back out of them so that CPO Gaffney and his assistants could perform maintenance routines on them; then they had to be reloaded, so as to leave room in the TSC racks for the four reloads which would be embarked subsequently, up at the torpedo depot. Electricians were working on the gyro, and ERAs had a job to do on the after periscope gland, which had been leaking unacceptably fast during the last few days off Tripoli. The engine room was strewn with dismantled bits of the port diesel, and in the control room battery-boards had been taken up for Roffey to top up some of the cells: you could only get around the boat by jumping or climbing over things or swinging Tarzan-like from overhead pipes. But by dawn most of the loose items were back in place and the chasms covered, so that Wykeham could pilot her out into the harbour for another day in hiding.

This next night she'd be embarking, as well as torpedoes, fuel, fresh water, lubricating oil and ammunition, while mainte-nance work was finished off. The same kind of operation was in progress in all the other submarines as well, and one boat had sailed at dawn.

Paul spent the day in the rock shelter, and at one point Shrimp Simpson called him over to the part of it that constituted his daytime office, to ask whether he'd had any news from his father.

'Not from him, sir. Only what was in that communiqué.'

Shrimp nodded. 'I heard that one. Sounded to me as if he'd done it again. Only ship to come out of yet another frightful mess . . . When you do hear from him, Everard, I'd be glad to know.'

'Aye aye, sir.'

He was leaving, when the telephone rang on Miss Gomer's desk. She said, 'For you, sir,' and handed it to Shrimp. His face changed as he listened: eyes hardening, lines deepening . . . He said, 'I'll be there as soon as I can.' He hung up, and told his secretary, 'P39's been hit, so I don't know how long I'll be. Pass the word, would you?' Then he left the shelter at a run. He had an old motorbike for his personal transport; by road from Manoel Island to Dockyard Creek on the far side of Grand Harbour was a distance of nine miles. And prowling German fighters tended to attack anything they saw moving on the roads.

P39 had been in dockyard hands since being damaged in an air attack during *Ultra*'s previous patrol; she'd been near-missed in the same attack that had sunk the fuel lighter, and by now her repairs would have been just about complete. It transpired later that she and the Pole, *Sokol*, had been lying opposite each other in Dockyard Creek, P39 at Store Wharf and *Sokol* at Machinery Wharf, when a bomb had slanted into the water midway between them; but its trajectory had carried it right under P39, where it exploded, splitting her hull athwartships. There'd been no casualties: all her crew had been in the dockyard shelter, in accordance with Shrimp's orders.

Paul was on the long gallery that evening at dusk, with the light fading across Lazaretto Creek and the submarines nosing back to their berths. It was going to be a busy night. Pete Chandler, third hand of one of the other boats, was among those waiting on the gallery: Paul had just accepted a cigarette from him, and they'd been talking about the loss of P39. In the dockyard, where boats under repair had to be, there simply was no cover: if the Luftwaffe saw them they were sitting ducks. P39 had been beached at the Marsa, but she'd be a total loss.

Chandler muttered, 'Like the ten little nigger boys, isn't it?'

'Oh, I don't know. It's the first loss for quite a while. And considering the amount of shit that's being flung at us —'

'*Unslaked?*'

'What about her?' Then he did a double-take: '*What?*'

'Only a buzz.' Chandler shrugged. 'It's said she's overdue.'

'Who's saying so?'

'It's likely to be a fact. There's certainly been a signal sent saying *Unslaked, report position*. And no reply. You know what *that* means.'

Jack had intended going on a route march with Trolley's keep-fit brigade that Tuesday, but a message came at breakfast-time from Lieutenant-Commander Hawkins that he was wanted at the naval HQ at 10 am. So the rest of the NTU team went along, in their new rubber-soled boots, leaving him behind.

He got to the seafront hotel building a few minutes before the hour, and was directed to the conservatory. The naval force commander was just leaving — for a conference with Colonel Newman, the military commander, Hawkins said. It was obvious there'd been some development during the night.

'Sit, if you want to.'

'Just as soon stand, sir.' Because Hawkins, with his gammy leg, was standing.

Hawkins said, 'Please yourself. Smoke if you want to. Here — have one of mine.'

'Thank you.' Jack provided the light. 'I gather something's happened, news of some kind?'

'Bags of it.' The lieutenant-commander nodded, smoke trickling from his nostrils. 'Three main headings, and the first bit's *good* news. The mix-up with the RAF has been fixed, we're told. They're increasing the number of aircraft to sixty-two, almost as good as the number they first thought of. So Chariot will go ahead as planned, and that's *one* thing settled.'

He nodded. 'Good.'

It wasn't his business anyway. They'd only told him about it because there'd been the possibility of the whole raid being cancelled. Hawkins sat down at right-angles to his desk, pushed his damaged leg straight out in front of him and began to massage it with both hands. He explained, 'Aches, sometimes. Bloody thing . . . Well, listen. Item two is somewhat alarming. Particularly from your end of the business. Or at least, it *may* be . . . Here, take a look.' There was a large print of an aerial photograph lying on the desk: he pushed it across. 'Taken yesterday afternoon. Notice anything new?'

If it concerned the NTU's part in the action, it was likely to be something in the St Nazaire Basin. It took him a few seconds to spot it, because in all the previous reconnaissance pictures there'd been a few small ships, harbour patrol boats or minesweepers, lying alongside the quays. But *these* were something different . . .

He pointed. 'Destroyers?'

Five of them, on the southeastern quayside. Identical shapes, obviously five ships of the same class, secured in two trots, one of three and one of two ships.

Hawkins nodded. 'Small destroyers. Torpedo-boats. Möwe class. Built between the wars. Just under a thousand tons, with 4-inch guns and 21-inch torpedo tubes. Thirty knots or so, when in good nick . . . Of course, the fact they were berthed in there yesterday afternoon doesn't mean they have to be there now, let alone at the end of the week. On the other hand it doesn't guarantee they won't be.'

He was thinking about it, and studying the photograph.

'Berthed just there, they wouldn't be directly in our light. I mean, in a position to stop us doing our job. I'd be a couple of hundred yards from the nearest of them, and Roy's troop would be between me and them. They'd blast the hell out of *him*, though.'

'They may not be there at all, by the time Chariot goes in. They could be a hundred miles away.'

'Or at sea to intercept us before we reach the target area.'

Hawkins agreed. 'The possibilities are numerous. And that's one the force commander will have in mind, obviously. What *your* thoughts should be directed to, Everard, is the chance of this bunch being there when you reach the quayside, and how you might vary your present intentions – what options you might have. For instance, if you found you had *two* E-boats to play with, you might use one of 'em to inconvenience these characters.'

'Not unless I had to, in order to shut them up before I got on to the primary job of attacking the U-boat pens. That's the number one consideration, isn't it?'

Hawkins smiled. 'Precisely.'

Trying him out?

'If they're where they are in this picture, their main threat is to Captain Roy's task, his No. 5 Troop holding the bridgehead here at the inner end of the Old Entrance. So they're also a threat to everyone else – my lot included – who are supposed to withdraw over that bridge, through Roy's position.'

He turned to the plan of the harbour layout: it was clearer than the rather murky photograph, some of which was obscured by cloud below the aircraft. And he realized that he'd understated the problem – and Hawkins was probably waiting for him to see it.

He turned back to him.

'*If* they're there, the withdrawal as it's planned would be a nonstarter. Two-thirds of the whole landing force would be cut off on the wrong side of that bridge.'

'If they're on that bit of quay, you're right.'

'If they were farther along, it'd be worse. For me, anyway. And for Roy as well, probably. In any case, there'd have to be an alternative plan for the withdrawal. All those commando groups might re-embark from – well, the outer end of the Old Entrance?'

'I dare say that's what the top brass will now be chewing over.'

'I suppose one *might* consider rushing the torpedo-boats,

capturing them? If *their* torpedoes and guns were used against the U-boat pens —'

'Hang on.' Hawkins shook his head. 'Complement of a Möwe is 120 men. Multiply that by five. Then even halve the total, to allow for one watch on all-night leave. And you'd be – how many?'

'Say my bunch plus Roy's —'

'Forget it. You don't know how many of you will be left on your feet by that time. And Roy's commando troop has its own job to do. What's more, if those ships are there, their guns will be manned long before you get to them. The alarm will have gone off loud and clear way before that.' Hawkins put the photograph away. 'This is simply a contingency for you to bear in mind – with a view, as you very properly said, to completing your own task even if they *are* there. Forewarned is forearmed, and all that.' He added, 'Especially so far as the withdrawal is concerned.'

Jack understood him. He suggested, 'Fifty to one against achieving it *and* withdrawing?'

Hawkins frowned. 'Not being a bookmaker, Everard —'

'Right.' He stubbed out his cigarette. 'I'll – ponder on it, anyway. And hope to God they won't be there on the day. It isn't likely they'd be left there for such a length of time.'

'I agree entirely.'

'You said there were three items, sir?'

A nod . . . 'The third is we've had a prognostication about the weather. It's likely to deteriorate in a few days' time. So the proposition of starting a day earlier than we've been intending is now being considered. A decision will be taken tomorrow, but it's on the cards you'll sail on the twenty-sixth instead of the twenty-seventh.'

The twenty-sixth would be Thursday. The day after tomorrow.

Paul hadn't realized how busy a night it was going to be. The first inkling of it came when *Ultra* was in the process of securing alongside Lazaretto and Ruck appeared, materializing out of nowhere, to announce that they had to have her ready to sail at sunrise. *Before* sunrise . . . Instead of tomorrow night.

Shrimp Simpson hadn't returned from the dockyard, but his Staff Officer (Operations) had telephoned to the house where Ruck had been a guest. All submarines that were anything like ready for patrol were to be pushed out as quickly as possible. So on top of the jobs already listed and prepared for they were going to have to store ship, finish all the minor tasks and top up the battery with a standing charge – because they'd be starting the patrol with a day's dived passage instead of with a night on the surface. And storing would have taken place tomorrow evening, alongside, before shoving off.

So there was some quick thinking to be done – most of it by Wykeham, who had to translate requirements into practicalities.

McClure arrived back, with the other half of the ship's company. Paul happened to meet him on *Ultra*'s casing: he was hurrying ashore on some errand just as the little Scot came strutting aboard. Paul told him, 'Best get cracking, Bob. We're sailing for patrol at 0500!'

He'd expected to give him a shock: but McClure looked pleased.

'Thank God. Sooner we get out of this bloody hole, the better.'

He was disappearing into the fore hatch. Paul called after him, 'Why d'you say that?'

'Because it's not fuckin' *safe* here, that's why!'

He got a more complete explanation later. The Ghain Tuffheia rest camp had been strafed that afternoon by German fighters. A naval pensioner who'd taken on the job of camp care-taker had made the mistake of hoisting a White Ensign on the flagstaff, and the Messerschmitt pilots had spotted it. Nobody had thought to warn the new caretaker, because nobody had expected him to do anything so daft. There'd been no casual-ties, because the camp had been almost deserted at that time, but Ghain Tuffheia would not henceforth be either restful or safe.

Still, there were other rest camps.

It was a marathon of a night. On top of everything else there was a recurring need to cast off and then reberth in accordance with their own and other boats' requirements. Two others sailed for patrol during the night: there were movements to and from the torpedo depot, and a need to be on the outside of the trot for fuelling, for instance, and on the inside – preferably – for storing. It was enough to drive anyone mad. But then Shrimp came back – about midnight – cheerful and indefatigable despite the extraordinary problems of this and every other day, running a flotilla and a complex base under siege conditions: under his benign, no-nonsense influence, frayed tempers mended and morale soared.

As one might have guessed, the convoy from the east was about to sail. The naval supply ship *Breconshire* and three merchantmen, escorted by the AA cruiser *Carlisle* and six destroyers, would be overtaken at sea by Admiral Vian with his flag in *Cleopatra*, her sister cruisers *Dido* and *Euryalus*, and four more destroyers. Six Hunt-class destroyers would join the escort off Tobruk as the convoy steamed westward, running the gauntlet of the Cretan airfields before entering the central basin where – according to Intelligence reports, Ruck told them – interference by enemy surface forces was considered likely. The Germans and Italians knew that Malta was down to about its last crust – even if the Maltese did *not* know it – and they'd be going all-out to stop the convoy getting through.

Ruck had other items of Intelligence to pass on. The enemy were planning to invade Malta in May, by which time they reckoned to have the island on its knees through starvation and lack of ammunition and fuel. A combined sea/air assault had been planned a year ago, but their invasion of Crete had forced them to postpone it. Now, the invasion force was being trained.

Ruck told them this during a short break for coffee in *Ultra*'s wardroom at about 0300. He'd come on board again when she'd returned from her visit to the torpedo depot: he'd left Wykeham to handle that, while he'd been closeted with Shrimp Simpson.

Oil fuel and fresh water were being embarked now, simultaneously; Fry, the stoker petty officer, was 'up top doin' his nut', according to Able Seaman Shaw.

Wykeham asked Ruck, 'Is it true about *Unslaked*, sir?'

Ruck stared into his coffee. March, *Unslaked*'s CO, was a close friend of his. He said quietly. 'She's overdue. That's all anyone knows.'

There was a natural tendency to think, *Could be a wireless defect, she might still pipe up* . . . But it would have been silly to have said it out loud, because the same kind of long-shot hope would be in everyone else's mind anyway. It was as if for the time being *Unslaked* was in limbo, and in a day or two it would be accepted that she'd gone. Or before that, if the enemy claimed a sinking in her patrol area or on her route back to base.

Wykeham said, 'She was going up through the minefield, wasn't she?'

Ruck nodded. There was a fixed route through that field, one long day's dived passage from off Cape San Marco to a position off Marettimo Island. It was in frequent use by 10th Flotilla submarines, and nobody thought much about going through there now.

'Are we headed that way?'

'With a convoy coming from the east, why would we expect surface forces to come round from *that* direction, for Christ's sake?'

Wykeham shrugged. 'I thought we'd still have to cover that Cape Bon supply route.' Blinking at Ruck . . . 'So we'll be off Taranto, will we, sir?'

Ruck just stared at him. Paul reached for a cigarette: McClure tapped him on the arm and pointed at the 'No Smoking' board that was hanging in the gangway. With the charging operation at an advanced stage the battery would be gassing, making it dangerous to strike lights. Wykeham asked Ruck, 'Messina, again?'

9

'Up periscope.'

ERA Quinn eased the lever up. A moment later Paul was circling to check sky first, sea second. A lively, tossing sea, white and heaving from the northwest, the direction of the Messina bottleneck, the direction an enemy was likely to appear from: the wind was taking the waves' crests as they tumbled, and driving spray at periscope-top level in an intermittent, lashing rain. It would call for sharp eyes to spot a periscope in that sea, even though you had to push it up a foot or so higher to see over the waves' tops.

He settled on the land, already clear-cut in sharp early morning light, to take bearings of Cape Spartivento and Cape dell'Armi. Furness, messenger of the watch, wrote the bearings down, blinking and breathing hard: then the periscope was slithering back into its hole, Paul moving to the chart table to pencil the fix on, ready for handing over the watch to Wykeham.

It was now 0610, and the bearings put *Ultra* thirteen miles south of dell'Armi. She'd dived just before 0500, and her course of 350 degrees was aiming her directly into the straits. Ruck had drawn this Messina billet again because Taranto, 150 miles farther north, was being patrolled by boats which had sailed earlier: they'd be in their allotted areas by this time, in the Gulf of Taranto and across the southern exit from the Adriatic.

Wykeham, whom Furness had shaken at five minutes past the hour, shuffled to the chart table and stared gloomily at the new fix and the pencilled track leading into the straits' funnel-shaped entrance.

'What's it like up top now?'

'Choppy. Nor'wester, three to four.'

'Well, that's something . . . Trim all right?'

'Spot on.' They'd dived her on the watch, without disturbing the first lieutenant's slumbers. 'If you don't believe me, come and find a fault in it.'

'In a minute.' With dividers, he was checking the boat's projected advance into the straits. Allowing for three knots, it would be four hours – this watch and the next – before dell'Armi was abeam, and *Ultra* would then still be as much as five miles offshore. So for the duration of *his* watch there'd be a lot of space in all directions. He mumbled as he turned into the control room, 'Only feels like about ten minutes since we were last here.'

It sounded as if he wasn't all that happy to be back. He'd brighten up, though, quite soon. He checked the trim, then had a look round through the periscope. Pushing the handles up, he nodded.

'All right, I've got it . . . Morning, cox'n.' CPO Logan glanced round from the after planes. 'Morning, sir.' He looked grumpy, too. Paul grinned as he left them, heading for some sleep before breakfast. All the new watch had the same bug-eyed look: you felt superior to them, being wide awake and with the prospect of getting your own head down – then breakfast and some *more* bunk time . . .

For all the roughness up top, twenty-eight feet underneath the surface it was rock-steady, warm and comfortable. And quiet, except for some fairly raucous snoring in the wardroom. Not sure who was doing it, Paul glanced first towards Ruck's bunk – but Ruck was awake, open-eyed, looking straight back at him. He murmured, 'Not me, Sub. Must be our tame West Highlander.'

'Ah.' Closer observation confirmed it. Paul said, 'What they mean by the skirl of the pipes, perhaps.' He sat down to pull his shoes off. Ruck asked quietly, 'Am I right in thinking he's getting over it?'

The RAF brother, Ruck meant. And there were times when McClure did seem to be getting back to his little old happy self. Paul nodded. 'He's not over it exactly, sir, but he's getting to live with it.'

He climbed on to his bunk. Six-thirty. Hour and a half's snooze now . . .

He wondered what might have happened to *Unslaked.* Where Hewson might be at this moment. It wasn't a good subject on which to allow the imagination much rope. But he and Hewson had been on the submarine training class together, up at Blyth in Northumberland, and they'd met again in the depot ship *Forth* in Holy Loch when both submariners had been doing their work-up and trials before sailing for the Mediterranean. *Unslaked* had come out a month before *Ultra* to join the Malta flotilla, and the Palermo patrol would have been about her seventh.

He didn't want to go on thinking about it. But there was a sense almost of obligation to, of wrongness in just cutting friends out of mind – *OK, they've had it, forget them* . . .

Breakfast was soya links – canned, skinless sausages – with canned tomatoes. Paul had acquired a taste for them, and he had a double helping because McClure ate only bread and jam before sloping away to take over the watch. Wykeham told Ruck when he came through, 'That seaplane hasn't been back in the last half-hour or so.'

'Good.'

Paul asked, 'Seaplane?'

'A Cant, as usual. Frigging around for most of my watch, while you were in dreamland . . . Who ate Bob's links?'

'I did.'

'Greedy bastard.'

'Anything on the surface?'

'Only the usual small fry. Nowhere near us, anyway . . . Pass the sugar, would you?'

McClure appeared, when Shaw was clearing the plates away in his strange juggler's fashion, to tell Ruck that two A/S schooners were coming south through the straits. 'Right ahead, sir, and coming towards.'

'No transmissions, I suppose?'

'No, sir.'

The schooners didn't seem to possess asdics, only hydrophones. They'd drift along virtually in silence, listening. But there could always be an exception to the rule. Ruck followed McClure into the control room, and from the wardroom they heard the periscope go up. Then a long silence. You heard the log ticking, and the hum of one motor at its slowest speed, and occasional movements of the watchkeepers. Finally –

'Down . . . Port ten.'

'Port ten, sir.' Periscope hissing down. 'Ten of port wheel on, sir.'

Ruck told McClure, 'Steady her on 270, pilot.' He came back and sat down. 'We'll let 'em go by, then turn north again.'

Paul turned in. Dozing, he half woke when McClure came to announce that the schooners had passed astern, and Ruck told him to bring her back to the course of 350 degrees. Then – he didn't know how long afterwards – McClure was reporting that the seaplane had returned; it was patrolling to and fro across the straits ahead of them.

'Keep an eye on it, pilot, and don't show too much stick.'

Wykeham commented, yawning from his bunk, 'Could mean something's coming through.'

'It could.' Ruck qualified the agreement: 'And it could mean damn all.'

Paul drifted into sleep again, vaguely aware that it might not be very long before it would be interrupted by an invitation to turn out and stand a watch. It was the process of turning out that one disliked, the effort of throwing off the soporific influence of the dived submarine's peace and quiet. The actual watchkeeping,

deep inside enemy waters as *Ultra* was here, was rather fascinat-
ing. There were usually a few small craft about, and you were
aware all the time that a target of importance could show up at
any moment: every time you poked the periscope up into the
daylight, there could be something there, and the element of
uncertainty contributed to one's enjoyment.

He came awake with that word and concept in his head.
Enjoyment?

That session of depthcharging during the last patrol had been
anything but enjoyable. And the probability that *Unslaked* had
been sunk was hideous. Yet one did, still, enjoy . . .

He'd mentioned it in a letter which he'd written to his father,
three days ago on the harbour bottom. *I truly do find this job fas-
cinating. It could be partly because the guys I'm with are such a terrific
bunch – the whole crowd, I mean, all Shrimp S's people, not just my own
lot. Which reminds me, your old friend Shrimp told me to give you his
warm regards, and he's keen to get news of you . . .*

'Shrimp's people' being a paraphrase for 'the 10th Flotilla', a
way of getting past the censors' rules.

He thought of a line in the letter from his mother: *I hope
you're not taking any silly risks —*

'Captain in the control room! Diving stations!'

Lightning evacuation – led by Ruck, a short head in front of
Wykeham. Paul made it too, to the other side of the fruit
machine before the rush arrived from for'ard. McClure was
telling Ruck excitedly, 'U-boat, on green two-oh!'

The periscope slid up into his hands as he lifted them. He
asked McClure, 'Where's the Cant?'

'Went out of sight northward, sir.'

Wykeham was fighting the trim as the shift of weights upset it.
Ruck snarling, 'Keep her *up*, for God's sake!' Circling, checking
all round, then finding and settling on the target . . . 'Starboard
fifteen. Stand by one, two and three tubes. Start the attack.
Bearing is – *that*. Range – *that*. I am – forty-five on his starboard
bow.'

Pool had read off the range and bearing and the periscope was shooting down. Paul had been expecting cruisers, or a battle-ship . . .

'Forty feet, group up, full ahead together.'

'Enemy course one-three-oh, sir!'

And the range was 4300 yards. More than two miles. Hence the turn to starboard and the extra speed, going deep so that speed wouldn't show up as a flurry on the surface, in order to get in closer, close the range on the target's track.

'Course for a 120 track, Sub?'

Paul cranked the dials round. *Ultra* nosing deeper and turning to starboard. He told Ruck, 'Oh-seven-oh, sir.'

'Steer oh-seven-oh.'

'Turbine HE port bow, four hundred revs, sir . . .'

Ruck stared at Newton, thinking about that. He made his mind up. 'Set enemy speed fifteen.'

'Fifteen – set —'

'Both motors full ahead grouped up, sir.'

Ruck motionless near the periscope, with his eyes on the stopwatch in his palm.

'Forty feet, sir.'

Three minutes passed, feeling more like ten.

'Group down, slow together. Twenty-eight feet.

Flow of acknowledgements; the depthgauge needles began to circle again, and vibration faded as the power fell off. Ruck looked at Quinn: 'Up.' He asked Newton, 'Bearing now?'

'Red five-oh, sir.'

He had the periscope set on that bearing before he put his eyes to it. Then adjusting by a degree or two . . . The height of the waves would make target-spotting less easy, when the target was as low as a submarine. 'Bearing – *that*. Range – *that*. I'm now sixty on his bow.'

Whipping round, looking for the seaplane; then he'd pushed the handles up, and stepped back.

'Forty feet, group up, full ahead.' Another burst to get in where he'd stand a chance of hitting. 'No zigzag, anyway. He's in too much of a hurry to get down to the convoy, I dare say.'

The range had been 3700 yards that time. Still not much less than two miles. McClure suggested, 'Enemy speed looks like sixteen knots, sir.'

Ruck nodded. 'Set sixteen. What's my DA?'

He'd adjusted the speed setting. He lined the dials up, and reported, 'Twenty-three degrees, sir.'

Wykeham murmured, 'Forty feet, sir, both motors full ahead grouped up.'

'Very good.' Ruck was timing it with the stopwatch again. *Ultra* quivering as the speeding screws forced her through the water. One minute . . . One and a half . . . Ruck looked up: 'Group down, slow together. Twenty-eight feet. Stand by one, two and three tubes. Target bearing, Newton?'

'Red three-two, sir!'

Nine degrees of travel by the U-boat, then, and Ruck's firing-angle would be on. He gestured for the periscope, as the boat rose towards the surface. Nine degrees extended over that range still gave the target quite a distance to run. Thirty-five feet; thirty-two; thirty . . .

'Stand by.' He set the periscope on the aim-off angle of twenty-three degrees to port, and Chief ERA Pool leaned over to hold it on that bearing. You could think of the enemy sub-mariners: feeling *safe* – smoking, chatting, sleeping, writing letters to their girlfriends . . . Ruck hunched at the periscope, waiting for the U-boat's bow to touch the vertical hairline in the lens. It would still be a very long-range shot, at so small a target.

'Fire one!'

A lurch, and a jump in pressure.

'Fire two!'

The same again. Newton reported, 'Both torpedoes running, sir.'

'Fire three!' He slammed the handles up. 'Dip it.' A glance at Paul:

'What's the running time for 3000 yards?'

'Two and a quarter minutes, sir.'

The dipped periscope returned like a yo-yo to Ruck's waiting

hands. His eyes at the lenses glowed greenish from the bright
reflection of the sea – because of the dim lights here under it . . .
Watching, Paul saw Ruck's face change, heard the sudden intake
of breath.

'*Damn* . . .'

Sharp concern in all the faces round him. Wykeham turning
too, uncharacteristically diverting his attention from the trim.
Ruck muttered, 'Turned his bloody arse to us!' Then, scowling,
switching to low power for an air search and swinging leftward:
circling on rapidly. Muttering to himself, '*And* the flaming seaplane's . . .' Slamming the handles up. 'Down. Sixty feet.
Starboard fifteen.' He shook his head, disbelieving the rotten
luck. The periscope was whistling down, flashing yellow, seawater
dribbles shiny in the grease on it.

Wykeham's acknowledgement of Ruck's order was quiet,
clipped: 'Sixty feet, sir.'

'HE astern, sir – reciprocating. It's – transmitting, sir . . .'

'Heard it, have you?' Ruck glanced angrily at Newton. 'I've
seen it.' His glare shifted. 'Stop starboard.'

'Sounds like' – Newton gulped, his Adam's apple wobbling –
'trawler, sir. Bearing drawing right —'

'It *is* a trawler.' Ruck told him, 'And there's another out
beyond it.'

'Starboard motor stopped, sir.'

'Steer two hundred degrees.'

Southward – but also out into the middle, where they'd been
before. Wykeham reported, 'Sixty feet, sir.' Creagh took the
rudder-angle off as the ship's head swung through due south.
Ruck asked Newton, 'Trawler bearing now?'

Explosion. Distant, muffled-sounding. Probably one of the
three torpedoes hitting the bottom or a rock. Newton paused
before answering Ruck's last question: and that crash would
have put the enemy on his toes, all right . . . 'Green seven-six, sir,
transmitting and drawing right.' Blinking . . . 'There's another
one, long way off, green six-four.' He licked his lips. 'Sir, this
set —'

'Course two-oh-oh, sir.'

Ruck told them, 'The seaplane was diving right over us. It may have seen the torpedo tracks, or the actual firing. Must have come out of cloud. But if the U-boat was following around the coastline' – he was addressing Wykeham, now – 'that's about where it would have turned. My own fault for just assuming it had to be heading south.'

Torpedoes were precious. When each one had to be brought through to Malta at considerable risk and effort, wasting them really hurt. Most of them came by the 'magic carpet', larger types of submarine acting as supply runners, bringing also aviation spirit in their ballast tanks.

CPO Logan muttered, 'Can't win 'em all, sir.'

Silence. Motor-hum, log clicking away, and the slighter clicks as Newton trained his asdics round. Ruck said, 'You're right, cox'n. Unfortunately.' He asked Newton, 'Where are they?'

'Green one-two-five, sir. Second one's on the same bearing but more distant. Both drawing right still.'

He thought about it for a moment. Then: 'One hundred feet.'

'Hundred feet, sir . . .'

'And we'll go to watch diving. Don't use the tannoy – pass the word I want dead quiet . . . Sub, don't drop any spanners while you're reloading those tubes, but do it like greased lightning. All right?'

'Aye aye, sir.'

'And I want to know as each tube's loaded.'

In case the process of reloading had to be interrupted, if a target appeared. Putting that U-boat out of mind, remembering they were here to intercept surface forces . . . Paul said, 'We'll load number three first, sir. It'll be the quickest, and you'll have three and four available.'

Number four tube hadn't been fired. Number three was the starboard lower one, and it was quicker to reload because for the upper pair you had to rig heavy horizontal bars across the compartment so the fish could be slid out sideways from the racks and then hauled across them into the tubes. The bars had to be set up at deck level for the lower pair as well, but it was a simpler, quicker job. CPO Gaffney had the bow-caps shut and the tubes drained down while the compartment was being cleared of hammocks and kitbags; then the bars – T-sectioned girders – were fixed in place and the hauling tackle laid out, from the rear end of the tube to the tail-end of the torpedo, and number three reload was manoeuvred out and lined up with the tube – which was empty by this time, with its rear door open, ready to receive it. Six torpedomen's weight on the block and tackle had the two-ton missile sliding forward, pausing at one stage for Gaffney to remove the safety-chock from behind its firing-lever. When the fish was fired, that lever in the top of its body would be knocked back by a projection in the top of the tube, sending twin hammers down on charges like shotgun cartridges that fired the engine: so the torpedo's two concentric propellers would be racing at the same time as a charge of high-pressure air punched it out into the sea.

Ready again: Gaffney as cheer-leader intoned, 'Two-six, *heave!*' The torpedo slid home into the tube, and before the rear door was shut Gaffney removed the clamp from its propellers. Paul reported to Ruck by messenger that three and four tubes were loaded. The bars were being shifted meanwhile to shoulder height, the level of the upper racks and tubes, and the tackle swiftly overhauled, ready for number one tube's reload.

The whole job took thirty-five minutes. It was probably a record. Paul climbed aft over the mountain of gear piled in the gangway, and reported to Ruck that all tubes were loaded. Ruck glanced at the clock, and raised an eyebrow. 'Not bad, Sub.' He was in the control room, and Wykeham was at the trim. It was eleven-twenty, halfway through what should have been Paul's watch.

'Take over, shall I?'

Wykeham glanced enquiringly at Ruck. Ruck ordered, 'Twenty-eight feet.' He told Paul, 'We've got what sound like four trawlers up there at the moment. Just wait a minute.'

Paul wondered what Newton had been about to say about the asdic set, an hour or so ago. Presumably it hadn't been anything important. He went into the wardroom, and sat down. McClure grumbled, 'Bastards are all over the place. *And* they know we're around.'

They'd at least suspect a submarine was present, after that explosion. And if the Cant had been right overhead when *Ultra* had fired those torpedoes, they'd have an idea *where* she was. Or anyway, where she had been . . . He heard Ruck's voice from the control room: 'Up periscope.' And Wykeham's reporting, 'Twenty-eight feet, sir.' He'd be using the small after periscope, with so many hunters up there on the surface. Paul heard the slither as it rose, then the soft thump of it stopping. That was the one with the leaky gland that had been fixed in Malta. A minute ticked by in silence while he visualized the periscope's top end, not much thicker than a walking-stick, cutting through tumbling, whitened sea.

'Down.' Then: 'Starboard fifteen.' More periscope activity: he must have shifted to the big one. Another minute passed before that one was hissing down.

'Fifteen of starboard wheel on, sir.'

'Steer oh-two-oh . . . Forty feet, Number One.'

The course of 020 degrees, twenty degrees east of north, would take them up towards the straits again. Ruck's voice was audible as he told Wykeham, 'One pair of trawlers is to the east of us, and the other's southwest. Bags of room up north of them.' He came through to the wardroom. 'All right, Sub, you can take over now.'

There was only about half an hour of his watch left; and nothing to do, at forty feet, except keep an eye on the trim. If anything happened on the surface only Flyte, the asdic operator of the watch, would know it . . . Paul went through, and stood beside Wykeham at the trim. 'Ready when you are.'

'She's all yours, chum. Forty feet, course 020, starboard motor slow ahead, port stopped. OK?'

'Right.' Wykeham left him, and Paul went to look at the chart.

There was a fix on it, slightly out of date: he up-dated it as a DR position, and marked the time of the reversal of course. Back in the control room, he saw that Flyte was looking agitated.

'Something wrong?'

Flyte shook his head: concentrating, and training the receiver to and fro. Then he pushed the phones off his ears.

'They've turned, sir. Green one-four-oh – bearing left. The other's coming towards, sir, green one-seven-five.' Phones on again, and frowning with concentration . . . 'HE increasing, sir!'

Ruck appeared, looking fed up. 'Twenty-eight feet, Sub. Let's see what they're up to.'

Paul moved over to stand behind the planesmen. 'Twenty-eight feet.' On his right, Flyte moved suddenly as if in discomfort. 'Turbine HE right ahead, sir – red five – E-boat or destroyer, sir, *fast* HE —'

'All right.' Ruck, waiting by the after periscope, watched the depthgauges as the needles crept past thirty-five feet: approaching thirty . . . He moved his hands: 'Up.' Glancing round, telling Flyte, 'Don't know why you sound so surprised. These are Italian waters, you've got to expect to find a few Wops around.'

Lovesay chuckled. Creagh glanced over his shoulder and grinned at Dracula Jupp. When Jupp returned the grin, you could see why he had that nickname.

'Twenty-eight feet, sir.'

Ruck circling now: checking the close surroundings first, then studying the positions and movements of each of the ships up there. Sending the small periscope down, moving to the big one.

'Port ten.'

'Port ten, sir.'

Swinging around, using the air search: and pausing to watch something on the beam. The seaplane, possibly . . . Completing the circle now, switching to high power and settling the periscope on that bearing of red five. Shifting slightly right . . .

'Torpedo-boat. Little old three-funnelled job. Nineteen-twenties.' He raised his voice. 'Pilot, get the *Jane's* out.

Three-funnelled Wop torpedo-boat. Five or six hundred tons with a very sheer stem.' He checked the bearing-ring and the ship's head as he pushed the handles up, and told Creagh, 'Steer three-three-five.'

To pass round the newcomer, obviously, up between him and the Sicilian coast. He ordered, as he moved to the chart table, 'Sixty feet.' McClure was there waiting for him, with *Jane's Fighting Ships* open at the pages of Italian destroyers and torpedo-boats. 'This one, sir? Generali class?'

The hydroplanes tilted again as the planesmen swung their brass controlling wheels, angling the planes to take her down out of the trawlers' way. It probably wouldn't change Ruck's intentions, Paul guessed, if another dozen A/S ships joined in up there. He saw himself as the hunter, not the hunted: those were simply nuisances to be circumvented.

'Isn't that really *something?*'

Harry Dixon, *Sauerkraut*'s Canadian first lieutenant, was gazing astern. The Cornish coast, he was referring to. Falmouth astern, and Manacles, Black Head and the Lizard to the west. Eastward, the land faded and disappeared in haze. It was a gentle spring day with a pale blue sky and a low swell running in on the port beam. Course would be altered to southwest shortly, as soon as they were clear of the land, and the swell would be on the quarter then, so there'd be less of the rolling which, Jack Everard suspected, might be making for discomfort among the troops.

But that coastline, that soft, haze-hung panorama: Dixon was right, it was about as beautiful as anything you'd ever see. *Too* beautiful – it made you think about coming back to it.

Like Fiona. To whom he'd written . . .

He turned his back on it. 'Yes. It's pretty.'

The Canadian stared at him – critically, obviously thinking what a philistine this was. Or what a bastard. Which would match Sharp's view, of course – for all the geniality and cooperation . . .

The Hunt-class destroyer *Atherstone* was leading, with the

motor gunboat in tow. Astern of her came the other Hunt, *Tynedale*, and then *Campbeltown* towing MTB 74. The MGB and the MTB were being towed most of the way because of their limited range, which was compensated for in the MLs by those auxiliary fuel tanks. *Sauerkraut*, bringing up the rear of this centre column, had all the range she needed because she was diesel-powered.

The MLs were in two flanking columns, one line of them on each side, and the force had its own air cover in the form of a single Hurricane circling overhead. But even with all this solid evidence all around him, Jack found it hard to take in the fact that they were on the way, that after all this time they were actually *en route* to St Nazaire!

This morning C-in-C Plymouth had signalled to the naval force commander, *Preparative Chariot*. That had been the signal to embark, raise steam, stand by. And at 12.30, *Carry on Chariot*. The MLs had chugged out of harbour past St Anthony's Lighthouse at 1400, and the three destroyers with *Sauerkraut* trailing them had followed an hour later. The naval and military commanders were taking passage in *Atherstone*; tomorrow night, before the force entered the Loire estuary, they'd be transferring to the MGB, which would then become headquarters ship and lead the force up the river.

Jack thought again, his eyes moving to the ML columns on either side, about wooden ships with petrol tanks on their upper decks. He was thankful now that Sharp's ML had become unreliable mechanically and that the E-boat had been available in its place. *Sauerkraut* and the MGB, and MTB 74, might stand *some* chance, he thought, of returning to that Cornish coast.

On Sunday, possibly. This was Thursday. The assault was scheduled to take place at 0130 Saturday, with re-embarkation about 0300. ETA Falmouth, therefore, Sunday.

For some. But Mountbatten *had* said 'We're writing you off' – *he* hadn't shirked it. And it was difficult to see much likelihood of any of the MLs coming out of it. If one or two of them did get away, it would be a miracle.

Lieutenant-Commander Hawkins hadn't agreed. Or probably he had, in his own mind, because he was an intelligent man and he'd been in action, could guess, surely, at how it was going to be, six miles up that river: he probably hadn't wanted to admit it. All he'd been ready to agree was that they'd undoubtedly incur *some* losses.

In his letter to Fiona, Jack had written that he expected to be in touch with her in about a week: that he'd either telephone or just turn up on her doorstep. He could imagine it: it was a happy fantasy, an escape, to shut one's eyes and picture it. Himself at the door of the flat, ringing the bell: and the door opening, and Fiona finding him standing there, just looking at her: she'd catch the mood, say something like, *You made it, then . . .*

Sharp told his coxswain, Shawcross, 'Come over to port a bit. You're too far over, man!' Shawcross shifted the wheel a little, without moving his eyes from the stern of the Hunt ahead of them. He was young-looking for a petty officer, quick-eyed and intelligent. Sharp called to Jack across the bridge, 'Like a joy-ride, isn't it? Didn't they pick the weather for us, begorrah?'

White Ensigns were whipping on the easterly breeze, bow-waves glistened white against grey hulls, sea and sky were near-matching shades of blue. *Sauerkraut* rolled stiffly to the swell, which had become longer and more regular as they drew away from land. Jack saw a signal-hoist rise to flutter at *Atherstone*'s yardarm: Shawcross had drawn Sharp's attention to it, and he had his glasses up to study it while at the back of the bridge his signalman ran the red-and-white answering pendant to the halfway point, meaning 'Signal seen but not yet under-stood.' It would be the change of course signal, though, the order to turn to the southwest for a run of about fifty miles to the point where they'd turn south. They were making thirteen knots, so that the next alteration would come at about 1900.

Sharp called, 'Answering pendant close up!'

Meaning he'd read it now, as well as seen it . . . Jack went below, to confer with PO Slattery and Sergeant Bowater. The latest reconnaissance photographs, which Hawkins had shown him this morning, had the five Möwe-class torpedo-boats still alongside in the St Nazaire Basin. He hadn't told his team about that particular problem yet, and now was as good a time as any.

Ultra had dodged trawlers all afternoon. With the watchkeeping rotation as it was, afternoons were pleasant – between the midday snack and teatime, all Paul had to do was sleep. But he'd wasted this one by only cat-napping, half listening to what was going on, mixing that with periods of semi-consciousness.

The torpedo-boat hadn't stayed with the hunt: it had gone on southward, looking as if it might be heading for Augusta. *Ultra* had been left with the two pairs of A/S trawlers probing for her, and there'd also been some schooners up in the narrows, in periscope sight only when the boat was on her northern limit. Ruck had set this as latitude thirty-eight degrees north; to have gone beyond it, into the more confined waters, would have served no good purpose and only played into the trawlers' hands.

The semi-wakefulness had been due, Paul guessed, to the general state of expectancy, the mind refusing to let its guard down. He'd been waiting for the alarm, the sudden order 'Diving stations!'

Which hadn't come by 1600, when McClure sent a messenger in to shake him. Paul must have heard him coming, because he was awake and sliding out of his bunk before the man had said a word. Yet tea and biscuits were on the table, and he hadn't heard Shaw crashing that lot down in his customary suave manner . . .

Ruck opened his eyes and told him, 'We'll start heading south soon, Sub. I want to surface at least ten miles clear of dell'Armi at about eight.'

Paul took a mug of tea into the control room with him. He asked McClure, 'What's cooking?'

'Bugger all.' The Scotsman stretched, drawing himself out to his full five feet and four inches. 'Twenty-eight feet, slow ahead grouped down on the port motor, starboard stopped. Course is

050.' He went to the chart table. 'We're here. Twelve minutes
ago. OK?'

'Where are the trawlers?'

'On the quarter and astern. There's nothing near us. I think
the skipper wants to skid out of it pretty soon now, and moving
out southeastward we'll be miles clear of all that garbage. Bloody
nuisance, they've been.'

'Seaplane?'

'It's around. Or its brother is. Off and on, you know.'

'All right, then.'

'Awake, are you?'

'Go on, piss off.' He walked into the control room, leaving his
tea on the chart table. Creagh grinned at him from the wheel,
and Lovesay looked round and nodded. Flyte, frowning as he listened to whatever he was getting from his headset, glanced up
abstractedly, like a man lost in thought. Paul stopped by the
for'ard periscope, lifted his hands, and Chief ERA Pool put his
hand down to the lever.

'Switched watches, Chief?'

Pool nodded. Smooth as a Fortnum and Mason floor-walker.
'Thought we'd have a change-round, sir.'

'HE astern – loud – all of a sudden – increasing, sir!'

He swung round, hanging on the out-turned handles: and
saw a trawler bow-on, high, rounded stem smashing through
the waves straight at them. A glimpse of another out beyond it –
but he'd already snapped the handles up. 'Forty feet!'

Lovesay repeated as he applied angle to the planes, 'Forty
feet, sir . . .' At the same moment Ruck arrived, and Flyte
reported 'Transmitting, sir!'

'Sixty feet. Starboard fifteen. Half ahead together.' Ruck
asked Flyte, 'In contact?'

'No, sir, I don't *think* —'

'Hundred feet, Sub.'

'Hundred feet, sir . . .'

The trawler's screws were audible, suddenly. They passed over
somewhere on the submarine's port side. Bubble well aft, needles

circling round the gauges. Creagh reported that he had fifteen
degrees of starboard rudder on. Ruck asked Flyte, 'How the hell
did he get so close without you hearing him?'

It *had* been close. Paul felt slightly breathless. He thought the
trawler must have had them in contact when he saw it, that bow
rushing at the periscope. It was extraordinary that Flyte hadn't
known it, if that was the case. And Newton had been slow getting
on to the trawlers this morning, too.

There was also McClure, who hadn't thought there was anything on the surface anywhere near them!

Propeller noises astern now . . .

'Steer one-five-oh. Hundred and fifty feet.' He looked round
at Flyte again. 'Where are they now?'

Flyte looked lost, or sick. 'I – can't seem to —'

'What?'

'I reckon it's the set, sir. Sort of off and on, like.' He tapped at
his headphones. 'Dead now. I think it was before, when I didn't
realize. Then all of a sudden —'

Ruck told the messenger, 'Get Newton.' He went over to the
asdic position, and Flyte passed him the spare headset.

'Course one-five-oh, sir.'

Screws chugged over. Out to port, but not *far* out. Either the
same trawler or its mate, and either in contact or not in contact.
It made a hell of a difference which, and there was no way to
know, if the set was on the blink.

Which it very likely was, and might have been since this
morning.

Depthcharges exploded on the port bow somewhere just as
Newton arrived and joined Flyte at the asdics. The explosions
indicated that the trawlers were, or at least had been, in contact.
They weren't close – but if it hadn't been for one or two you'd
heard during the Tripoli patrol they might have *seemed* close.

Ruck said, 'Diving stations.' He left Newton to deal with the
A/S equipment, and he hadn't said a word to McClure: he'd be
sorting *him* out later, no doubt, in private. He leaned against the
ladder, with a foot on its bottom rung and his hands up on one

above his head, looking like a man who couldn't for the time being indulge in the luxury of anger.

Paul reported, 'Hundred and fifty feet, sir', and switched the telegraph to 'stop pumping': he'd got her about right but she'd be light for'ard now, from the hands having shifted to their action stations.

Wykeham muttered, 'All right, shove off.'

He moved away, as Newton told Ruck, 'Definitely not working, sir.'

'The point is, can you fix it?'

U-class boats didn't carry engineer officers, let alone EMs, electrical mechanicians: they didn't have room for them. Hence a Chief ERA as head of the engineroom department, while the more specialist skills had to be called on from the base staff. Newton didn't know – unless it was some simple fault, like part of the external wiring.

'Do what you can.' Ruck ordered, 'Shut off for depthcharging.'

Screws were coming up the starboard side. A slowish, quite distinctive rhythm. He waited, draped on the ladder like a dummy hung up to dry. Listening with half-closed eyes, judging his moment. Watertight doors were swinging shut between compartments.

'Group up, full ahead together, starboard twenty!'

The other one might still be holding them in contact. No pings had been audible here inside the boat: but that didn't prove anything. Differing conditions, perhaps a different kind of asdic set . . .

'Twenty of starboard wheel on, sir.'

'Both motors grouped up, full ahead, sir.'

At times like this, voices tended to become quieter, tones flatter.

For Ruck, Paul realized, it would be a matter of getting the timing exactly right. He wouldn't want the enemy to detect his sudden avoiding action before the loss of contact hid it. Then he'd count on the exploding charges to provide him with an extra minute or two's cover.

Like – *now.*

The noise was deafening: the percussions coming like blows. A whole series: seven – eight – nine . . .

Total, nine.

'Group down, slow together. Stop starboard. Steer two-one-oh.'

That was another problem. *Ultra* had to get well away from the coast before she could surface to charge her battery. But under attack like this she obviously couldn't hold a straight course or maintain a constant speed. She had to crawl – as she was doing now – and spurt, as she'd been doing a moment ago, and dodge . . . And if she did manage to get out far enough, when the enemy knew for certain she was here – well, there'd be a night hunt too.

'Port motor slow ahead grouped down, sir.'

'Course two-one-oh . . .'

Southwest. Southwest was the course Ruck wanted. At least they weren't being driven in a totally wrong direction . . . Completing that other thought-sequence, though – if you were kept down all night, or most of it, it would mean starting the next day with a near-flat battery. All right if you were just going to plod up and down a patrol-line very quietly: but if there was any action, grouped-up business . . .

Newton was on his knees at the back of the asdic cabinet. Flyte had been replaced by Parker, the PO telegraphist.

Propeller noise, astern. Closing. Heads lifted, listening, as the sound developed into a regular *scrunch-scrunch-scrunch*, coming up the starboard side again. McClure murmured behind Paul, 'Hang on to your hat, Yankee-doodle.' Paul looked round, preparing some rejoinder, but the sound of the screws had suddenly begun to fade and he and McClure were staring at each other, forgetting each other's presence or even existence as they listened to it. Depthcharges might be in the water, floating down: most likely another batch of nine – any second now . . .

Nothing, except the underwater silence. The propeller-noise was a memory, an echo in the brain.

'Port ten.'

Ruck spoke quietly, and Creagh replied in the same low tone, 'Port ten, sir.' Light gleamed on the brass wheel turning in his hands. 'Ten of port wheel on, sir.' Almost a whisper.

Ruck told him, 'Steer one-five-oh.' Back to the course he wanted, now. He glanced round, at tense but slightly hopeful faces. 'Anyone so much as sneezes, I'll shoot him.' He asked the two harassed-looking characters at the asdic set, 'Any joy yet?'

'Don't know *what* to make of it, sir.' Parker shook his head. Pinkish scalp showed through thin, pale yellow hair. 'Job for 'em inboard, I reckon.' By 'inboard' he meant 'in the depot ship'; it made no difference that it happened to be a shore base.

'Course one-five-oh, sir.'

Ruck told Parker and Newton, 'Leave it now. Leave it switched off.' He looked at the clock: it was coming up for 5 pm. 'Silent routine. Pass the word quietly.' He meant not by telephone, but through the bulkhead voicepipes from compartment to compartment. 'We'll stay at this depth for one hour, then come up and —'

He'd stopped talking. Listening, to a distant churn of screws. A murmur: it grew – then faded. He waited a few moments, to make sure of it, then began again: 'One hour, then we'll go up and see what's what. *If* they leave us alone that long. Settle down, everyone.' He let himself down, to sit on the deckboards with his back against the slope of the ladder. Quinn sat too, and Pool, and the telegraphman. And if anything came south through the straits now, Paul thought – also squatting – nobody'd know it. Victory to the trawlermen, who'd have ensured some surface force a safe passage. But Ruck had no option, he *had* to get his submarine out to sea.

With or without asdics, Paul guessed, *Ultra* would be coming back inshore tomorrow. You could bet on it – on a whole day dodging around – deaf, most likely, and when she had to go deep, blind as well.

The hour dragged by. Two dreads lingered in his mind: one was the sound of the trawlers closing in again and finding them,

the other the likelihood of Bob McClure agitating for a game of
noughts and crosses. To make this less likely he edged away a bit
and turned his back on him, pretending to be asleep while he
listened – as everyone else was doing – for those screws. But it
was all right: at six, when Ruck ordered 'Open up from
depthcharging' and brought her up cautiously to periscope
depth, sky and surface were clear of enemies.

He pushed the handles up.

'Forty feet. Relax to watch diving, Number One. We'll surface
at eight.'

McClure had the first surface watch. It was rough: the boat was
slamming through the waves, and night air sucking down
through the tower was cold, made colder by the salt water
coming with it. Wykeham had proposed rigging the 'bird bath',
a canvas affair that fitted round the ladder to contain the splash-
ing, but Ruck said it wasn't worth it. He might have had a
premonition of what sort of night it was going to be.

Before eight-thirty a pair of MMM lights swung to the vertical position: McClure dived the boat, and what sounded like an
E-boat or Mas-boat passed over the top ten minutes later. Ruck
surfaced her again at nine.

Supper, consisting of hash with boiled potatoes, was ready at
nine-thirty. *Ultra* was steering south, to put a few extra miles
between herself and the Measures, with a standing charge on
one side to feed the battery. It was a case of starting from
scratch now, because an interrupted charge was useless. To do
any good it had to be maintained over a period of hours and
gradually reduced as the density of the electrolyte neared its
ceiling.

Ruck leaned back in the wardroom chair, and spoke in the
direction of the galley. Hoagy Carmichael's 'Stardust' was tin-
kling from the loudspeaker, a tenuous link with some other,
utterly remote world.

'Very good hash, Shaw!'

With the boat staggering around as she was, you had to hold

on to it as well as eat it. Shaw's stubbled countenance appeared round the bulkhead.

'I'll convey your compliments to the chef, sir.'

Wykeham muttered, 'My God!'

Ruck asked Shaw, 'Going to be a *maître d'hôtel* after the war, are you?'

'Gentleman's gentleman, sir, I thought.'

He'd withdrawn. Wykeham said, 'He's been reading Wodehouse. Sees himself as Jeeves, in a smart house in Mayfair, up to his goolies in buckshee port.' He looked at Ruck. 'Likely to be a bit tricky tomorrow without asdics, sir?'

Ruck hesitated. 'Well —'

The klaxon roared: ear-splitting, beating engine noise and the boat's violent, sea-bashing motion. Ruck and Wykeham vanished: Paul hung back to let the rush get by. The racket of the sea was all directly overhead, as her hull slipped under the waves leaving only the tower for them to hammer at; as he arrived in the control room McClure was just appearing, feet-first and soaking wet, and the needles in the gauges were circling past the twenty-feet marks. By this time the boat was quiet and steady, under all that turbulence.

'Looked like an E-boat, sir, reciprocal course, on the port bow.'

'Forty feet. Group down.' Ruck turned to McClure. 'Same fellow coming back, perhaps. Think he saw us?'

'No *reason* to think so, sir.' McClure muttered to Paul, unzipping his Ursula jacket as he edged past him, 'It's a real bitch, up there.'

It was where they had to be, though. Ruck gave the E-boat a quarter of an hour to get clear, then surfaced again. If it had been sitting up there waiting for them, he wouldn't have known: with no asdics, and the periscope useless in pitch darkness and bad weather, he'd had to take a chance on it . . . He said afterwards, shedding a wet oilskin in the gangway opposite the wardroom, just after 10 pm, 'Let's hope that's the last of it.'

Wykeham put his hands together and intoned, 'Amen . . .'

From the speaker over his head a girl singer was insisting huskily that all she needed was to know in the night the nearness of you. He opened his eyes and murmured, 'If I were in a position to oblige you, madam, be sure I *would*.' Paul was getting dressed for his watch: an extra sweater, and a towel around the neck under the Ursula. You'd think the jacket's hood would stop water going down your neck, but it never did. Sitting, now, to slide the trouser legs over his seaboots, so the boots wouldn't fill with water. In a U-class submarine's bridge you weren't far above water level even when the sea was flat: when it was rough, you were virtually *in* it. And the deck you stood on, in any submarine's bridge, had brass-bound holes in it, so as to let water run down when she surfaced; but water could fly *up* through them just as easily.

Ruck said, 'I hope not to see you again for a couple of hours, Sub. But for Christ's sake pull the plug if you have the slightest reason to.'

'Aye aye, sir.'

'And keep an eye on those bloody shore lights.'

With luck they'd be out of range of the Mysterious Measures by now, he thought, as he climbed up through the hard rush of air into the wet, bucking bridge . . . McClure told him that Ruck had given him hell for not having known those trawlers had been closing up on them. Up here on the bridge, after they'd surfaced at eight, he'd fairly chewed his balls off, he said . . . OK, so he'd left it too long without shoving the periscope up: he hadn't had any way of knowing the fucking asdics had gone for a loop, had he?

He went below, to his ration of corned beef hash . . . Those lights were only pinpoints, hardly visible even through *dry* binoculars . . . Salt water bursting over the bridge was more or less continuous, and from time to time green sea came solid, dumping itself right into it.

Searching, straining his eyes into the wet blackness, knowing how easy it would be *not* to see some threat close at hand: imagining *Ultra* as a dark, plunging shape in the overlapping circles of some enemy's binoculars. If you let yourself *feel* it, there was a hollow in your gut. But awareness of danger was, surely, essential to survival.

Twin points of light still horizontal . . .

He swung back, to search the sea ahead again: white-streaked, heaving. *Ultra*'s long and slim, bat-eared bow soared while her afterpart buried itself in the sea; then the bow came crashing down, smashing and ploughing black water into white foam that rolled aft engulfing, exploding upwards, outwards, overhead and underfoot, solid first and then its residue like heavy rain as her forepart came clear and began its climb again, the submarine rolling hard the other way after her dizzy tilt to port. Inside that forepart, that long gyrating tube of steel pointing like a finger at the clouds now, men were *sleeping* . . .

The towel inside his jacket was already soaked. It felt better to have it there when you went up on watch, but it never did any good. Jammed between the front curve of the bridge and the for'ard periscope standard, eyes slitted into flying sea, muscle-power exerting itself in natural opposition to the boat's unremitting attempts to dislodge him, he thought that one factor in *Ultra*'s favour tonight was that Italians weren't exactly celebrated as foul-weather sailors. They'd tend to be inside their harbours, or in sheltered water. Although that E-boat —

German, probably; E-boat as distinct from Mas-boat. So *that* thought hadn't got far . . . *Ultra* was listing hard to starboard, leaning over almost to the horizontal and then hanging, as if in two minds whether to swing back or to carry on over, turn turtle: and light sparked – grew – fierce, white, right overhead, flood-lighting a wide circle of surrounding sea. He heard one of the look-outs shout, 'Starshell!' and he was already turning and opening his mouth to shout, 'Down below!' Shutting the voice-pipe cock and a green wave slopping over as the dark figures behind him jumbled into one mass melting downwards, *Ultra* standing on her tail now as if to look up and see what the hell that flare was; Paul was in the hatch, a thumb pressing the klaxon knob while the other hand grabbed the underside of the heavy lid to drag it down over his head. Klaxon-roar down below and sea thunderous around the tower; one clip on, now the other: his fingers, stiffened by cold, fumbled as they slid the retaining pins into the clips. He slid clattering down the ladder.

Ruck was asking the look-outs, 'Starshell? *Sure?*'

Paul told him, 'More like an aircraft flare, sir.'

'Sixty feet.'

Steadying, as she nosed down into blessedly calm water.

From HM S/m *Ultra*'s log, night 26/27 March . . .

2250 Dived for aircraft flare.

2308 Surfaced. Co. 150°, 300 revs stbd, standing charge port.

2313 Dived, shore d/f lights vertical.

2328 Surfaced. Co. 150°, 300 revs stbd, stdg chge port.

0100 Altered co. 320°.

0445 Dived in posn 37°50'.5 N, 15°33'.4 E Altered co. 005°.

They'd dived on the watch – in Paul's watch. It had come as a surprise to be shaken for it at 0400 and realize there'd been no alarms since he'd turned in, half an hour after midnight. Now they were at periscope depth and nosing up towards the Messina Straits again with Cape dell'Armi eight miles on the bow; daylight was growing greyly from the east and the weather looked as if it might be moderating. There was shelter in here, of course, from the nor'wester.

Ultra's telegraphists had intercepted a signal at 0130 this morning to S10 from one of the boats patrolling off Taranto, reporting that heavy surface units had passed southward during the night.

'Up periscope.'

ERA Summers sent it up. The small after periscope, to start with. Without an operator on the asdic stool, the control room looked half empty. And it was a peculiar feeling, to have no hearing: you realized how much you'd relied on that machine and how handicapped you were going to be without it. He'd completed the search, left the small periscope to find its own way down into its well, crossed to the big one as it rose. Pulling the

handles down, switching to low power, to start with an air search.
Then, still in low power, a quick all-round inspection of the sea,
for anything at close range. For the third, slower search, he
switched on the magnification.

Still half dark. He could make out the lighthouse building on
dell'Armi well enough, and the left edge of land where the
coastal railway ran north through Reggio Calabria, but this was
only because of the land's height and the fact that the daylight
was getting to it before it affected the sea's surface. Periscope
range at sea level couldn't be more than four or five miles at
most, he guessed. Or three . . . 'Dip it, please.'

The brass tube slid down, paused, rose again.

Ahead, where the straits were, was an emptiness floored with
undulating sea and roofed with grey cloud, framed by a hard
edge of land on the right and a less distinct land-mass to the left.
He circled away from it, slowly right around, encountering nothing except one lonely gull gliding above and around the
periscope. Its curved yellow beak opened and shut soundlessly as
it squawked, banking black-tipped wings to the up-draught from
the sea. He settled on the hazy area of the straits again.

Two small, dark smudges. Like midges on a dirty window.

Gone now. You could easily imagine things, when you looked
too hard . . . Then he saw one of them again . . . the one to the
right. It had a white speck under it that appeared, then vanished, came again before he lost it altogether. The eyepieces
had misted: he reached up to the wad of periscope paper skew-
ered on a wire hanging from the deckhead.

Much clearer. And he could see them both.

Destroyers? 'Down.' He jerked the handles up. 'Captain, sir . . .'

10

Jack Everard woke suddenly – in *Sauerkraut*'s chart room, a
tiny space like a cupboard with a bench-like berth in it. He
threw off the blankets and reached for his boots and sweater.
Coming up for 7 am – on 27 March: Friday . . . The Chariot force
would be at about the limit of its run south: in fact they'd be
roughly on the same latitude as St Nazaire, though 160 miles
west of it. The intention was to circle southward and then turn
up, only changing to a direct course for the Loire entrance after
dark tonight.

They'd passed Ushant – seventy-five miles west of it – at midnight. It had been a pleasant evening, with moments of hilarity.
As Sharp had said – like a joyride. Yarning, playing cards and
cribbage: with all navigational responsibility in the hands of the
force navigator – an RN lieutenant by the name of Green, who
was in *Atherstone* – there'd been no strain on anyone. The training had been hard work and seemed to have been going on for
ever, and right ahead of them was the cliff-edge, the great leap
into the unknown; now, in this interval, with not a damn thing
you could do about any of it any more, there was time to draw
breath, crack a joke, sing a few songs . . . Songs had included
solos by Sergeant Bowater – his favourite numbers, repeated
several times, being 'Trees', 'Without a Song' and 'Old Man
River'.

Probably the same sort of thing had been going on in the

other ships as well. Although the MLs, those carrying commandos, must have been overcrowded. *Sauerkraut* was well off in that respect, since she had only two more than her normal German complement on board.

Jack left his little cubby-hole and went up into the bridge. Sharp and Dixon were both there, and Shawcross was on the wheel. Dixon saw him first, and nodded. 'Morning, sir.'

Sharp turned, then: 'Ah . . . Sleep well?'

Sharp seemed better at sea. Less idiotic, Jack thought, in direct ratio to distance from land.

The force was in its anti-submarine formation, the disposition for daylight passage that was designed to look like an A/S sweep. In the centre, *Campbeltown* with the MTB in tow had *Tynedale* and *Atherstone* on her quarters; ahead, and spread back in echelon to the beams, the sixteen MLs formed a screen, spaced out ahead and down the sides in a shallow inverted V. *Sauerkraut* was keeping station astern of *Tynedale*; on her starboard beam, two cables' lengths away, the MGB was in tow of *Atherstone*.

Last night, when Jack had turned in, the force had been in night cruising order, three straight columns plugging southward under a hazy-looking moon. The moon would be full tonight, for the assault: the two requirements, a spring tide and a full moon, happening to go together.

'When did we open out like this?'

'About three-quarters of an hour ago . . . Pretty sight, eh?'

It was. The morning was clear and bright: the ships and launches dipped and swayed to a low, blue swell, bow-waves curling sharply white.

'Flag-hoist on *Atherstone*!'

Dixon reported it, with his glasses up. It would be the order for altering course southeastward: and it was coming right on schedule, since the time was just on 0700. Answering pendants were already either close up or pausing at the dip on all the other craft. Sharp called back to his signalman, 'Close up!' He told Shawcross, 'Follow *Tynedale* round, when she turns.'

Dixon said, 'Executive signal.'

The flag-hoist was dropping, fluttering bright-coloured down from the Hunt's yardarm. All the answering pendants were coming down too as the leading ships put their wheels over. The MLs would have to adjust their speeds as well as courses, the inside ones slowing and those to starboard speeding up, to maintain formation on the turn. Jack took out his cigarette-case: 'Smoke, Tubby?'

'Thanks.'

Sharp had dated the blonde Wren, Maureen, for next Wednesday evening. It happened that Wednesday would be April Fools' Day, but he said she hadn't caught on to that. And in any case – he'd suggested tentatively, wanting Jack's reaction – 'We *might* make it, don't you agree?'

'Why not?'

Before Wednesday, though, if they 'made it' at all – long before that he, Jack Everard, if he was alive and mobile and back in England, would be in London, and the hell with Falmouth . . . But he didn't think much of Sharp's taste in women – preferring that blonde to Paul's little number, Sally . . .

Early yesterday evening, when they'd been steering south-westward down the coast of Cornwall, he'd explained to Sharp – and afterwards separately to Dixon, because the Canadian had to be in a position to take over if Sharp was killed – that if the Möwe-class torpedo-boats were still in the St Nazaire Basin when the attack went in, re-embarkation would have to be from the Old Entrance, not the Old Mole. He'd been discussing it with PO Slattery and Sergeant Bowater first, then invited Sharp to join them – down below, with the E-boat rolling quite a bit at that stage, Sergeant Bowater feeling the effects and trying not to show it.

'Main point as far as you're concerned, Tubby, is that if the commandos find they can't hold this bridge' – he touched the plan of the port layout – 'because of fire from the Möwes, then none of the people who've landed that side of it will have any hope of getting through. We, and all the commandos working on that side of the Old Entrance, will need to be taken off about here, instead.'

Sharp had seemed suspicious of it, as if he thought Jack was changing the plan on his own say-so. He'd wanted to know why he hadn't been warned about it before.

'It's a new development. We've been hoping they'd shove off out of the way – then there'd have been no need for any variation. Maybe when the time comes they *won't* be there – in which case you stick to your original brief, naturally.'

'How'll I know, one way or the other?'

'Well, you'll be told, for Christ's sake. By the naval force commander. I suppose you stick to the original intentions unless you get orders to the contrary. OK?'

'Seems a bit vague, doesn't it?'

'I'd have thought it was quite explicit.'

Sharp pointed at the jetty in the St Nazaire Basin. 'If they're here, how the hell can you do *your* job?'

'That's what the three of us have been chewing over. And the short answer is we ignore the bastards.' Slattery laughed; Bowater managed a smile. Jack explained, 'Captain Roy's commandos, No. 5 troop, will be a lot closer to them than we'll be. OK, so we may get some interference from them too, but it needn't stop us commandeering the E-boat and firing its torpedoes at our target. Here – the completed section of submarine pens, the south end of the new construction.'

'Wouldn't it be about as useful in the long run, and a lot easier particularly if the Möwes are there, to fire them into uncompleted pens?'

Sharp was suggesting this because the unfinished part of the U-boat shelter was right opposite the supposed E-boat berth. There were five pens not yet roofed and nine finished, reported to be in use. Jack explained, 'In the operational pens there'll probably be some U-boats. Crewless, because they take the crews off to La Baule every night.'

'Sounds as if they're expecting us!'

'Cosseting their precious submariners. Just a precaution. But any U-boats in those pens are just as much our targets as the pens themselves. Think how much effort – ships, men, weeks at sea, etc. – it takes on average to sink one U-boat. We might bag a couple in one go – *and* smash up their shelter.'

'Pity we couldn't get my *Sauerkraut* into the basin, use her fish as well.'

'Signalling ahead to the Germans to open the lock gates for us?'

'I know it's not on.' Sharp sounded testy. 'Just a pity, that's all. Obviously we couldn't get inside, and in any case we've got to be outside to re-embark you.' He shrugged. 'In one place or another, now.'

'That's another point, Tubby,' Jack explained. 'Whether it's at the Old Mole or the Old Entrance . . . It'd be very neat and convenient if we could perform our task, fall back to the embarkation point and find you waiting for us, step aboard and buzz home . . . But actually, things don't work out like that. There'll be a lot of casualties, of men and craft, and very few of the landing force can reckon to go home in the ships they came in. Our own NTU party may very well be split up. It'll be all sixes and sevens, and largely a matter of pot luck – first come, first served.'

'You're saying I fill up with anyone who's ready to take off?'

'What else could you do? Tell a crowd of wounded commandos their tickets are for different seats?'

'Well, I take the point, but —'

'Is that orders, sir?' Slattery asked Jack. 'Survivors embark in whatever's there with room for 'em?'

'Yes. It's how it'll turn out, anyway. As I see it, the only likely survivors in terms of transport will be this boat, the MGB and the MTB. And if we can get ourselves back aboard this one, fine, obviously . . . But I wouldn't rate any of the MLs' chances very highly.'

'Nor would the ML skippers.'

Sharp had said it. He added, 'The ones I've talked to, anyway. All that bloody fuel on deck . . .'

He'd muttered later, on the bridge, 'Should've brought Maureen along . . .'

It *had* been an enjoyable evening. Even with Bowater's singing and Leading Torpedoman Merrit's mouth-organ . . . Jack flicked his cigarette-stub away down-wind. The MLs were all in station again now, settled on the new course. They'd be on this one until midday.

'*Tynedale*'s flashing, sir!'

Shawcross had seen the Aldis-lamp flashes – not *Tynedale*'s but *Atherstone*'s as she acknowledged her consort's message word by word. Then *Atherstone* asked *Tynedale*, 'What did you see?' Jack had read that himself: he went out of the enclosed, minuscule bridge and up on to its roof, for a better field of view. Most of the NTU team were farther aft, grouped around the stern Oerlikon . . . He had a better height of eye from up here, but unfortunately no binoculars . . .

Tynedale was under helm, turning away to port. *Sauerkraut*'s signalman yelled, 'U-boat on the surface red nine-oh, sir!'

It looked like a floating box, out on the port beam, a long way off. A U-boat's conning-tower . . . *Atherstone* was casting off the MGB and turning to follow *Tynedale*. Exhaust smoke coughed out of the MGB's stern as it got its own engines going, and Sharp had cut *Sauerkraut*'s speed to give *Atherstone* room to pass ahead.

The U-boat was still there, on the surface and apparently at rest. Either it hadn't seen the Chariot force or it was busily reporting their numbers, course and speed before it dived. *Tynedale* already dwindling into that far distance, and *Atherstone* with a pile of foam under her counter as she cracked on speed . . . If the U-boat hadn't seen the MLs and *Campbeltown*, Jack guessed, it mightn't spot them at all now, since the two Hunts were right in the line of sight: and when the Germans woke up to *their* presence, they wouldn't have time to spare for much else.

The crack of *Tynedale*'s 4-inch guns was a plain statement that she'd caught the U-boat napping. Which was just as well. The one thing Operation Chariot would *not* be able to survive would be to be recognized or suspected as a raiding force and reported, so that German coastal garrisons would be alerted.

Those muffled thumps were depthcharges. Sharp panted, joining him on the bridge roof, 'It must have dived. Thought they'd have got it *before* it . . .' He had his glasses trained on the scene out there. He shouted, 'They *have* got it! It's come up again!'

Blown to the surface by those charges? Jack took Sharp's word for it. All he could see were the end-on shapes of the destroyers – although another outbreak of gunfire seemed to confirm what he'd said. Sharp told him, 'Can't see much now. It broke surface, then *Atherstone* was in the way and now it's gone.' He offered Jack his glasses. 'Want a decko?'

The raid would still go ahead, Jack thought, even if the U-boat *had* sent off an enemy report.

'Keep her up!'

'Sorry, sir . . .' Wykeham had let her dip to thirty feet. Getting her back up now, though. Ruck was at the periscope, although the ship's company was still at watch diving. Course was 005 degrees, with one motor slow ahead. The battery had only had a partial charge, as a result of the night's various alarms, and it was essential to conserve its power.

'Three of the bastards, now.' He folded the handles up. 'Down.' Glancing at the depthgauges, seeing the needles static at twenty-eight feet now, he told Wykeham, 'It still doesn't look like anything more than an A/S search.'

There might be something more interesting cooking up, and there might not be. When Paul had spotted the two destroyers he'd thought *Here it comes, the target we've been waiting for* . . . But they'd gone back northward. Now, in the middle of the afternoon, they were working their way southward again and there were three instead of two. And unless there was something good coming along behind them, they weren't in the least welcome.

Lacking asdics, *Ultra* could only know what was happening by staying up at periscope depth and watching it. Once they were forced to go deep she'd be the booby in the game, blind and deaf and hunted by enemies who had eyes and ears.

Ruck nodded to CERA Pool, and the periscope began its upward slither.

'Stand by for a fix. You there, pilot?'

McClure came out of the wardroom, and propped himself against the chart table. 'Standing by, sir.' Ruck circled first, an all-round search; then he paused to inspect each of the destroyers in the narrows to the north. Now he was taking bearings – a right-hand edge of land, the dell'Armi lighthouse, a left-hand edge. Back on the destroyers: and then air search, all round.

'Down.' He went over to the chart table. 'They're searching every inch up there. Must think we're crazy.'

'What kind of destroyers, sir?'

'Biggish. Could be Aviere or Oriani class . . . Where does that put us?'

McClure drew in the last of the three bearings. Ruck touched the chart with the end of a pencil. 'Our Eyetie friends are here. Well to the north. We can stay as we're going, for a while.' He looked round. 'Number One – we have three destroyers, between green two-oh and red three-oh. Keep tabs on them, and also a good eye out for seaplanes. If there's any change I want to know *prontissimo*.'

'Aye aye, sir.'

'I'll be having a mug of tea.'

While he had the chance, Paul thought the implication was. He was on edge – expecting developments, whatever he'd said about it being only an A/S search. He came through now; and McClure left the chart too, flopped down on the bench beside Paul. Ruck muttered, taking the chair, 'Bloody asdics. It's infuriating not to be able to handle one's own simple maintenance.'

Next door, the periscope hissed up.

Ruck called, 'Shaw? Tea, please. And bread and jam. Make it fast, will you?' He asked McClure, 'Why are asdics called asdics?'

'Search me.'

'You know?'

Paul shook his head. Ruck told them, 'Anti Submarine Detection Investigation Committee. Set up in 1917.'

'*That* long ago?'

He nodded. 'The system wasn't developed until much later, between the wars. At Portland. We gave it to the Yanks in 1940. They had a system of their own called sonar, that wasn't nearly as good, so they switched over to asdics although they went on calling it sonar. Unfortunately we also gave it to the French – in '39 – so the Germans got it when France surrendered. And of course they've passed it to these locals. And to the Japs . . . *Shaw!*'

'Coming, sir!'

Rattling some cups, to prove it . . .

Wykeham called, 'Captain, sir?'

Ruck shot through. The others sat still, listening. Shaw appeared and hovered with a laden tray; Paul beckoned to him and he put it down, more quietly than usual. Wykeham's voice carried from the control room: 'They're coming towards, sir. Two on the port bow and the other's about dead ahead.'

Periscope's hiss; click of its handles opening out. Shaw still standing in the gangway, listening.

'Starboard ten.'

'Starboard ten, sir . . . Ten of starboard wheel on, sir.' That was West, one of the torpedomen, on the wheel. Periscope still up. At least there was broken water up there, so *Ultra* did have *something* going for her . . . Ruck's voice: 'One Cant seaplane now.' Click of the handles. 'Dip.'

They heard it sink, stop, come up again.

'Steer oh-nine-oh.'

'Oh-nine-oh, sir . . .'

Eastward, to sneak out of the Italians' path. Or to try to . . . McClure poured two mugs of tea, and Paul took his to the chart table where he could see what was going on. Ruck was completing a low-power circuit and settling with his sights trained on the beam, the direction from which the destroyers were coming: slightly abaft the beam, as *Ultra* settled on her new course.

'Course oh-nine-oh, sir.'

'Slow ahead together.'

To get out of their way a little faster.

'Dip.'

Then it was up again and he'd switched to low power, circling. He muttered, '*Two* Cants now. We've been upgraded.'

Paul looked round at McClure. There had to be something
coming through, surely, with all this activity. Didn't there?
McClure muttered, 'Looking for *us*. They know we're here –
unless they're bloody daft . . .'

'Dip again, Chief.'

The destroyers couldn't be all that close, but he was being
very cautious with the periscope. The seaplanes, of course . . .
He'd begun a new air search. Cants were ideal for A/S work,
because they were so slow-flying. Like kites drifting around. He
was making a second quite rapid circuit in low power; switching
to high power now and starting again, more slowly, down the
port side first where the destroyers were, pausing to check on
each of them and then swinging on. Looking astern now – at
Sicily – and sweeping on, round to the starboard quarter and
slowly up that side.

He'd stopped, caught his breath. Back the other way: to and
fro . . . Then he'd snapped the handles up. 'Down. Starboard fifteen. Diving stations!' Paul, flattening himself against the side of
the fruit machine as the attack team came rushing to their stations, saw Ruck laugh – a short bark of it, shaking his head . . .
He told Wykeham, 'Coming the wrong bloody way – *northward*!'

'But what —'

'Five destroyers, and a cruiser's foretop astern of 'em.'

He'd finished being chatty, though. 'Up . . .'

Surface forces coming north – *from* some convoy action, if
there'd been one?

'Steer one-four-oh.' Turmoil subsiding, and the periscope
rising to his summons. Paul saw him glance at the unoccupied
asdic stool: he'd be thinking something like *Of all the times to go
deaf* . . . But he'd gone calm too. He'd been taken by surprise, but
the tactician and mathematician were in control now – assessing

the problem, deciding how this game could best be played.
There'd be an entirely different sort of game later, but for the
moment he'd only be thinking about winning *this* one. Spinning
round, his weight hanging from the periscope's spread handles,
pushing himself round with his toes against the rim of its well,
his body an extension of the periscope itself. The three destroyers north of them would be coming up astern – on the quarter
now, possibly *just* clear astern . . . Ruck knew: he could see;
everyone around him had to guess. He'd completed another fast
circuit and now he was motionless, studying the northbound
squadron.

'Start the attack. Bearing – *that*. Range – *that*. Target is a
cruiser. I'm – five degrees on its starboard bow. Down.' Moving
swiftly to the other periscope, the little one, he told them,
'There are two cruisers. Looks like one of the new Regolos
astern.' He snapped the handles up. 'Sixty feet. Half ahead
together!' Propeller noise ripped overhead as she dipped her
bow, driving deeper: he'd cut *that* fine enough . . . The range was
twelve thousand yards – six miles – and the enemy warships'
course 360. *Ultra* was only five degrees on her target's bow, so
unless the Italians zigzagged one way or the other she'd be well
placed for an attack. The course for a ninety-degree torpedo
track would be 270 degrees.

The destroyer had passed over and the sound of its fast-
revving propellers had faded ahead. Several pairs of upturned
eyes had seemed to watch it pass – eyes watching white-
enamelled deckhead and the orderly maze of piping, minds
seeing a destroyer's keel and thrashing screws. Those three had
swept the narrower part of the straits, and now they'd have been
whistled up to join the northbound pack.

'Set enemy speed twenty-five knots.'

Paul turned a knob on the fruit machine. 'Twenty-five knots
set, sir.'

'Sixty feet, sir.'

Ruck nodded: emerging from a brief period of thought – or
mental arithmetic. He took down the tannoy microphone, and

thumbed its switch on. 'D'you hear there. Captain speaking. We
have two Italian cruisers approaching from the south. Still some
distance away. I'm going for the leading ship, which I *think* is
either the *Giovanni delle Bande Nere* – however the hell that's pro-
nounced – or her sister ship the *Luigi* something. They've got
destroyers screening them, and two seaplanes over them, so we
may get a few whumpfs later. In fact we'll shut off for
depthcharging now, and be done with it.' He switched off. Then
switched on again. 'Stand by all tubes. Depthsetting twelve feet,
TI.' Hanging up the microphone he told McClure, 'Check what
the *Bandy Knees* draws, in *Jane's* . . . Twenty-eight feet, Number
One.'

Watertight doors were shut and *Ultra* was nosing up towards
the surface.

'All tubes ready, sir!'

He had the after periscope, the small one, coming up. Needle
in the gauge passing forty feet – thirty-five . . . The periscope was
right up and he had his eyes pressed to it as the boat rose; he'd
be seeing the polished rolling underside of the surface before
the top lens broke through sudden turbulence into an explosion
of light and the wavetop-view seascape and skyscape . . . Spinning
round; then he'd finished with it, transferred to the big one, fingers twitching impatiently for it as Quinn brought it shooting
up.

'Bearing is – *that*. Range – *that*. I'm —' he checked the stac-
cato flow of information. 'Damn him, he's altering!' In low
power now, a fast circuit; then back on the target . . . 'Right. I'm
now – right ahead of him. *Down*.' For about three seconds he was
getting the problem straight and its solution settled in his mind.
Then: 'Sixty feet. Group up, half ahead together. Port fifteen,
steer oh-nine-oh.'

'The *Bande Nere*'s mean draught is fourteen feet, sir.'

'Fifteen of port wheel on, sir!'

Depthsettings of twelve feet were about right, then. And enemy
course was now 015 degrees. Ruck was at the track chart, beside
McClure, as McClure put on the second range and bearing.

'What does a Regolo draw?'

He checked. 'Thirteen feet, sir.'

Ruck nodded. He could shift target if he had to without adjusting the settings on the fish.

'Enemy speed looks more like twenty-six, sir.'

'Set that.'

Course for a ninety track would be 285 degrees.

'How long like this to take us 800 yards off track?'

'Four minutes, sir.'

And they'd been running for one minute already. Ruck went back into the middle of the control room. At the end of the fourth minute he'd turn inward on to his attacking course: he'd be inshore of the target, between the cruisers and the Italian coast as the squadron cut past that headland.

With not much room to spare, Paul guessed.

'What's my DA?'

'Thirty-eight degrees, sir. Red three-eight.'

Two minutes, since he'd altered course and put on speed. *Ultra* trembling, as she always did, from the grouped-up effort – from a battery that hadn't had its full charge last night . . .

Three minutes. A burst of propeller noise astern and above them as a destroyer passed over, close. Ruck let out a breath hard, as if he'd been holding it for a long time.

'Forty feet.'

'Forty feet, sir . . .' The hydroplanes swung to bring her up. Ruck said, for general information, 'Most of the screen's on the seaward side. Ahead of them and down their port side. Only one other this side.'

Wykeham reported, 'Forty feet, sir.'

Ultra had been running blind for three and a quarter minutes.

'Group down, slow ahead together.'

Cutting it short of the four minutes he'd intended. If there'd been no changes of course up there, he'd be nearer 700 yards off track than 800. Off-track in this case being the distance the torpedoes would have to cover after they left the tubes. They ran at forty knots, so over 700 yards the running-time would be thirty-one seconds . . . His thoughts froze for a moment as screws scrunched overhead.

Transmitting? In contact, even? Without asdics, you didn't *know . . .*

But if that had been Ruck's 'only one other', was *Ultra* now *inside the screen?*

'Both motors grouped down, slow ahead, sir.'

'Twenty-eight feet. Port twenty. Stand by tubes.'

Turning and rising, to attack; Ruck standing ready at the after periscope. 'What should the target bear now, pilot?'

'Two-four-oh, sir!'

'Up.' He'd flicked his fingers; Quinn lifted the short steel lever and the wires hissed around their sheaves.

'Twenty of port wheel on, sir.'

'Steer two-eight-five.'

'Two-eight-five, sir . . .' Creagh eased the rudder angle.

Thirty-five feet. Thirty-three. Dead quiet: *Ultra* could have been alone . . . Ruck had the periscope trained to the right bearing, inching the periscope around to hold it there as the boat swung to her firing course. At thirty feet he put his eyes to the lenses.

'Course two-eight-five, sir!'

'*There* . . .'

A smile, or a grimace of satisfaction: half a dozen other pairs of eyes saw it. Imaginations picturing the cruisers and the pack of destroyers, the periscope-top poking out of the waves between the warships and the Italian coast.

'Twenty-eight feet, sir.'

Studying his target. Then circling fast. Back on the cruiser; and pulling his head back to check the bearing-ring. Sweat gleaming on his forehead. Paul repeated, in case he needed the reminder, 'DA red three-eight, sir.'

Charlie Pool's hands, over Ruck's shoulders, held the periscope on that aim-off bearing. Ruck would see the target cross that line of sight, and his torpedoes would go out on a course thirty-eight degrees to the right of it, the way the tubes were pointing now. Torpedoes travelling at forty knots and the cruiser steaming at twenty-six would run to meet each other.

Paul reached to his left, to the edge of the chart table, thinking, *Touch wood* . . .

'Stand by.'

The torpedoes were the ones he'd seen loaded yesterday, with their polished steel warheads and long sleek bodies gleaming in blue shellac. They were about to leave home. Lying there now in their tubes, about to perform the function they'd been made for, groomed for. Alternatively, to miss, lie rusting for years to come in the silted bottom of the straits . . . He watched the taut, muscled face, the intent, day-glistening eyes. Wykeham concentrating on the trim: to allow the boat to dip below the ordered depth, blinding Ruck at this crucial moment, would be the crime of crimes . . .

'Fire one!'

Muttering: something about a seaplane. Then: 'Fire two!'

Lips moving: judging by his expression, cursing an inquisitive Cant. Eyes seeming to burn with that reflected light in them. 'Fire three!'

No asdics, for confirmation that the fish were running. Ruck's lips parting again: and a pause, before – 'Fire four!'

Men gulping, swallowing, to clear their ears after the four successive jumps in air-pressure. Ruck had slammed the handles up: 'Dip it.' About to allow himself the luxury of seeing his torpedoes hit?

Or *not* hit . . .

'Running-time on 750 yards will be' – the periscope came back into his hands – 'what, half a minute?'

'Thirty-four seconds, sir.'

He'd pulled the handles down, jammed his eyes against the lenses, a split second before an explosion from ahead rocked the submarine.

'*Got* him!'

Then a second one. At such close range, the boat *felt* them.

Ruck announced, 'Abaft the second funnel . . . I'd say that'll do it . . .'

Sink her, presumably he meant . . . Silence now. A gap of more than the firing interval. Still, even *two* —

Three!

'That was – what the hell . . .' Scowling, at the periscope . . . Then, 'My God, one of the screen! A destroyer, out on the beam, she's – Christ, she's *gone*!' He'd banged the handles up, and stepped back. 'Sixty feet. Port ten, steer' – he thought about it for a second – 'two-seven-oh.'

Laughter, comment, congratulations . . . He shut them up. Creagh repeated, 'Steer two-seven-oh, sir.' West – across the straits, probably passing close across the tracks left by the ships he'd torpedoed. Hoping the Italians would expect him to retire the other way, east or southeast?

There was a sense of triumph: echoes of the torpedo-hits rang in memory. And rising behind that, now, awareness that as likely or not *Ultra* would have to take her own medicine.

'Make that a hundred and fifty feet.'

'Hundred and fifty, sir.'

'Course two-seven-oh, sir.'

Ruck had the Tannoy microphone in his hand: he tapped it to make sure it was working. 'D'you hear there. We just scored two hits on the leading cruiser. The third hit sank a destroyer. My guess is that two hits with that depthsetting on a 5000-ton ship doing twenty-six knots will almost certainly sink her. How a fish set to twelve feet managed to hit a destroyer drawing at most nine is a question for CPO Gaffney, not for me . . . Now we're likely to get a bollocking, so – silent routine. Not a whisper.' He switched off. 'Stop one motor when the trim can stand it, Number One.'

'Aye aye, sir.'

Going the wrong way *might* fox them. And it was highly desirable, with so many destroyers up there, to do so – to get away undetected. Those weren't trawlers, they were fleet destroyers, crack ships manned by professionals; and if they did locate her,

Ultra's deafness would severely limit her capacity to take effective avoiding action.

Ten past five . . .

Ruck had adjusted the course to 250 degrees as soon as he'd reckoned to have passed the Italian squadron's tracks; since then *Ultra* had been motoring very quietly southwestward across the southern approaches to the straits, her snout pointing towards the Sicilian coast about halfway between Taormina and Riposto.

More than an hour had passed since the attack: there'd been no asdic contact, no charges dropped. Twice, destroyers had passed close enough to be heard. Perhaps asdic conditions were poor, with the sea churned up by recent bad weather; and to start with there would probably have been survivors in the water, which would have inhibited the destroyers or preoccupied them.

Hitting a shallow-draught destroyer with a deep-set torpedo: Ruck had come to the conclusion that the destroyer might have been pitching, her bow deep in the sea, when that fish had reached her after passing between the two cruisers. That, or the torpedo's depthkeeping hadn't been too accurate . . . He glanced up at the clock now: it was a good half-hour since they'd heard the last propeller noise.

There'd been eight destroyers, and *Ultra* had sunk one. At least two would have continued northward with the other cruiser, and another two would very probably have busied themselves rescuing survivors. They'd have gone off, too, to land them at Messina. Leaving three. But then again, Messina was only fifteen miles away, and some of those others could very easily return to join the hunt.

'How far have we come, pilot?'

McClure got to his feet. 'Must be roughly in the middle, sir.' He checked the log, for the distance run, then bent over the chart to put on a DR position.

Ruck said, from his customary position – seated – by the ladder, 'Let's have both motors slow ahead now.'

Chief ERA Pool passed the order aft, by way of the bulkhead

voicepipe. In silent routine, the telegraphs were too noisy to be used.

The depthgauge needle, in the one gauge that wasn't shut off, was motionless at 150 feet. There was no sense of movement whatsoever. Warmth, silence, and surprise at having been left alone all this time; hope growing that it might be possible to creep away, having got this far.

Pool came back from the bulkhead pipe. 'Both motors slow ahead, grouped down, sir.'

'Thank you, Chief.'

McClure told him from the chart table, 'We're seven miles two-two-eight degrees from the dell'Armi lighthouse, sir.'

Ruck got up. Stretching to ease cramped muscles, he went over for a look. He muttered, after a few moments' considera- tion, 'Might come round to south now, I suppose.'

Paul hoped he wouldn't. It would be the most direct route away from this now over-populated area, and it would also be the course for home, and in the circumstances – the convoy opera- tion would be over by now, *Ultra* had only one torpedo left, and these waters would be distinctly unhealthy for a day or two – 'home' did seem the obvious place to head for. But it was also what the enemy would be expecting, he guessed. And so far this westerly course had *worked* . . .

On the other hand, he realized, since it was now getting towards 1730, and the usual surfacing time was about 2000, if they did *not* turn south how could *Ultra* be far enough off the coast to surface even a couple of hours later than usual?

'Well.' Ruck came back from studying the chart. 'We'll start moving out. Want to be up in time for supper, don't we? Even if it's a late one.'

CPO Logan muttered, 'Not *too* late, let's hope.'

'Hungry, cox'n?'

'Well, sir.' The wide shoulders shrugged. 'Put it like this. I wouldn't say no to a nice juicy steak – touch on the raw side – with onions an' French fries and a couple of grilled tomatoes, and a pint or two of —'

'Bloody 'ell.' Lovesay, on the fore planes, couldn't stand it. 'I *mean —*'

Screws churned over the top. The first they'd heard for nearly three-quarters of an hour.

Nobody spoke, or looked at anyone else, until Ruck said quietly, 'Port ten.'

'Port ten, sir.' Creagh had almost whispered the acknowledgement. 'Ten o'port wheel on, sir.'

'Steer one-eight-oh.'

South. If they'd altered a few minutes ago, Paul realized, they might not have been treated to that shock . . . No sound now, anyway; it had come, and gone. But which way to turn, or when – blind and deaf, you might as well spin a coin . . . Then he heard the pings: little squeaks, like a creaky shoe walking on the outside of the hull. He'd lifted his head to listen to it: meeting Ruck's eyes, and seeing Ruck listening too.

'Course one-eight-oh, sir.'

'Very good.'

Propeller noise to port: and over the top again. Attacking . . . Ruck leaning against the ladder, looking displeased. He told Wykeham, 'Use telegraphs now.' The screws passed over in a sudden rush. He snapped, 'Group up, full ahead!' All through the boat, in the other compartments isolated behind shut and clipped watertight doors, they'd have heard the destroyer go over, and they'd feel the burst of speed by which Ruck aimed to get out from under the charges which would now be floating down . . .

The pattern exploded astern. Only one charge was quite close, throwing the trim out so that the planesmen had to work hard to get the bubble aft again and regain the depth. A lot of cork came down, littering the deckboards.

It wasn't only the submarine that had been shaken. Brains had, too. Reality had returned. Awareness that any notion you could sink cruisers in confined waters and just walk away unscathed had been ridiculous.

'Group down. Slow both motors.' Staring at the depthgauge.

Knowing that whatever he decided it would be just another gamble.

'Two hundred feet.'

'Two hundred feet, sir.' The hydroplanes swung over. The operators moved their wheels to apply dive angle or rise angle, and miniature hydroplanes in the indicator dials followed the movements of the planes themselves – which were in effect horizontal rudders fore and aft. *Ultra*'s bow tilted downwards. No sounds from the surface. If she'd had asdics there'd have been plenty: Ruck would have known when the next attack was coming and from which direction, and where the ship was that was holding them in contact . . . As things were, he only knew it when it happened: as it would again, in a minute, or two, or three. Sound here inside the boat dropped to a quiet murmur as the power came off. The men at the various controls were blank-faced, carefully expressionless.

Screws churned over. From astern. It had come abruptly, ceased abruptly. Whether or not it had been an attack, or just one of them happening to pass over . . .

'Two hundred feet, sir.'

Overhead, the sea exploded. The separate charges in the pattern of five seemed to run closely on each other's heels, making one drawn-out eruption. The submarine, already nose-down, was diving deeper, the echoes of the crashes ringing, her steel reverberating like a gong struck with a hammer.

'Half astern together.'

'Half astern together, sir!'

To slow her, take the way off her, the forward impetus that was also driving her downward. Wykeham and the planesmen hadn't been able to get her bow up: she was passing 260 feet – 270 . . . Screws running astern . . . Logan had had his after planes angled to drag her stern down and thus tilt her upwards, but with stern-way on he'd need to reverse them. Wykeham had got the pump going on the midships trimming-tank.

Levelling, at last. 'Stop together.' Depth 285 feet. She was only tested to 300. 'Slow ahead together.'

'Two-fifty feet.'

'Two hundred and fifty, sir.'

You paid for everything, always. If you drank too much you paid with a hangover, if you whored around you got a dose, if you sank an Eyetie cruiser you got this. They'd sunk a destroyer too, and those were the destroyer men's chums up there: *they'd* have some ideas about exacting payment.

Screws scrunched over, eighty yards overhead.

'Port twenty. Half ahead starboard.' To turn her faster as she circled away to port. 'Steer oh-six-oh.'

'Steer oh-six-oh, sir . . .' Creagh's 's' sounds were sibilant, because of his jagged front teeth. Ruck ordered, 'Slow together.' He added, glancing round at them all like a father with his family, 'Always sounds worse than it is. That lot wasn't *really* close.' There were nods, here and there. Wise nods of experience, dutiful ones of acceptance. Then upheaval, thunderous and vicious, the submarine flung upwards and over to starboard as if she'd been rammed and knocked sideways. Charges still exploding as the lights went out: in pitch blackness you felt the bow drop, deck angling steeply, and the gyro alarm began to shriek. Paul had been thrown across the gangway and McClure was on the deck at his feet. Emergency lighting flickered and glowed weakly. McClure, struggling up, pushed himself aft towards the cage where the gyro switches were. Several other men had been thrown off their feet. With the gyro toppled, Creagh would be steering by magnetic compass. The main lights came on again as that raucous alarm bell cut out, but the boat still had a steep bow-down angle.

'It's Q flooded, sir!'

Quinn, pointing out to Wykeham that the quick-diving tank's indicator light was flashing: hence loss of trim, the dive, the angle on her. 'Outboard vent must've been blown open, sir.' He'd got it shut again now, and Wykeham asked Ruck quickly, 'Blow Q sir?' You *had* to – unless you wanted to test the chart's accuracy, the sounding of about a thousand fathoms here. *Ultra* was at 375 feet and still diving steeply. More depthcharges exploding – astern, comparatively shallow-set. Ruck ordered, 'Blow Q!'

A/S men on the surface would hear it. But they already knew where their target was.

Bow coming up. Depth four hundred feet. McClure came shambling back from his trip to the gyro gear, muttering, 'Bloody hell, I mean, fuck *this* for a lark', and shaking his head as if he felt things had really gone too far. Four hundred and five feet on the gauge, but she'd be rising now. None too soon. Quinn shut off the air to Q and reported it blown; he and Pool were glancing around the inside of the pressure-hull as if expecting leaks to show. Quinn was bleeding from a gash on his forehead: he'd obviously been thrown against something sharp. She *was* coming up now, but she was still a hundred feet below her tested depth.

Ruck sat down on the asdic stool. 'Hundred and fifty feet, Number One. Report damage from compartments.'

Screws churning over.

'Starboard ten. Group up, full ahead together.'

How many destroyers up there hunting, Paul wondered. One team in action and another standing by for when that lot's depthcharges had been used up? With Messina so close they could go home for more, run a shuttle-service.

Motors grouped up, speeding. 'Steer east.'

'Steer east, sir.'

Logan murmured, 'Never did like Italians.'

Depthcharges bursting like a roll of thunder on the quarter. The more nasty ones you heard, the less the off-target ones disturbed you. This lot rolled the boat a bit and shook some more cork off the deckhead. Ruck said, 'Losing their touch.'

Too much to hope they'd lost their target.

'Group down. Slow together.'

'Chief.' Wykeham glanced round at Pool. 'May be something wrong with the after pump.'

'Permission to go aft, sir?'

Ruck nodded. Pool went to the watertight door and began to

wrench the clips off it. Ruck called, 'Tell 'em I hope we'll be out of this before much longer, Chief.'

'Course east, sir.'

Rising past 240 feet.

And past five-thirty, too. On what day? Paul found his mind dug its heels in, resented being asked the question. Because *this* was the world, not the one outside where they had days with numbers and names on them? Who bloody *cared*! 200 feet on the gauge. He forced an answer out of his memory: it was a Friday, and the twenty-seventh day of March, 1942. Coming up quite fast. There'd be pressure in Q tank, from having blown it, and at some point they'd have to vent it. You could vent it inboard, but the internal pressure then, on top of the torpedo-firing, would be a long way above normal. If you vented it outboard you'd send a great bubble to the surface and give away the boat's position. If they didn't have a good idea of it already.

Screws passing over. Gone.

That mental disturbance a minute ago: was it because the only thing that mattered was surviving this, so that a question not directly related to that end was an irritation and unacceptable?

Neurotic: better watch it. Trouble was, he realized, having no work to do; in present circumstances he didn't have a thing to do except stand around and listen.

Still grouped down. Worried about the battery, of course. If this went on into the night there'd be good cause to worry, too. And *wouldn't* it, if there were enough destroyers up there to share the work and cover all possible directions of escape?

Reports coming in from the other compartments were of only minor breakages – light bulbs, and the TSC depthgauge blown out, and a leak on the after heads, where the hull-valve had been blown off its seating. Chief ERA Pool was back. Braidmore, a leading telegraphist, was reclipping the watertight door behind him. Pool reported, 'After ballast pump's had it, sir. It's the suction-rubber —'

A pattern of depthcharges exploding overhead, shallow-set but noisy . . . He finished as the rumbling crashes died away, 'I'd say it's the suction-rubber, sir. Pressure from outboard —'

'All right, Chief. Thank you. What about the heads?' Ruck glanced round. 'Stop starboard.'

'Quinn here'll fix that in two shakes, sir.' Pool grinned, Quinn scowled. He was constantly having to work on the blowing-gear of the heads, and it was a job he detested.

'Starboard motor stopped, sir. One-fifty feet, sir.' Wykeham reached to the order-instrument. The loss of the after trimming pump wasn't any disaster, in normal circumstances, as long as the for'ard one didn't stop working too. The trouble was, one defeat did so often seem to lead to another.

Propeller noise, very faint, just for an instant . . .

'Seems to be the second eleven batting now.' Ruck got up off his stool. 'Let's see if we can't lose the bastards . . . Starboard fifteen —'

'Starboard fifteen, sir.' With that motor stopped, she'd turn fast. Creagh reported, 'Fifteen of starboard wheel on, sir.'

'Steer south.'

Paul could hear asdic pings again. Perhaps they'd been audible before and he hadn't noticed them; but they were there again now all right. He thought, *Second eleven's learning fast* . . . He saw Ruck's expression harden as he heard it too. So it *had* just started.

Screws churned over, as *Ultra* swung around to starboard. Right over the top and as sudden as a passing train.

'Group up, full ahead together!'

He remembered a nightmare concept he'd considered, during the last patrol – of no amount of dodging doing any good, the enemy always there and in contact no matter what tricks you tried . . .

Ultra vibrating, noisy under grouped-up motor-power. Precious, to-be-conserved battery-power.

'Both motors grouped up, full ahead, sir.'

'Course south, sir!'

They'd have tracked her, on that turn. The one holding her in contact would have.

'Starboard twenty.'

Depthcharges thundered on the port quarter. Then one closer, abeam: she seemed to shift bodily sideways, recoiling from the shock of the explosion. Lights had flickered, then steadied: she'd rocked back, and the sea was quiet again.

'Twenty of starboard wheel on, sir.'

'Stop starboard.'

No pings now. Not audible ones anyway. *Ultra* mouse-like, circling away to starboard, driven by her port screw alone. Circling as quietly as she was able, out of the churned-up water. Ship's head on west now, and circling on: Ruck, standing behind Creagh, had his head bowed, listening. She was pointing north now, towards the Italian coast, and still swinging.

'Midships.'

'Midships, sir.'

Easing the rudder-angle off.

'Meet her, and steer northeast.'

'Meet her, sir.' It meant putting the rudder the other way, to counter the swing. 'Steer northeast, sir.'

One mouse, blind and deaf and with several minor injuries, trying to steal away . . .

In a lousy direction, too, from the point of view of being able to surface when the dark came – for that very reason it probably wasn't a direction in which the cats would expect any mouse in its right mind to be crawling.

'Course northeast, sir.'

Six-fifteen. In about an hour and a half it would be getting dark up there.

At six-thirty, everything was still quiet. Wykeham murmured, 'Looks like you did it, sir.'

Ruck was on the asdic stool. He moved off it, to sit on the deck with his back against the ladder. 'We'll give it an hour.' He pointed upwards. 'If *they* will. Until seven-thirty.'

Everyone sat. Some – including Paul – dozed, occasionally. He was dreaming about a girl called Sally, a very pretty little Wren he'd known in Scotland: she had a way of kissing that could go on for hours and, since kissing was all she'd do, could just about drive you mad. In the dream she'd just taken her mouth off his and whispered, 'All right, I *will* go to bed with you,' and Wykeham, still on his feet behind the planesmen, announced, 'Seven-thirty, sir.' Paul opened his eyes, acutely disappointed, and saw Ruck getting to his feet.

'Let's have a look at the DR now, pilot.'

'Here, sir.'

Paul looked at it too, over Ruck's shoulder. He had a crick in his neck, possibly from his activities in that dream, the kissing . . . If McClure's figuring was accurate, *Ultra* was now six miles off shore, roughly midway between dell'Armi and Spartivento. Ruck muttered, taking measurements with the dividers, 'Last night's experience suggests we should be a good twelve miles off the coast, to surface clear of those Measures. That's minimal. On the other hand we must get up there as soon as possible, or the battery'll give up on us. *But*' – he was talking to himself, aloud – 'it'd be silly to steer south from where we are now, because that's precisely where they're looking for us. So, making it southeast so as to skirt around them – making say four knots, with the set – right, pilot?' McClure agreed. Ruck used dividers again. 'There. We'll be twelve miles off at – 2145.'

He came back into the control room. Paul was thinking about the destroyers hunting around for them farther south, and the chance of being caught again. At this stage, it would probably be fatal.

So it wouldn't happen. Another thought in the back of his mind was that the sooner he could get back to sleep and take Sally up on that offer, the better.

'Number One – bring her round to southeast, and open up from depthcharging.' Ruck glanced at the telegraphs: the starboard motor was still stopped. 'Slow ahead together. Relax to watch diving – but I want *quiet.* Cold supper . . . All things

being equal, we'll go to diving stations at 2145 and surface at
2200.'

Soon after nine-thirty, Ruck and Paul got dressed for the bridge.
Red lighting had been burning in the wardroom and control
room for the past hour; so that your eyes would adapt themselves
more quickly to the dark. And it was quite enough to see by:
poker dice, for instance, were perfectly legible.

Not that Paul had played, this evening. First there'd been
supper to eat, then he'd been for'ard seeing to the loading of
their last torpedo into number four tube.

Ruck's intention was that when they surfaced he'd go southeastward at full speed on the diesels for the first hour, to put
another dozen miles behind them; then the battery could have
a standing charge from one engine until the dive at dawn. The
battery was so near to being flat that Wykeham didn't want
Roffey to take readings: however bad it was, there was nothing
he could have done about it.

At 2140, Ruck told Wykeham to take over from McClure and
bring the boat up to forty feet. She'd been at 150 all this time.
McClure, relieved as officer of the watch, paused at the chart to
lay off Ultra's return courses to Malta. The run southeast first,
which would take her to a point twenty-five miles off Cape
Spartivento, then the turn southwestward, and he had her surfacing tomorrow night, the twenty-eighth, just fifty miles short of
Malta. He said to Paul – Ruck had gone through to the control
room – 'Probably enter about midnight.'

'Bloody shame. Nobody'll see the Roger with its two new red
bars.'

'Oh, fuck the Roger, let's just get there!'

As if Malta was some kind of sanctuary . . . Perhaps he'd forgotten he'd been machine-gunned in the rest camp, and that
they were bombing the Sliema flats now?

Or perhaps he only wanted to hear from home. From his parents, to know they were all right, recovering from the news of his
brother's death. That might well be it.

There'd be positive news about *Unslaked* too, by now.

Wykeham asked Ruck, 'Diving stations, sir?'

The prospect of getting up there, into dark, cold air, and the diesels driving her out into open water clear of enemies was – well, *fantastic*. After the hours of helplessness . . . Ruck nodded, with a glance at his watch.

'Yes. I do believe that's —'

He'd checked.

Looking round, Paul saw him standing quite still and looking upwards, frowning slightly, listening . . .

Screws came over in a rush and passed down the starboard side. Before the sound diminished and disappeared, they'd begun to slow. Nothing, now – except the soft hum of one motor running on the last vestiges of battery-power. Dim red lighting glowed on stubbled, anxious faces. Paul thought, still watching Ruck, *It's passed over: he'll still surface, make a run for it in the dark – won't he?*

Ruck motionless, still listening. Head down, eyes half closed. Then he sighed: and Wykeham whispered, 'Oh, *bloody* hell . . .'

Asdic pings. And Ruck's expression, as he glanced up. For less than a second, Paul could read the truth in it: this surfacing *had* been their last hope.

11

'Flashing.' Dixon leaned into the enclosed hutch of the E-boat's bridge. 'Fine on the bow here.'

And right on cue . . . Sharp, and Jack Everard, moved over and saw it too – just to the left of *Campbeltown*, whose dark shape *Sauerkraut* was tailing at eleven knots with the Chariot force now in its shape for the passage up-river. That flashing would be coming from the bridge of the submarine *Sturgeon*, who'd been sent on ahead to position herself as marker, marking the departure-point for the final stage, the run-in to the target.

Just after eight o'clock this evening, in the early darkness, the force had stopped and redisposed itself into the assault formation. *Sauerkraut* had moved up astern of *Campbeltown* and lain waiting, rolling gently to the swell, while the launches formed columns in line astern on either side and the MGB ran alongside *Atherstone* to embark the force commanders and their staffs. From there on the course had been northeast, towards the river mouth: the MGB leading, torpedo-carrying MLs flanking her, the other pair bringing up the rear of the columns and MTB 74, no longer under tow, riding hard astern.

Atherstone and *Tynedale* were somewhere back there in the darkness. They'd been tailing the force this far, but now they'd drop back and spend the night patrolling, and be here to cover the withdrawal in tomorrow's dawn. Two other Hunts were being rushed to join them, too, from Plymouth, because those

five Möwe-class torpedo-boats were reported to have sailed from
St Nazaire and to be at sea now – somewhere or other . . .

'There's *Sturgeon*.' Sharp passed Jack his binoculars. 'Red
three-oh. See her in the gaps between the MLs.'

A low, black shape: displaying no flashes now. She'd done her
job. And the force navigator had done his, too, leading the ships
to this point after all the southward detour and half a dozen
course changes. All he had to do now – he'd be in the MGB with
the force commanders – was guide them into the river and over
its shallows to their target.

If *Campbeltown* did make it across those mud-flats . . .

C-in-C Plymouth's signal about the Möwes had come just after
5 pm. Good news for Jack and the NTU, but potentially bad
news for the force as a whole. The success of the operation
depended on achieving total surprise, and a naval battle in the
Loire wouldn't exactly help.

But with luck, the torpedo-boats would be right out of the way,
steaming off on some other errand. In which case, they'd have
timed their departure very nicely.

Tynedale and *Atherstone* had kept that U-boat down, hunting it
with depthcharges, for two hours this morning; then they'd left the
area on a southwesterly course, so that if it had surfaced to send off
an enemy report signal it wouldn't have endangered the security of
the operation. By 11 am, under gathering cloud – the weather was
deteriorating, proving that forecast's accuracy – the two destroyers
had been back with the rest of the force, in day-cruising order.
Then there'd been some French trawlers to cope with: three were
boarded and their crews taken off before they were sunk. *Tynedale*
had dealt with two, and the MGB with the other; it had been necessary because those trawlers sometimes had Germans on board
with W/T equipment.

One ML had dropped out, with engine trouble, but its commandos had been transferred to one of the torpedo-carriers,
who'd started with no troops on board.

Now the submarine's dark shape had disappeared astern.
Looking at it, Jack had had thoughts of young Paul, knocking

around the Mediterranean in some more or less similar craft. And wondering whether Paul *would* have written to Nick about Fiona: not that it would make any damn difference now . . . He came in from the wing of the little bridge, and gave Sharp back his glasses. Roughly thirty miles to go, now . . .

In the bridge wing again an hour later, not long after 11 pm, he heard the drone of bombers going over. Cloud-cover was shutting out the moon they'd expected, and it might interfere with the RAF's diversionary attack on the port. After all that high-level fuss . . . But in the last of the daylight this evening, clouds had also hidden this force from any reconnaissance flights the enemy might have had up.

He'd called his team together to give them the good news about the Möwes. Bowater had asked, 'Then after you've shot off the torpedoes, sir, will you bring the boat in like you thought you might before, along where the torpedo-boats have been?'

'I don't know, Sergeant.' He shrugged. 'Depends how it works out. We may go alongside, or just abandon her and swim, or if we haven't had to use the plastic we might have time to pack her with it and send her off on her own somewhere. But if you're not on board with us when we shove off, you fall back to the commandos' bridgehead. Or to cover elsewhere – depending . . . You'll see for yourself what we're doing, and you'll just have to use your loaf – whether to stay with the commandos and withdraw with them, or join us, or get the hell out on your own.'

Dewar had promised, grinning, 'We'll be there to fish you out of the drink, I'd guess, sir.'

You couldn't spell it out in detail. So much depended on how the take-over of the E-boat went, how much opposition there was, how long it took to get the boat off the quay and to a firing position opposite the U-boat shelter. The naval section of the NTU would have to be on board the E-boat, obviously – Jack and Slattery driving it, ERA Pettifer looking after its engines, and the torpedomen first casting off the securing lines and then preparing the torpedoes for firing. The Marines might end up on board too, or they might be left on the quayside – just depending what

the situation was when they got there. There'd be guns directed
at them from across the basin and also quite possibly from other
ships tied up around its sides, and there might be Germans on
the quays and in the surrounding buildings. The Marines' job
was to fend off opposition and provide protection to the naval
party while they did *their* job, but it was impossible to say exactly
what this would involve.

They all understood this; they'd discussed it dozens of times
and practised it a dozen different ways. It was still natural
enough, at the last minute, to go over it again, making sure that
all the answerable questions had been answered. Jack added, 'If
we were being shot up at the south end of the basin, there'd be
no point your trying to join us. You'd be better trying to give us
covering fire from the commando area.'

In the northeast, at midnight, gun-flashes were visible: St
Nazaire's AA defences in action against the RAF . . . The landing
party checked their weapons and equipment. It wasn't a pleasure-
cruise any more, and there were no songs left to sing.

He was below, sorting his own gear, when *Sauerkraut*'s engines
stopped. He rushed up to the bridge, and as he arrived the boat
was getting under way again.

'What happened?'

'*Campbeltown.*' Sharp lowered his binoculars. 'She hit the putty
and just about stopped.'

It happened again a few minutes later. The ordered speed was
still eleven knots, and she slowed suddenly to about half that. It
wouldn't be any joke to run aground on this high tide. If she
stuck now, she'd *stay* stuck.

'She's off. Half ahead, cox'n.'

Dixon said, with glasses up, 'Northern shore's in sight.'
Pointing. 'There, on the bow.' He had a flat way of talking that
matched his phlegmatic, down-to-earth character; the steadi-
ness was a contrast to Tubby Sharp's more volatile
temperament . . . But this was crazy, really: they'd come 450
miles across open sea, as strange and noticeable a collection of
craft as you could imagine, and they were expecting to take an

alert, intelligent enemy by surprise? And to make an assault in wooden boats with petrol storage on their decks? Take *that* for granted, as if it could reasonably be expected to work out as planned?

Air activity seemed to have petered out. They'd seen gun-flashes, and searchlight beams like pencils of far-off light, but if there'd been any bombs dropped they must have been little, quiet ones. And now, *everything* was quiet. At 0045, on Saturday 28 March . . . Boat's engines grumbling, swirl and splash of the Loire water, the night tide rising to its peak.

Time passed slowly. Time *hurt* . . .

Campbeltown hadn't grounded again, after that second scrape. Pretty soon the explosives expert in her would be activating the time-fuse in what had been her for'ard messdeck. She was intended to blow up at some time between 5 am and 9 am.

By which time, Jack thought, so many currently insoluble questions would have been answered, passed into history and the more immediate simplicity of life or death.

'Hey, damn it!' Tubby Sharp – indignant . . . 'Put those bloody things *out*!'

Searchlights, on the shore . . . One on each bank: and the banks weren't as far apart here as they had been lower down. Sharp yelled, 'Don't you know this is supposed to be a *surprise*?' Against those beams you could see the two columns of MLs silhouetted like black cut-outs. The beams swung to meet each other – and joined, a wide road of glaringly bright light clear across the river. *Astern* of the little armada plugging on towards its target . . . Then both lights suddenly switched off. Sharp said, '*That's* better.' He snorted. 'Bloody cheek!'

Speed of advance fifteen knots now.

At 0110 Jack went below to get himself ready. Whitened webbing, ammunition, blue torch, Colt .45 by courtesy of the commandos, Lanchester sub-machine gun through the kindness of the Royal Marines. He cast an eye over the others, checking that they were properly kitted up, including the three torpedomen's haversacks of plastic explosive.

Everyone very quiet now. Ready, and yet *not* ready. Needing to get on with it, as if there was a time-fuse in each one of them.

'We're all set, then.' They agreed. He warned them to stay below, under cover, until he gave them the word to come up. Hesitating on the point of wishing them luck, he decided it would have been meaningless. They knew as well as he did what they were up against and how much luck they needed. Looking at them, he realized suddenly that he really did *know* them – and was one of them . . . It was a revelation: they were ten men of entirely disparate types and backgrounds, but they formed one entity and he was part of it, as well as its leader. Looking at them he was also seeing himself – clearly, perhaps for the first time ever. Understanding this, his mind opened to a second revelation – that he understood *Nick* Everard too, with the same suddenly cleared view: almost as if he *was* Nick . . .

He was back in the bridge at 0120, ten minutes to zero-hour. Sharp told him, 'Two miles to go. You lot ready for the off?'

'Ready enough.'

And still no guns were firing. This crowd of small ships steaming up an enemy river – nobody seeing them, nothing opposing them?

0122: a searchlight flared out from the shore to port. *Campbeltown* suddenly, brilliantly illuminated. More searchlights coming on: the whole force was flood-lit. He held his breath, thinking, *Here we go* . . . But the ships, lit up, were still chugging up-river, closing on their target. From the leaders black water folding back, swirling white and rolling outwards, heaving in their wakes and outspreading to wash both shores. Ships astern, like *Sauerkraut*, pitching steadily across the wash. As lit up as players on a stage – with German gunners on those banks as audience. *Campbeltown*'s German Ensign was clear to see in the brightness surrounding her: and with those slanted funnel-tops she did look German.

Flashing now – morse, from the port area, a challenge calling on the ships to identify themselves. Sharp observed, 'It's going to get noisy in a moment, boys. Oh, my nerves . . .' Shawcross and Dixon laughed. But *Campbeltown* was flashing an answer to the challenge: she had a German-speaking signalman on board and he'd been primed with the signal-letters of the torpedo-boats she resembled. He was also ready with a claim – in fast German morse – that the squadron was about to enter harbour 'in accordance with previous orders'.

He wasn't saying *whose* orders.

The shore station had acknowledged that message. Searchlights were being switched off, one after the other, their beams dying back across the river's surface.

Dixon muttered, 'Would you *believe* it?'

A light AA gun opened fire, somewhere ahead. Possibly from the Old Mole. And another outburst of flashing from *Campbeltown*. Protesting . . .

The firing ceased. Force Chariot pushed on towards the port area. Just a few minutes now to touchdown. Then, suddenly, several shore guns opened fire. More joining in – as if they'd all simultaneously realized that they were being duped. Tracer arcing out at the ships: shells whirred over. *Campbeltown* was hit immediately: a searchlight held her in solid white light as the German flag came tumbling down and a White Ensign rose rather grandly in its place. Under her own colours she was free to fight now. Her guns blazed into action, and the whole force was returning the German fire: pompoms, Oerlikons, bigger guns, commando mortars, Hotchkiss, Brens . . . Searchlights from the shore blinding gunners and helmsmen. *Campbeltown* was being hit repeatedly but she was dishing it out too and holding her course and speed. Tracer criss-crossed multi-coloured as the force poured its heavy fire-power, the abundance of Oerlikons particularly effective, against the shore defenders.

Sharp was at the controls beside PO Shawcross, both men shielding their eyes against the searchlights and watching *Campbeltown*'s stern, keeping *Sauerkraut* glued to that wake; and *Campbeltown* following the MGB which was passing the end of the Old Mole now – *that* close, point-blank, and a gun on the end of the mole still in action . . . Abaft the E-boat's beam to port was the long eastern arm of the *avant-port*, and then the warehouse area; the heaviest volume of fire seemed to be coming from ahead, but several searchlights had been shot out and as the E-boat swept past the end of the Old Mole that gun on it was hit and wrecked. Another at the shore end of the mole was in action, with tracer-streams from several MLs' Oerlikons licking at it. *Campbeltown* taking a lot of punishment, and abreast the mole she'd altered course; Shawcross was putting his wheel over now, to follow her round to port. She'd have a straight run from where she was now to the dock caisson – if she didn't blow up before she got there. The MGB with the force commanders on board would peel off to port, leaving the destroyer to press on. It was 0132 now: two minutes *past* zero-hour. The port column of MLs was curving away to land their commandos on the Old Mole – or try to – and one of them was already on fire. Jack was looking that way when tracer came streaming low from some-where ahead and part of *Sauerkraut's* bridge roof shattered and flew away, with a lick of flame spreading aft. The MGB had turned to port, brightly illuminated by searchlights and gun-flashes; explosive bullets lashed across the E-boat's forepart, the screen on her port side disintegrated: Dixon had yelled some-thing and dived over towards Sharp. *Campbeltown* going strong, holding on, guns all in fast, continuous action: he was looking at her, seeing a shell burst orange-red on the side of her bridge, when she hit the centre of the lock gate. Bullseye . . .

Dixon bawled, 'Come around to port a little!' Shouting it at Shawcross. Jack let Sharp down: he'd fallen back against him with a wet pulp where his head had been. Dixon was at the throt-tles, slowing her, getting set to slide in alongside *Campbeltown*, who was at rest now, embedded in the caisson. One of the star-board column of MLs, burning, swung in close across *Sauerkraut's* bow, out of control. Having avoided her, Shawcross obeyed Dixon's order. Half a minute, and they'd be alongside, but going aft to get his team up Jack saw several other MLs in trouble. The after part of this E-boat's superstructure was burn-ing too. Slattery was in the hatch, with his tin hat on – which

Sharp had *not* been wearing, Jack realized – and the others grouped behind him. Jack asked him, 'Got my Lanchester?'

'Here, sir.' Romeo Merrit passed the gun out, and Jack fixed it on the webbing harness to leave his hands free. Tracer everywhere and noise building. He shouted to Slattery, 'Hang on a minute.' No point having them up too soon, and a lot of point keeping them under cover. *Campbeltown*'s flash-lit bulk loomed closer, higher; an ML close to port, heading into the Old Entrance, was being hammered by what looked like Bofors fire, and commandos who'd been ready to jump ashore were going down in heaps. It could happen here, too: *Sauerkraut* slewing in, with her stern still on fire, towards the destroyer's waist. Tracer hammering at the superstructure over their heads, ricocheting away in streams of lethal, screaming colour and shells or mortars exploding up there too. But she was their bridge to the dockside and they had to get on to her and over her. He yelled to Slattery, 'Come on!' and poised himself to jump the closing gap.

Echoes of the last crashes still quivered in his skull. There'd been about ninety charges dropped since the Italians had found them again at ten o'clock. It was nearly 2 am now and there was no sign they might let go.

They'd lost her once – for about ten minutes. At least, inside *Ultra* they'd *thought* they'd lost her.

'Two hundred feet.'

'Two hundred, sir.'

'Port twenty.'

Creagh's wheel whirled. 'Twenty of port wheel on, sir . . .'

Depth and course were the only things Ruck was varying now, in his attempts to evade the attacks. There was no question of using bursts of speed, grouping up the batteries. It was one reason there wasn't so much chance now of the destroyers losing her again.

'Steer one-double-oh.'

'One-oh-oh, sir.'

Calm, low-key. Ruck set the tone. He couldn't stop himself sweating, but from his general manner you'd guess he still saw reasonable prospects of getting away.

There did have to be such prospects, too. Paul couldn't shift this out of his mind, the plain but inexplicable certainty of it. He didn't want to lose it, really, only he just kept feeling for it and finding it still there, like a rock that wouldn't budge. There was no justification for it that he could see: but then he was, he reminded himself, inexperienced, ignorant, whereas Ruck and Wykeham knew a lot about this business and obviously *did* expect to get her away from the tormentors.

Screws over the top again. *Scrunch-scrunch-scrunch* . . .

Coming down now: canisters floating down, while their pistols filled —

And detonated, burst . . . A noise that could have been the submarine's hull bursting: the blast threw her about, shook her . . .

Angling down again as the residue of noise boomed away. She'd been changing depth from 150 to 200 feet, and she was passing 200 now at a steep bow-down angle. Fore planes hard a-rise, after planes scooping to drag the stern down, get the angle off. That pattern had been near them and disturbing, but it had been shallow-set and a bit ahead of her. There'd been several worse, in the past few hours. Nothing breakable and loose was intact inside her now: even the glass faces of shut-off gauges had been shivered into splinters. Levelling . . .

The Italians might run out of charges?

Otherwise – apart from the senseless conviction that survival was something you could count on – what way out *could* there be? There was no chance of surfacing, so the battery couldn't be charged and soon she'd have no power at all. And the air, which was already wearing thin, couldn't be renewed. After a certain time you'd suffocate. This wasn't speculation, it was fact. It would be getting towards daylight up there in about three hours, and you couldn't surface in enemy waters in daylight, even if the hunters went away – which they would *not*, of course . . .

'Two hundred feet, sir.'

'Very good.'

Ritual acknowledgement in a soothing tone.

The after periscope gland was leaking badly again, worse than it had off Tripoli. It was supposed to have been fixed in Malta before this patrol, but obviously the fixing hadn't been thorough enough. A couple of dives out of control down to 400 feet and more, plus the hammer-blows of pressure from close depthcharges, must have dislodged some of the packing. Chief ERA Pool had his eyes on it nearly all the time, as if he was expecting it to get worse.

Ruck glanced over towards the helmsman. 'Starboard fifteen.'

'Starboard fifteen, sir . . .' Grunting to himself as he spun the wheel. 'Fifteen of starboard wheel on, sir.'

Until now, Ruck had only made alterations when charges were actually on their way down. He was varying his tactics now: trying anything that occurred to him because his old, well-tried dodges hadn't worked?

It was that nightmare concept coming true: the brick wall whichever way you turned. And one disability leading to another: the loss of asdics, now a dying battery and air turning to poison. That leaking periscope gland wasn't anything much – not for the moment – nor was the fact that the after ballast-pump was out of action. Not yet.

Pings. Squeaking on the hull. Tiny, nasty . . . Better not to hear them if you could help it. But you couldn't help it: you listened because you wanted them *not to be there* . . .

Screws coming over again. *Ultra* still circling. The screws passed over, and he could hear the pings again. Usual routine: one ship holding *Ultra* in contact while the other one attacked. While holding the contact, it would be reloading its depthcharge throwers and resetting the depth at which the next pattern but one would explode. But there could easily be more than two ships up there.

'Midships.'

He'd put the rudder the other way, Paul guessed, when the

charges began to go off. As they would at any second now. McClure began to sing in a jerky whisper, 'Hold tight, hold tight —'

'Hold that Tiger.' Harry Roy . . . Or was it Alexander's Ragtime Band? Wykeham was the expert in that area. Alexander's best-known, most-played dirge was the music-goes-round-and-round-and-it-comes-out-here thing. McClure wagging his head to the whisper-singing, with his eyes shut. The exploding charges punched her bow upwards and flung her like a dart towards the surface. Ruck snapped, 'Open one main vent!' Because letting her break surface would be doomsday – they'd ram or blow you to bits. He was on the deck, on his hands and knees: he wasn't the only one who'd been thrown across the control room. Quinn wrenching the lever back. The point being that the explosions might quite likely have driven air into the tank from underneath through its open kingston: you had to vent it to let that air out. She was levelling – at eighty feet. Seventy-five . . .

'Open two, three, four and five main vents.' Then, immediately, 'Shut main vents.' Because leaving them open was dangerous, one of the great thou-shalt-nots . . . Screws passed over – louder-sounding, because she was closer to them, nearer the surface. But getting down: passing the hundred-feet mark. Ruck checked the ship's head, realizing he hadn't given Creagh a course to steer: 'Starboard twenty.'

Hundred and twenty feet.

The pattern went off to port. *Ultra* rolled away from the pressure-waves. The deckhead leak spurted, then slowed again.

'Can you do anything about that, Chief?'

'Not much, sir. Not as would help for more than a few minutes.'

'We'll just have to live with it, then.' It had slowed more, anyway. 'Steer oh-two-oh.'

'Oh-two-oh, sir!'

Creagh sounded bright and chirpy. Ruck muttered to Wykeham, 'D'you realize we've still got pressure in Q?'

'Yes.' Wykeham nodded. 'Realized it a minute ago, sir, when I was thinking about flooding it to stop us breaking surface.'

They couldn't vent it now, anyway, because of the air bubble it would send to the surface. It would be dark up there still, but the Italians would have searchlights on the water, watching for the fruits of their unpleasant labours.

Nobody knew what the weather was like up there now. It was about eleven hours since they'd had a periscope up.

Screws raced over. *Right* over, by the sound of them. And if they went on for long enough —

'Hundred and fifty feet, sir.'

Vickers-Armstrong would be gratified, he thought, if they could have seen their handiwork standing up to such a battering. But it couldn't last for ever. Sooner or later, he warned himself, there'd have to be one final pattern, one really close one; the thing was, to be ready for it. Not to be caught off-guard . . . And still, even recognizing the facts of this situation, there was the hope, the idea that something like – well, the destroyers using up all their charges, or —

A depthcharge burst to port, close enough to rock her violently the other way and throw her bow up; then one that sounded as if it must have exploded almost *on* the fore casing seemed to fling her astern. She was standing on her tail-end like a seahorse, ringing with the crashes and – he thought, jammed between the bulkhead and the chart table – *finished* . . . Three more charges then, all around her, shaking her and buffeting her so that the deckboards lifted, rattling, and slammed down again. The lights went out and he heard what sounded like woodwork snapping somewhere below or to his right. The boat was tilting over now, toppling bow-down, men and objects sliding and banging around and the sound of loudly spurting water.

Emergency lights came on. In the others it wasn't a switch that had thrown off this time, it was simply that the bulbs had been smashed in their sockets. Wykeham told Ruck, 'Pretty sure some battery-containers went, sir. I *think* in number one.' The luminous needle in the gauge showed they were passing two hundred feet: she had a steep bow-down angle again and she was going downwards fast.

'Full astern together!'

'Full astern together, sir!'

For how long? Half a minute, before the batteries gave up the ghost?

A whistle from the voicepipe in the after bulkhead. Pool went to it and answered the call. A voice reported thinly, 'Voltage is falling off very fast, sir!'

'Stop together.'

'Stop together, sir . . .'

Still going deeper. Minimal lighting throwing deep shadows. Light caught the leak on the gland, gleamed on spouting, cascading seawater. Ruck told Quinn, 'Blow one main ballast.' Quinn wrenched the valve open on the panel. It was all happening very fast, all within seconds of the final crash of that last pattern, but each word or move in isolation, and set in the weirdness of the circumstances, seemed to mark the passage of a much longer time. It would be different, Paul suspected, if he'd had work to do.

'One main ballast blowing, sir!'

Yelling, to be heard over the rush of HP air. Which the Italian A/S men might well be hearing too. Guessing, if they did hear it, that the submarine they were hunting was in trouble. Depth now 340 feet.

'Stop blowing!'

Quinn jammed the valve-wheel shut. He used a wheel-spanner, his personal possession, as highly polished as old silver. *Ultra* was on an even keel at 365 feet. Now 362 . . .

'Slow ahead port.'

'Slow ahead port, sir . . .'

'Get Roffey in here to check the battery tanks . . . Ship's head?'

'Oh-two-three, sir.' Creagh's tone was apologetic for being three degrees off the ordered course. Ruck moved over to the chart table, and Paul moved out to give him room. Ruck wanted the battery tanks checked to find out whether it was true that some containers had been cracked. If they had, acid would be leaking out of them into the tank they stood in. Then if salt water got into the same tank, you'd get chlorine gas seeping up through the deck.

Chlorine . . .

It killed fast, and painfully. There was already a peculiar smell, and it very probably was gassing from the batteries, but it wasn't chlorine. Not yet. This sort, from a played-out, damaged battery, was heavy, hung close over the tops of the cells. He *thought* he remembered being taught this . . . Ruck said from the chart table, 'Two hundred feet, Number One.'

Screws pulsed over. The same warning every time . . . Ruck's tone had been normal, unflustered; he looked haggard, but so did most people after the tension and sleeplessness of the past twelve hours.

'Two hundred feet, sir.'

Wykeham's voice was normal too. And shallow-set charges were exploding ahead. The first bad shots for quite a long time.

'Want me, sir?'

Roffey: rotund, harassed-looking. Worried for his precious battery. And who wasn't . . . Ruck told him, 'Check both tanks for cracked containers, would you?'

If there were some cracked, he'd find acid in the bottom of the tanks. Pool had dragged the A/S stool over to the after periscope, and he was standing on it to get at the periscope gland in the deckhead. He was soaking wet, taking the whole brunt of it. It wouldn't have been so bad if the water had run straight down into the periscope well, but at the rate it was leaking now even the well would have filled up before long. Two resulting factors would be, first, chlorine gas, from the salt water getting into number two battery tank, and, second, the fact that the boat would be taking in extra ballast, and she lacked the battery-power to run the pump and compensate for it.

Nobody would know how it had been, down here. Submariners who'd been through very bad attacks would have a good idea of it, could guess; but it would always be, ultimately, a private matter. For *Ultra* as for *Unslaked*, and all the others who'd gone before them and would come after. You took your story with you.

'Two hundred feet, sir . . . Open one main vent?'

'No. Hang on with that for the moment.'

'She's light for'ard, sir.'

'Can you hold her down on the fore planes? Lovesay?'

'I reckon, sir. Just about.'

Screws rushed over. Ahead, Paul thought. Ruck might have thought so, too; he told Creagh, 'Starboard fifteen. Steer oh-nine-oh.' If a batch of depthcharges was floating down ahead, why motor into them when you didn't have to? He was talking to McClure now . . . 'All right, we *can't* be very certain of it, but we must still be roughly about – well, say in this patch here.' He'd pencilled a circle on the chart. 'Agreed?'

McClure nodded. He grew stubble unevenly: Paul had told him only this morning that he looked like a badly worn lavatory brush. If he and Ruck were right about *Ultra*'s position, she was quite close to Cape Spartivento and southeast of it. They'd been on mostly easterly courses all through the first hours of this long period of persecution, and there was also a southeasterly set just here. Ruck tapped the chart with a pencil. 'So we've got shallow water north of us. All along here. Look – two miles out, and less than fifty feet.'

So what? Lie on the bottom? Until the air gave out completely and you suffocated?

Depthcharges shook her slightly, from the port side. Ruck ordered, 'Port fifteen.'

'Port fifteen, sir —'

'Steer oh-two-oh.'

Making for those shallows . . .

The fore planes were at twenty degrees of dive, to hold her bow down. With the voltage right down that screw wasn't turning very fast, and the less movement she had through the water the less effect the planes had. Quinn had joined Pool in working on the periscope gland, both using the same stool and the same huge steel wrench, leaning outwards to put their combined weights on it. Like some circus act: and both of them dripping wet. Pool grunted, 'Tight as we'll get her, Tom.' Quinn disengaged himself by half-falling backwards; Wykeham caught him, held him up. Pool said, getting down more safely, 'We've taken up what slack there was, sir.'

And the leak *had* slowed. Ruck nodded. 'Well done. I've a new job for you now, Chief. And you, Sub.' Paul moved closer. 'Chief, get a couple of stokers and all the open-ended cans they can lay their hands on, and fill up the cans with oil. Old engine oil, lub.-oil, anything. As many containers as can be packed into one torpedo tube. Sub, you round up some loose gear. Clothing, your own cap, at least one sailor's hat with a submarine ribbon on it, a shoe or two – anything else that floats. Cushions, a locker door, one of the wardroom curtains . . . Get it all up for'ard and tell the TI to load it all into one empty tube. With Chief's oil. Then he's to keep the bow-cap shut and wait for further orders. Get it?'

He nodded. Wykeham said, 'She's getting hard to hold, sir.'

'We'll vent it when we fire the tube. We'll vent Q at the same time.'

Wykeham's glance met Ruck's: and Paul saw that look, saw it meaning, *Last resort* . . . For all their calmness, that was how it was. And the object would be to make the Italians think they'd sunk her: they'd see oil and gear, following the air-bubbles. It might fool them, as long as they were watching the surface for signs of that kind – which they were likely to be doing. They'd have searchlights on the water after each batch of depthcharges exploded; and it wasn't so long to dawn now, anyway.

But even if it did work – *Ultra* couldn't surface, and the battery was dead, and the air wasn't going to sustain life much longer. What he'd be telling them with those signs would be no more than advance notification of the truth . . .

Screws scrunched over: faint, not directly overhead, audible for only about two seconds. Paul squeezed past McClure, to get

to the door leading for'ard and unclip it. Roffey, on its other
side, was already pulling clips off – the door could be secured
from either side – in order to return to the control room. He
told Ruck, 'Most of the containers in number one section's
cracked, sir.'

'Check this one now.'

At slow grouped down, the one motor was barely turning that
screw, barely giving the boat steerage-way.

Depthcharges burst: claps of thunder in the middle distance.
Off to starboard and rather shallow-set again: more sound than
danger . . . Wykeham looked round at Ruck again, his raised eyebrows expressing a possible admissibility of hope. Ruck wasn't
buying any of it: and he was right not to, because – suddenly –
you could hear the asdic pings. His head moved, indicating the
surface, drawing Wykeham's attention to them. Little trilling
squeaks, as one of the hunters found her again and fingered her.

First fingers, then claws . . .

Up for'ard, talking to Gaffney in the TSC, Paul heard it too
and tried to shut it out. The torpedomen had been confined
behind their watertight door for a long time: they were full of
questions that weren't easy to find answers to.

The pinging ceased.

Italian A/S man deciding it hadn't been a submarine contact,
moving on to search elsewhere?

Asdics did, frequently, pick up false contacts. But then, false
hopes weren't hard to come by, either.

Smoke drifted, gunflashes and searchlights flaring through it:
the noise of fighting and wrecking was still mostly behind them –
eastward – but there was also a lot of machine gunning from the
right now – in front as well, sporadically, he guessed from the
other side of the basin – but it was getting quite heavy to the
right. That would be where assault and demolition parties would
be pressing through to the top end of the Normandie Dock and
from there to the swing bridge at this end of the Penhouët
Basin: that bridge had to be destroyed quickly to stop German

troop reinforcements getting into the port area. Jack's team
were against the wall just short of the corner – close to their
target but on their own, the problem being that as soon as they
moved round it they'd be easy meat for the guns on the other
side of the basin. The E-boat, if it was there, would be roughly
two hundred yards from this corner. They'd come ahead of the
commando assault party instead of following it up: it was his
own fault, he knew, for landing too soon. There'd been demolition parties as well as assault parties landing from the destroyer,
and as it had turned out he'd been right on their heels, even
among them: so No. 5 Troop wasn't in position yet, and around
that corner the NTU would be unsupported instead of having
commandos just along the quayside to take and return a lot of
the fire – if not all of it – from across the water . . . He told
Bowater to stay where he was, and moved back. 'Slattery?' He
was there; so were Pettifer and Lloyd, Rayner and Merrit, each
torpedoman loaded with a pack of plastic explosives as well as his
other equipment. Jack told them, 'Hold on here for a minute.
I'm going with the others for a shufti along the quayside.' He
asked Pettifer, 'You OK?' The ERA nodded, still panting from
the fast sprint. He was older and heavier than the rest of them,
and he was also the one member of this bunch who could not be
spared. Jack could be dispensed with, because Slattery could
take his place, but Pettifer was a lot of eggs in one basket, thanks
to ERA Wolf having dropped out. Too late to worry about that
now: too late to worry about anything . . . A shell struck the
building somewhere above them, showering brickwork; he'd left
them, and he and Bowater, with Corporal Dewar and Marines
Bone and Laing, were running at a crouch for the corner.

  Campbeltown had still been under heavy fire from all directions
when he'd led the team across her. There'd been dead and
wounded soldiers all over her, and fires below decks which her
naval crew were fighting to put out in case the flames spread to
the huge explosive charge in her for'ard messdeck. There'd
been problems getting from the destroyer's crumpled stem
down to the caisson in which it was embedded: steel ladders

provided for the purpose had been shot away, and dangling ropes were smouldering. They'd got over, anyway, and over the caisson to the dockside. Demolition teams were already starting work there, under heavy fire which their protection parties were returning and in places eliminating. The opposition had been coming from both sides of the *Forme Ecluse* and from the roofs and upper floors of buildings; shells were exploding in *Campbeltown*'s superstructure, some of her Oerlikons were still in action, tracer ricocheting off her . . . Even if her gunners weren't stopped by the enemy, or called to evacuate over her stern – as they would be before long – they'd have to cease fire soon or they'd be hitting their own people as the surviving commandos swarmed ashore and began to attack their various targets.

Jack had been running then, with the naval party behind him and the Marines in a loose covering formation around them; off to the right Captain Roy's troop was attacking the pumping-house, a great concrete cube lit by flashes and searchlight beams sweeping over. The German guns on its roof were the commandos' primary interest, after which they'd move on and a demolition section would move *in*, to blow up all the pumps and gear. The NTU couldn't very well have stopped and waited for No. 5 Troop to finish that job on the rooftop guns, largely because there was no cover here; and with an empty quayside ahead, and the tempo of the action quickening and thickening all around, the natural thing was to push on towards the objective. It was his own plan that was at fault, a misconception about timing which had escaped everyone else's attention too. The hell with it: split milk . . . Mortar shells crumping down close to the right. Behind, grenades were being lobbed up on to the pumping house roof, and machine guns were creating a solid, continuous blare of noise; on his left, down in the approaches to the Old Entrance, a burning ML swung helplessly across another's bows. A lot of things were going wrong, but you'd expect that; a lot of other things would go *right*, and the great success already scored was that *Campbeltown* was securely lodged like a giant time-bomb in that primary objective, the lock gate.

He wondered whether Trolley had got ashore: a lot of them
would not have. Running fast, crouching, zigzagging along the
dockside; noise building to incredible heights behind them and
action spreading to the left as well. Laing spraying an upper
window with bullets from his Lanchester as they pounded under
it: glass shattered and a gun ceased fire.

About eighty yards from where they'd rushed off the caisson
a commando demolition party was disappearing into some kind
of blockhouse, their own protection party covering them: the
blanco'd webbing was a hell of a good idea, you could recognize
your own side a mile away . . . Bowater and Dewar, leading,
began shooting, still running while their guns blazed: their
target was a group of helmeted Germans who'd appeared from
the right, from an open archway in that eastern end of the same
building beside which – farther along – the naval team were
waiting now. Flash lit them, and two of the Germans went sprawl-
ing; one darted back into the archway and disappeared, and
three more went sprinting down the jetty. Dewar sent another of
them skidding on to his face: one of the survivors stopped then,
turning, with his arm back over his head. All four Marines were
firing at him and he didn't stand a chance, but the stick-grenade
came flying, was in mid-air as he died. Dewar got his boot to it,
full-toss, and sent it over the edge of the quay. The racket was
solid and deafening: when guns fired you saw it but heard nothing different, for the rest of the noise absorbed it; and you had
to ignore the bedlam, all the surrounding action and its racket
and confusion, keep your mind on your own objective. At the
corner, with the battle going on behind them and only enemies
in front, there'd been a chance to pause and recognize discre-
tion as having the edge on valour – for a moment, a breath or
two, a thought . . . The objectives being, one, the E-boat if it
existed, two, the U-boat shelter, and neither being achievable by
tearing straight round the corner and having his men cut down
on an exposed quayside.

But at this point, Jack discovered as soon as he got round the
corner with the Marines, it wasn't exposed. The quay had two

sheds built on it, between the front of the buildings and the water's edge. They were both narrow; the nearer of them – in front of him now – was about ten yards long, and the one to the right was more like sixty. With an eight-foot gap separating them.

He pointed at it. 'There.'

Sprinting for the gap . . . He went flat, between the sheds, and the four Marines flopped down around him. He crawled forward. Bowater muttered, 'Not E-boats, are they?'

They were harbour patrol-craft. Launches, with no fixed weapons. They weren't important. He got over to the far side of the gap: there was a lot of noisy action on the right now, the Penhouët direction. Diagonally to his left across the black, oily water of the St Nazaire Basin he could see the great bulk of the U-boat shelter. To the left again was a blockhouse which was clear to see because of a searchlight on another building beyond it: there were guns on *that* roof. Oerlikons by the look of them, and they were spouting tracer-streams at some target on this east side of the basin. Either No. 5 Troop moving up to its holding-area at the bridge, or troops working on the other side of the Old Entrance – where, come to think of it, the military commander would by now be setting up his headquarters post. Those guns could be engaging any target between the Old Entrance and the Old Mole, and they'd be a problem for Roy's commandos.

To the right – north – of the patrol launches, two minesweepers lay side by side, and helmeted sailors were standing by their guns. Those, undoubtedly, were *his* problem.

He pointed them out to Bowater, and made sure he'd seen the guns. There'd be heavier weapons – 4-inch or 2-pounders – on the ships' foc'sls, which of course one couldn't see from here: the ones visible were machine guns in the bridge superstructure.

Bowater had nodded. 'E-boat?'

'Probably higher up. You'll have to take care of this lot for us. While we're rushing the E-boat – *if* it's there . . . Let's get the others up here.'

They left Dewar and Laing in the gap, and Bone went back to

collect the naval party. Jack and Bowater ran on behind the big shed, up to its northern end. He guessed that Roy's troop would be at the bridge by now. The battle was in progress in all directions, totally enclosing them – except for their front, the water that was to be *their* battleground – in noise and flash. He remembered that when they'd first had the bad news that there were five torpedo-boats in here, the military commander had proposed rushing them from the quayside, and the idea had been turned down because there wouldn't have been enough men available. Now, these two armed minesweepers would have to be dealt with in much the same fashion by the four Marines.

They got to the end of the long shed just as the flash of a huge explosion ahead and to the left lit the underside of the clouds like a light flaring in a tent. That could have been the Penhouët Bridge going up, he thought; or maybe the inner gate control post. The commandos would be fairly chewing the place up by now. And the teams from *that* area would be falling back along this quay, when they'd finished, so it would be just as well to have the minesweepers' guns knocked out.

From the corner, he saw the E-boat. Right there in front of him, and armed as *Sauerkraut* had been before they made the changes to her: a one-pounder AA gun aft, and a 20-millimetre for'ard of the bridge, between the torpedo tubes. There was an officer or petty officer in the outer wing of the bridge on this side, and a sailor in silhouette at the 20-millimetre. No other sign of life, and he could have shot both those men from where he was standing now, flat against the end wall.

He would, too. In a minute.

Beyond the E-boat to the right the quayside was empty for a hundred yards. Then a cluster of small ships right at the end, filling that corner. He could make out three tugs, and another of those harbour-protection launches. There was a giant explosion beyond them, a vertical shoot of flame as some dock installation disintegrated; then it was one blur of sound again, one constant roar of guns, grenades, mortars and explosive charges. From the corner of the shed he saw tracer arcing both ways across the

basin at its other end; so No. 5 Troop *was* at the bridge now. He
edged back into cover and told Bowater, 'I'll stay. Send the naval
party to me. Soon as they're set we'll go for the E-boat, and you
cover us by attacking the sweepers from the other end. We'll
have a go at the sweepers' for'ard guns on our way to the E-boat,
too. You can board them if you need to, or do it from the quayside. When we're away, you're on your own. OK?'

Bowater took off.

Jack guessed, *Three minutes* . . .

Ultra, barely alive, settled slowly towards the seabed. Without
anyone having any clear idea where the seabed was.

One torpedo tube was still loaded with containers of oil, and
wreckage and personal effects, letters, some copies of *Good
Morning*. The reason the tube hadn't been fired was that it
seemed – *seemed* – the Italians had lost contact, about an hour
ago. They seemed not to have regained it even when Ruck had
taken the risk of venting the for'ard ballast tank, which he'd
had to do eventually.

You used that word *seemed* in your thoughts because there'd
been so many moments of disappointment since yesterday afternoon, and nobody was counting on anything now. Only a raving
lunatic *could* have. Even if the Italians *had* lost her – which wasn't
certain, or could be just temporary, more a matter of mislaying
than losing – there remained the facts that she'd exhausted her
one battery section that wasn't smashed, had several minor items
of damage and – most important of all – that this thinning,
carbon-monoxide-loaded air was all her thirty-two officers and
men had to breathe.

For how long? He told himself, needing to face the truth, *For
longer than it can possibly keep us all alive.*

Hundred and ten feet.

Wykeham ordered in his quiet, rather lazy tone, 'Open and
shut the flood again.'

The flood-valve on the trimline for'ard he was working with,
admitting a few gallons at a time into the midships trimming-tank.

Passing the order by word of mouth because the order-instrument needed electrical power which they didn't have to spare. Although she'd get heavier as she sank, he was having to take in ballast now because he'd deliberately been keeping her light; when she got heavier he wasn't at all sure there'd be enough power to run the ballast-pump to get the weight out of her again. It was about as vicious a circle as anyone could have dreamed up.

There were no cracked containers in the after battery tank. Only in number one, the for'ard tank. This was lucky, because if there'd been loose acid in the tank under the control room there'd have been salt water in it too, from the leak on the periscope gland, and that would have ended the whole thing long ago, by chlorine gassing. Ruck had mentioned it, adding something about counting their blessings.

Watertight doors were open now between compartments. A very few emergency lights provided faint radiance between areas of darkness. When those lights died there'd be a few hand-torches.

'Flood opened and now shut, sir.'

Hundred and twenty feet. She was lowering herself very slowly still: you might think – if you were imaginative to that extent – *unwillingly* . . . If Ruck and McClure were right about the position, she might touch bottom at any moment. If they were wrong by more than a mile or two, which wouldn't be difficult, she wouldn't find anything but water under her. In view of the lack of power, Ruck probably wouldn't let her go too deep in this search for a resting place, because without the use of her motors he'd have only the bottled reserves of high-pressure air to rely on for getting her up again, and if you had to do it more than once you'd be using up that air. When it was gone, you'd have *nothing*. With the last of it, the best he'd be able to do would be to blow her to the surface, order 'abandon ship' and probably – he himself – activate the explosive self-destruction charge. It was at the after end of the control room: he'd have to set its time-fuse going, then open main vents. It was possible he'd have time to get up the ladder himself before she dipped under.

If the Italians did regain contact now, they'd win. If they hadn't won already. They'd have a target which they'd already clawed so badly that she'd only be able to wallow around and take further punishment until it finally split her open.

Hundred and twenty-five feet.

According to the chart she *could* have been in less than a hundred feet of water. If she was out near the edge of the coastal shallow patch, it might be more like a hundred and fifty or two hundred. Beyond that, she wouldn't touch any bottom before *three thousand.*

Ruck motionless, feet spread, his hands on his hips, watching the luminous depthgauge dial. Wykeham's taller figure drooping slightly as he shifted his weight to one side. The planesmen sat squarely on their stools, their hands resting on brass control wheels that were useless now because of the lack of steerage-way.

A soft, almost imperceptible bump from for'ard. A small shiver that ran through the fabric of the boat . . .

Wykeham looked round at Ruck. One hundred and thirty-six feet. Ruck nodded. 'Put a few pints in for'ard, to hold her.'

'Shut O, open H suction and inboard vent.'

A little more weight in that for'ard trimming tank would anchor her forefoot to the bottom.

'Cox'n.' CPO Logan glanced round. Ruck told him, 'Get the trays out, will you? Protosol. And don't be mean with it.'

'Aye aye, sir.' Logan got off his stool. Protosol, lithium hydroxide, was a chemical that was supposed to absorb carbon monoxide and make the air last longer.

'All hands turn in now, and keep still and quiet. We've got to stick this out until it's dark enough to surface. No unnecessary movement, no talking, no damn all . . . Long as we don't take any breaths we don't need, we'll make it.'

'Shut H suction and inboard vent.' Wykeham asked Ruck, 'Fall out diving stations, then, sir?'

Ruck nodded. 'No need for watchkeepers.'

Lying still, you used less air. And if the enemy came back there'd be nothing anyone could do about it. Except fire that tube full of muck: and the destroyers would still drop a few more charges right on the spot, just to make sure . . .

Ruck went for'ard, to have a word with the torpedomen. CPO Logan and his assistants were already setting out protosol trays and pouring the white crystals into them.

The E-boat's for'ard gunner was dead before they'd moved from cover. PO Slattery's shot, that had been, as an opener to the assault. Two E-boat officers in the wing of the bridge were cut down within seconds of the gunner's death, probably before they'd realized they were under attack; there was no possibility of hearing individual shots or bursts in the surrounding roar of action. By that time Jack, Slattery, Pettifer and Lloyd were halfway across the open stretch of quayside, while Rayner and Merrit stayed back to spray the minesweepers' foc'sls and bridges with Lanchester fire. The sweepers' gunners would be under simultaneous attack by the Marines – who now had it all to themselves: Jack and Slattery were in the E-boat's bridge, Pettifer in its engineroom, Lloyd was getting the lines ready for casting off, Rayner checking the torpedoes' pistols and other detail, and Merrit was searching the boat for more Germans. There'd been several shots from below, so he must have found some.

'Both fish are armed and ready, sir!'

Rayner yelled it from the bridge window on the starboard side. Jack had given Pettifer enough time: he pressed the starters and the engines fired. He shouted, 'Let go fore and aft!' He couldn't hear his own voice, but Rayner knew what was wanted; he was on the boat's bow and Lloyd was on the jetty casting off. All gone for'ard – Lloyd had given the hand signal and now he was running to the stern. Merrit came up into the bridge and shouted in Jack's ear, 'No problems, sir.' This was the feeling he had too: that it was all so easy and smooth-running, going just as they'd practised it so often; and they weren't even going to need the plastic explosive . . . Glancing round to check on how Lloyd was doing he saw him stumble and then pitch forward across the bollard. Merrit rushed out. Rayner was on the quayside, first casting off and then, kneeling more or less on Lloyd's body, firing in short bursts at the inside minesweeper: and twisting away, doubling over his gun, dropping it and falling sideways. Merrit yelled into the window, 'All gone aft!' and Slattery came pushing in from the wing of the bridge. Jack put the port engine ahead and the wheel to starboard, so she'd nose in and swing her stern out; then he centred the wheel and put both engines full astern. Slattery was putting new clips into his Lanchester and Jack's, and Merrit, outside, had settled himself down at the 20-millimetre. Opening fire to starboard, sending a solid stream of tracer at the minesweepers' bridges as the E-boat shot stern-first away from them. It must have been from the sweepers that the two torpedomen had been shot; what had been going on with Bowater and his squad was anyone's guess, but they obviously hadn't knocked out those guns. Merrit had ceased fire. Jack stopped the starboard screw and put the port one half ahead, and wound on a lot of starboard rudder. The guns on the far side of the basin, beyond the U-boat shelter, were still in action, firing steadily across the water. The sky was alive and flickering with fires and gunflashes: there were several fires burning between the St Nazaire Basin and the river. 'Both engines ahead now!' he yelled at Slattery. 'Tell Pettifer to come up!' The out-side minesweeper was shooting at them, tracer flashing over high, then lowering but curving away astern as the E-boat picked up speed. Merrit came crashing in from that port side: 'No more bastard ammo!' He dumped his pack of plastic. Jack had had ideas of using all that stuff to convert the boat into a small bomb-ship, a miniature *Campbeltown*, after he'd fired its torpedoes – which, in about thirty or forty seconds —

Pettifer was beside him. He'd wanted him to be up here where he could get away with the rest of them, after they'd fired; the engines were all right, and there was nothing more for him to do down there. Jack looked over at Slattery, who was at the torpedo-firing panel, identical to the gear in *Sauerkraut*. He shouted at him to stand by, and the PO raised a thumb signifying 'ready' . . . One of the guns on the far side was shooting at them now, tracer sending up a long, fast line of splashes across black, reflective water, firing at them across the front of the U-boat pens. How they'd know, those gunners, that this E-boat was manned by their enemies – well, of course, if they'd seen the action with the minesweepers . . . But more guns were joining in now – from that far end of the basin – from some ship berthed where the Möwes had been during the past week. A searchlight stabbed across the water, blinding him: before it had come on he'd realized that the ship was under way and that it was almost certainly another minesweeper – coming at them down the length of the basin, or heading to cross the E-boat's bows? It had something like a Bofors, 40-millimetre, pumping shells at them, fireballs in a flat trajectory, muscling in on the tracer from that blockhouse roof. He'd only just have time and room, he saw suddenly as he realized how fast that ship was coming, to get this boat round and fire: and even then that bloody thing would ram or —

Didn't matter: long as you got the fish away first. He spun the wheel, hard a-starboard. With an even chance of getting a clear shot, with seconds to spare, into the front of the completed part of the U-boat shelter. Just *about* make it, if —

Shells hitting, all along the port side as he swung her to the firing course. The E-boat jolting and shuddering – and flames behind him, smashing timber, and a hit right in front of the bridge, a huge circular expanding thrust of flame. That side was *all* flame and Slattery was in it – he'd have been killed outright in the shell's explosion but now he was just part of the blazing wreckage. Merrit recoiling, after an attempt to get to the torpedo control panel: roar of flames as well as gunfire and Pettifer was trying to get over there too, covering his face with his forearms and forcing himself into the flames. All in those few seconds: the wheel was centred and the boat was on her firing course. He flung himself over to the burning starboard

side – Pettifer reeling back from the furnace where the torpedo control panel was: the swelling fireball engulfed *him* too,
and the minesweeper struck aft, rolling the E-boat over and
swinging her around to port, the blazing forepart lifting, lighting the entire basin as she began to fill through her shattered
stern.

12

Mid-morning in Perth, Western Australia, time-zone minus eight . . .

The white-haired man in the dark suit said, glancing up at them both and smiling, 'I hereby pronounce you man and wife.'

Foot of the rainbow . . . Even if it was actually a parquet floor in Perth's Town Hall. And there was no time to waste now thinking about the letter he'd only just managed to get written and posted to Fiona: explaining – or trying to – and apologizing . . . It was time now for nothing but letting his heart and soul rest in the sight and feel of Kate beside him, Kate's slim figure in pale blue, and a floppy blue hat on her backswept light brown hair. He'd thought when he'd first set eyes on her, on the bridge of his destroyer *Tuareg* in the Aegean a year ago, that she looked very much like Ingrid Bergman; but he'd been wrong. Out of the army nurse's uniform, and not having just been dragged off a Cretan beachhead that was under attack by German paratroops, she made Ingrid Bergman look like *anybody* . . .

'Hello, there.'

'Hello, Nick.'

You were supposed to kiss: but the hell with that, they'd done it a thousand times – *remember Cairo, last September*? – and they'd be doing it a million more. Now, he wanted just to look at her, photograph her and this moment in his mind: her wide-set grey eyes, rather wide, curvy mouth, the small indentation that

appeared on one side of it and not the other when she
smiled . . . He was fifteen years older than she was and he had a
scar, still fresh-looking, that ran from his left eye to the corner of
his mouth. He'd collected it in the Java Sea, a month ago. Beside
her he felt old – and damaged, like his ship that was in pieces in
a dock a few miles away. Kate looked – well, the stock word for
brides was 'radiant', and he couldn't have found a better one . . .
Behind them her mother, Mary Farquharson, said quite loudly,
'You're supposed to kiss each other now.'

He heard Ted Farquharson's rumbling laugh; and on his left,
Jim Jordan's chuckle. Jordan had acted as best man, but last
night's stag evening had been held on board *Defiant*, because
Jordan's destroyer, the USS *Sloan*, was dry, like every other US
Navy ship.

He murmured, still looking at her, 'I suppose we'd better.'

'I can stand it, if you can.'

They kissed lightly, formally. By mid-afternoon they'd be
alone, and that would be the time for kissing: in the Esplanade
Hotel, where he'd reserved a suite with an outlook across the
Swan River. In case anyone wanted to look out. Tomorrow they'd
be taking the train to Tambellup – 240 miles southeast – where
Kate's father would meet them and drive them out to his farm.
He raised wheat and sheep, and it was a farm, he insisted, not a
sheep-station, which was what you found up north and farther
east. But it was a farm, Nick gathered, about the size of the West
Riding of Yorkshire. You looked south from the house and
garden, Kate had told him, to the Stirling Range, a crescent of
blue mountains halfway between Tambellup and Albany on the
south coast.

Jim Jordan shook his hand. 'Congratulations, Nick . . .
Somewhat changed circumstances from a month ago, huh?'

A month ago both their ships had taken part in the battle of
the Java Sea, and both had been lucky enough to survive it.
Then, pushing their luck a bit farther, they'd got away, under the
noses of encircling Jap squadrons, *Sloan* through the Bali Strait
and *Defiant* through the Alas Strait. Four other American

destroyers had escaped via the Bali passage ahead of *Sloan*, but that made up the full tally of survivors. Just *one month* ago . . . Java had fallen, and within ten days the Japs had poured 200,000 troops in.

Jordan kissed the bride. Nick kissed Mary Farquharson. Bob Gant, *Defiant*'s second in command, shook Nick's hand . . . 'Every happiness, sir. But I'd guess that's pretty well assured.' Then Gant was leaving, beckoning to the other *Defiant* officers who'd be forming a guard of honour now on the steps outside. Representatives of the ship's company were also filtering out. There were forms to be filled in and witnessed, for the registrar. Ted Farquharson, who was a big man with a broad face and iron-grey hair, embraced his daughter. Nick heard him growl, 'There'll be no arguing with you now, I suppose, now you're *Lady* Everard . . .' She was laughing and hugging him and he was muttering, 'I don't know *what* I'll do . . .'

Kate would be staying here in Australia – permanently, he hoped. There'd be plenty of work for nurses in Aussie hospitals, with the Japanese swarming all over the southwest Pacific and the Allies preparing for the long, tough process of driving them back where they'd come from. In recent weeks there'd been a scare over the possibility of an invasion of Australia, but informed opinion seemed to regard that danger as having passed now. The Jap carrier-launched air attack on Darwin in late February had caused enormous damage – the element of surprise had been as total as it had been at Pearl Harbor – but it looked as if that was about as far as they'd be allowed to come. The first huge convoys from the States were already pouring men, weapons and warplanes into the Australian ports, and more convoys were on their way; it was the start of the great build-up, and there was a theory that the Japs might already have over-reached themselves, might logistically have bitten off more than they'd be able to digest. General Douglas MacArthur, who'd fought a tremendous though doomed rearguard action in the Philippines, had just arrived in Australia to take over as Supreme Commander SW Pacific.

The tide would turn now. Or rather, it would *be* turned.

Ted Farquharson had asked Nick last night, on board *Defiant*, 'I suppose they wouldn't leave you out here? No chance of this ship staying?'

'I wouldn't think so. This is the American strategic area now. And we've got more on our hands than we've ships for anyway. Indian Ocean, Mediterranean, North and South Atlantic, and the Cape route to protect – and the Arctic, the Murmansk run, which is about all that's keeping the Russians going . . . I doubt there'd be the slightest chance of it, Ted.'

'Pity.'

'You'll look after Kate for me, that's the great thing. I'm grateful. She'll be safe, and making herself useful, and I won't have to worry about her. Much better than if I lugged her off to England and had to leave her there alone most of the time.'

'I'm glad you look at it that way, Nick. And naturally we'll be happy to have her around. I still wish they'd leave you out here as well.'

He didn't know yet where he'd be taking *Defiant* when she was mended and fit for sea. To Colombo, Ceylon, perhaps, or to Kilindini in East Africa, where the newly formed Eastern Fleet was being established now, or back to the Mediterranean – which he'd have liked, for the chance of seeing Paul – or even possibly to the USA for the full refit his ship did really need. Perhaps back home to England . . . In due course, they'd tell him. Meanwhile, *Defiant* was conveniently immobilized, and he could count on having about three weeks with Kate.

Mary Farquharson said quietly, aside, 'Shame you couldn't have had a church wedding, Nick.'

'Yes. Kate would have liked it.'

It hadn't been possible, because a dozen years ago he'd been divorced. And if that was the church's attitude, so be it. He thought he had a reasonably sound idea of his own status as a Christian, and he didn't believe the bishops or synods could be any more omniscient or infallible than, say, the Board of Admiralty. Which, on occasions over the years, he'd seen displaying fallibility to a marked degree. But for Kate's sake he was sorry they hadn't been able to do it in church.

'The marriage could be blessed, Nick, if you'd like that.'

He nodded. 'I'm sure Kate would.'

'Well, when you're out with us on the farm, if you'd permit it I might arrange for a ceremony at home? And a reception after, for our friends and neighbours to come and meet you?'

'You're very kind. And – yes, as long as Kate would like it —'

'Kate like this, Kate like that . . .' Kate's father, muttering as he joined them. The form-filling was all finished, and everyone was ready to move off to the hotel where champagne would be waiting in coolers. Ted grumbled again, 'Now she's Lady Everard, my life's going to be pure hell. I can see *that* coming from forty miles away.'

On the town hall steps, sun glinted on the arch of naval swords. Cameras flashed. Kate's arm in his, her weight against him. He wondered how long it would be before some of the pictures appeared in London papers, whether there was any hope his letter might reach Fiona before she saw them.

Down the steps. Grins from Gant, from Sibbold the doctor, Charles Rowley, Greenleaf, Chevening, Haskins the Captain of Marines . . . A crowd of sailors cheered: civilians clapped and called good wishes. Turning into Barrack Street where the cars waited . . . After a few days out at Tambellup they'd be moving into an hotel at Cottesloe, which Kate had said was a good place to stay; it also had the advantage of being close to *Defiant*'s dockside berth in Fremantle.

Eventually, there'd come a time to say goodbye – for God only knew how long. That would be – quoting her father – *pure hell* . . .

He told himself not to think about it. To forget everything, except Kate and the sheer, blinding happiness he had now.

13

M orning after, in St Nazaire . . .

Jack wondered what the French were thinking of it: and whether the news would have broken in London yet. Probably not; Fiona *wouldn't* know. Thoughts drifted, rather: you had to make an effort to keep them in line. Of course there'd have been no announcement made yet – if there were any surviving ships they wouldn't be far off the French coast yet . . . Daylight, as he stepped out into it, on to the minesweeper's deck with a German soldier pointing a rifle at him, was messy, stained with smoke still rising from a dozen different points. Stench of burning: and he was still feeling sick, as well as weak, from the quantity of filthy harbour water he'd swallowed.

The whole place was overhung with smoke. Blinking around at the greyish morning light he recognized the odour as being from burning oil and petrol. Fuel storage tanks on the other side of the Normandie Dock had been one of the commando targets – underground tanks, between the dock and the river. But there'd been the burning MLs on the river too . . . It was obvious, looking around at the general panorama of destruction, that the landing force must have achieved virtually all it came for, despite the ML losses. It was also a fair bet that not many of the raiders could have got away – unless they'd fought their way inland, which was an alternative the commandos had had in

mind. Down to the south, perhaps into Spain, had been Trolley's
idea.

He didn't remember being hauled out of the basin, but
apparently a boat from this minesweeper had found him. It had
also picked up Pettifer and Merrit. Merrit had been hauled out
dead, and Pettifer had died since; Jack had identified both
bodies and given the intelligence officer their names.

That was all he'd given the bastard, except for his own name
and rank. He'd given that much to the naval lieutenant, the
minesweeper's skipper, before this Wehrmacht sleuth had come
aboard and taken over the interrogation. The naval people had
been very decent: their doctor had bandaged his head while
he'd been still unconscious, and applied some kind of lotion to
the worst of his burns. The burns were quite bad, and now he
had his clothes on the ones on his arms and torso were painful.
He hadn't looked in a mirror yet.

He wondered where he was being taken now. The German
army captain had been distinctly unpleasant during the past
half-hour, annoyed by his refusal to answer questions. He'd
made a fuss about a number – 'name, rank and number,' he'd
insisted, were the items a prisoner was obliged to divulge. Jack
had explained that he was a commissioned officer and didn't
have one, and the intelligence officer – a man of about thirty,
with a narrow, balding head and sharp features – had threatened
that he could have him shot for refusing to supply it. Jack had
said, 'Fine, so have me shot. I still don't have a number.'

The commandos had done their job, but he'd failed in his
own. He'd also thrown away the lives of at least five good men in
the attempt. He'd been too slow, hung on too long. When he'd
realized that ship was coming straight at the E-boat he ought to
have turned at once, even though it would have meant firing on
the slant. The torpedoes would have done *some* damage.

'You are an officer of the Royal Navy?'

He'd nodded. Giving them his rank had already told them
that much.

'Then why were you performing the duties of a soldier?'

'Was I?'

'On land, fighting?'

'They tell me I was in the drink.'

It riled him . . . Jack had been wearing only a blanket at the time, and his face hurt when he spoke. There was ointment – or lotion – on it. The naval man had muttered, *à propos* the bandage around his head, 'You will not for a long time require to have your hair cut.' That was the doctor, who'd been with the captain of this ship: the one that had rammed the E-boat was in the outside berth, alongside, but it was this one who'd sent the boat to look for survivors. Rather surprising . . . Presumably the water had saved his life, by extinguishing the flames. It was speculation; he didn't know much about what had happened, except that he'd been unconscious at the time and wouldn't have suffered if he'd been left in it to drown. You had no choice: and he'd just as soon have changed places now with – say – Pettifer, or Slattery, or any of the others. They'd been his people, and he'd lost them: there was a feeling of guilt in that – as if he, of all of them, *should* have died.

When the interrogator had decided to take him ashore, they'd given him his gear back. The clothes had been warm – they must have been in the sweeper's engineroom to dry, he guessed, but the process hadn't got far. Now, in the breeze that was carrying all the smoke out to the river, he was shivering with cold and worried about his clothes sticking to the burnt areas of his body. He hadn't been listening very closely in there to the questions and complaints, partly because he wasn't thinking of talking to them anyway and also because he'd had his mind on the others, who'd been killed. He hoped to God the Marines had come through all right. He felt particularly badly about Slattery and Pettifer, who were married men – *had been* married men. He'd asked Slattery once – on that Cornish hillside, during a turnip shoot – why he, with a wife and baby son at home, was going in for this kind of job, and Slattery had seemed surprised at being asked. He'd said finally, 'Well, they're – they're like the *reason*. I mean, it's *for* them, sort of thing . . .'

He was being directed down the minesweeper's gangway to the quayside. A thick column of dark smoke was rising from the warehouse area. There were soldiers in helmets, carrying rifles, standing around on the quay. On guard against a new attack? He was thinking about stable doors and bolting horses when he heard a rifle-shot from the direction of the Old Town. One, then silence. Everyone listening and looking that way . . . The intelligence officer shouted something, and the guard behind Jack gave him a prod with the rifle barrel: one of the other soldiers called something to his friends, glancing at Jack and jerking a thumb towards the Old Town. They were grinning, looking at him, and one of them drew a finger across his throat. It was towards the Old Town they were expecting him to go, apparently. There didn't seem to be any fires in that area: the smoke was coming mostly from around the Old Entrance and the Normandie Dock.

Normandie Dock, alias the Tirpitz Dock, alias the *Forme Ecluse.* He knew for sure that its operating and pumping machinery would have been destroyed, but he didn't know whether *Campbeltown* had blown up yet. It was nine-thirty now, and the time-fuse had been supposed to set off that very large explosive charge by nine at the latest. One would surely have heard a bang that size – even miles away you'd hear it and feel it. And if it had gone off while he'd been unconscious, wouldn't the Germans have had something to say about it?

It would be terrible if the device had failed; or if they'd found it and deactivated it . . .

Walking – they were marching him towards the Old Town – his clothes rubbed against burnt flesh and hurt like hell. He was walking peculiarly, like a duck, in his efforts to reduce the friction. If they didn't shoot him, he expected he'd end up in some hospital, and then, presumably, a POW camp. *Did* they shoot commandos when they captured them? If they classified him as one, which they might . . . There *had* been threats, in German propaganda broadcasts.

The building they stopped at wasn't far from the south end of the basin. There were soldiers on guard outside it, and steps up to a doorway which looked as if a bomb had gone off inside it. German officers were hurrying in and out, like bees in the entrance to a hive. Another building close by had been wrecked – by some internal explosion, it seemed – and every wall in sight was scarred and pitted. There wasn't a window anywhere that had glass in it.

He wasn't to be privileged to use that front entrance. There was another, steps leading down into some sort of basement. Two guards stood beside it with rifles at the ready. A stretcher was carried past by trotting soldiers: the body on it was covered by a blanket and German army boots stuck out at one end. His escort prodded him forward towards the basement steps: his interrogator, climbing the other ones, was straightening his cap and brushing down his tunic as if about to appear before his seniors. The soldier poked Jack again, harder than before: he stumbled forward, down the steps, and through a doorway with an arch on it.

Dim light, a crowd of men, conversation ceasing, heads turning. Commandos: prisoners . . .

'Hey, Jack!'

Frank Trolley. He was wrapped in a blanket. Gaunt, bony face and close-cut hair: he might have been some variety of monk. Bruised face, split lips . . . Grinning a welcome, holding out a hand: Jack took it with his left, the one that wasn't burnt. Trolley was staring at Jack's face: so were others round them.

'God's teeth, what's happened to you?'

'Only burns. I've got them all over, so don't shove me around.' He guessed his face would be like raw meat, a rump steak *saignant.* 'You OK, Frank?'

'Went in the drink, then fell into ill-disposed company and got beaten up, somewhat . . . Did you pull it off, your stunt?'

He shook his head. 'Got the boat away, but then we were shot up and rammed, halfway to the target. My own damn fault.' He shut his eyes, reliving it for one ghastly moment: Slattery in the flames . . . He added, coming back to earth, 'All my chaps were killed.'

'Not all.' Trolley jerked a thumb. 'There's a couple here. But I'm damn sorry, Jack —'

'Lieutenant Everard?'

Corporal Dewar, pushing through the crowd. And the red-headed Marine, Bone. 'How'd you make out, sir? Where's old —' His expression changed, as he got a clear look at him. 'Oh, crikey . . .'

'What about Bowater and Laing?'

'Sarn't Bowater got shot in the legs, before we'd hardly started. He's with the stretcher-cases, wherever they took 'em. Laing's dead – I saw it, sir, he was charging up the gangway like a mad elephant and they shot him off it.' He was finding it hard to look at Jack as he spoke: his eyes kept sliding away to Trolley. Bone was the same. Dewar asked him, 'What happened, sir?'

He was describing it, or attempting to, when the Wehrmacht interrogator came in, with two armed soldiers for his protection and also a German naval man, a lieutenant-commander or commander, in tow. At first he couldn't see Jack, because of the ring of commandos round him. He shouted, 'I require the Royal Navy officer!'

Nobody took much notice of him. Trolley muttered, 'Last bloke we had in here was promising we'd all be shot. They found we were wearing our fighting-knives' – he tapped his left thigh – 'and it seemed to upset them. I told him "There's a war on, chum" . . . You'd better see what the sod wants, hadn't you?'

Jack wanted to know a few things first: he asked quickly, quietly, 'Has the *whumpf* gone off yet?'

Trolley frowned: 'They don't know about it, as far as we can tell. For Christ's sake don't —'

Jack broke in, 'Don't worry . . . Has anyone at all got away?'

Trolley nodded, edging forward with him through the packed room. The interrogator had spotted Jack's bandaged head and pointed him out, and the soldiers were pushing through to get him. Trolley whispered, 'Some by boat and some into the hinterland. Mum's the word, though, eh?'

'You! You Royal Navy officer!'

'I'm coming.' The soldiers closed in on him: he moved his hands outward to space them away, not wanting contact on his burns. He looked round at Trolley. 'See you, Frank . . . Dewar – Bone – good luck.'

Outside there was a truck waiting, and they pushed him into the back of it. Both the guards got in with him and sat with their guns pointing at his head, and the naval man climbed into the front with the driver. The truck lurched forward, swung around in a U-turn and headed up towards the St Nazaire Basin, then along the eastern quayside past the minesweepers. There was a diving-boat out in the middle, opposite the U-boat pens, and he guessed they'd be locating the E-boat, prior to raising it. They'd enough trouble now without sunken ships cluttering the place up: with the locks out of action this basin would be tidal, and at low water the U-boat shelter might not be usable. The truck stopped where it couldn't get any further – at the blown-up swing bridge at the Old Entrance – and everyone got out. There was a footway over the gap now, a plank and two wire cables to hold on to: they filed across it, the commander leading and then Jack with one guard in front and the other behind him. Fifty yards ahead was the smaller of the two dockyard sheds which only a few hours earlier he and his team had used for cover; at least, and thank God, Bowater was alive. And the two others . . . They turned right as they approached the shed. Ahead and on the left then was the corner that had been their first stopping point after they'd landed.

The commander dropped back to walk beside him. He was short, dark, rather dapper. Probably on some shore staff.

'Your intention was to attack submarines in the shelter?'

His English wasn't at all bad. Jack said, 'I gave that other fellow my name and rank. I've nothing else to say.'

No argument, from this one. A shrug, a hint of a smile. Probably not a bad sort. Except that, if their positions had been reversed, *Jack* wouldn't have given up so easily. The army one might have told him Jack had refused to talk, so the attempt had been perfunctory, just so he could say he'd tried . . . Ahead, the

ruin of the control post for the outer gate, the winding-gear
that moved the caisson to and fro, reminded him of seeing the
commando demolition boys diving into it, when he and his team
had been belting up this same dockside. It occurred to him that
they were bringing him dangerously close to the caisson, which
had *Campbeltown* stuck in it with more than four tons of explosive
in her for'ard messdeck and a time-fuse that was already overdue
in blowing.

If you were close to it when it went off, he thought, you
–wouldn't know a thing about it. It would be an easier death
than Slattery's or Pettifer's had been . . . With sudden fore-
knowledge of what was about to happen he told himself you
must not, repeat not, let them guess you're scared of it.

Passing the control post now. Completely wrecked. Between
it and the river end of the *Forme Ecluse* was the huge slot into
which the caisson, when it had been in working order, used to
be hauled on its rollers when they'd wanted to open the lock.
The slot was about a hundred and seventy feet long, nearly forty
feet wide and about sixty deep. They were marching along
beside it now, and ahead of him he could see *Campbeltown*.
There were Germans all over the place, even all over *her*. Forty
or so uniformed officers, actually on the ship and the caisson,
apparently inspecting the damage. But just standing around,
most of them, military and naval officers in long greatcoats and
high-fronted caps. Gawping like tourists. Quite a lot of other-
ranks around too, and even a few women – garrison officers'
wives, he guessed.

It occurred to him that they were all either raving mad, or
quite abysmally stupid.

Approaching the end of the caisson, the commander glanced
back at the escort and ordered 'Halt!' He told Jack, 'Wait here,
please.' He advanced to the edge of the dock, on the river side
of the caisson, a position from which he could call up to some of
the officers on *Campbeltown*'s foc'sl.

Campbeltown battered, lacerated, scarred. Beautiful old
warhorse, he thought. And what a bullseye!

You could visualize that slow-working fuse. Acid at work on copper. It could blow at any second: literally, every tick of the clock was one you might not have heard.

And such a crowd of people . . .

To his left he could see the pumping house that had been No. 5 Troop's first objective. It was scarred and scorched, with a litter on its flat roof that would be the remains of gun positions. Inside, there'd be total shambles. Much the same applied to the whole of the port area – machinery, defences, ships inside the locks, fuel tanks, bridges, dock gates . . .

'You will please come.' The commander was back. He spoke to the guards, evidently telling them to stay here, then beckoned Jack and led him forward to the end of the caisson, where ladders had been placed. They began to climb, up on to the caisson. Just hours ago, he thought, stepping off the ladder, he'd led his men over this same massive structure: in the dark, lit by gun-flashes and shellbursts, explosions —

Which could have been *nothing*, compared to the explosion that was coming at any moment now. Before he'd completed his next thought, it might blow. He thought, *OK, so let it* . . .

There was another lot of ladders up here, leaning against *Campbeltown*'s bow. Crumpled, smashed-in bow. Much easier getting up now than it had been getting down. Hard to believe they'd managed it, without ladders . . . He wondered whether, if the Germans did get to know about the horrifically destructive force lurking under this steel deck on which they were standing, they'd be able to do anything to defuse it. Presumably they'd have to open up the steel tank that held the twenty-four depthcharges. But the tank itself had been enclosed in concrete . . . There'd have to be some point of access, all the same, because otherwise the raiders couldn't have got at the time-fuse to activate it during the approach up-river.

On the foc's'l, the commander marched up to a group of army officers, clicked his heels and saluted. The fattish character in the middle looked like at least a brigadier. He had also,

Jack thought, to be quite an idiot . . . It was a reasonable guess
that he'd sent the commander to bring Jack along, though less
simple to guess what for . . . He was asking a question now –
that senior man was – shouting it directly at Jack Everard. The
others frowning disdainfully, as if they didn't much care for his
appearance.

He was glad he'd had the sense not to look in a mirror.
There'd been one in the cabin in the minesweeper, and he'd
been careful to stay away from it. His face felt as if it had deep
cracks in it.

The spasm of shouting finished. The whole crowd up here
were staring at Jack now – goofing at him and muttering to each
other. He thought, *Trespassers will be blown to bits* . . . It would have
been almost worth telling them about the charge they were
standing on, just to see the rush for those two ladders, the panic
and probably some broken necks . . . He looked enquiringly at
the naval commander.

'The *Herr General* demands that you explain how you believed
you could destroy this dock, so large, by damage from a vessel so
small. Answer, please!'

He was aware that he might still be suffering from having
been knocked on the head, grilled and then half-drowned,
that his mental powers might still not be at their sharpest. But
even allowing for some impairment of the wits it was difficult
to believe that so many people could be so completely unimag-
inative. If this had happened the other way about – for
instance, if German assault troops had attacked the King
George V dock in Southampton and left a destroyer embedded in it – wouldn't everyone assume there'd be a bomb in the
bloody thing?

The biggest bloody bomb imaginable? Right under one's
bloody feet?

He wanted to laugh, but it might have given the show away.
Even to these clowns . . . It might also have come out as a scream.
He told himself, *This is what it was all for. It's why Slattery and the
others are dead.*

And the general's face wouldn't be any prettier than his own was, in a minute.

He looked at the commander. 'Why ask *me*?'

'Because this is a naval affair. Ashore' – he gestured – 'military. Here' – he tapped the deck with his foot – 'ship, naval business. Please to answer the *Herr General*'s question?'

The people weren't only on the ship and caisson. All round, on quays and docksides, Germans of all ranks milled around, some of them picking up spent bullets and anything else that caught their eyes. Like hens pecking around in a farmyard. He pointed at the caisson, where the destroyer's stem had carved into its steel.

'Isn't that bad enough damage?'

The commander interpreted what he'd said. Some of the staff officers laughed. The general glanced at them frostily before he shouted more German at Jack. The commander interpreted, 'The *Herr General* says you British are a very stupid people. In one month, we will have working again this dock!'

'Oh.' He stared – stupidly – at the caisson. 'I'd have thought it was a bigger job than that.'

Again, translation. The general, staring contemptuously at Jack, grunted something to the officers around him. There were nods and smirks . . . But a new thought had struck the naval man: he swung towards Jack and asked him sharply, expectantly, 'Is there *explosive* in the ship?'

'Is what?' He blinked at him, while the question sank in. He looked puzzled by it. Other English-speakers had heard the question and repeated it to each other in German; all, including the general, were looking back this way again, and there were some fairly alarmed expressions as well as one or two surreptitious movements towards the ladders. Jack asked vaguely, 'Explosive? How could there be?'

One of the steel barriers that had been added as protection for troops on deck was just behind him. He glanced round, then sat down on it. Touching his bandaged head. 'I have to rest. I'm sorry.' Relaxing: very clearly not in any hurry to move. *Or* taking

much notice of that silly question about explosives. He heard the
general rap out some order, and the commander's '*Jawohl . . .*'
Then a hand on his shoulder, which hurt; he flinched away from
it.

'We go now. Later you may rest.'

There was sympathy in the man's expression. Jack got up
slowly. They had to be allowed to see he wasn't in any hurry to
leave; but also they must *not* see that he wanted them to notice it.
Actually the general had turned his back now, and was lighting
a cigar, while a young officer with a box camera prepared to take
snapshots. *Hold it. Smile, please . . .* He thought, *It's a dream, all
this. Script by Lewis Carroll.* He followed the commander to the
ladders. But another group of officers had arrived and they were
on their way up, had to be allowed to get up here before anyone
could start down. Two of them were in Luftwaffe uniform. Jack
remembered the Luftwaffe off Crete, about a year ago: the fighters strafing boats and rafts, killing swimmers in the water. One
particular boatload of dead and dying men he remembered with
extraordinary clarity: he could see it, see the bodies washing to
and fro, as he watched the flyers climb over *Campbeltown*'s stove-
in bow.

Acid burning through copper. Just down there, under their
feet. He wondered whether Nick might ever hear about this.
Difficult to see how he could, really, when no eye-witness could
possibly survive to tell the tale. Nobody within half a mile, he
guessed.

He wished to God he'd been quicker getting the boat round
and the fish away. Such damned *waste . . .*

The commander had spoken . . . Jack glanced at him, ques-
tioningly, waiting for a repetition, but with Pettifer and Slattery
and their families in his mind. The German said, 'We go now.'
Below them, gazing upwards and cradling their rifles, the two
guards waited. He thought, *Stick around boys, you may be lucky . . .*
Then he was on the ladder, climbing down.

It would be *dreadful* if the time-fuse had failed. Acid somehow
diluted or the copper impure and too resistant? Or if it hadn't

been activated properly in the first place? He walked slowly across the top of the caisson, skirting around a pair of quite intelligent-looking officers who were almost certainly engineers. They looked away, with shocked expressions, when they saw his face.

How would Fiona react, he wondered? That scene he'd imagined – himself at the flat in Eaton Square, pressing the bell, and Fiona opening the door, and —

And *nothing*. That stuff was still eating its way through the copper. He was on the caisson, right beside it.

But *otherwise* – well, by the time she saw him his face would have healed, presumably, but if his guess was right he'd still be no Adonis. Which – come to think of it – wouldn't make much odds, because she'd have married Nick.

Wouldn't she? Didn't this change everything? Being a prisoner – and Nick before long getting back to England. How would she hold him off, or explain, or find the courage to tell him she'd changed her mind and intended to marry his young half-brother who was caged up for the duration and had a face like some sort of gargoyle . . .

Prisoners of war escaped though, didn't they? You didn't have to accept the condition as permanent.

He'd have to tell her, when he was allowed to write, about his face.

He climbed down the next ladder, from the caisson to the dockside, and as the guards moved forward he turned and looked back up at *Campbeltown*'s battered forepart. Still thronged. And still quiescent . . . 'Come, please!'

He nodded. 'All right.'

Returning now by the same route. It was about 250 yards to the plank footbridge across the Old Entrance; then into the truck again, and they were driving back to the place they'd started from. Expecting, every yard of the way, that colossal detonation.

The truck stopped, and they ordered him out, then pushed him towards the cellar steps. The commander, from the other steps, nodded curtly and went on inside. Down below, Jack was immediately surrounded, with Trolley to the fore again, wanting to know where they'd taken him and what for, what was going on . . . He told them, 'I was hauled on board *Campbeltown*. She's still intact and stuck in the dock gate. It was a general who sent for me – wanted to know what the point of it all had been, just making a dent in their bloody caisson, and all that . . . *Campbeltown*'s fairly smothered with brass-hats. About forty officers – they're even taking snapshots on her now. And I'd guess there must be at least a hundred or two Germans on the docks around her, as well as —'

Campbeltown exploded. Like the most enormous clap of thunder he'd ever heard. For about a minute the earth was shaking, and so was the stone building over them. Part of its outside masonry – a balcony or something – was crashing, cascading down.

Echoes dying. But objects still falling, out there. Shouts, whistles blowing, the panic starting. In here in the cellar, a very different noise – forty or fifty commandos laughing, cheering, whooping, going mad . . .

There was a line that Paul remembered from the prayers for burial at sea: *When the sea shall give up her dead . . .*

That was how it felt. Finding yourself stirring, emerging, with the other near-corpses. Stirring, anyway. Emerging was something else again: the sea hadn't offered to give up a damn thing, yet.

Hand-torches were the only sources of light. Faces caught in the splashes of it were white, dull-eyed. There'd been a lot of vomiting in recent hours; the other symptoms were headaches and high pulse-rates and general weakness.

The control room clock had stopped. Wristwatch time made it 1940. So it would be dark enough now, up top.

He leaned against the fruit machine. On Ruck's orders he'd got himself dressed for the bridge, and Ruck was similarly prepared. The two Vickers gunners were standing by, with their guns and a ready-use pan of ammunition each, and the 3-inch gun's crew had also been told to muster. There might be Italians waiting for them on the surface, or there might not be: they could be searching elsewhere, or they could have convinced themselves they'd made a kill, and gone home. Whether or not they were there now, *Ultra* couldn't be dived again, once she got up there. There was air in the bottles to blast her to the surface, and once she surfaced her diesels would take her homewards. If she met enemies, she'd fight: she had her guns, and one torpedo.

Torchlight flickered over the diving panel. Quinn switched it off again. Ruck ordered, 'Stand by to surface.'

Wykeham said, 'Check main vents.'

'Chief.' Ruck addressing Pool. 'Clutch-up main engines.'

They were within two or three miles of the Italian coast. Surfacing now, if she found she was alone she'd go flat-out seaward on the diesels. If a shore D/F station – the Measures – fixed on her and sent an E-boat out along the beam – well . . .

Well, what?

Stay up, and use the guns, of course. The 3-inch and the Vickers. Vickers GO, the letters standing for gas-operated. He could take those guns to pieces and put them together again in six minutes flat with a blindfold on: he and Creagh had had races doing that. In the 1914 war Vickers GO had been the guns they'd first synchronized with fighters' propellers for ahead-firing; they were still very good guns with a high rate of fire, despite having been around for so long. How long? Subtract say sixteen from forty-two . . . The brain didn't function too well when it was starved of oxygen. A few of the hands were sicker than others, *really* sick. But once she got up there and they had the engines running, sucking fresh air into her compartments and expelling the poison through the engines' exhausts —

Too bloody marvellous to contemplate. Just wait for it. *Hope.*

'What?'

McClure. Down by Paul's elbow somewhere. Asking *What?*

when he hadn't said a word. At least, he didn't think he had. He felt around in the dark for McClure's head, and patted it like a dog. He promised him, 'I'll stand you a haggis when we get back, Shortarse.'

Creagh's voice said, from the wardroom area, 'Gun's crew ready, sir.'

'Good.' Ruck had heard him. His voice answered Creagh's, 'I hope you won't be needed, layer. Just stand by down here.'

'Main vents checked shut, sir!'

Wykeham reported in his lazy tone, 'Ready to surface, sir.'

Voices in the dark. Faces lit occasionally, weirdly, by torch-beams, in this steel tube on the seabed, with air in it that wouldn't sustain life for long.

'Sub.'

'Here, sir.'

'I'll want you hanging on my legs.'

'Aye aye, sir.'

Because of the pressure there was now in the boat. If he was on his own when he opened the top hatch he could be blown out like a human cannon-ball.

'Can you see what you're doing, Quinn?'

'Oh aye, sir.' Quinn flicked his torch on and off as proof of it, then put it back in his mouth, so as to have his hands free to operate the HP blows.

'Main engines ready, engine clutches in, sir.'

'Very good. Number One – soon as the hatch is open, half ahead on main engines, three hundred revs.'

'Aye aye, sir.'

'Winters.' Leading Torpedoman Winters was on the wheel. Ruck told him, 'Soon as we have steerage-way, bring her round to southeast.'

'Southeast. Aye, sir.'

The lower lid was open. Janaway flicked a torchbeam upwards for Ruck to see.

'Take her up slowly, Number One. Try doing it on number four. Surface!'

'Blow four main ballast!'

Quinn's torch glowed in his mouth as he wrenched that blow open and air went thumping down the one-inch-diameter HP line.

She wasn't moving. She felt dead, like the air inside her.

The blowing seemed to have been going on for a long time, and to have had no effect at all.

'Stop blowing!'

Quinn shut the valve. He stood waiting, ready for the next move, looking round at Ruck with one hand still on the wheel-spanner on that valve. Ruck was staring at the depthgauge, watching for some movement.

Nothing.

'Check four main vent.'

In case it might be open, despite having been reported shut. Then all that air could have been blowing out into the sea, wasted, instead of driving water from the tank to make her buoyant. That bottled air was *Ultra*'s only asset, only way of getting up, ever; you might as well open your own veins as waste it.

Chief ERA Pool came back. 'Number four main vent is shut, sir.'

'Thank you, Chief.' Ruck told Wykeham, 'Let's try blowing one, three and five.'

This *had* to work. There was no damn reason why it shouldn't. But then, there was no reason why blowing number four tank hadn't worked, either.

Air roaring now; torchlight touching faces here and there: some of them, since they hadn't expected to be illuminated, showed anxiety to live.

She wasn't moving.

'Stop blowing!'

Silence, when the flow of air cut off. That was a hell of a lot of it gone already, to no purpose. He couldn't understand it. If he'd been taking his final submarine-course exams now and a question had required him to explain such a situation, he couldn't have. He heard Ruck mutter, 'There must be some —'

She'd quivered. Like a dog stirring in a dream: a little shake. Then she was still again, like a dead creature on the seabed.

Wykeham suggested, 'We've taken a slight bow-down angle, sir, d'you think?'

It was hard to judge, and the fore-and-aft spirit-level was useless because depthcharging had split the bubble up. Paul thought Wykeham might be right, though.

Ruck asked McClure, 'What's the bottom here, pilot?'

'Supposed to be sand, sir.'

'That's what I thought. Funny sort of *sand*.' He chuckled. Several other men laughed with him, and Paul was one of them – for no reason that he could have explained. Ruck told Quinn, 'Blow one main ballast.'

'Blow one, sir!'

He had the torch in his hand as he did it. Light flaring round. And this time, she *moved*: her forepart seemed to jerk free suddenly and begin to lift, the angle growing steeply . . .

'Stop blowing?'

Quinn shut the air off. Bow still rising.

'Blow four main ballast!'

Now she was coming up. Needle moving in the depthgauge: hundred and thirty-four feet – thirty-two . . .

'Stop blowing. Open number one main vent.'

Because of the bow-up angle. Quinn's hand went to the top-most vent-lever and pulled it out towards him: you heard the thud as the vent banged open.

'Shut!'

He slammed the lever in again. She was on an even keel, more or less, and rising steadily. Passing the hundred-foot mark, and accelerating as she rose, through the natural effect of becoming lighter as depth and density decreased.

Sixty feet. Coming up *too* fast. But it was better than being stuck on the bottom – in mud, or silt, or whatever had been so loath to let her go.

Ruck muttered, 'It's a great life if you can stand it.' On his way to the ladder. 'You all right, signalman?'

Janaway nodded. His grin was wolfish in the torchlight. Face bearded and running wet with sweat, sick-looking. The grin was a grimace. He said thickly, 'Better every minute, sir.'

'Needle and thread tomorrow. Two new red bars on the Roger. Right?' He looked round. 'Come on, Sub.'

Thirty feet. Twenty-seven . . . Paul climbed, following Ruck. The idea of having clean air to breathe was staggering. *Dreaming* this? High on the ladder, he clamped his arms round Ruck's knees. Not seaboots: it would be embarrassing to be left hugging a pair of boots and to have mislaid one's captain. He could hear him easing the pins out of the clips and then the clang as one clip swung free. From below, Wykeham's voice called, 'Twenty feet!'

He repeated, 'Twenty —'

'All right, I can hear . . .'

'Fifteen . . . Fourteen . . . Twelve . . . Ten . . .'

Ruck eased the second clip towards him. Pressure inside the boat lifted the hatch fractionally off its seating: despite a weight of solid water on the other side of it, only the clip's leverage was preventing it flying open. Air leaking out . . .

'Eight feet, sir!'

Air pouring up now, roaring up the tower: a strong wind of it, foul-smelling and fog-coloured, flooding out like pus from a boil. Paul's weight hanging on Ruck's legs. The hatch crashed open. Ruck yelled, 'All right, Sub!'

He let go, hearing from below Wykeham's yell of, 'Start main engines!'

Air – salt-wet, fresh, cold, dark air . . . He was out of the hatch, in the sea-swept bridge. Dragging the voicepipe cock open. Ruck was a black silhouette revolving slowly, glasses at his eyes . . . He'd lowered them, muttering, 'All clear, thank God.' Stooping to the voicepipe: 'Four-two-oh revolutions. Up Vickers gunners.' The diesels had already coughed themselves into loud, grumbling life: *Ultra* herself, rolling to the swell and beginning to forge ahead, was suddenly, astonishingly, alive . . .

Paul had his glasses up, sweeping across the bow. Ruck too, searching the dark sea and hazy impression of a horizon to starboard. Both of them silent, concentrating, straining their eyes through the binoculars and the darkness – knowing this was the only way, now, they'd *stay* alive.

Postscript

In the raid on St Nazaire there was no *Sauerkraut* and no direct attack on the U-boat shelter. Whether such an attempt could have succeeded – perhaps using the harbour-defence launches, of which there were several in the St Nazaire Basin that night – may be arguable. The raid as it did take place is described here as Jack Everard would have seen it if he'd been involved in such a sideshow.

Of the assault craft only three MLs and the MGB got back to England. The totals of British killed and missing were Navy eighty-five, Army fifty-nine. Many others were taken prisoner. Estimates of the number of Germans who allowed themselves to be blown up with *Campbeltown* vary a great deal; one account puts the figure as high as 380.

The main target was destroyed, and the 'Tirpitz dock' was out of action for the duration of the war. Sir Winston Churchill described the operation as 'a deed of glory intimately involved in high strategy'.

Ultra is a fictional submarine, and so is *Unslaked*, but in other respects I have tried to draw a lifelike portrait of the 10th Flotilla and its work. I admit that in order to tie up the two themes of the novel I have 'fiddled' some dates: for instance the convoy operation from Alexandria (in the course of which Admiral Vian fought his magnificent Second Battle of Sirte) was completed a few days before the attack on St Nazaire, so *Ultra* would have been back in Malta before Jack sailed from Falmouth. And some events in Malta – for example, the strafing of the rest camp and the bombing of the Sliema flats – have been switched from April into March. I did this because such happenings illustrate the conditions under which the Malta base operated, and the story had to be set in March.

I am not sure that 'Mussolini's Mysterious Measures' were in operation in March 1942. They certainly were a few months later. For this kind of detail, which one might have forgotten, I have been able to make use of a notebook which I kept during my own first submarine patrol. I was a midshipman, allowed to go along for 'submarine experience'; I kept watches as a look-out, as a planesman, in the motor room, etc., but having no diving-stations duties there was time to make notes during attacks. The patrol was from Malta, in HM Submarine *Unbending*, in January 1943. In the Messina Straits her captain, Lieutenant E. S. Stanley, torpedoed a 9000-ton troopship within half a mile of the beach near Cape dell'Armi. *Unbending* was then heavily depthcharged and kept down for thirty-six hours, protosol being spread on trays to improve the air. She finally returned to Malta with defects listed in my notes as: *Periscope will not rise. After pump out of action. Bubble split up. After plane indicator and shallow gauges out. Gyro fell over. Battery containers cracked.*

Upholder, whose captain was Lieutenant-Commander David Wanklyn VC, DSO★★, was lost in April 1942 on her twenty-fifth Mediterranean patrol. *Urge*, commanded by Wanklyn's close friend Lieutenant-Commander E. P. Tomkinson DSO★★, survived her by only a fortnight. Tomkinson had heard, from a distance, the depthcharge attack that destroyed *Upholder*.

'Shrimp' Simpson left Malta at the end of January 1943, and the ship in which he was taking passage to Alexandria was torpedoed and sunk by an Italian submarine. He survived, later to become Flag Officer (Submarines), and he retired in 1954. He farmed in New Zealand for some years and died shortly before his 'professional autobiography', *Periscope View*, was published in 1972.